As soon as the handle
open of its own acc
slowly as if someone
drawing it open. Sno
took a breath, half expecting Philip to be there.

And as the door opened, she froze.

For a moment she saw nothing inside. Nothing. No light, no shade, no colour. Just a pale nothing-ness.

Then, way below her, she saw the sea, as if the door of the room had opened into the air above the Atlantic Ocean.

Snowy screamed as her balance deserted her and frantically wheeled her arms trying to remain up-right and searching for something solid to hang on to.

There was nothing there.

Screaming at the top of her voice, she began to fall.

STEVE HARRIS

BLACK ROCK

VISTA

First published in Great Britain 1996
by Victor Gollancz

This Vista edition published 1996
Vista is an imprint of the Cassell Group
Wellington House, 125 Strand, London WC2R 0BB

A catalogue record for this book is
available from the British Library.

ISBN 0 575 60082 9

Printed and bound in Great Britain
by Cox & Wyman Ltd, Reading, Berks

96 97 98 99   10 9 8 7 6 5 4 3 2 1

Black Rock is dedicated to three special people:
Steve Harris the younger
(first I stole his name . . .)
Suzanne
(who keeps the squirrels away)
Florence
(still a real sweetie)

CASSELL PLC

As usual, a lot of people need thanking for letting me pick their brains and for their badly needed support. So thanks to: Sue Strachan (for telling me what a book rep did between shopping trips); Geoff Barrs (the dribble of some knowledge) and Mrs Sarah Barrs; Phil and Barb; Paul and Sheila; acam@cix (for advice on *Futility*); Jack Verglas (for my reputation as a misogynist); Chris Long (for untold support); Simon Wady (for hilarious calls); Richard 'just wait here for two years' Evans (for publishing this); Jo 'it's a boy's book' Fletcher (for publishing this); Darren Jones, John Overall and the *Invasion* crew (for keeping me busy); Pauline Clarke (my biggest fan); Hilary Morris; Ratboy (my smallest fan); Steve Crisp (for another fine illustration); Debbie, Jason and Harry (for being the neighbours from Hell); Tony Wheeler (for being one of God's own); Loei (for the 35mm entertainment); Duke 'n' Cindy (for protecting me); Colin Rowe (for helping me add up the Peter Perfects); The Cix Friends of Dorothy (for warmth and intelligence); Durham University SF society; Mark Chadbourn; shellgrip, debwilde, piharris, rupertg, quill, dave__the__mage, imurphy, pan, quill, cassidys and spear, all @cix (for their support), and all my readers, whoever and wherever you are.

'The getting in is easy; it's the getting out again you have to worry about.'

Peter Perfect

Chapter One

Black Rock

The house wasn't haunted.

It might have looked as if it had been designed and built solely for the purpose of housing ghosts, and it certainly seemed to have been planted in a landscape crafted to heighten its visually disconcerting effect, but it *couldn't* be haunted.

And sitting in her red Ford Sierra estate on the shingle forecourt of the house, Snowdrop Dresden – known to her friends as Snowy or, depending on how recently she'd broken something, Dropsy – began to list the reasons why.

The first of these – *There are no such things as ghosts* – would normally have been enough. Snowy was not one of those people who lie in bed at night interpreting the noises of the house settling as spooks or creatures that go bump in the night. From the moment her book hit the floor and her head hit the pillow, Snowdrop J. Dresden slept the sleep of the dead. The expression *fast asleep* when applied to her was a gross understatement. Her ex-boyfriend Martin had coined the far more accurate term, *full speed asleep*. Consequently, Snowy didn't often think about ghosts.

But sitting here looking at the big dark house – although the word *mansion* seemed more appropriate – the simple denial of the existence of ghosts didn't seem enough. This house – Black Rock according to the crumbling sign at the gate – seemed to argue back.

So Snowy made a rational, and somewhat cynical, list of extras. The place looked as if it had been invented by the world's most uninspired horror writer: *Take one Victorian house, double its size, find a spooky location on the coast of*

9

North Cornwall – *any outcrop of rock protruding into the Atlantic will do* – *place house on rock with the wild sea behind it and make it look as if it's squatting there, ready to pounce. Put a dark, roiling sky above the sea. Two hundred yards to the left you can see the ruins of King Arthur's Tintagel Castle; for miles to the right the bare cliff winds away. The nearest building, a small farmhouse, is three hundred yards back up the hill towards Tintagel. A narrow path leads towards the ruined castle, which itself is a good quarter of a mile from the village.*

That was another good reason the house couldn't be haunted. Real haunted houses would look just like any other ordinary house. Maybe a sixties semi, or one of those prefabs they made after the war. If ghosts were the spirits of dead people, they wouldn't be confined to big foreboding houses, would they? People died all over the place so how come only houses like this seemed to feature ghosts?

'And there isn't a spooky atmosphere, either,' Snowy added, nodding.

This might change when she got out of the car, she realized, and, fighting off a tingling in her spine which threatened to become a fully fledged shiver, she pushed open the door.

There was no spooky atmosphere.

It might have been late October and the clouds might have been building up out at sea and threatening lousy weather, but the breeze was warm and welcoming, the air was fresh and clean and, now she was out of the car, the house looked a great deal friendlier. It looked somewhere you could be snug and secure no matter what the weather. It looked like a place where you could make love on a fur rug in front of an open fire while a blizzard whirled outside and glowing coals from the fire wouldn't even dare to pop and shower your naked bottom with sparks.

Smiling to herself at this unbidden sappy image, Snowy reached back into the car for her briefcase. She was not renowned for her innate spacial awareness or sense of direction. She was half an inch short. Her fingertips brushed the handle, but didn't quite grasp it. Her hand came away from the case with the nails of her middle and ring fingers broken.

The two little curves of translucent nail looked like sickles with ragged cutting edges. Snowy looked at them and swore. *My best ones yet*, she inwardly complained, taking one of the nails between her teeth and tearing it off.

She glanced at the house. No one was watching her and the house itself didn't feel as if it was watching her either, so that was another one in the eye for the haunted house thing.

She tore off the other broken nail, retrieved the case, slammed the car door and realized she hadn't taken the key from the ignition.

Some days, Dropsy, she told herself, suddenly irritated, *you're like an old-fashioned Vaudeville act looking for somewhere to perform.*

And her irritation grew because her own mind had just seen fit to use one of Martin's favourite disparaging remarks about her. Now she found herself picturing his face and her irritation grew to anger. Martin had been banished from her mind for over two months now. She did *not* think about him any more. It was all over and good riddance to bad rubbish.

His face hung there in her mind's eye, though, his features not a bit blurred by the passing weeks. The first few times he'd gone on business trips to the States, she'd had trouble hanging on to the memory of how he looked. His image would gradually diminish until all she retained was a pink oval face with thinning sandy hair and a gingery moustache. Back then, she'd loved him more than anything else in the world and had dearly wanted to hold on to that fading view; now, when she wanted to forget, he remained more sharply defined than ever, that infuriating 'told you so' expression of male superiority fixed to his face.

Well, Martin could 'go fucking whistle', as he'd been so fond of saying of other people. Snowy now told him so, aloud. She also told him that she might be a little scatter-brained and clumsy occasionally, and she might have trouble telling her left hand from her right, or north from west but she was intelligent, compassionate, loving, caring, generous, a distinguished seller of personal computers, a damned good-looking woman, an animal in the bedroom (no thanks to 'Call me Mr Missionary') and perfectly able to exist in a world where there was no such thing as a freelance science-fiction editor, bigot and male chauvinist *extraordinaire* called Martin Dinsey.

Snowy glanced at the house again, turned away and told Martin's image (now looking distinctly pale and shocked, the way he had the day she'd stood before him armed with that mother of all weapons, a wooden rolling-pin) that she wouldn't pee on him if he was on fire and that he could take his Ferrari Dino (which she'd never been allowed to drive because, 1, she was a woman, and, 2, it was *his* car and *he'd* paid for it and wasn't going to share it) and get out of her life before she did him some serious damage.

I could have killed you, Martin, Snowdrop called after her ex-lover's fading image. *Could have and would have. Now go away and stay away. It's all over!*

She straightened her skirt and dusted off her jacket, rearranging her face into its proper professional expression of polite confidence. Inside this big, old haunted house was a someone called Mr Winter, who wasn't going to be a ghoul at all, but a perfectly nice (and possibly rich) man who wanted to buy a personal computer system. A very expensive one. And he would buy from her because she was incredibly good at her job and was going to offer him exactly the system he required. Then she could go home happy and spend the evening pleasing herself.

Snowdrop Dresden walked up the shingle forecourt towards Black Rock smiling, because feeling good about herself came much more easily since Martin's passing than it had ever done before. Snowy thought she was going to like it inside the house. It felt a little as though she was going home.

She stood in front of the big oak front door looking for the bell while she treated herself to a quick fantasy in which *her destiny had brought her here*. Snowy had done a lot of fantasizing over the past year while her relationship with Martin had decayed. They had begun as fantasies which could have been entitled, *How it's going to be when I've sorted out my life*, and turned into epics concerning Martin and violent death. Like an unused muscle in need of exercise, her mind had been loath to accommodate this mode of thinking at first, and then had gradually become toned. These days it had quickened to the point at which it could provide her with a story and background whenever she fancied; on the road, in the office, or alone in her bed and feeling randy. Sometimes these were short vignettes, and sometimes they came to her so rounded and rich in detail she thought she might be able to write them up into a novel one day.

The one that came to her now painted Mr Winter as a tall, good-looking man in his mid or late thirties, assertive and craggy faced. He would be warm and welcoming, like his house. His eyes would be ice-blue, his smile melting. He would take her to a large, white room with a huge oak desk and piles of electronic equipment and Snowy would imagine him pushing her gently down on to that desk and blush. He would explain that he was a freelance computer software designer or playwright or screen-writer and show her his credits. He would laugh a lot and seem shy and hustle her down to the lounge where that log fire would be burning and that inviting fur rug would lie before the hearth. He would make her tea with pure Assam leaves and they would sip while she sold him a top-of-the-range Pentium system. As she closed the deal, he would ask her if he could take her to a restaurant some time when she wasn't too busy . . .

The part of Snowy's mind which wasn't busily turning an ordinary working day into a perfect future, and Mr Winter into Mr Right, informed her that a sharp fireman's hatchet would make barely a dent in Black Rock's solid front door. Rapping on it with her knuckles made no discernible sound at all. There was a huge brass knob in its centre and one of those little spy-hole things set in the wood at head height, but there was no letter box, no bell and no knocker.

And no keyhole or lock, either, Snowy added, frowning to herself.

This last observation unsettled her a little. The fact that there was no apparent method of opening the door from the outside was odd, to say the least.

Maybe the brass knob opens it somehow, Snowy told herself, bending forward to inspect it. A lion-like animal with a gargoyle face was embossed on it. The creature was truly

13

ugly. The part of Snowy that always noticed cobwebs and dust in other people's houses realized that the knob was unbelievably clean. There were many corners and angles in that representation of a demon, and in the real world, in houses that weren't haunted, these would be the places that didn't get clean when you polished.

So it's new, she told herself.

But she didn't think it *was* new and she didn't even think it was brass any more – for one thing, its colour was too deep.

The knob appeared to be solid gold.

Bullshit! Snowy told the wide-eyed little girl inside her, who was threatening to leap out and take over. *Get on your bike and ride!*

Fingerprints! the awed little girl cried in a mixture of astonishment and delight, and for a few moments Snowy did not understand what she meant.

If Snowdrop J. Dresden had not been the kind of woman who refused to believe in ghosts or haunted houses, at this point she could well have decided that perhaps discretion was the better part of valour after all, and left Black Rock ... because for the past twenty seconds or so she had been handling the demon door knob and there wasn't a single fingerprint upon it.

Snowy reached for it again, watching closely this time. The moment before she made contact with it, the warmth of her approaching fingers misted the cool metal. She laid her hand on it. The misted area spread around the edge of her hand, then vanished. She took her hand away quickly. The door knob was totally unmarked.

Snowy suddenly realized she'd been standing here for quite some time. She rapped on the door again and while she was waiting, took her Ultraglow compact from her handbag and opened it. She checked her face in the mirror, told herself – as she always did – *Yeah, that's the same face you had when you left home this morning and my God, it's still beautiful,* then placed a thumb firmly in the centre of the mirror, rolling it and peeling it away carefully, the way the cop did it after she'd been busted for the one and only joint she'd ever smoked in her life.

Vi-o-la, mad-man, she thought, *ein fingerprinten!*

The print, made with the same thumb that wasn't greasy enough to mark the door knob, was perfect. Like the ones she'd given the police in Exeter all those years ago, this one wasn't an oval dab, but almost rectangular where she'd rolled it. The whorls, hooks and twists of her print were clearly visible.

She applied the same thumb to the door knob.

The knob misted as her thumb approached. She rolled it and removed it. There was no mark whatsoever.

Used up all your finger-grease?

Snowy tried the mirror again.

Nope, still plenty of that left.

She tried the door knob again.

Then she shook her head. 'Well, *that's* a bit of a mystery,' she said aloud.

But it wasn't necessarily a mystery of the genus *Supernaturalis*, or even *Bermudus Triangalis*, it could be one of that arcane art *Electronic Engineering*. Lurking in Snowy's past, along with the drugs bust and several other things she would rather not remember, was her crowning achievement, a degree in electronics. Because of this, she favoured the latter explanation of the door knob's refusal to accept her fingerprints. It was obviously some pressure-sensitive gizmo used to open the door and probably coated with some grease-resistant stuff. The fact that she'd never yet heard of such a thing didn't necessarily preclude its existence. Electronics, although difficult to wrap your mind around when you started trying to understand strange things like Josephson Junctions and the Double Slit experiment, was a practical science: the odd actions of minute particles might not be easy to understand, but someone who did could harness an effect and do something useful with it (like making the computers she sold, for example).

Snowy rapped out a few Morse code messages on the hard door: *Let me in, Hello, it's me*, and *Open Sesame* but none had any effect.

Except that when she looked again, something *had* happened. To the were-lion embossed into the knob. She was (almost) certain it had been open, the last time she looked; now it was closed and the creature's gargoyle head wore a self-satisfied smirk.

Snowy looked at it for a second, feeling a variant on the old *déjà-vu* sensation – which she knew was caused by an occasional glitch in the optical pattern-recognition part of your brain. This feeling wasn't so much, *I have lived through this before*, but rather as if the world about her had subtly altered – as if to accommodate her within an alternate history it had prepared earlier.

There was a sharp metallic *click!* from behind her and Snowy spun around, suddenly certain that Mr Winter was out on the forecourt, watching her.

No one was there.

Way up on the hill where the nearest farm building stood, a black dog leapt up on to a trailer and froze, facing in her general direction. It was so far away Snowy could not make out the breed but she got the distinct feeling that it was some kind of a pointer and that it was pointing at her.

She looked back at the long, steep track she had driven down to get here, then at the black clouds which were sweeping in off the sea and wondered how you would get back up that track in a vehicle if it rained. The track – which was barely more than a widened footpath – was unmade and had been pretty muddy on the way down. If it rained hard, she was going to spend a good long time sitting in the car and listening to the wheels spin while she fought to keep the car from sliding off the edge of the track and falling down to the rocky ground below.

The rain was coming, but it might not fall for another hour or so. The quicker she got inside Black Rock, the quicker she would be out.

So how do *I get in?* she asked herself, then yelped when a voice from behind her spoke.

'The getting in is easy. It's the getting out again you have to worry about.'

During the few seconds it took her to realize that the voice

16

belonged to Mr Winter, several scattered thoughts bounced across Snowy's mind. The most important of these were that not only had Mr Winter opened that huge door without making any sound whatsoever, but that he had apparently read her mind.

Snowy quickly told herself that she must have spoken the words aloud.

'Sorry, did I frighten you?' Mr Winter asked with what sounded like childlike amusement, then, without waiting for a reply, said, 'And you must be the lovely Mizz S. Dresden. I've been looking forward to meeting you.'

Mr Winter looked just as he had in Snowy's fantasy, but a little older perhaps. Tall, early forties, handsome, ice-blue eyes and a smile that almost certainly saw to it that when Mr Winter wanted company in his bed Mr Winter got it.

During her travels Snowy had noticed that money seemed to rub off on people. Many of those who had serious amounts of it also had a certain aura. At first she had thought that it was simply due to their expensive clothes and jewellery, but you often saw them dressed in jeans and tee-shirts and could still tell. Whatever it was, Mr Winter had it in spades.

I think I might enjoy this one, Snowy told herself, put out her hand and said, 'Pleased to meet you, Mr Winter. Call me Snowy.'

Mr Winter's hand was warm, dry and firm, just the way Snowy liked. If you got a wet-fish job, or the one where they just squeezed your fingers, you were in for trouble. If you got one that left you worrying about broken bones, you weren't going to make a sale. This was good. Mr Winter gently let her know he had strong hands and she equalled his pressure, letting him know she was no mug.

'What a charming name,' he said, holding her gaze just as he had in her fantasy. 'After Snow White, I presume?'

Snowdrop shook her head, but even then his eyes didn't let her go. Butterflies flitted across her insides and vanished. 'No, it's Snowdrop,' she said, 'after the flower.'

'Snowy Dresden,' Mr Winter said quietly. 'You were named after a beautiful sight – Dresden in the snow.'

When she tore her eyes away from his, she remembered the

door. It was behind him, and it was still closed. Perhaps he had simply materialized this side of it.

'What did you mean,' she asked, 'about getting out again being the problem?'

Mr Winter smiled. 'Just a little joke. And for your information, the bell-pull is set in the wall, on your right, as you walk into the porch. It's one of those old-fashioned rod-and-wire ones that jingles a little bell in the kitchen. It came with the house. Most people go right to it, so I haven't considered fitting an electric one.'

Snowdrop went and looked. *Yep, there it is, Dropsy, you just missed it!*

Out across the valley between Black Rock and the hill behind which Tintagel hid, she saw the farm building again and the old trailer. The black dog was still on it, still pointing at her. It looked like a statue.

'I'm sorry,' Snowy said, feeling very silly indeed. If it was there now, it must have been there when she arrived. She wouldn't be getting her Observer badge from Akela this weekend, that was for certain.

'Never mind,' Mr Winter said, 'I saw your car outside, and here we are. Would you like to come in?'

Snowy nodded. 'I couldn't understand the door,' she said. 'How does it work?'

For a moment she thought she might be in for trouble because Mr Winter completely ignored her question and her nod and asked again, 'Would you like to come in?'

In the seconds that followed, Snowy seriously considered turning around and high-tailing it out of Black Rock before it was too late. She realized she was seeing what she wanted to see, and not what was really there. That was what the odd *déjà-vu* sensation had been about. Suddenly she didn't like any of this, not the silly haunted house, its cut-off location, the impenetrable and silent front door.

Don't be stupid, she told herself. *You're just having an attack of the screaming-meemies because for the first time since you threw Martin out you've seen someone you fancy.*

'Yes, I do want to come in,' she said, ignoring the warning bells that rang in her head. 'But what about the door?'

Mr Winter smiled. 'It's my front door,' he said, 'and when I want it to open, it will.'

Snowy watched him carefully.

'It isn't locked,' he said, turning away from her. 'It never is.' He looked at her over his shoulder. 'All you have to do is push in the right place,' he said. 'And now I've told you all this, you'll be able to break in and sneak up on me whenever you want. Watch!'

He leaned to one side so that Snowy could see, placed his left hand on the door knob, his right on the wood where the lock should have been and pushed gently.

The door swung slowly open, moving with the sedate smoothness of a solid steel bank-vault door. It moved soundlessly, which knocked another nail into the coffin of the haunted house theory.

And behind it, standing half-way down the long dark hall, pointing at her with its nose while it held one paw off the ground, was the dog she'd seen on the farm trailer, perhaps twenty seconds ago.

Except that it couldn't be the same dog, because the trailer was probably a quarter of a mile away – and even if it *had* managed to run that distance in those few seconds, it would have had to pass her to get inside the house. The plateau on which Black Rock was built was almost circular and, except for the quadrant she had been standing in, was surrounded by sea.

Snowy took a step back to the edge of the porch and looked back at the trailer.

And there it was, minus one black dog. She shivered.

'I'd like to introduce you to Diamond,' Mr Winter said, when Snowy rejoined him in the doorway.

The dog stood frozen in the hall, just as it had done on the trailer, pointing at her. It was a big dog, maybe a cross between a black Labrador and a Doberman with a bit of greyhound in its history. It didn't look particularly friendly. Its eyes reflected the light from the open front door, making them shine white and blank.

'Do you mind dogs?' Mr Winter asked.

Snowy eyed Diamond. 'Normally I rather like them.'

'Good, because I have no control over Diamond. He's not mine.'

'Whose is he?' was not the question Snowy wanted to ask, but she asked it anyway. What she really wanted to ask was, Does he bite?, or more particularly, Is he going to bite me?

'He's a stray,' Mr Winter said. 'Comes and goes as he pleases. He can get into the house whenever he wants. I put food down for him and he eats it and that's about as far as it goes. I've called him Diamond after Isaac Newton's dog who destroyed several years' worth of his master's work when he upset a lighted candle. This merchant has recently pulled off a similar trick with my computer, which is why you're here.'

Snowy looked at the dog and the dog looked back at her with those glassy white eyes. Its lip wasn't curled and it wasn't growling, but it wasn't exactly wagging its tail and it wasn't pointing at her for nothing, either.

'Is he going to bite me?' Snowy finally managed.

'Oh, of course not. He's pointing at you because he likes you. Call him, he may come, although it can't be guaranteed.'

Snowy wasn't sure she wanted the dog anywhere near her, but she called him anyway.

The dog remained rock solid.

'Use his full name. It's Diamond Ambrose Anstey.'

You must be joking, kiddo, get on your horse and ride outta here! Snowy thought, and did it anyway.

The dog sat down. Its tail wagged. Once.

Snowy tried again. It was a mouthful to call in a happy voice, and if it wasn't even Mr Winter's dog, why had he bothered to name it so elaborately?

This time the dog stood up and padded towards her. When it reached her, it turned around, sat down on her feet and looked at her over its shoulder with such a pained expression that Snowy could have cried for it. It looked like a dog that had seen hell itself.

Snowy put her hand on its head. Diamond shuffled and leaned against her legs, looking up at her with soulful eyes.

'See, he likes you,' Mr Winter said. 'Now, if you would like to step across the threshold, I'll close the door.'

Feeling slightly uneasy about committing herself to going

right inside, and not knowing why, Snowy nevertheless pushed Diamond off her feet.

The dog leaned back against her, a little harder. It looked up at her with a pleading expression.

'I don't think he wants me to come inside,' Snowy said lightly.

'Get away, Diamond Ambrose Anstey!' Mr Winter ordered in a voice which wouldn't have sounded out of place if he had been casting out demons.

The dog looked at him disapprovingly, then got up and trotted back down the hall.

There was no excuse now, but still Snowy hesitated. The little girl inside her felt very strongly that Mr Winter might not be Mr Right at all, but the evil queen dressed up, and ready to feed little Snowy a very rotten apple indeed.

She thought about this for a few seconds, then rejected it. This was an ordinary working day, and there was work to be done.

As Snowdrop J. Dresden was later going to discover, she had just spent the last twenty minutes setting herself up to make the mistake of her life. Perhaps, if she had allowed herself to believe in ghosts, she might have saved herself a great deal of trouble and agony. But Snowdrop did not believe in ghosts.

If she had listened to the voice of her intuition, or to what Mr Winter had said about the door, or to the message the dog was trying to pass to her, she might have refused to enter the house and things would have turned out very differently. But Snowdrop refused to listen.

Later, she would replay the whole scene over and over to herself and would wish she *had* believed in ghosts and that she *had* taken notice of her intuitive voice, but most of all she would wish that she had swung the car round and backed it up closer to the front door as she had originally intended.

Because if she had done this she would have seen the house in the car's mirrors. And that would have been enough to save her because you could only see the *real* Black Rock when it was reflected. What you saw when you looked with your eyes, was *what was*, or *what might be*.

What you saw when you looked in a mirror would have been enough to make you leave immediately, prevent you from ever getting within ten miles of the place for as long as you lived and shocked you so deeply you would probably never get rid of the nightmares.

But, as Snowy would later discover, a lifetime's worth of nightmares would have been a cake-walk in comparison.

Now, standing on the threshold of Black Rock, she made her decision.

She took a deep breath and swept past Mr Winter into the hallway.

But like the man said, it wasn't the getting in you had to worry about, it was the getting out again . . .

Chapter Two

Peter Perfect's Ghosts

The *real* Sarah-Jane Dresden, the one who had not been christened Snowdrop, sat in her red Ford Sierra looking at Black Rock and feeling confused and unsettled.

But she wasn't parked upon its shingle forecourt, watching the dark sea-sky roiling behind the house, she was sitting in a car park in Falmouth with a Coke beside her, a half-eaten Cornish pastie in her left hand and twenty-four manuscript pages of an unpublished novel in her lap. Sarah-Jane was reading *Black Rock*. Again.

Since she had discovered the rough, pencilled-over manuscript in her flat, she had surely read through it once for each of the twenty-four pages and now she was reading it again.

Sarah-Jane, who was known to her friends, not as Snowy, but as Essenjay, S'n'J, or Drezy (which sounded a little like Dropsy, she supposed), knew that those writers who were considered shining stars were set above the masses of also-rans because of their good characterization. A lot of sins were forgiven in the face of good characterization. As Martin would have said, 'If you have a crap plot, and great characterization, you'll sell. If you have a great plot and crap characterization you'll sell. If you have a great plot and great characterization you'll sell big; but if you have neither, you may just as well put that revolver to your head and pull the trigger.'

According to Martin, the trick was to get your readers to identify with your heroes. If you made your characters think and say what 'real' people did, your readers would warm to them.

And Sarah-Jane Dresden had identified with Snowy Dresden very strongly indeed.

If it was meant as a joke, she told herself for the thousandth time since finding the manuscript, it didn't work. For one thing, it was too good, too well written, in spite of the fact that Martin had inscribed derogatory remarks in the margins of almost every page like Mr High-and-Mighty editor. For another, he had made it much too obvious that Snowy Dresden, who fell into the hands of ghosts at the end of Chapter One wasn't just based on S'n'J, it actually *was* her.

If this was in print, I could sue the bastard! she told herself.

She assumed that towards the end of their stormy relationship, Martin had finally felt threatened enough, and inspired enough (and God knew, he was always promising to swap hats and write a book instead of editing them) to fictionalize her. Presumably he'd felt it was his only way of tipping the balance of power in his direction.

The thing that really made her nervous, was not that the pages in her lap described in quite graphic detail some of Martin's violent feelings towards her (although this surprised her in such a mild man), but that during the writing Martin seemed to have developed second sight.

He had always been full of tales about how writers could pre-empt, or in his wilder flights of fancy, maybe *bring about* the future. His science-fiction writers had predicted many developments in technology and political events and one of his horror writers – 'These books are disgusting, but they sell in cart-loads and bring in the dosh' – had written a novel about a man who believed he could become immortal by slaying people, only to find that two years later a real-life psycho was caught attempting the very same thing. And this wasn't a copy-cat moron who'd read the book – it turned out that the psycho had never heard of the author, let alone the novel.

Those things proved that it was possible for authors to predict events, but they were almost always generalizations. You postulate a man killing to become immortal, and the laws of chance said that sooner or later someone would come along and do just that – and yippee, you predicted it. It was a bit like predicting the arrival of a bus after you'd seen the timetable.

What was spooky about the start of *Black Rock* (and Sarah-Jane thought that spooky looked like getting to be the word of day on this particular Thursday in October) was that in its twenty-four double-spaced pages Martin had used details of Sarah-Jane's life about which he could not have known. On one page, for instance, Snowy referred to a morning, years ago, when after a night on the town she'd woken up in bed, naked and entwined with her best friend Ellen. After untangling herself she had spent the rest of the day wondering what, if anything, had happened during those drunken hours.

This had actually happened to Sarah-Jane.

And she'd never told Martin.

In *Black Rock*, the reader learnt that this encounter had precipitated a brief lesbian affair (*more about this later, folks*, Martin might as well have written at the end of the paragraph) which was where Martin's gift of 'second-sight' veered off into sheer sexual fantasy. In real life, what followed had been nothing so exotic. The humdrum conclusion was that both girls had piled into bed drunk and since they were eighteen and insecure about being away from home for the first time, they had cuddled up together for comfort.

Put that in your pipe and choke on it Martin, Sarah-Jane hissed, glaring at the offending page.

The manuscript was laser-printed and had neat page numbers, a header at the top of each fresh sheet with the book name and chapter heading, and a footer at the bottom of each with the author's name and address. And the fact that the name and address in question wasn't Martin's (or hers) had to have been another of Martin's silly jokes. No one else on earth could have known Sarah-Jane Dresden in such detail, so Martin had to have been the author.

S'n'J didn't get the joke though. Why would he choose the name 'Peter Perfect' as an alias and Black Rock, Tintagel, North Cornwall, as an address?

Scowling, she sipped her Coke. There were other discrepancies with the damn thing too.

Martin, blast his eyes, had done quite a hatchet job on the pages in his customary razor-sharp 2H pencil. From the first page onwards he had written such acid comments as: *stretch my credulity a little further, why don't you?* and, *horribly convoluted*. He had objected to Snowdrop's entering the house with, *you don't expect me to believe any woman in her right mind would actually go inside this house, do you?* To top it all, his final verdict was: *a hackneyed idea for a crappy ghost story. Reject.*

Which was surely not something any writer would do to their own story. Apparently he'd started a novel about her and then, for some unknown reason, had seen fit to pretend it was the work of someone else.

To compound the mystery, there were numerous spelling corrections, and annotated sentences in a different hand and grade of pencil. Which could mean either of two things. The first was that Martin was suffering from a multiple person-ality disorder (of which she had seen no sign during their four years together) and the second was that the pages had been written and annotated by someone other than Martin.

The first was implausible, the second, impossible.

When S'n'J was a bright young thing at college in Exeter, she had entertained romantic hopes of becoming a private eye. She knew how to be discreet and she had an almost insatiable curiosity. Some of her friends had called her Parker, as in Nosy. But when she left college for her first two years of work in the real world – as an assistant in a bookshop – her hopes began to fade. The real world had a way of grinding you down and making your once fantastic hopes and dreams become as workaday as everyone else's. Some-where between her second year at the bookshop and the job coming up as sales representative for Ace Publishing (Pub-lisher of the Year 1992 and still heading their letters such – without the year, of course – three years on), she'd quit thinking of being an investigator, and started thinking how nice it would be to have somewhere she could call her own. And a dog, maybe, and a car – and if a suitable one happened by, a man too.

And shortly after starting work as Ace's Western Area sales

rep (territory: Bristol to Land's End and a thousand miles a week to cover), she had all of them except the dog. And since then, she'd thought no more about becoming a private dick (or a private fanny, perhaps, if you wanted to be coarse).

Until she discovered the manuscript in her flat.

When she'd first found the unstamped A4 envelope under the recently departed Martin's side of the bed, she'd pulled out the contents far enough for a quick glance and had decided that if Martin wanted his manuscript, Martin could damn well phone and ask for it and if she was feeling particularly magnanimous she *might* send it to him.

Martin had phoned. Oh how he had phoned – every single day for a fortnight. But he'd had other things on his mind than work. Such as what he wasn't going to do to his little Essenjay if only she would have him back!

But his little Essenjay was not the same girl she'd been when he'd first moved in and brought the sprouting seeds of his nasty little habits with him. His little Essenjay was a good deal more worldly-wise these days. She now understood the wisdom of that old saw, *You can't make a silk purse out of a sow's ear* and although not female, Martin was undoubtedly an ear of the porcine variety. She told him this, along with the fact that she didn't believe his promises of reformation; of how he would become a model partner.

It served him right, of course, but it had also alienated him. Eventually he'd concluded that his days of dominance over this particular little girl – who needed an authoritative father figure to keep her in her place – were well and truly gone and he had ceased calling.

And good riddance to him, Sarah-Jane thought, defiant, even now.

The problem was, that now she'd read the manuscript, she wanted to talk to him about it. Maybe to tell him it was much better than he realized and to encourage him to persevere with it, but mainly to ask him why he'd signed himself as Peter Perfect (Penelope Pitstop's boyfriend, she thought, from Wacky Races) and why he'd written his address as Black Rock.

So phone him up, she told herself, and looked at the cellnet phone which lay in its leather case on the car's passenger seat. She doubted that Peter Perfect (and he'd probably chosen the name because he thought he *was* perfect) would speak to her. And if she left a message she didn't know if he would return her call.

What Sarah-Jane Dresden *did* know, was the reason she was hesitating. A conversation with Martin might not turn out the way she wanted it to. Martin wasn't just going to talk about the weather and the famous twenty-four page sample of an unwritten novel called *Black Rock*. Martin was undoubtedly going to broach the taboo subject of *Me and You* and that was something she needed less than a six-inch nail driven between each of the pupils of her eyes.

But today was the last day this week that Martin would be in the office at Ace Publishing. Because he was freelance he only spent Tuesdays, Wednesdays and Thursdays at Ace.

And Sarah-Jane badly wanted confirmation that he'd written the pages.

Except that what you really want, my girl, is confirmation that he didn't write it, isn't it?

But she ignored this because it was absurdly romantic wanting to believe that there was an actual place called Black Rock. And even more ridiculous wanting there to be a man inside it who'd sat down and written accurately about her without even knowing of her existence.

Shaking her head, because when you seriously started to entertain such fancies you had a job to sort out where fiction ended and reality began, she reached for the phone. She *had* to know.

The Ace switchboard operator completely ignored her request for connection to Martin and plumbed her through to Del Blass, the marketing manager, and for her sins, her boss.

'Blass, marketing,' his voice said. 'Drezy, nice of you to phone. Got a problem?'

'Only if you're not answering Martin's phone,' Sarah-Jane said. 'I asked for his office.'

'How's tricks?' Del asked. 'Any problems down your way?'

'No Del, none, now look . . .'

'The new Kaminsky subbing in okay for Christmas?'

'Like hot cakes, surprise, surprise,' Sarah-Jane said. Lulu Kaminsky's already sky-high sales had trebled since someone had pushed her down one of London underground's tallest escalators and killed her. Aided by Melvyn Bragg and a South Bank Show special entitled, 'Who Killed Kaminsky?' Lulu's first posthumous book, *Clarissa*, was set to break all sales records since God was a kid. Lulu Kaminsky was already the world's *numero uno* shopping and fucking novelist; now she would be a record-breaking *dead* one.

'Good,' Del said, and Sarah-Jane could picture his huge head nodding slowly. Del was one of those people you crashed into full speed ahead and hyped up and bounced off feeling mellow and cool.

'Now look, Del, can you put Martin on the line please?' Sarah-Jane said, quickly before he could calm her any more.

'I'm not in his office, I'm in mine,' Del said. 'How you feeling Drezy? Okay?'

'I'm fine, Del. Just put me through to Martin, and I'll feel a damn sight finer.'

'Is it work related?' Del asked.

'Yes Del,' Sarah said.

'Oh,' Del said sounding disappointed. 'Thought there might be a chance, y'know . . .'

'Of a reconciliation?'

The trouble with the publishing industry was that the fuel that ran it was intrigue and scandal. Everyone knew everyone else and word spread like wildfire, not just through the publishing house you worked for but all the others too. Almost everyone in the industry knew Martin Dinsey the country's most respected science fiction editor, and everyone now knew that he'd been blown-out by some jumped up bitch of a sales rep.

'Absolutely no chance,' Sarah-Jane said. 'Will you put me through to him now?'

Del hesitated. 'The switchboard has been instructed to divert your calls to me,' he said. 'I'm . . . uhh . . . supposed to explain to you that Martin doesn't want any contact with you.'

'Well, I have a question I want to ask him about one of his books,' Sarah-Jane lied, 'and I'd like him to answer it for me.'

Del sighed. 'Hold on Drezy, I'll see if he'll speak to you.'

The line went dead and Sarah-Jane waited.

When it clicked into life again, she'd already said, 'Look Martin, I want to talk to you about Black Rock,' before the person on the other end cut in.

'It's me, Janie,' Janie Sanderson said. 'Martin's gone to lunch with Mike Sharland. Something to do with a telly deal for Gray Eliot's *Replicant* book.'

'Shit,' Sarah-Jane said.

'What's up? You weren't pining, surely?'

'No.'

'He'll be disappointed if he finds out. He's convinced you're a shadow of your former self since he left you,' Janie said.

'Sounds like him all over, that does. Since *he* left *me*.'

'He wants you back y'know. He's stricken.'

'He can stay stricken.'

'I think it did him some good. Not that I'm advertising him or anything. I certainly wouldn't want to live with him.'

'You're slurring my character!' Sarah-Jane said. 'Everyone's entitled to one mistake.'

'Yeah, but I wouldn't like to see you making it again. What did you want to talk to him about, anyway? Something about a rock, wasn't it? It must have been urgent for you to have phoned *him*.'

'Black Rock,' Sarah-Jane said. 'I found this twenty-four page sample of a book called Black Rock in my flat after Martin left. It's a haunted house story, apparently and I . . . well, I just wanted to ask if he wanted it back.'

'Uh-huh,' Janie said, 'I'll give him the message. Okey-dokey?'

'Fine.' Sarah-Jane said, quickly weighing up the odds. If she told Janie she would phone Martin back, the Ace bush telegraph would be afire within seconds. She and Martin had apparently become the literary world's equivalent of Charles and Di.

Sod it! she thought. 'Look, Janie, I'll ring him back this afternoon,' she said.

'Ohhh-kay,' Janie said, presumably already searching under her desk for her tabla-drums or whatever they used to spread the word.

'Speak to you soon,' Sarah-Jane said, and rang off.

And that was yesterday. Sarah-Jane had not called Martin back as she had promised, because for one thing she thought she might inadvertently be sending him signals which he would undoubtedly interpret to read 'she wants me back', and for another, the private dick in her had decided to take action.

There was a very easy way of finding out if 'Peter Perfect' was Martin or someone else. Last night she had actually dreamed of Black Rock – as a windblown, godforsaken place, shining like a beacon in the eye of a storm. And this morning she had woken, knowing she was going to travel miles out of her way in order to visit the spot where Black Rock was set.

You're obsessed, the Girl Guide voice of her conscience informed her.

There's nothing wrong with a little obsession, now and again, Sarah-Jane thought back. *Just look at . . . just look at . . .* and was unable to bring to mind any great historical figure who hadn't paid the price of their obsession. There had to be some, but she couldn't quite bring them to mind.

In fact, if she was truthful with herself, she was having trouble bringing *anything* to mind since she'd found the manuscript. Except the manuscript itself, of course. She was suckered, just as the writer had intended. She really *did* want to know what happened to Snowy. Wild goose chase or not, she had planned her whole day so that she could get some work done and still have time to drive over to Tintagel and check out the location.

She'd last been to see the ruins of King Arthur's Castle when she was a little girl, and she certainly didn't recall seeing any spooky houses nearby. The rock – Barras Nose it was called in the manuscript – might be there, but there would be no house upon it. It was all National Trust land there anyway.

So I'm going to be disappointed. So what? I can stand in the Castle and look at the empty piece of rock where Martin set his haunted house and wonder how he suddenly became so inspired.

Sarah-Jane turned over page twenty-four's cliffhanger (where Snowy was about to be violated by an extremely nasty apparition), tidied up the thin stack of pages and fed them back into their envelope.

But you'd like it better if Black Rock really turned out to be standing there on top of Barras Nose, wouldn't you? her Girl Guide voice chipped in. *You'd like to walk up that shingle drive with that house crouching before you and lay your fingers on that solid gold door knob, wouldn't you? You'd like to meet Mr Winter, too. Very much.*

'And I wouldn't be frightened, either,' she muttered.

Just like Snowdrop.

'Because there are no such things as ghosts,' she said, starting the car.

As she drove out of the car park, Sarah-Jane's stomach filled with butterflies.

Chapter Three

Martin's Confession

Martin Louis Dinsey, renowned and respected editor of science fiction, fantasy and a couple of hack horror-writers that he preferred not to talk about, threw the office door open, yelled, 'Hiya gorgeous!' at Janie Sanderson, flung himself down in his chair and began to pull off his tie.

From where Janie sat, it looked as if the lunch had been a good one. She scowled at him, touching her two loose front teeth with her tongue. Drunks were not her favourite animals today.

Martin smelled like a distillery. Which was a change from the reek of Tennent's Extra she was used to at home, but still not good. It was still booze.

For the last hour, Janie had been trying to write a cover blurb for a romance and it wasn't going well. *An epic saga of a noble nineteenth century family's fall from riches to the gutter*, she'd written, *and of the youngest daughter's climb back into society. Kitty's path from kitchen maid to lady of the night, to companion of the Prince Consort, is a marathon struggle against the tide of the times. Betrayal, jealousy, lust* and here Janie had run out of steam: *and broken dreams . . . bugger bugger shit bum bollocks, I'm crap at this. Get the author to send in a draft.*

She considered reading it out to Martin and asking him what he thought, then changed her mind. He would say it was a piece of shit, just like he always did.

Martin swung round in his chair. Janie could feel his eyes boring into the back of her head. She turned to face him and realized there was a certain truth in the expression 'tanked-up'. Her colleague looked like a hollow man, almost filled with liquid. You could all but see the booze slopping about behind his eyes. His face was swimming – there was no better way of describing it.

Janie's husband, her own personal drunkard, and presently her number one worry, never looked like this, no matter how much he drank. And he drank a lot.

'Busy?' Martin asked.

Janie nodded. The action made her lip hurt and she mentally cursed her husband and thought, *No more, Billy-Joe.*

'Yeah,' she said wondering if Martin had noticed anything about her – like her fat lip or the slight bruise on her right cheekbone. 'You?'

'Gotta cut twenty per cent outta this turkey Davy Rosenburg just delivered,' Martin said, pointing at the pile of pages on his desk. 'Horror crap. S'called *Lucy's Birthday*. Nearly half a million words. Dunno why anyone buys his stuff. S'crap an' full of padding. Any calls, darling?'

Janie, who was most certainly *not* his darling, looked at her pad. There were three calls. The first was from Davy Rosenburg threatening violent retribution if Martin didn't phone him immediately. The second was from an agent setting up an auction for a first novel from an sf writer who was 'going to be bigger than William Gibson'. And there was the one for which Martin had been waiting for over two months. From Drezy.

When she told him that Rosenburg had threatened to kill him, Martin shrugged and grinned and said, 'He's a pussycat'. But he sobered up inside two seconds when he heard that Sarah-Jane had phoned.

Janie watched this take place and distantly wished that there was a magic phrase she could say to good old Billy-Joe which would do the same.

'What did she want?' he demanded, the slur completely absent from his voice. He looked like a little boy who'd lost his mummy at a carnival and had just been told by a policeman that she was on her way to collect him: anxious and hopeful.

'She just wanted to ask you something about a manuscript you left in her flat.'

Martin's face became stricken. He nodded slowly, looking as if he suddenly understood the worst. 'She was annoyed. Christ, I wish I hadn't done that. But I was livid with her. Bloody thing was good, see? Even I could see that and I hate haunted house books. Christ, I'm a wanker. Why'd I do it?'

He's right about the wanker bit, Janie thought and said, 'Slow down Martin. You lost me somewhere. She wasn't annoyed, she was quite calm. What are you on about?'

'The *book*,' Martin said plaintively. '*Black Rock*. That's just about scotched any chance I had. I wish I'd just said I liked it.' He clapped his hands to his face, doubled over and heaved a sob.

Janie didn't much like him, but she liked seeing him cry even less. She wasn't the kind of girl who found it easy to clasp a weeping companion to her breast and say, 'There there.' All she did was become embarrassed for the distressed person. Anyway, it should have been *her* sitting there weeping.

Some of us have to soldier on, she thought. *Even when we have split lips, loose teeth, bruises all over us and a pain in our ribs each time we breathe in.*

While she looked at Martin's shuddering back, wondering what to do, a demon spoke up inside her and suggested, quite calmly, that she ought to whack him over the back of the head with her computer keyboard while she had the chance because he would probably never make such a good target again. Janie almost giggled, then hated herself for it. *No, I don't suppose the keyboard wire's long enough to reach anyway,* the demon said before it departed.

She scooted her chair a little closer to Martin, hesitated for a moment, then reached out a hand, intending to touch him, but not knowing where. His arms were folded in under him and his back was too far away to reach, which left his head as the obvious place. Janie could see his shiny pink scalp beneath his thinning hair and didn't really want to come in contact with it, but she swallowed her pride and her reservations and did it anyway.

Martin jumped as if he had been shot.

'S'okay,' she said quietly, 'I'm here,' she added, wondering what kind of consolation that was for him.

'Oh, Janie,' Martin's muffled voice said from somewhere beneath the folded-up tangle of arms and legs that he'd made of himself. 'I still love her.'

You shouldn't have been such a shit to her then, was the obvious reply, but Janie did not say it. She said, 'I know. I *know*.'

Martin unfolded himself and sat up. 'You don't understand what I've done,' he said sadly, shaking his head.

'You're right there, Martin,' Janie said. 'I haven't a clue.'

'*Black Rock*,' he said.

'Yeah, I've gathered by now that Black Rock is the word-pairing of the day. You'd better explain its significance.'

'I *wrote* on it,' Martin said, as if writing on a manuscript was a sin akin to chiselling a smiley face on one of the tablets bearing the Ten Commandments.

'That's what editors are for, isn't it?' Janie replied.

'It was good.'

'Yeah, you said that. Nod if I have it so far. You had this bit of manuscript – twenty-four pages, so Drezy said – and it was called *Black Rock* and you wrote on it.'

Martin looked at her in torment.

'You didn't nod.'

For one ugly moment she thought he'd slipped into a catatonic trance. 'Martin?' she asked.

He nodded.

'Right. Now tell me why you shouldn't have written on it.'

'Because it was good.'

That never stopped you before, she wanted to say, *or me, come to that*. But Martin hadn't finished yet.

'It said it was written by someone called Peter Perfect, down in the footer, it said, Peter Perfect, Black Rock, Tintagel.'

'Yeah?'

'But it was such a stupid name and the address belonged to the haunted house in the story . . . so I knew.'

'Knew what, exactly?'

Martin shook his head. 'It didn't come in the post you see. The envelope was sealed but there was no stamp on it, or addressee written on the front. So I knew. *She* left it there on the mat.'

'Sarah-Jane left it there?'

Martin nodded. 'Sarah-Jane *wrote* it. That's why she used a silly name and address. She wrote the first few pages of a novel – something that could have been excellent – and left it for me to find. And I played the game. I didn't mention it to her. I picked it up and read it and wrote some editorial comments on it. It was good, but I said it was crap because I was mad with her when I read it. I left it under the bed where I thought she'd find it, but she didn't and I forgot all about it. Now she's seen what I wrote on it there's no chance of a reconciliation.'

Two large tears formed in the corners of Martin's eyes. Janie watched them gather, no longer thinking of her colleague's distress or her own troubles at all. The words that swam in her head pushed everything else aside:

Sarah-Jane Dresden has begun to write a book.

Janie felt a moment of literally insane jealousy because this was the very thing *she'd* been promising herself she would do any day now, knowing she'd never get around to it. Then she felt a sudden surge of warmth for her friend who had started a book that wasn't going to be an ordinary 'I wish I could write a book' book, but one that – in Martin's own words – 'could have been excellent.'

In the moment of editorial competitiveness that followed, Janie had to stop herself asking if Martin had a copy that she could look at. Then she started to play Agony Aunt again.

'I think you should phone her and tell her the truth,' she advised.

'You do?'

'Yes, I do. Turn round, pick up that phone and tell her how good you think her writing is. I'll vacate the premises while you do it, if you like.'

'Thanks Janie, I'll ring her mobile now,' Martin said. 'And you can stay too, if you like.'

Janie liked.

Chapter Four

Romantic Interlude

Sarah-Jane's mobile telephone was supplied and paid for by Ace Publishing. This was not an act of kindness by Ace. In fact, some of the sales force regarded the sudden introduction of the mobiles as an act of treachery by their employer. A tighter rein could now be kept upon the sales staff. Which meant no more bunking off to go shopping, no more POETS days (Piss Off Early Tomorrow's Saturday) and no excuses about not getting messages. If Marketing Director Del Blass sent you a memo, you could say you didn't receive it – if he left a message on your ansaphone, you could lie that the machine was cranky, but if he spoke the words of his urgent message in your very ear, the only excuse you had later was that you forgot.

Sarah-Jane had mixed feelings. Sure, it was equivalent to having Del sitting in the passenger seat of your car, but Del didn't make a point of ringing you every five minutes and if you did your job you didn't have a lot to worry about. You could still fit in those little trips to the shops and wherever you were (theoretically, at least), you had instant contact with the world at large. This was a good thing.

Because although Sarah-Jane didn't believe in ghosts, she did have *some* fears. For example, walking back to her car in any one of a hundred dimly-lit and deserted multi-storey car parks, her red Ford Sierra estate always seemed to be a good fifty yards away from the stairs and there was always a heap of boxes or promotional stands in the back which would magically transform their outlines to resemble a figure. Waiting for her. And the phone was handy because Sarah-Jane would wait a few seconds, her fingers ready to turn on the phone and punch three nines if that vague shape on her back seat moved so much as an inch.

But it was not yet dark and Sarah-Jane was thinking not about finding men in her car, but bad-mouthing the woman in the Austin Allegro that she'd been stuck behind for five miles on the A384 to Launceston. She muttered curses by rote while she treated herself to a frame of Snowy Dresden's world; a scene starring Mr Winter and the fur rug in front of the fireplace. Sarah-Jane's imagination was fertile but she wasn't above stealing someone else's fantasy if it suited her. And the gothic romance Peter Perfect had set up in *Black Rock* suited her.

When the phone began to bleat, she jumped and felt absurdly guilty – as if she'd been caught masturbating.

Which was true – up to a point, she told herself.

She pulled over, put the car in neutral, applied the hand-brake and leaned down towards the passenger's side of the car for the mobile. The seatbelt locked. Sarah-Jane fought a brief battle with it before getting it undone. She leaned over, grabbed the bleating phone then lost her grip on it.

Dropsy! she scolded.

And stopped dead, staring at the phone.

Suddenly she didn't want to answer it.

Because something had gone awry.

In Sarah-Jane Dresden's twenty-eight years on the planet Earth, she had called herself Dropsy exactly *no times at all.*

But it wasn't just that. She also had the distinct feeling that when she put the phone to her ear she was going to be listening to the dulcet tones, not of Del Blass, but of Mr Winter himself; suddenly fictional no more, but alive and kicking. She was sharply aware that in the story Snowy had felt as if reality had subtly altered to accept her into a new version of it.

The odd sensation of fear and excitement ceased at the moment the phone stopped ringing.

Just being silly, Sarah-Jane told herself. *Get on your bike and get outta here!*

She used this other Snowy Dresden expression purposely, as though consciously adopting it would sap whatever power that fictional world might have. Then she grinned. The trouble with fictionalizing yourself, she thought, was that after a while, you wouldn't be quite sure where fiction finished and reality began. Like the man said, getting in was easy, it was the getting out again you had to worry about. But it wasn't as if she was going to visit a *real* place called Black Rock and a *real* Mr Winter, merely the real location upon which her ex-lover had sited his fantasy haunted house. What kind of trouble could you get yourself into by visiting Tintagel Castle? Other than falling off it into the sea?

The phone didn't ring again until Sarah-Jane was on the A39 at Camelford. This time there was no sense of foreboding. But this time its ringing hadn't broken into one of her fantasies.

'Look, Essenjay, I'm calling about the book.' Silence.

For a moment, Sarah-Jane didn't have the faintest idea who it was. Then she twigged. Martin, of course. How could she have forgotten his voice so easily?

'*Black Rock*?' she asked, knowing that was exactly what he meant. He thought his use of her as his heroine had offended her.

'Yeah . . .' he said and paused the way he always did before he said something nice to her. Handing out a compliment always seemed to hurt him badly – almost as if he were being forced to open his belly with his fingernail and pull you out a length of intestine which he badly wanted to keep for himself.

Sarah-Jane pre-empted him. 'It's good,' she said. 'Very good. You should be pleased.'

'I *am* pleased,' Martin said.

'You don't sound as if you are,' she replied.

'It's difficult for me,' he said. 'Y'know.'

Sarah-Jane didn't quite know whether he meant that writing it was difficult for him, now that she and he were parted, or that it was difficult for him to ask her if he could continue with it without her eventually suing him.

'You carry on,' she said brightly. 'I'm flattered.'

Silence.

'I said I'm flattered,' she repeated. 'You carry on. Do what you want to do. I don't mind.'

'I phoned to say I was sorry,' Martin said.

'It's OK, really Martin. I don't mind.'

For some reason Martin still didn't sound as if he believed her. 'You don't?' he said. 'You're sure?'

'Sure I'm sure. I won't sue you.'

Martin chuckled then and Sarah-Jane wasn't sure why. Relief perhaps. 'I'd like to talk to you,' he said.

Sarah-Jane was instantly on her guard against any onslaught he might be planning. She would not be emotionally blackmailed. 'You're talking to me now,' she said, knowing that this statement might not be true for very much longer. Her finger was a millimetre from the switch and if Martin started on his favourite subject, 'Us', he would be talking to a dead line in very short order.

'You're playing hard to get,' he said, almost certainly with a smug expression on his face. She could picture how he looked sitting in his office in 'doing deals' mode. She suddenly remembered why she'd threatened him with a rolling-pin and thrown him out. Martin had a good side, but it was his bad side she was reminded of now. If he was trying to get back into her favour, he was going about it entirely the wrong way. A red rose every day for a week would have been a start. An apology for his awful behaviour, accompanying said roses, might have softened her still further – and if the week's last rose had brought with it a receipt which said he'd added her to the insurance for the Ferrari, she might have begun to believe he'd changed.

'So what?' she said, suddenly bored with the conversation. If Martin wanted to novelize all her personal details, let him. As long as he kept out of her way, anything was fine by her.

'I want to publish it,' Martin said with a distinct question in his voice. That question asked: *Aren't you just ecstatic?* and it was probably present in the voice of God when he explained to Job what all the tribulations had been about.

'Oh, go whistle, Martin,' Sarah-Jane said mildly and rang off.

When the phone rang again, she ignored it. She did so all the rest of the way to Tintagel. The book would be good, and if it was published she would buy herself a copy, because

Martin had achieved the writer's goal of making her really want to know what happened next.

But as far as screwing the author went, well, she'd tried that and didn't damned well want to do it again.

Big headed bastard, she thought as she drove into Tintagel. *He's writing a book about me and he's publishing it himself and he expects me to be thrilled.*

Then her Girl Guide added, *but you* are *thrilled. You've driven all the way over here just to look at the place in which the book is set.*

Sarah-Jane no longer really knew what she felt about the whole thing. All she knew was that the Girl Guide spoke in the eminently reasonable voice of her dear departed mother.

Tintagel in late October looked much the same as all the other small towns in Devon and Cornwall: closed. There was one gift shop still open, but most of the hotels and guest houses were shut down for the winter. Barring the few late trippers, only the natives were here now and Tintagel had changed back from a pretty little tourist village to a drab-looking farming community. Bude, where Sarah-Jane lived, looked much the same at this time of year, but bigger.

She drove down the main street, past the silent Tintagel Toy Museum and the closed Wooton's Country Hotel. King Arthur's Bookshop stood at the top of the walk down to the ruins of King Arthur's Castle and appeared to be shut for the winter too. Sarah-Jane followed the road round to the right, heading towards the hotel which stood on a cliff on the edge of town. Where the row of houses ended, the road turned sharp left towards the sea and terminated at the hotel. This hotel was called The King Arthur. Sarah-Jane remembered it from the last time she was here years ago. It too was closed.

She drove on to its shingle forecourt, turned off the engine and sat looking up at the hotel. It was large and imposing and she suddenly realized that Martin's Black Rock might be based on this. He'd merely shrunk the hotel to the size of a mansion because since King had published *The Shining* you could no longer do haunted hotels without being accused of plagiarism.

A huge gut-twisting disappointment settled over her. She didn't know exactly *what* she'd expected to find, just that there should be more than this.

But there it was, the dark Atlantic sky behind it threatening a storm.

But it doesn't look as if it's crouching and about to pounce, she observed.

It didn't. It just looked like a hotel that was shortly going to be undergoing some maintenance.

Sarah-Jane got out of the car and walked up to the door. There was no gold knob on it and it was glass-paned. The inside of the hotel looked like the inside of a hotel: lobby, reception, thick carpets, chairs, you name it. Sarah-Jane did name it. Several times. She felt cheated.

Back on the forecourt she walked over to the building's left-hand side. Beyond the fence which bordered the parking area, the land fell away swiftly down to the sea. It wasn't a cliff on this side, just a steep hill which led down to the tiny bay where all that Tintagel had in the way of a beach lay. She couldn't see the beach, but remembered that it was less than a hundred metres long and access to it was almost impossible.

Looking across at the Castle ruins, she was more impressed. She didn't know who had built it, but it was a good place for a castle. It stood high on a double hill which was shaped like a figure eight and apart from the valley that led to its foot, was entirely surrounded by the sea. The beach – presumably where the inhabitants of the Castle had moored their boats – lay close by and would have been easy to defend. Anyone foolish enough to invade would have a major problem on their hands. You send an army down a heavily defended narrow valley, and pretty soon they're going to be dog food. And troops attacking from the sea would have had to swim to the base of the rock, and then face a very steep climb indeed before they even got to fight.

'Can I help you, love?'

Sarah-Jane spun round, stifling a yelp. A man in paint-splattered workman's overalls was standing behind her.

'Sorry, did I frighten you?' he said, using the words of Mr

Winter. But Mr Winter he was not. He was short and stocky and quite a bit too old. 'Anything I can do?'

'Uhh . . . well, I don't really know,' Sarah-Jane said, feeling stupid. 'I just came up here to, uhh, look around.'

'If you want to get to the Castle, there's a way down, but you have to go back through the village. There's a car park by the side of King Arthur's Bookshop.'

'No, I . . . I was looking for a place called Barras Nose. D'you know it?'

'You're standing on it, love. Or at least a part of it. Was it the hotel you were looking for?'

Sarah-Jane opened her mouth to speak, then snapped it shut again, knowing there was more to come, and knowing exactly what it was going to be.

'. . . or Black Rock?' the workman finished.

During the pronunciation of those last three words, the man's voice took on an entirely new tone. It was both sly and knowing: the voice of a Transylvanian villager who has had plenty of vampire hunters stop him and ask him the way to Castle Dracula and who has never seen any of them again.

You're imagining it, Sarah-Jane quickly told herself. *You didn't switch out of fantasy mode properly.*

This had to be true. What other reason could there be for her heart to hammer and her head to swim like that of a girl about to open her first male zipper? Simply because she now had confirmation that the place existed?

'Black Rock, actually,' Sarah-Jane said, hearing the faint tremor in her voice and feeling ashamed of herself. As if there was anything wrong in wanting to be the heroine of a gothic romance!

The workman held her gaze and nodded slowly. 'Down there,' he said, pointing behind him at the hotel as if it were transparent and the land showed through it. 'Down the hill. It's that big lump of rock at the bottom, stuck out in the sea.' Then he added the old traveller's joke: 'You can't get there from here though.'

'Where can I get there from?' Sarah-Jane asked, mesmerized. The man was staring at her so intently he might have been attempting hypnosis.

'Go back up the road to where the corner turns and instead of turning with it, you turn left against it. There's a little road that looks like it goes into the caravan site, but if you keep left, you'll see a muddy track. You can take a car down it, but there's something you may want to ask yourself before you do that.'

'And that is?' Sarah-Jane.

The workman smiled. ' "Can I get my car back up again?" ' he said.

Sarah-Jane nodded. 'Thanks.'

The man looked at her for a few seconds longer, then, as if deciding business had been concluded, abruptly turned away. Sarah-Jane watched him go, her brow furrowed. About half-way back to the hotel's entrance, he stopped dead, looked round and called, 'Best of luck, love,' then went on his way.

You don't suppose he was trying to tell you something, do you? Sarah-Jane's Girl Guide asked her.

Like what, d'you suppose? she answered mentally. *Beware the Ides of October? Don't forget your stake? I doubt it most sincerely. He was probably trying to let me know that when I get the car stuck and ask for help, he'll be the one with the Land Rover charging twenty-five quid to tow me out.*

Sarah-Jane went back to the car, trying to control her excitement. There was nothing to be excited about, when you thought about it. The workman had merely said that Black Rock was down there. Just that it existed. And the way he'd spoken suggested she would find only a lump of rock stuck out in the sea. He hadn't mentioned a house or its owner, so there was nothing to get worked up about.

Not yet, anyway.

Sarah-Jane paused at the top of the hill where the 'muddy track' began and looked down it at the sea. You couldn't see the bit of Barras Nose called Black Rock from here because the track wound round behind the hill on which the hotel stood, so there was still nothing to set the pulse racing.

There was, however, something to be concerned about.

She sat in the Sierra with the engine running and asked

herself the sixty-four thousand dollar question as suggested by Mr Weird the builder.

Will I be able to get my car back up again?

The track wasn't mud, it was the kind of gravel-clay mixture her dad called 'hoggin'. It was also very steep and very narrow and looked as if it would become slippery the moment any rain fell. She decided she should just go for it anyway. So what if the track only gave her a foot either side of the car? She was a good driver, wasn't she?

About half-way down, the mobile began to bleat. Sarah-Jane glanced at it, cursed and brought the car to a standstill which ended in a two-foot skid. She yanked on the handbrake and snatched up the phone.

'Essenjay, look, we seem to have a bit of a misunderstanding,' Martin said, without any preamble.

'I'll say we have!' Sarah-Jane snapped and turned him off.

She put the car back in first and rolled slowly down the steep track, keeping the phone on her lap. What she expected to happen next, happened at the exact moment she saw the white farm building set into the side of the hill.

The phone rang again.

Still rolling, she picked it up, turned it on and held it to her ear. Her eyes darted from the track to the farm building and she distantly noted that it was inaccessible from here – you'd have to cross a good two hundred yards of steep valley and hill to reach it. There had to be another track down to it that she hadn't noticed.

'Drezy, look,' Janie's voice was saying. 'Martin really did mean what he said about the book. You ought to be thrilled.' The line had developed a distinct hiss since the last time Sarah-Jane had answered it.

'I *am* thrilled,' she said, 'I'm just about tickled pink, but I absolutely don't want to talk to him any more.'

'He means it when he says he wants to publish it,' Janie said. 'And he isn't just doing it because he thinks it's a way back into your heart.'

The hiss was more pronounced now.

'It isn't and I'm thrilled for him,' Sarah-Jane replied. 'Just tell him to keep on . . .' She was going to add the words 'writing it,' but she had apparently entered one of those famed zones through which microwave signals seemed reluctant to pass and the line had gone dead. At the same time she began to feel dizzy. And scared. When her head cleared she was left with a disconcerting feeling that *everything had changed*. Especially as she could now see the trailer parked outside the white farm building. And the big black dog on it, still as stone and pointing.

At her.

The wide-eyed little girl inside Sarah-Jane woke up and was delighted. *It's all coming true!* she said. *Look, there's Diamond Ambrose Anstey, King of All the Dogs!*

She shivered. This wide-eyed little girl part of her had come within an ace, she was certain, of calling her 'Snowy'.

So the dog's real, so what? she asked herself. *So Martin came here for a look round on one of those Saturdays when he used to vanish and refuse to say where he was going. And he saw the lie of the land and got inspired, and there just happened to be this big black dog hanging around. So what?*

But if the dog was real, and pointing like it did in the book, it meant that Martin's imagination hadn't stretched as far as inventing it. Which also meant that perhaps his imagination hadn't stretched as far as inventing the house either.

The dog – whether it was called Diamond or not – still gave her something approaching the creeps. It wasn't natural for dogs to stand as still as that, for as long as that, pointers or otherwise.

Except that he's no ordinary dog, the little girl slipped in before she could stop her.

Bullshit, S'n'J told her good-naturedly and suddenly felt a little better about things. She glared up at the dog, told herself it was just a mangy mutt, and let the car roll down the track, a little further around a bend.

And there it was: the site of Martin Dinsey's famous haunted house – the lump of rock itself.

It was no hallucination: there was the house exactly as she had envisaged it while reading the manuscript – two storeys high, wider than Vistavision and looking for all the world as if it was ready to pounce. For the first time in all her years,

Sarah-Jane Dresden gazed upon a building that looked as if it possessed life.

S'n'J smiled. She knew exactly how Martin must have felt at exactly this point on this very track. It not only looked as if it was haunted, it looked as if it was *supposed* to look that way – as Martin had written, it was like some horror hack's version of a haunted house.

'So what do you do now, my girl?' she asked herself. 'Go down there and ask them if they want to stock the new Lulu Kaminsky novel?'

You could always say you were looking for Mister Winter, her inner voice suggested. *That'd be true!*

Anyway, she was already committed. It wasn't possible to turn the car around without driving up to the house and you'd have to be pretty nifty at reversing to go backwards all that way up a steep and narrow track. Apart from anything else, she wanted to go down there to see if there *was* a big reinforced door with no letter box and no lock, just a shiny door knob that looked like gold.

But the house won't be called Black Rock, that's a for-certain, she told herself. *It'll be End of the World House, or Atlantic Mansion, or Sea View or something like that. Martin wouldn't have used the house's real name. Its owner might sue.*

Of course it would be very nice indeedy if the house *was* called Black Rock and was inhabited by a Mr Winter, as per the imagination of Martin Dinsey, but that was heading towards fantasy-land . . .

And besides, you don't have a computer system to sell, she thought, putting the car into gear and following the track down the hill.

The weather-beaten sign on the gatepost said '*Black Rock*' just as it had done in the text, the house's forecourt was shingle and S'n'J parked where Snowy had parked.

Well, it might have looked as if it were a huge hunched grey animal, but there was no bad atmosphere. The place felt safe.

S'n'J knew that if she did nothing else, she was going to have to get out of the car and look at that front door, because there really was no letter box or lock on it – not that you could see from here, anyway.

You're crazy, she told herself, but she turned off the car's engine anyway. She put the keys in her jacket pocket. *I'm getting out of the car and I'm going over there and I might even knock on the door*, she told herself, *because so far, none of this has been a lie. So far, everything in the book has been true, which isn't what fiction is supposed to be about. And I'm curious as to the reasons why.*

Knowing that it was too much to ask that a man called Mr Winter lived inside the house, Sarah-Jane reached over to pick up her telephone, fumbled and broke two fingernails.

It's all coming true, Dropsy! she told herself and no longer knew whether she should be shocked or delighted. What she *did* know was that she was filled with that delicious kind of anticipation she used to feel back at the beginning of her relationship with Martin when he was due down to Cornwall after his three day stint at Ace. She was also aware that there was a small part of her busily totting up the list of *coincidences so far* and reducing the odds against the rest of the first chapter of *Black Rock* not happening. It looked very much as if fiction was somehow changing into fact. Snowy's romantic experience suddenly seemed to have a very good chance of happening to Sarah-Jane.

Shouldering open the stiff car door, she looked at the house, marvelling at it, and at herself. Because what they would say in books at this point (and what Martin had said in *his* book) was that the person standing in front of the house would be overcome by an emotion of *belonging* – as if they'd finally come home. At this point, even if the story was incredibly good, you'd find yourself curling your lip and thinking, *Oh yeah, very likely!* The real marvel was, that now she was standing here, the sensation didn't seem clichéd at all. She really did feel as if she belonged. It was stupid and her own lip curled as she realized it, but it was the curled lip that went away, not the sensation of being home.

This means, young lady, that according to the usual principles of hack fiction you're pretty certain to end the story haunting Black Rock until the end of time. Either that or you're a ghost already!

S'n'J grinned, because she felt good – better, in fact, than she had done since giving Martin 'the flick' as they said on 'Neighbours'. But also because she had mentally begun to sing Kate Bush's 'Wuthering Heights': *Heathcliff, it's me, Cathy, come home* ... It seemed to fit the circumstances somehow.

Must read the book one day, Snowy, she told herself. *I may find I'm in that too!*

She chuckled. The warm Atlantic wind tousled her hair and the first warm raindrop touched her nose. The storm had started, apparently. She didn't care. Sarah-Jane Dresden was beginning to have fun.

But hadn't you better turn the car around? her Girl Guide voice suddenly cut in.

There *were* actually such things as ghosts, S'n'J suddenly decided, and she had proof of it. When her mother died, she left behind a ghost and its sole purpose was to haunt her only daughter. It lived inside her daughter's head, pretending to be the Girl Guide voice of her conscience. If they'd handed out medals for being a spoilsport, this ghost's metaphysical chest would be weighed down. It made sure you were wearing clean and unfrayed underwear, that you brushed your teeth, and amongst its many other sins, it had been responsible for S'n'J spending her first night with Martin alone in the spare room when she'd badly needed to shag him till he screamed for mercy.

The trouble with mothers was that they still pushed you around even after they'd stepped off this mortal coil.

S'n'J knew that this voice would nag at her exuberance until she did what she was told so she got back into the car. It said in the book that if Snowy had turned her car around and looked at Black Rock in its rear-view mirrors, a different story would have been followed (or no story at all!). S'n'J's Girl Guide insisted that she check it out and Be Prepared.

As S'n'J started the car, she searched the windows of the house in case *he* was in there, looking out at her. The windows were dark and nothing moved behind them.

Undaunted she turned the car through a hundred and eighty degrees and brought it to a standstill on the spot she had started from. She had intended to turn off the engine, but her Girl Guide wasn't having it.

Up on the hill in front of her, where the farm stood, the big black dog was still on the trailer, still pointing at her. It must have altered its position by about ninety degrees from when she saw it earlier, but she got the strange feeling that it hadn't moved a muscle. It seemed to her that the animal was some kind of canine optical illusion – like those oil-paintings you saw whose figures looked directly at you wherever you happened to be in the room. The dog probably wasn't pointing at her at all – it just looked as if it was.

As long as it doesn't come down here looking for a fight, I don't mind, S'n'J told herself, and turned her attention to the rear-view mirror.

All it showed was a section of Black Rock's grey wall. The wing mirrors gave a wider angle of view, but were tilted for the road, and angled too low to help.

Nothing much changed so far, she told herself bobbing about like a boxer to give herself different angles of view.

Like many people who drive for a living, S'n'J would have broken your fingers for you before allowing you to screw up her mirrors, but she couldn't get a clear view of the house without moving at least one of them. She grabbed hold of the internal mirror and manipulated it.

Her mouth dropped open.

The two windows she could now see were patterned with a coating of frost.

S'n'J twisted round and looked over her shoulder. The windows were *not* frosty.

She looked in the rear-view mirror again, her heart beating fast. *Impossible!*

The frost was not the thick rime you had to scrape off the windscreen on a January morning, but delicate filigree traceries, the centres of which seemed almost to describe a fleur-de-lis. Both windows were similar, but not identical, and she began to wonder whether the frost effect was a pattern etched into the glass

But that surely had to be what it was. The patterns were etched into the windows, perhaps by hand. She still didn't know why they appeared plain when you looked straight at the windows though.

S'n'J adjusted the mirror so that she could see another downstairs window on the left-hand side of the house. This too was frosted but the design seemed to be of feathery arcs. There was no frost at all on the panes of its partner on the right-hand side of the house. Instead there appeared to be an oblong of darkness that reflected no light whatsoever. It could have been painted there in matt black.

Frowning at this optical illusion, she drove the car away from the house, stopping close to the gate. From here she could see the upstairs windows in the mirror. The one on the right also appeared to be a black hole in the wall.

Except that when she actually got out of the car to look directly at them, the missing windows *were* present. None of them was frosted, they all had curtains, open and friendly, and not one of them twitched suggesting a hidden watcher.

There was evidently no one at home, or she would have been spotted by now and asked what she was doing on private property.

On any ordinary day, Sarah-Jane would have been worried about trespassing, and it would have occurred to her to be dead careful because she was some distance away from civilization and anyone could come screaming out of that house and lay into her. But this, apparently, was no ordinary day. She felt safe here. As if she belonged.

And besides, there's something very interesting going on here, she told herself, getting back into the car.

The Girl Guide spoke up as she sat down. *The only reason you're hanging around here is because you're waiting for Mr Winter to show up and sweep you off your feet and down on to his fur rug in front of the fireplace. These things don't happen in real life. No one is coming to sweep you off your feet!*

But like her namesake, Sarah-Jane could imagine it. Very clearly and in fine detail. Mr Winter's hard body, his soft and warm skin. His gentle and experienced hands.

A picture of Martin grew in her mind then. Martin, standing naked in front of her, his shoulders slumped forward from years at a desk, his small, slack belly looking like a pink bum-bag tied around his waist and a five-and-a-half-inch erection (he was one of those men who incessantly measured, perhaps expecting further growth) sticking up at an angle of forty-five degrees or so and looking a bit like the neck that you pulled out of a frozen turkey. 'Do you want to suck my lollipop, little girl?' he asked in her mind. At the time, it had been funny. Looking back, she felt only distaste.

Because he was crap at sex, she told herself, angling the wing mirror on her side of the car so that she could see the upstairs window on the left side of the house. *Because he didn't like having me on top because it threatened him.* S'n'J had never called him Mr Missionary to his face but towards the end she'd thought it a great deal.

There had been a time when none of this mattered. Unfortunately, S'n'J had been a bit green then and it didn't for one moment occur to her that that little thing called 'quality of life' was important. A couple of years with Martin had taught her differently.

The only orgasms you got were the ones you gave yourself, S'n'J needlessly reminded herself as she pushed the image of Martin off the retina of her mind's eye and replaced it with one of Mr Winter, who could probably make you come yourself to death.

Then Sarah-Jane found the upstairs left-hand window with the rear-view and her fantasy shattered.

This window was thick with frost.

And it shone with a dazzling golden light.

In quick succession, three thoughts whickered across the empty plane of S'n'J's mind. The first was that Mr Winter was in this room and you could be certain of that because of the depth of the frost. The second was that the level of light inside the room would be enough to chase any semblance of a shadow out of Wembley Stadium. And the third was that the light was not internal, but a reflection of the sun.

'All of these things are impossible,' she whispered to herself. 'I am looking North. The front of the house faces

South. The sun doesn't reflect on that window. Ever. Even if it was shining, and the sky wasn't dark with rain cloud, there is no way the sun could reflect in that window. There is also no earthly way it could be as bright as that inside the house, and in the real world, the one that you don't seem to be doing a very good job of keeping in touch with just recently, men called Mr Winter do not frost up their houses merely by being in them.'

She began to wonder if there'd been a large whack of ergotamine in her lunchtime pastie and she was tripping out of her brain. It was either that, or the house was enchanted.

Looking into the light, Sarah-Jane told herself that her retinas would be getting a tan, and grinned.

Before she was *completely* magicked, she supposed, she ought to put her head outside the car and look at the shining window without the use of the mirror. It was difficult to break away and for a few moments she understood how a moth must feel when presented with an unshaded hundred-watt lamp. When she tore herself away, she felt a snap inside her head, as if someone had pinged the centre of her brain with an elastic band. Distantly she told herself it had to be something to do with her pineal gland which was the thing that sensed light and dark. Left over from ancient times, the gland told you to hibernate when the days got short. S'n'J thought it had a point.

She stuck her head out of the car and craned round at the offending window. Two huge blue and yellow after-images of it swam on her retinas, but through them she could see that the window was not lit. Or frosted.

Her left temple throbbed – there was a blunt instrument in there that would doubtless soon turn into a pointed one. S'n'J rubbed the hollow beside her eye, wincing. She glanced at her watch and was surprised that fifteen minutes had passed since she'd arrived.

Now you know what really *happened*, she told herself, suddenly disappointed. As in all the lousiest books, everything had been a dream. She remembered feeling tired and she remembered leaving the engine running, and now she thought about it, she also remembered what James in Cars

Inc. had said when she'd gone in for her new front tyres a fortnight ago: that the exhaust downpipe was blowing and wanted fixing pretty damned quick. He'd asked her if she could smell the exhaust coming into the car and when she'd said no she couldn't, his reply was, 'That's how it kills you.' S'n'J had nodded dutifully, said she didn't have time to have it done now, but would get back as soon as possible to have it fixed, and since then she had entirely forgotten about the leaky pipe.

She told herself that she was lucky that one quick nightmare and a headache to follow were the only things she had to worry about. If she had slept a little longer with that good old carbon monoxide coming in the car, she might not have woken up at all.

Turning off the engine, she climbed out, feeling a little shaky and disorientated, and breathed deeply. The air tasted very fresh and clean and damp; it had begun to rain. It wasn't quite the storm she'd expected though, just one of Cornwall's famous light and steady drizzles.

It felt good on her skin.

Chapter Five

Janie

Sometimes – usually on the days that Martin was in the office – Janie Sanderson wished she'd stayed in bed and called in sick. Today hadn't yet turned into one of those, but its status was *borderline* and edging towards *why didn't you stay home?*

The reason she almost never stayed home, even when she felt poorly, was back there lurking in her house in Bracknell.

It was called Billy McAllister and it purported to be a musician. Three years ago, in a fit of what she could only describe as juvenile optimism, she had married him.

The oft-quoted piece of wisdom which ran along the somewhat sexist lines of, *soon as you marry this gorgeous* Vogue *model she'll turn into a horrible old drudge because she no longer has to bother being lovely*, also worked in reverse, Janie had discovered. Billy (also known as Billy-Joe after the famous song in which his namesake jumped off the Tallahassee Bridge – and sometimes Janie wished he'd live up to the song) had been in full possession of a very good day job as an analytical chemist when they'd married and he'd been handsome, debonair, and fun to be with. But a week after they'd moved into their new home Billy-Joe had jacked his job.

And since then he had been a 'professional musician' – which in reality meant that he did one gig a month if he was lucky and brought home about thirty quid – minus what he'd drunk, of course. Which, in turn, meant that Billy lived off Janie.

It had been OK in the early days when Billy hadn't yet developed his aversion to housework, cooking or washing up, but the subsequent two and a half years had been different. It got to be wearing after a time.

These days Billy was the regular couch-potato; transfixed by television, turning to fat and chugging down all the cans of liquid refreshment he could lay his hands on. Janie had developed the ability to pick out the smell of Tennent's Extra from fifty feet, and like many wives before her, had discovered that when your spouse was crossing the slender border between *drinker* and *alcoholic*, communication became impossible. Nowadays there were only two ways Billy wanted to communicate with her: with his dick and with his fists. And quite often, one of these modes of expression would lead to the other. Because as much as you might want to, you couldn't communicate with a woman *that* way when your dick resolutely pointed south and swung like a dowser's pendulum.

Because she loved him (or at least loved what he had been) Janie had tried to make Mr Flaccid into Mr Stiff. She had stroked, caressed, pulled, nibbled, licked and sucked like a hoover, all to no avail. And guess who collected the blame? She'd emasculated him, he said, that was why he couldn't get a hard-on for her. After which he would rap home the message on her body with those parts of him that did still work.

It had gone far enough now. Last night's enthralling episode was the last she wanted to be in. You couldn't say that Janie Sanderson hadn't stood up and taken her lumps like a woman (or a man come to that) but last night the rules had changed from *blows to the torso only* to *open season* and while she could carry a stabbing pain in her ribs or big purple bruises on her abdomen, there was a limit and that limit had been exceeded last night.

If Janie put her tongue to her two upper front teeth she would be able to move them both, easily and to an extent which frightened her. If she ran her tongue between those loose teeth and her top lip she would feel the cuts there, caused by the penetration of the loose teeth under the impact of Billy's delicate musician's hand. Her top lip was swollen to what seemed like the size of a bicycle tyre.

So far nobody seemed to have noticed the fat lip, which was good, but it had to end here. Janie didn't intend to spend the next weeks, months or years concocting stories about how she'd walked into doors or fallen down the stairs.

THE BASTARD'S GOT TO GO, she typed on the screen in capitals. HOW DO I GET HIM OUT OF THE HOUSE?

ANSWER: KILL HIM STONE DEAD AND CHUCK HIM DOWN THE WELL.

She looked at the new plot-line for her life, and grinned.

It hurt.

'Who you gonna kill?' Martin asked.

When Janie looked round she found he was standing right behind her. Normally she knew when he closed in on her. His ego arrived before him. But today, said ego was somewhat shattered. He'd offered to publish a book the love of his life had written, and she'd told him to go whistle, which wasn't how you were supposed to treat the famed Martin Dinsey.

'Kill?' Janie asked, turning back to the screen to buy herself time while she frantically tried to concoct a suitable story. No one here knew about her trouble with Billy.

'Yeah. If it's a reference to me, I think I oughta know.'

Janie looked up at him and saw that he meant it. If she hadn't spent the last five years dealing with writers, she probably would have thought he'd thrown a cog. Ninety-eight per cent of writers had egos the size of China through which ran a streak of paranoia which was as black as tarmac and a hundred miles wide. Apparently it rubbed off. It had on Martin anyway.

'Is that what she said when you spoke to her?' Martin asked.

Janie shook her head. 'No, Martin. It's nothing to do with Drezy.'

'What *is* it to do with then?' he challenged.

Janie thought about it. And realized why *she* was an editor instead of a writer. Lies didn't come easily to her. She sighed. 'Billy,' she said.

Martin frowned, peering at her screen. 'Billy, as in your Billy-Joe?'

She nodded.

'You're gonna kill him?'

She nodded again, resignedly.

Martin's lips flickered into the closest approximation of a smile she'd seen since he'd learned that Drezy had called. 'Fallen out?' he asked.

'Of an aeroplane,' she replied. 'At least I hope he has.'

Martin nodded. 'Men,' he said, and stood there, swaying slightly and brimming with booze.

At least he doesn't smell of Tennent's, Janie thought, hoping he wouldn't ask any more questions about her private life.

'Did you get hold of Drezy yet?' Janie asked, changing the subject.

'Phone's in a dead spot.' He shook his head. 'I can't understand her. It's almost as if she didn't *want* me to publish her damned book,' he added in a wounded tone.

'Perhaps she doesn't,' Janie replied.

'Because it's me, I s'pose,' Martin reasoned.

Janie shrugged. 'I'd take the book off your hands if *that* was going to be a problem,' she ventured.

When Martin finally spoke it was with the dangerous tone of a sheriff telling you you had until sundown to get out of town. '*I* found Black Rock, *I* get to publish it,' he warned.

Janie shrugged

'But she doesn't seem to want that.'

'I wonder why,' Janie said, innocently.

Martin ignored this. 'She can't be holding out for more money because we haven't offered her any yet. But if she didn't want it published, why did she leave the damned thing where I'd find it?'

'Maybe she just did it to prove something,' Janie said. 'What if she wanted to show you that she wasn't as dumb as you thought? That would be the best way of doing it, wouldn't it? You find an unsolicited manuscript, you read it, you rate it. *Voilà!* One happy Drezy.'

Martin shook his head. 'I didn't think she was dumb,' he said. 'She knew that.'

I doubt it very much, Janie thought. *That isn't the*

impression I got from her. 'Well, perhaps she felt insecure,' she said, biting her tongue before she could add, *Because you probably treated her the way you seem to treat all women. As inferior beings*. She could have gone on to illustrate that by referring to his list of authors which, as yet, did not include a single female.

Martin sighed. 'Maybe she did,' he said with that infuriating expression which said: *women, huh, they ain't just a different sex, they're a different species*.

Janie sighed too. She could no longer be bothered with the mystery of Drezy's book and why she didn't want it published.

'She wants it published,' Martin said. 'She must or she wouldn't have shown it to me.'

'You're certain it was *her* work, are you?' Janie asked.

Martin nodded. 'Positive. Look, I'm going to try ringing her again.' He went back to his desk.

Janie suddenly felt very weary. *None of this is necessary*, she thought. *Not the trouble between Martin and Drezy or the trouble between me and the uncrowned king of the rock guitarists Billy McAllister. All this heartache could be avoided if men would just loosen up a little and treat women how they'd like to be treated themselves. We're not a different species, inferior, inscrutable or genetically inclined to servitude, we're just like men except for the variance in sexual equipment. And the aggression, of course . . .*

She touched her loose teeth with her tongue and made a decision. As from tonight Billy was history. She would go home, pick up a few things and leave the house – and him in it. She could get him to leave later. She would tell Jill, the Editorial Director, she was going to be working from her mother's for a few days.

'Damn!' Martin shouted and slammed the phone back into its cradle. 'I've . . .' he tailed off, shaking his head.

Janie waited.

'I've got this odd sensation,' Martin finally confided. 'A horrible feeling that Essenjay is in trouble. Big trouble.' He looked ashamed. 'It's not like it's my imagination working overtime, just because the phone won't work,' he said. 'It's more than that. It's like a piece of my brain has turned into a kind of rectangular box made of bright crystal,' he said, looking at her carefully to gauge her reaction.

Janie had never seen Martin embarrassed before, but he was blushing like Bashful from the seven dwarfs.

'I can't explain it any better than that,' he said, continuing in spite of himself. 'It's like this bright rectangle in the centre of my brain and in it, I can see this big house.'

'Looks like a haunted house,' Janie said. 'Made of grey stone. Two storeys high, grey slate roof. Seven windows and a door. There's sea all around it. It's Black Rock, isn't it?'

Half-way through her first sentence, Martin's jaw began to fall. By the time she'd finished, it was almost on his chest. 'How did *you* know?' he asked in wonder.

Janie didn't know how she knew. All she knew was that it was unsettling. Janie had heard that craziness was infectious and if Martin had it, she didn't want to wake up in the morning and find she had it too.

'I thought I was going insane,' Martin said. 'But I can't be if you can picture it in exactly the same way. I can see it there now, hunched like it's going to pounce. Only I can see Essenjay standing in front of it, looking at something. I can't see what the thing is, but it's dangerous. And it's going to hurt her.'

Janie's point of view was a little different, but not much. She could picture the house, she could picture Drezy standing in front of it, and she knew there was danger involved, but she didn't think it was just Drezy who was going to get hurt if this Black Rock thing wasn't sorted out soon and put to bed. She thought it was going to be all three of them.

'Can I ask you a question, Martin?' she said. 'One to which you will reply truthfully.'

'Yes.'

'Scouts honour?'

'Dib dib dib,' Martin said grinning and giving her the scout's two-fingered salute. In that moment he looked quite insane.

'Did *you* write *Black Rock*?' she asked.

Martin looked absolutely astonished. '*What?*'

'Answer the question, Martin. This might save us a lot of trouble later.'

'No, I did not write *Black Rock*,' he said.

Janie nodded. She was tempted to believe him. But only tempted.

'So why did she promise not to sue you?'

Martin shook his head. 'I'm as puzzled about that as you are,' he said.

'She's in the book, isn't she?' Janie said.

Martin nodded. 'Yeah, she is. I don't know how you knew unless she showed it to you, or told you.'

Janie nodded too. Drezy *was* in danger, but not from a haunted house. She was in danger from Martin. At some point during the couple of months since they'd split, he had departed from reality in a big way. He'd started writing a 'haunted house' book, in which Drezy played a part. She had seen some of it and consequently she had been nonplussed when Martin had phoned her and offered to publish it. It all fitted. You *would* be nonplussed if an editor you knew wrote a book with you in it and then told you *he* was going to publish it. And if, when he made that phone call, he treated you not as if you were a character in it, but as if you actually *wrote* it, you would be dumbstruck. And you might not want to speak to him again.

Janie Sanderson solves another mystery, she told herself. But for some reason she didn't feel any better about things. She could still see Black Rock itself etched on her mind's eye, and she still had the distinct feeling that Drezy was in immediate danger.

Chapter Six

Sarah-Jane Takes a Tumble

After about thirty seconds of standing in the rain on the forecourt of Black Rock and breathing deeply, some of the wool began to clear from Sarah-Jane's head, leaving room for the doubts to creep in. She either had to believe she'd been poisoned by the leaky exhaust, or that Black Rock really was different when viewed in a mirror.

While she didn't feel a bit poisoned, S'n'J thought that Lewis Carroll's Red Queen, who practised believing two impossible things before breakfast every day, would have had trouble with the other alternative.

There was a part of her that badly wanted to drive away, scattering the pages of the manuscript as she went. She didn't *need* to know what happened to Snowy Dresden, or what Black Rock actually was. But another part of her knew a more basic truth. Needing something was a mile away from *wanting* it.

And S'n'J *wanted* to know.

She got back inside the car and stared across the valley to where the big black dog still pointed at her.

Where the supernatural was concerned, Sarah-Jane Dresden was not a woman who took fright easily. She could sit through the spookiest of films then happily wander through her flat in the dark without so much as a thought about the vampires or ghouls waiting for her in the shadows. But she also knew that she possessed the potential for becoming a Born Again scaredy-cat; she was by no means fearless now, where dark car parks were concerned, but she wasn't frightened by the supernatural because it didn't exist.

But if she looked again, and those windows were frosted

and that brilliant light was shining out from upstairs, she was going to be forced to change her views.

S'n'J took a deep breath, held in and looked up at the mirror.

The upper window, which had earlier shone with a blinding light, was now just an ordinary window.

She let her breath out in a long, relieved sigh. *One down, six to go*, she told herself, moving the mirror so that she could see the window above the front door. This was all fine and dandy too. The chances of seeing something wrong were steadily diminishing. Especially as the right-hand upstairs window – the one that had earlier looked like an empty black rectangle – was present and correct.

Smiling, she angled the mirror so she could run through the rest of the house. Same story. Disappointing even, in a perverse kind of way.

It wasn't until she'd finished checking and was turning the mirror to its original position that she realized she'd just seen the edge of something she didn't recall from before. Something that had moved. Skittered, perhaps.

Don't look back! her Girl Guide voice suddenly ordered. *Don't look back because if you do something will go wrong. If you do, it'll be too late to stop!*

Ignoring this advice in much the same way as Lot's wife had ignored it before her, and for the same reasons, S'n'J turned the mirror back.

And felt that odd sensation of reality changing again. It was almost as if the very air had split, swept the rent in itself over her, then knitted together behind her, so that she was on the wrong side of the old reality. Or in an entirely new one. It was not a pleasant sensation, and if she'd been the screaming type, she would have screamed then. Not a long throat-tearing screech of terror, but a short, sharp yelp of surprise. As it was, she just said, 'Oh my!'

Because the impossible had just happened again.

Her brain, obviously not used to such quick changes in the world about her, first interpreted what she saw lying on the wet shingles as a very large black bird, crashed to earth and dying, its wings twitching their last. Then she decided it was

64

the black dog, bigger than it should be, and broken beyond repair.

The truth was just as surreal.

It was a man sprawled there as if he'd just fallen. He was on his back, his limbs at crazy angles, and he was dressed like Fred Astaire: top hat, white tie and tails. And white spats on patent leather shoes. Except that the hat, crushed beyond redemption, lay nearby, and one of the shoes was half off his foot.

S'n'J couldn't see his face, and couldn't tell if he was alive or dead, but she knew exactly who he was.

Mr Winter.

A ghost from a bygone age.

None of this can be happening! she complained, frightened to look any more and yet frightened to take her eyes off the mirror in case the view changed again when she looked directly at the scene.

Steeling herself, she tore her eyes away from the mirror and looked over her shoulder out of the car's rear window.

The man was neither ghost nor optical illusion. He still lay there, one of his coat tails flapping lazily in the breeze.

Oh Jesus, God and little fishies! she thought, *He was on the roof watching me and he fell off.*

She climbed out of the car, her body no longer waiting for her mind to tell it what to do; it was responding to an emergency and acting of its own accord. If there was anything she could do to help the man on the ground, she would do it.

S'n'J went round to the far side of him, because his face was pointing at the house and because she didn't want to start pulling him about in case his back was broken. She spotted the blood dripping from his mouth and swore. There was so much of it that he'd either bitten his tongue half off or he had internal injuries. It wasn't lung blood, though, which was good. It wasn't bright enough for that.

S'n'J squatted down beside him, entertaining a brief fantasy that he was going to jump up and grab her (*like an ugly jack-in-the-box*) which would be par for the course if this had been contained between the pages of a horror story. A quick visual check-over confirmed that this man was too badly broken to do that. One of his thighs had a thirty-degree kink in it, his right femur was surely snapped in several places, both his thumbs and his right shoulder appeared to be dislocated and his knuckles were badly lacerated. In short, he looked like someone who had fallen off a roof and landed badly. Even his clothes were ripped and smeared with the green moss from the roofing tiles. He was not going to be jumping up at anything for a good long time, certainly not up at her.

But it *was* Mr Winter. There was no detailed physical description of him in the pages of *Black Rock*, only the way Snowy had visualized him, but he fitted the picture that had formed in S'n'J's imagination, right down to the last detail.

She laid her fingers on the side of his throat, feeling for his carotid. His skin was cool and moist with the rain, but his heart was beating. And he was breathing quite regularly. This wasn't a man about to pop his socks.

S'n'J pulled open one of his eyelids. His eye was rolled up. She could just see the edge of his smoky grey iris. She let the lid drop again, then prised his mouth open and felt inside. His tongue wasn't bitten off and none of his teeth were loose, but there was plenty of blood about in there. She wasn't sure where it was coming from unless it was from the back of his nose – he was breathing through his mouth, so it could be. He wasn't inhaling it, either, so it was unlikely to be coming up from his stomach, unless he'd puked this lot. S'n'J wanted to roll him on his side and put him in the coma position so the blood ran out, but she was worried that his back might be broken and didn't want to make it worse if it was. If he was conscious she could get an idea as to its state, but he was still out cold. The best thing she could do, she decided, was to call for an ambulance.

She looked at him for a few seconds, frowning. Then she gently slapped his cheek in a kind of patting motion. He didn't stir. She hit him a little harder and when this didn't work she went back towards the car to call for help. She could keep her eye on him while she waited for the ambulance to come. She wouldn't let him choke.

Ignoring all the questions queuing up in her head that

badly wanted answers, S'n'J snatched the phone out of the car, dropped it, retrieved it, distantly reminded herself about being a Vaudeville act looking for somewhere to perform, turned it on and punched three nines.

Up on the trailer, across the valley, the big black dog still pointed at her.

It wasn't until nothing happened, that S'n'J remembered that she was in a radio dead spot. The only other option was to try to get inside the house and use the phone in there. If Mr Winter had got out he was going to have to be able to get in again, so he would have left a door or window open. Probably round the back of the house.

And failing that, the mobile might work round there.

But having decided on this plan of action, she realized that now she'd discovered there was a *real* Mr Winter, she was reluctant to let him out of her sight, even to make a phone call.

Because you think he might disappear again, the way the frosty windows and the bright light did?

'Something like that,' she muttered, and had another idea.

She went back to the prone body of Mr Winter and began to search his pockets. Contrary to what she might believe having read those manuscript pages, the front door *had* to have a lock, and the key to it might just be in one of the pockets of Mr Winter's tail suit.

Thirty seconds later, S'n'J was heading down the path at the side of the house with her mobile. There had been a lot of interesting things in Mr Winter's pockets – including a foil-wrapped ribbed condom whose shelf-life had expired in 1993, a gold-plated flick-knife, two HB pencils, a British Rail ticket to Waterloo, the ignition key to a Porsche and a big bullet for a handgun of some description, but no door key. And she'd found no money, wallet or identification of any sort.

The muddy path that led down the left-hand side of the house – the side that gave you a clear view of the ruins of King Arthur's Castle – was about eighteen inches wide and next to a steep drop to the sea. It wasn't steep enough to call a cliff, but S'n'J had no doubt that if you stumbled you were going into the water because there was no protective fence.

Round here, the wind was a little more keen and whipped the drizzle into her eyes. Squinting against the rain, and keeping her right hand in contact with the wall of the house at all times, S'n'J proceeded with extreme caution.

There was a small, raised rocky garden at the back. At some time someone had obviously dumped topsoil upon the rock, walled it in with two courses of bricks and half covered it with turf. It hadn't been looked after. The grass was long and the flowerbeds were thick with weeds. There were several items of wooden garden furniture too – a rotten table, two falling-apart chairs and a bench seat that looked as if it had been added recently. Between this and the back of the house was a small flagstone patio.

S'n'J stopped, wiped her face and looked carefully at the house. There were windows here in the same configuration as the ones at the front, but there was no door.

Not entirely surprised, S'n'J turned on the mobile, mentally crossing her fingers.

The phone didn't work. There was no blip when she turned it on and no hiss of static afterwards.

Bugger! she thought.

The battery couldn't be flat because the phone had held a full charge when she left home this morning, so it should have made some sort of noise, even if it was only a buzz or hiss. Feeling a numb kind of panic, she held it to her ear. If you listened carefully you could hear a similar sound to the one made by a seashell if you held one to your ear. The distant roar of the sea.

Great, S'n'J thought, *my mobile's connected to the Atlantic . . .*

And as if the phone was alive and knew that it had only a limited amount of time before she turned it off, it acted.

And suddenly blasted her ear with a raging full-volume screech.

Afterwards, S'n'J thought it had sounded like a high-speed saw tearing through metal. Now, she simply reacted to the pain and moved so quickly there wasn't time for thought.

She threw the phone down before the sound had time to burst her eardrum – and probably mince her brain too.

It hit the wet flagstones, bounced and finally came to rest in a shallow puddle.

S'n'J looked at it for a second, simultaneously realizing two things. The first was that the terrible noise had stopped; the second – and lesser – realization was that she'd almost certainly broken an expensive piece of kit that belonged to Ace Publishing.

When she retrieved the phone, there was a crack which ran almost its entire length and it was wet, but the power light was still on. Glaring at it, she shut it off and stuffed the phone into her jacket. She could think about the damage later. The important thing was to get help and get it fast. If Mr Winter came to and started trying to move, he could well cripple himself.

If he isn't crippled already, that is, she told herself.

She hurried to the other end of the patio and followed the path round the far side of the house. The door had to be up there.

Except that it wasn't.

This side of the house was identical to the other – no doors, no windows. Which meant, S'n'J thought, that Mr Winter must have either come out of the front door and climbed up on to Black Rock's roof, or climbed out from an upstairs window.

Later, S'n'J, would tell herself she should have seen the significance in this and she would mentally kick herself for being such a dummy. As it was, she made a snap decision. She would break into the house and use the phone inside to call an ambulance.

Back at the rear of the house she peered into the lounge window. Her mind had already furnished the room. And here it was, real: big, open fireplace, fur rug and two leather sofas.

She gazed in at it and shivered. Not a cold-water-down-your-back shiver, but one of delight. The optimistic side of her was busily telling her that sometimes things *could* be perfect and just as you had imagined them.

One of the good things about having access to everything

Ace published was that over the years you picked up many snippets of exotic information. Sometimes these proved useful.

This was one of those times. When you wanted to enter a building through a window and you didn't have any method of forcing it, you could break a hole in it that was just about big enough to put your hand through and open the catch. The noise wouldn't be too great – which wasn't her major concern here – and there wouldn't be too much broken glass. All you did was to tap gently on the pane with a pointed object. Or in S'n'J's case a good-sized chunk of Barras Nose rock pulled from the moist earth behind her.

She chose her spot, and tapped gently.

The windowpane clinked like steel when the rock hit it.

She frowned and tapped again. It really did sound like a hammer hitting metal. And a fairly solid piece of metal at that. *Things don't always work out just like they do in fiction*, her Girl Guide voice told her, somewhat needlessly.

Suddenly maddened, S'n'J tried again, this time swinging the rock from a distance and with a lot more force. In the moment before the rock touched the glass, when it was too late to stop, a thought struck her: when the piece of Barras Nose went through the glass, her hand would still be wrapped around it. The consequences of this didn't require extra thought. Her fingers and wrist were undoubtedly going to be slashed. The only question was, *how badly?*

The rock hit the glass, making a *tink!* noise and bounced off. The resultant shock wave tore through S'n'J's hand and up her arm. The rock flew from her fingers.

'Oooo . . . .you bloody . . . bastard!' S'n'J spat, clenching her teeth and shaking her hurt hand. When the pain eased, her hand felt hot and fat and her elbow ached.

Bullet-proof glass, her mind informed her as she strode purposefully towards the rock. *You won't break it with a brick.*

But she snatched the rock from the ground, walked into the overgrown back garden, targeted the window and launched the rock at it as hard as she could.

The rock bounced off with that all-too-familiar *tink!* noise and flew straight back towards her with a speed and precision that it had no business having. The window seemed to have absorbed none of the rock's kinetic energy at all. And it didn't seem to have simply bounced off the window either, but appeared to be tracing its inbound course in reverse – like a video playing backwards.

Cursing, S'n'J leapt to her left, dodging it. The strange thing was that when the rock reached the point where she estimated she'd started her swing to fling it, it ran out of energy. It reached the point where her hand had been, stopped travelling through the air and fell straight down into the wet grass.

There was only one thing left to be done and that was to drive up to the village and summon help.

Half-way along the muddy path – which she wasn't treating with quite as much caution this time – S'n'J's legs betrayed her.

Not so long ago, Sarah-Jane had leapt to her own defence when Martin had accused her of being clumsy. 'I may not be a ballet-dancer, but *I am not clumsy! I am as sure-footed as a mountain goat!*' she had told him. But those criticisms that hurt the most were the ones which contained a grain of truth, and although S'n'J wouldn't have admitted it under torture, she was not only *not* as sure-footed as a mountain goat, but she was somewhat prone to falling over.

It was something to do with her skinny little ankles. They might, on the odd occasion, have drawn admiring glances, but they were predisposed to turning themselves at the slightest provocation. If there was any unevenness on an otherwise flat surface, she would be sure to find it and catch it with a foot, which would turn up sideways, twisting one of those ankles almost to the limit.

This happened now.

S'n'J's right foot – the one nearest the drop to the sea – flipped up sideways, placing her whole body weight on her ankle joint. It hurt and if there had been time for her to yelp before she went down, she would have.

She toppled sideways to her right. On the periphery of her vision the angry grey sea rose towards her and through the horrible out-of-control feeling adults always experience during a fall, S'n'J's mind blasted one petrified thought into her mind: *YOU DON'T WANT TO FALL IN THAT SEA!*

But she didn't think she was going to be able to stop herself.

She hit the steep slope four feet down and began to slide, head first. Down there, a hundred feet below her, the Atlantic was ready to swallow her.

She threw out both her arms in front of her and ploughed her spread fingers into the thin grass, while she dug her feet in like anchors.

But she wasn't stopping.

I'm going to die, a small part of her thought calmly. It wouldn't be death by drowning though – she was a strong swimmer. It would be death by being driven on to the rocks by the swell of the sea.

S'n'J made a passing grab for the root of a bush with her numb right hand, felt her fingers slide off it, and knew that it was all over.

The telephone saved her life.

Ace Publishing's crap mobile phone was not the new slimline kind. It was one of the old bulky ones. And when she'd stuffed it into her jacket pocket in disgust, it still protruded from the top.

Now it caught in the root of the bush she had tried to grab. The root hooked between the protruding head of the phone and S'n'J's jacket and she slid to a standstill.

It wasn't until she heard the tell-tale sound of tearing material, that she realized what had happened. A sob that she didn't know was coming escaped her lips and she drew a deep breath. *There's still hope. Still hope for at least one happy ending today*, she told herself, reaching back for the root.

She fastened her fingers around it and tested it, knowing it was going to give way.

It didn't.

Her head was still spinning with the sensation of falling and sliding out of control, and beneath her the sea looked as if it hadn't given up hope of having her, so she waited, fighting off the urge to scramble back up in careless haste.

When she'd caught her breath, she carefully manoeuvred herself so that she was facing up the slope instead of down. The climb back up to the house was probably less than fifteen feet – although it seemed further – and there were quite a few pieces of rock protruding through soil that she was sure she could use for hand and footholds. All she had to do was move very slowly and try to forget that up there was a man in need of urgent medical attention. It wasn't going to do either of them any good if she fell off.

S'n'J's right shoe was about half-way up and she climbed carefully towards it, distantly aware that reality didn't always mimic fiction. This particular turn of events hadn't taken place within the pages of *Black Rock* – not the pages she had anyway. Mr Peter Perfect, bless his cotton socks, had missed a good one here.

S'n'J reached the shoe and stuffed it into her free pocket. Like an experienced mountaineer, S'n'J took her time choosing her route, then took her time placing her hands and feet and tested before she let anything take her full weight.

She didn't allow herself to relax until she was sitting in a puddle on the path with her back against the wall of the house.

Sarah-Jane ached all over and was aware that everything was going to hurt twice as badly tomorrow. She didn't have a single long fingernail any more, the palms of both her hands were bleeding, as were her knees; her tights were in holes, her skirt was soaked in mud and split to the waist into the bargain, and somewhere on her forehead there was a cut which was bleeding steadily.

And the ankle that had caused all of this (S'n'J imagined it sniggering) didn't hurt a bit.

She concluded that she'd been a very lucky girl indeed and began to thank God, then thanked Marks & Spencer instead. It had been the good quality of their jacket that had brought her to a halt. She put her broken shoe on to her cut and bleeding foot. The heel was broken so she was going to be walking like a woman with one leg longer than the other, but the alternative – walking in bare feet – sounded more painful.

And you know exactly what's going to happen next, don't you? she asked herself as she struggled up and stole a glance at the Atlantic, which was presumably feeling cheated. *You're going to walk around the corner of the house and Mr Winter will have gone.*

S'n'J felt this without a shadow of a doubt. That was the reason she hadn't wanted to drive back up to Tintagel to phone for help in the first place – he was bound to have vanished the moment she took her eyes off him. Even she knew *that* much about how stories developed.

But this wasn't a story. This was real life – even if back there she *had* thought for a while that she *was* Snowy and that the story told by Peter Perfect was hers. Now, she'd decided that fiction was always much more gentle than brutal reality. That was why people read it. It didn't hurt like the real thing.

And if this isn't a story, Mr Winter can't have vanished. If this is reality he'll still be lying there, probably dying by now.

S'n'J hobbled along the path to find out, holding her breath as she turned the corner.

And there he is, gone!

Except that this wasn't a fairy tale and he wasn't gone. S'n'J moaned, feeling rather like she did in her nightmares: needing to act quickly but feeling as if she were stuck in treacle. She hobbled over to him, knelt beside him and tried again, without success, to wake him.

Plan B, she told herself, trying to fight off the feeling that she was not only losing ground and time, but also her self-control. She stood up and hobbled back to the Sierra.

It won't start now, she told herself confidently as she reached for the key.

But if God, or Peter Perfect, was arranging things for her today, he wanted to keep her guessing: the car started on the first turn of the key.

S'n'J drove slowly and carefully back on to the narrow track down which she had come, conscious that her judgement wasn't up to scratch. Since she'd fallen off the path –

and almost to an early grave – everything seemed off-kilter, as if the world had altered its standard settings concerning gravity and space.

When she reached the point where she'd first seen the dog, she realized that she wasn't going to have to drive all the way back to Tintagel to summon help after all. She had been speaking to Janie on the mobile at this point on her way down the track. It had only cut off completely when she'd passed the level of the white farm building where the trailer and the dog were.

If the phone (*God bless it!*) still worked, she would be able to make the call from here. She brought the car to a halt, snatched the phone from her pocket and was about to dial when it began to trill.

S'n'J stared at it in disbelief, suddenly *knowing* who it would be. She hit the button and put the phone to her ear.

'Look Essenjay, I don't know what's wrong . . .' Martin started.

And before he could complete his opening gambit, S'n'J cut him off short. 'You may not know what's wrong, but I *do*,' she hissed, 'and I need an ambulance so get off the line while I call one!'

She punched the button and shut off the phone. When she turned it on again, Martin was still there. 'What's *wrong*?' he bleated.

'RING OFF MARTIN!' she demanded. 'RING OFF AND DO IT NOW. THIS IS URGENT!'

For once in his life, Martin did as he was told rather than as he would have liked.

S'n'J turned the phone off, then on again, and punched three nines.

'Emergency, which service do you require?' a calm voice asked.

'Ambulance,' S'n'J said, trying to match that serene tone and failing miserably.

'Hold please caller, I'm putting you through,' the operator said.

'You require an ambulance?' an efficient male voice said.

I know that already, S'n'J thought, 'A man's fallen off the roof of his house and he's bleeding and unconscious,' she blurted.

'Could you give me the address please?' the man asked.

They're not going to get here, S'n'J thought as she told him the address. *They won't be able to find it.*

'And the man's unconscious after a fall and you think he's suffering injuries?' the operator enquired.

'*Yes,*' S'n'J said through clenched teeth.

'And you're there now are you?'

Hurry up, why don't you? 'Yes,' she said. 'A little way away. I'm in my car. I had to drive out of a telephone dead spot to make the call.'

'Could I have your name, love?'

'Why?'

'For the record.'

He thinks it's a prank call. They're not going to send anyone, she thought, then replied, *but they* have *to. Even if they think it's a false alarm they have to send someone, just in case. They've got to send someone.*

S'n'J's vision swam for a second. 'My name,' she heard herself say with the utmost clarity, 'is Snowdrop Dresden. I live at Black Rock, Barras Nose, Tintagel.'

'Be there right away,' the ambulance coordinator told her and rang off.

Engulfed by an awful feeling of dislocation, S'n'J hardly heard him. She felt as if she'd just woken up on the planet Xarg where all words had a slightly different meaning. The only useful thought in her head at that moment was that she'd have to move her car because pretty soon there would be a sizeable ambulance coming down here and she was blocking its path.

But you don't have to go back down there at all. You can just put the car in gear and keep on going the way you're facing. That'd be the better idea.

And S'n'J agreed. Until she'd finished her pastie and driven out of the car park in Falmouth, everything had been going swimmingly for her. Or at least predictably and normally. In a couple of very short hours she had come close to crashing her car, she'd suffered hallucinations, discovered an injured man it was almost impossible to help, and nearly lost her life.

But she put the car in reverse gear anyway.

Because you didn't abandon an injured man.

Don't do this! her Girl Guide pleaded. *Leave now, while you still can.*

Backing towards the forecourt of Black Rock, S'n'J thought about this. Perhaps she should quit while she was ahead. Perhaps.

But you won't. You won't because the house is exactly as you imagined it and so is the injured man. You won't because that wide-eyed little girl inside you believes in happy sappy endings. And she won't let you go home while there's a chance, however slim, that she might be right. She's a kid trying to stay awake on Christmas Eve to see Santa because even though she knows it's her dad in a red coat, there's a million to one chance that the real *Santa will come this year.*

S'n'J backed into the drive and pulled up. The house was not haunted because there was no change when she looked at it in the car's mirrors. And Mr Winter was not a ghost because he had not vanished. He still lay in exactly the same position he'd been in when she left.

If there were any ghosts present, she decided as she got out of the car, they were of the canine variety. The moment before she backed across the perimeter of Black Rock, her friend the pointing dog had been up there on his trailer. Now, less than twenty seconds later, he stood at the corner of the house. It would have been impossible for the world's fastest greyhound to have travelled that distance in the few seconds that had passed.

When the hairs at the nape of S'n'J's neck finally stopped prickling and a logical explanation came to her, she began to smile. It was obvious now. So obvious she could barely believe she hadn't thought of it before.

There were *two* dogs. Not one ghost dog, but two ordinary ones. One of them stayed near the white farm building across the valley and leapt on to the trailer to see what was going on each time it heard her car's engine and the other was simply skulking around down here. The fact that both dogs were never in view at the same time held no significance whatsoever. If she waited long enough, they would be.

'OK hound, I've got you sussed,' she called, still a little unsettled at its immobility.

The dog did not move.

S'n'J began to hobble towards Mr Winter.

And stopped dead in her tracks when the noise started.

Afterwards, when she tried to piece together the sequence of events that followed, S'n'J found she had a problem, not only with fitting everything into the few seconds of time that passed, but with fitting those events into her view of reality.

S'n'J had heard dogs howl and she knew what the lonely voice of a wolf sounded like, but she had never heard an animal howl with such power, or in a tone which suggested such desolation. The banshee wail froze her to what seemed like absolute zero. It was a sound that hurt your soul to hear, that made you wish for a quick, clean death instead of the aeons of torment it suggested. S'n'J suddenly understood the true meaning of the word 'fear'.

She tried to turn her head towards the dog but her neck was rigid, the muscles bunched and locked solid. Her eyes were the only part of her that she was able to move and they swung slowly towards the corner of the house, moving like ice-breaking ships in the Arctic.

The dog was sitting up in a kind of begging posture, head thrown back, jaws wide, its paws not dangling prettily, but stretched towards the sky like the arms of an evangelist reaching for God. To the left of it, out over the coast between here and Tintagel Castle, the clouds which raced in from the sea were no longer travelling at a constant altitude, but sweeping up in a graceful curve, to perhaps two hundred feet, then sweeping back down again, hitting the coastline at ground level and swamping it with a fast-moving fog. Out in the sea, at the same point that the clouds began to rise, a large foaming wave was forming. The wave appeared to have no forward momentum. It was not rushing towards the land gathering volume, but standing still in a fairly well defined peak and simply growing taller and more curved. Water curled from the top of it making it look a little like that surfer's favourite, a *tube*, but the lost mass wasn't stopping it growing.

Like the massing wave out at sea, a thought was forming in S'n'J's head. It was the single terrified word of a woman whose grasp on sanity is growing weak: *Impossible*.

And the dog howled. On and on, way past the point at which any natural dog's lungs should have run out of air.

S'n'J sensed movement to her right and tore her eyes away from the dog just in time to catch sight of something fluttering. She saw it only on the periphery of her vision; it was gone in a moment and she wasn't sure what it was. Except that she *was* sure; she just could not allow herself to believe it.

It was Mr Winter.

He had folded up. Not folded up like a man hit in the stomach, but literally. She had just witnessed Mr Winter crease like a large piece of black and white paper. As if unseen hands had reached down, pressed him flat and packed him away. He had been creased across the centre of his body, bent double, then creased down the middle of his spine and bent double that way. And folded and creased, again and again, faster and faster, his size diminishing until he was on the point of vanishing.

When the dog finally ran out of air to howl with, the silence that followed almost made S'n'J collapse. She wanted to cry, and perhaps faint too, but instead she gasped and screwed her eyes shut, tensing herself for a repeat perform-ance – which didn't come. She opened them again in time to see the huge wave collapse on itself and form two smaller ones on either side of where it had been. And in time to see that the clouds were now racing further inland.

During the moment her eyes had been closed, the dog had vanished.

And when she fought off her paralysis and turned back towards Mr Winter, he had gone too.

It occurred to her – but only very distantly – that she should go and search for him in case he'd woken up and staggered round the side of the building. S'n'J instantly rejected this course of action, realizing she was no longer

79

running under the heading of Miss Logical. In fact, Miss Logical had taken a long hike from which she might never return. She was now Miss Hanging-on-to-her-Sanity and like her Girl Guide always said, it was better to quit while you were still ahead.

She glanced at the spot where Mr Winter had been (all that remained was the blood on the shingle), hobbled the few yards back to the Sierra, started it up, gunned the engine and left.

If there was only one thing she was sure of at this moment in her life, it was that if all the wild horses in the known universe were roped together and tied to her, they would never drag her back here again.

Chapter Seven

Martin Makes a Call

Pinned to the cork board behind his desk in Ace's offices, was Martin Dinsey's motto. It said:

WE TURN THE IMPOSSIBLE INTO REALITY

If you had told Martin that it was stolen from a computer ad, he would have shrugged and nodded. He didn't know where the words had come from, and he didn't care. What he *did* know was that they fitted, quite perfectly, the literary task he and his authors regularly undertook. Turning the impossible into reality.

The motto was the key to his success. Over the past fifteen years as an editor, Martin had become an icon of the fantasy genre. The sub-genres included sword and sorcery and horror and Martin handled them all. And excelled.

He had a bloodhound-like nose for a good read, and knew how to make a good read into an excellent one. And that often meant cutting, which was where he'd gained his nickname, 'Snips'. But more often, it meant reconstruction. Martin liked to think of himself as the Isambard Kingdom Brunel of literature. But instead of designing suspension bridges, he designed the suspension of *disbelief*. He helped turn the impossible into reality.

Now, he was faced with the disconcerting feeling that he'd worked his magic motto on himself. Somehow, he had turned the impossible into reality. And not *literarily* this time, but literally.

He couldn't quite put his finger on the moment it had happened, but his mind had jumped the points and changed tracks. Which only went to show that if you lived most of your life in the realms of fantasy, sooner or later you wouldn't be able to tell the difference between that and reality.

And that had surely happened, because Martin now believed that during the walk back from the Gay Hussar restaurant to Ace's offices, a crystal had formed in his brain. A single tiny speck of ice. And while he had walked, it had grown. Not slowly, like the sugar or alum crystals in science at school, but amazingly rapidly. And then it had stopped being a crystal, and shaped itself into a rectangular block, which looked something like an empty paperweight. In his mind's eye, where the block still hung, he could see it clearly. He could even feel the cold radiating from it. And when he peered into that block, he could see . . . nothing at all. Just emptiness.

Earlier, an image of Black Rock had hung there. Then the image had changed, like a movie cutting from one scene to another, and he'd watched Essenjay fall down the side of a steep hill towards the sea. Then, before he'd seen what had happened to her, the image had cut back to the static frontage of the house again. And after he'd spoken to her on the phone when she'd told him to get off the line because she needed an ambulance, the image had cleared, leaving the block blank.

It had stayed blank since.

The disconcerting thing was not that the block had stayed blank, but that it had stayed at all.

Martin, who spent his whole life in one author's pretend world after another, did not believe in the supernatural. Or in alternate universes, parallel time streams, demons, were-wolves, dragons, or any of that other shit that Ace's readers soaked up like sponges.

What he *did* believe in, was the scientific explanation of life which left no room for afterlife, before-life, reincarnation or the supernatural. These irrational beliefs were merely the products of brains which had genetically mutated into some-thing more than simple survival computers which drove people to eat and reproduce. The human brain had expanded itself to the point where it always had to be telling itself stories, and extrapolating from them. And like even the best

82

computer software, the brain had a few bugs lurking. Consequently your brain could turn traitor and make you believe things for which there was no empirical evidence.

And this was surely what had happened to him – the pressure of his failed relationship had caused his brain to strip a few cogs, ergo the psychic ice block that now stood in his mind's eye, waiting, like a blank computer screen.

But Martin liked to think of himself as resourceful and conjured up a vision of an industrial hot-air blower. In his mind's eye, he turned the blast towards the ice block.

Which not only didn't melt away, it didn't so much as drop a bead of water.

He then tried pneumatic drills, heavy machinery and finally a nuclear explosion, but nothing worked. And if he was truthful with himself, he had to admit that the result he'd obtained was entirely the result he'd expected. None of the mental images he provided seemed even a tenth as substantial as that of the ice block.

Which left him with a big problem.

Martin 'Snips' Dinsey, was sitting in the hall of his ex-wife's house in Ladbroke Grove with the telephone in his hands, certain he'd gone mad.

'Did you get through?' Angela called from the kitchen.

For a moment, Martin wasn't certain he'd even dialled Essenjay's number. He had been trying to recall the twenty odd pages of *Black Rock* he'd read, but they were vaporizing in his memory.

Angela opened the kitchen door and peered down the hall at him, frowning. 'Martin?' she called.

Martin looked up at her, blankly. She was dressed in cycling shorts, Nikes and a baggy cotton sweater, and there was a pan of something steaming in her hand. It smelt like bolognaise, but Martin didn't remember her saying she was going to cook it. Angela was pretty. She wasn't thin, but you couldn't describe her as overweight either. 'Voluptuous' was the word Martin used to use.

For a moment, he tried to summon up some of the love he'd once had for her, and when that failed, some of the lust. It didn't work. It would have been much simpler if it had; he could have fallen into her arms. This was what she'd been hoping for since he'd split with Essenjay and moved back in as her lodger. It was too late, he supposed. Things had moved on and he now looked on Angela as little more than a friend.

'What?' he asked. The kids were in the lounge playing Sonic the Hedgehog II, and squealing and shouting advice over the racket it was making. The whole thing should have been a picture of domestic bliss. And if it hadn't been for that sales conference at which he'd first met Essenjay, it still might have been.

'Did you get through?' Angela repeated, absently stirring the steaming pot.

Martin shook his head.

'Oh,' Angela said, 'You'd better come and eat then. It's nearly ready.'

While Martin was trying to decide whether or not she looked smug, he tried the number of Essenjay's next door neighbours, Janet and Dave, wondering if he should have come back here at all.

It only made things more complicated. The kids wanted to know why he and Mummy slept in different rooms for one thing, and whether he was here to stay for another. Then there was Angela. She hadn't crept into his room in the dead of night yet, but he kept thinking that she would, soon. And a part of him wanted her to. The part that hadn't been anywhere warm and wet except the bath for the better part of ten weeks. Martin knew that if *that* started again he was going to have all sorts of trouble breaking off for the second time. There might occasionally be such a thing as a free lunch but there was certainly no such thing as a free shag.

'Hiya, you're speaking to a genuine genius, what can I do for *you*?' Dave Bett's voice said in Martin's ear.

If there was one thing Martin was certain of, it was that Dave was no genius and never would be — at least while he had a hole in his arse. A genuine mental midget would have been a more apt description.

'Hi, it's Martin,' Martin said.

'What, Martin, *the* Martin?' Dave enquired, his tone cooling.

'Yeah,' Martin replied. He had never said anything derogatory about Dave – not in his presence anyway – but he didn't have to. Martin was not good at concealing his innermost feelings about people at the best of times, and when faced with someone who had the brains of an ironing board was unable to prevent himself from using his superior intelligence to tie that person up in knots. Dave might not have been able to put his finger on what it was he didn't like about Martin, but somewhere along the line he'd begun to feel inferior. And people didn't like to feel like that – which was one reason Martin did it.

'Oh,' Dave said. This time his tone read: *why are you phoning me, you arrogant motherfucker.*

Martin said, 'Look, I'm a bit worried about Essenjay . . .'

And Dave, seeing his opening, quickly cut in, 'Well, she wasn't very worried about you the last time I spoke to her.'

'That may be,' Martin replied, 'but I called her earlier this afternoon and something had happened to her. She said she needed an ambulance and rang off. Now I've been trying to contact her ever since. Her mobile won't respond. I thought she might be in hospital, but when I tried her home phone, it's constantly engaged which suggests that she's in. I'm a little worried about her condition and I was ringing to ask if you'd seen her today.'

There was a silence, presumably while Dave digested this information. 'Saw her this morning when she went out,' he finally said. 'She seemed OK then. Full of the joys of spring in fact. Hang on a mo.' Dave clapped his hand over the mouthpiece of his telephone but his muffled voice could be heard as he shouted to Janet: 'Hey Janny, you seen Sarah-Jane tonight? Only that twat Martin's on the phone. He says he can't get hold of her.'

Martin listened to the pause, during which, he assumed, good old Janny was telling Dave that it wasn't surprising that twat couldn't get hold of her because Sarah-Jane no longer wanted to have anything to do with him. Then he heard Dave shout again. 'Yeah, I know, but he says she's had an accident. Ambulance case. Go and knock her up and see if she's in. Yeah?'

Dave took his hand off the phone and said, 'Janet's just going to knock on her door. D'you wanna hold on, or will you call back?'

'I'll hold on,' Martin said, 'if you don't mind.'

Dave grunted, presumably because he *did* mind. But he was being a good neighbour and if that meant letting Martin hold on, that was what he was going to do. 'She won't be two shakes,' Dave said.

'Thanks,' Martin replied.

'What have you been up to, then?' Dave asked.

'Not a lot,' Martin replied.

Silence.

Angela came out of the kitchen carrying two plates of spaghetti bolognaise, passed Martin, nodded at the food and entered the war zone. There was a brief squeak of protest from one child, and Sonic the Hedgehog fell silent.

'You didn't have to pull the plug, Mum,' the other child complained. 'We were half-way through the labyrinth zone. We'll have do it all over again.'

'Not tonight, you won't,' Angela said and closed the door.

Ours is still in the pot, Martin told himself. *She's waiting for me to be free so we can eat together.*

He didn't feel hungry at all. He was still hopelessly in love with Essenjay, she was in some sort of trouble, and there was a large, immovable block of ice in his mind which, presumably, was going to feed him the latest details about what was happening – when it got bad enough.

'Is she back yet?' Martin asked.

'Nope,' Dave said.

Silence.

Inside the lounge, the six o' clock news began.

Martin's mental box of ice shimmered as if a light had been turned on inside it. He frowned, willing the block away. A picture began to form there, pulling itself together from pastel shades of colour which seemed to slide into the crystal block from nowhere. It didn't happen rapidly, but it was difficult to discern what was taking place.

'Be back soon,' Dave predicted.

Martin didn't speak. The picture had solidified now – if

that was the right word. (It seemed more as if it had slid together like angled geometric pieces which fitted to one another to make a whole.) And what he was now looking at, while he sat here and listened to Dave's measured breathing, was another picture of Black Rock.

Except that this time he was looking at the inside of it. The lounge. The lounge was just as he remembered it from the book – if indeed he *did* remember it, and he could no longer be certain. It was big and there was an open fireplace with a sheepskin rug in front of it, and leather sofas and deep pile carpet. Essenjay was there in that room. Alone. But it was what she was doing that seemed strange. She was touring the room adjusting things.

Except that she wasn't simply tidying up, the way she would at home; sling this cushion *here*, chuck these magazines *there*. Essenjay, who normally tidied only when her belongings approached critical mass, wasn't just tidying a room that was already tidy, she was doing it with the utmost care and a kind of furtiveness.

In Martin's mind's-eye block of ice, he watched her, as she went about her strange business; altering the position of an ornament by a few millimetres, twisting another by only a few degrees. And while she worked, she kept glancing over her shoulder. As far as Martin could discern, she was alone in the room. Now she was dragging one of the heavy sofas around so that the seats faced the front windows.

Then Martin began to understand.

If what he was seeing was real – and he wasn't sure about *that* – Essenjay had been feeling the pressure of their parting as keenly as he had. If he'd cracked because he imagined he could see her doing things from afar, then she'd cracked too.

What she was suffering from here was obsessive compulsive disorder syndrome. It was a fairly common behavioural complaint of the type which often began with the subject feeling that their hands were dirty and ended up with them showering twenty or thirty times a day. People under pressure often developed it. Martin knew a little about it. He'd read of a man in Gloucester who believed he was responsible for all horses. If he didn't line up all his belongings each morning

87

before nine so that they pointed north, a certain amount of horses would die in agony.

And this was what his image of Essenjay was doing. She was moving the furniture and ornaments so that they all faced a certain direction.

Because she was obsessed.

Who are you trying to kid, kiddo? Martin asked himself. *It's you who's sitting here having visions, not Essenjay. It's you who's obsessed, not her.*

He grew increasingly uncomfortable.

'Oh, here she comes now,' Dave suddenly announced and Martin jumped

'Hello Martin?' Janet had evidently grabbed the phone from her husband. 'There's a light on, but if she's up there she isn't answering the door. What did you say was the matter with her?'

'When I called her this afternoon she told me she needed an ambulance,' Martin said.

Then Janet asked a question which stopped Martin dead in his tracks. It shouldn't have done, because as he frequently told his colleagues, he was knife-sharp. It left him feeling a little better in one way, and a lot worse in another. The question was so simple he didn't know how he'd managed to miss it.

'Was the ambulance for herself?' Janet asked.

And suddenly Martin knew that it *wasn't*. If he'd half a brain, he would have realized that straight away. People who were injured didn't tell you to get off the line because they had to get an ambulance quick, they told you they were hurt and needed help. And they didn't sound so snotty either. In any work of fiction presented to him, Martin would have picked up on this instantly. In real life things weren't quite as cut and dried. In real life you had your own emotional and mental welfare to take into consideration on top of everyone else's.

'She didn't say,' Martin replied, feeling very stupid.

'Oh well, there you are then,' Janet said. 'Nothing to worry about by the sound of it. The ambulance must've been for someone else. Like I said, her light's on upstairs, so she's been home since it got dark. She's probably gone to the pub or something. I shouldn't worry, Martin. I'll tell her you were concerned when I see her. Perhaps she'll ring you. Does she have your wife's number?'

'I'm not at my wife's,' Martin lied. He didn't know how Janet had discovered where he was staying (perhaps Dave had heard the kids earlier or Essenjay had heard a rumour and told her) but he certainly didn't intend to admit it. It wouldn't look good if it appeared he'd run home to the wife the moment Essenjay had thrown him out. It would make him look exactly like the stereotypical philandering husband.

'You're not?' Janet asked.

'No,' Martin said. 'I'm with friends. Essenjay can reach me at the office if she wants.'

'Okay,' Janet said, sounding as if she didn't believe him. 'I'll tell her.'

After she rang off, Martin remained crouched in front of the telephone until Angie came out of the lounge and laid a warm and somehow comforting hand on his shoulder. 'Food?' she asked.

Martin looked up at her, saw the pain in her eyes and knew how she felt. She wanted him like he wanted Essenjay.

There was no sense in it. If he was God – or Cupid, or whoever controlled these things – situations like this would not arise. If he'd been God, Angie and the kids would never have happened; it would just be him and Essenjay and she would feel the same way towards him as he did towards her. But there were parts of Angie's character he would have grafted on to Essenjay first. Like Angie's subservience. She had never wanted to share his possessions the way Essenjay did. His car was *his* car. It wouldn't have crossed Angie's mind to ask to be insured to drive it. Or to operate his Bang & Olufsen stereo, or his computer without his permission. Or to want to spend his money as though it belonged to her.

Suddenly he was angry. Any fool knew that women should support their men rather than imbuing themselves with the same status. And even if Essenjay *could* write a book – and even if it promised to be a damned good one – it didn't make her equal to him. Who had the power to decide whether or not the public got to read that book?

And now he was angry at Angie too. Because she had a bovine expression and because having two kids had given her a slack belly and stretch-marks, but most of all he was angry because her spark had gone. Standing there before him, she looked like a woman whose spirit had been broken.

'WHAT DO YOU WANT FROM ME?' he demanded, slamming the phone down.

Angie jumped back a foot, then cringed like a dog who knows it's been bad. She didn't say anything at all.

'WELL?' Martin said.

Inside the lounge, the sound of the television faded. The kids had turned it down. They would be at the door now, listening, their eyes wide and fearful. It was a scene Martin had played out many times before and he didn't like it. Because it upset Angie and scared the kids, but most of all because he couldn't stop himself. And the reason he couldn't stop himself was the same reason masochists willingly submitted themselves to torture: it felt so good. Martin, who was famous for his volatile temper, lit up like a high-power halogen bulb when it happened.

'I just wanted to know if you want to eat now,' Angie said in a tiny voice.

'No you didn't,' Martin hissed. 'What you wanted to know was, am I ready to come back to you yet, wasn't it? What you wanted to know was when your meal-ticket is returning.'

Martin waited. The tension struck him as sexual. The game was domination, powermongering. Not physical, but mental. Except that it wasn't a game, it was real. And he had no control over it, no sense of playing a role.

Essenjay hadn't taken kindly to his attempts at dominating her. Essenjay had hit him with a rolling-pin, just as she'd described it in her book. And if he wanted proof, he only had to dip his head and look in a mirror. Just beneath the peak of his thinning hair was a large, livid scar where the rolling-pin had split his scalp. You could still see where the eight stitches had been.

'Dinner,' Angie mewled in her little voice. 'I just wanted to know if you wanted dinner.' Her voice was steady, but there were tears running down her face.

Martin glared at her for a few seconds as his anger passed. Then he dismissed her with a weary gesture.

And Angie went, leaving him alone with the phone and his ice-crystal vision of the woman who, for some unknown reason, he loved.

Essenjay was now in the hall of the house, facing the front door. The door seemed to have no handle or letter box. And no hinges, either. It was just a huge black door, studded with brass points. Martin couldn't even discern where the door ended and its frame began.

Essenjay made what looked like a magical pass with her right hand and spoke some words. Then she frowned and waited. Then she repeated the process.

And then the image vanished.

But the ice block in Martin's brain remained. Either he'd gone bananas, or there was such a thing as telepathy and he was getting a demonstration. And telepathy was easier to accept than madness.

Fuck the phone, he thought, and tried to contact Essenjay by the power of his mind, concentrating just the way a character in one of the books he edited might have done. He even put the tips of his fingers to his temples.

Essenjay, can you hear me? he asked. Or broadcast, or whatever you did when sending mental messages.

He tried again, raising the volume this time. *Essenjay, are you all right?* he asked.

Contact was not made.

Then he quit. It was all so stupid. Telepathy was for hack writers and film-makers. If the imaginary ice block in his mind wouldn't go away, it wasn't because Essenjay was trying to contact him, but because a part of him didn't want it to go away.

Or maybe it was a kind of conscious dream-state. The reason he felt Essenjay was in danger had nothing to do with the part of his mind that was dreaming. It had everything to do with the fact that Essenjay had told him herself that she needed an ambulance. The rest was imagination.

Even the picture of Black Rock he'd had before he first called her meant nothing in psychic terms. His mind might have stripped a cog, OK, but it hadn't suddenly become imbued with the mystical power of ESP. It was mere coincidence that he'd imagined she was in trouble and had then phoned her only to find she was.

She didn't say she'd fallen half-way down something almost steep enough to be called a cliff, did she? he asked himself. *She didn't say she was hurt either.* Which meant the whole thing had been a gigantic misunderstanding, caused purely by the mental cog he'd somehow stripped.

Not convinced, Martin phoned her again.

And almost suffered a heart attack when her line clicked open.

He had already started to blabber how relieved he was that she was OK when he realized he was engaged in conversation with her answering machine which said, 'Sarah-Jane cannot come to the phone at this precise moment because she is currently in her boudoir being entertained by several members of the Chippendales. If you would like to leave a message and your number, she will call you back as soon as possible – if she isn't too tired, that is.'

Martin listened, fighting his rising anger at her whimsy, and after the tone left a message asking her to call and let him know if she was all right.

If Bude had been a couple of hours closer to London, he would have leapt in the Ferrari and driven down to find out for himself exactly what was going on.

Martin shivered. At some point during the day, his clear and incisive mind had turned into something akin to mashed swede. He was no longer sure who or what his anger ought to be directed at. He didn't know if he was angry at Essenjay for not taking his calls when she could have done, or angry at Angie for trying to entrap him again, or what. All he knew was that he was livid.

And that there was a surefire way to assuage his anger.

He stood up, went into the lounge, pointed at the children and said, 'You and you, bed!'

He didn't expect any complaints and he wasn't disappointed; even though it was only eight o' clock and it was a Friday, their staying up late evening, neither child complained. Both of them looked up at him with something in their eyes which might have been fear and might have been hatred. He preferred to think it was fear.

The children got up, gathered up their belongings and headed for the door.

'And when you get upstairs, tell your mother I want her.'

Martin sat down and waited. Angie would understand the summons, that was a certainty, but there was a chance that she would either refuse point blank to come down, or she would waltz in with a list of things she wanted *him* to do to her: *touch here, stroke there, kiss this, lick that.*

And that kind of thing he could do without.

He grinned when she did come in. She had showered and was wearing only her bathrobe.

'They said you wanted me,' she said, sounding both hopeful and beaten.

'And they were right,' Martin said.

The combination of his anger, his sexual frustration and the anticipation he'd felt while awaiting her arrival almost drove him over the edge. He was iron-bar hard and throbbing.

'You want to make love,' she said.

Martin shook his head, standing up. His penis tented his trousers. 'No,' he said, 'I want to fuck you. Now take off your robe and lie down.'

Angie seemed to want the same thing, and lay down on the carpet on her back, knees raised, legs spread.

Martin looked at her and for a moment despised himself. Then he shed his trousers and boxers, went to her, knelt between her legs and entered her. She was warm and wet and a little loose – exactly as he had anticipated. He positioned himself on his elbows, looking down into her face and he thrust at her, hard. Angie winced.

'This doesn't mean anything,' he told her, thrusting again, harder this time. 'It doesn't mean I love you and it doesn't mean I want you back. It just means I want to fuck you.'

Angie shut her eyes and bit her bottom lip as he whacked

himself into her for a third time. A gasp escaped her and Martin thrust again, so hard his pubic bone was going to be bruised in the morning.

Angie's arms came up and tried to enfold his neck; Martin caught them and pressed them back to the floor, squeezing her biceps as he drove himself into her.

After the fifth angry thrust, he realized that the ice block in his brain had gone. After the sixth he thought of Essenjay, who wouldn't just lie there and be fucked, but who would fuck him in return, and even rake skin from his back like an animal. After the seventh he realized that *this* was the right way: the man on top proving his dominance, proving his masculinity.

After the eighth violent thrust, Angie gave a little squeal which either meant it hurt or she'd come. Martin didn't know which.

And from then on he was a furious pile-driver until the moment of his orgasm approached, drawing closer with each stroke. And just as his muscles were strained tight and he closed in on the exorcism of his rage, the telephone began to ring.

Martin was out of Angie and into the hall before it had rung three times. He snatched the receiver off the base and held it to his ear.

'Martin?'

Martin looked down at his throbbing penis. 'Essenjay?'

The line went dead.

'COW!' Martin shouted. And flung the phone back into the cradle. It bounced out again and he left it swinging by its cable and strode back into the lounge.

Angie had got up and put on her robe.

'Get back on the floor,' he commanded.

Angie shook her head. 'Enough,' she stated. 'I'm finished.'

'Enough? What do you mean, *enough*?

'You heard me, Martin. I'm not prepared to compete with that girl. You either want me or you want her. I'll have you back if you want me, and you can stay here. Or if you want her, you can go. You can't stay here and have both. You can't stay here and have us both.'

94

Martin's anger reached fever-pitch. There was life in the old girl yet. 'It's ultimatum time, is it?' he said, keeping his voice calm, the way he did when he explained to his authors what was wrong with their crappy books.

Angie nodded. 'You've had your fling and it's about time you began to realize that it's over. She doesn't want you.'

Martin nodded. She was right of course. That was what angered him even more.

'I'm sorry,' he said, still biting down on his rage. 'I've been the world's champion arsehole over the past couple of years. You're right, it's over between me and Sarah-Jane. Has been for six or seven months, really. We were just raking over the embers towards the end. It's you I want. That's why I came back here. I've been hoping we can get together again. I'd like you to take me back. What else can I say?'

Martin supposed he ought to feel like a lying toad, but he didn't feel any guilt whatsoever. All he felt was a raging anger which could only be fucked away.

Angie nodded wordlessly.

Chapter Eight

Escape from Black Rock

It was during the frantic drive away from Black Rock that she hit the black dog, Diamond Ambrose Anstey.

It just appeared before her on the track, suddenly and without warning. It didn't solidify out of a shimmering haze or unfold itself the same way as Mr Winter had folded himself up ... One moment the track was empty, and the next, the dog stood there. Pointing at her.

S'n'J didn't have time to react. The car was only moving at around twenty miles an hour, but by the time she'd found the brake and clutch, it was all over.

The sound of the impact was not the soft thud S'n'J anticipated. It was closer to the metallic hammer-blow you heard when one car bumped another car from behind at low speed. A solid *thonk!*

What happened next was that the car skidded to a precarious halt on the very edge of the track. Cursing, S'n'J backed up.

The dog should have been in front of her. When you ran over things, they either came up the bonnet at you, or got pushed along by the car.

But the dog wasn't lying at the edge of the track, dying or dead.

It wasn't there at all.

S'n'J climbed out of the car. The dog was not in the road behind her. She got down on her hands and knees on the wet ground and peered under the car. It wasn't there either.

Which meant it had to have been knocked down into the valley.

Except that the dog was not in sight anywhere in the valley. Neither was it up on its trailer on the other side of the valley.

I'm sorry, Diamond Ambrose Anstey, she thought. *If that was you I ran over and killed, I'm truly sorry. You didn't hurt me and I'm sorry I had to hurt you.*

Then, no longer feeling like Miss Hanging-on-to-her-Sanity, but rather like Miss Lost-it-Completely, she returned to the car and drove away.

Up on the main road through Tintagel, she had to pull over to allow an ambulance to pass. She stared at its flashing lights as it squeezed by and didn't realize until it had gone that it was the one she had summoned.

That's one more false alarm for them, she told herself. They weren't going to find any customers down there now, that was for sure.

By the time she was half-way back to Bude, S'n'J was a little less mentally frazzled. As she got further away from Black Rock she began to think more clearly.

She realized she was driving in one shoe and decided it might be better, all things considered, if she was to take that shoe off and drive barefoot. She pulled in to a lay-by, turned off the car's engine, removed the shoe, nodded to herself that this was going to be more comfortable and that she was going to be okay now, and just as she thought she had everything under control, suffered a five-minute-long attack of what her mother would have called *the tremblies.*

Except that she didn't just tremble, she shook violently.

S'n'J breathed deeply, tried to relax and told herself it was only to be expected. She had almost fallen to her death; she'd seen an injured man fold himself up and vanish and she'd run over a dog that didn't seem to exist. And that wasn't even counting the hallucinations of the frost on the window, the brilliant lights or what had happened to the sea and the sky.

Funny stuff, carbon monoxide, she told herself, opening the window a little further, and tried on a grin. It didn't fit and when she checked it in the rear-view mirror, what stared back at her looked more like a killer clown in a cheap horror flick than good old Sarah-Jane. She fought back the tears which wanted to visit and rode out the tremblies.

When they'd ceased, she felt sane again. Shocked but sane. As far as she could see, the problem was not going to be getting the image of Black Rock out of her head, but coming to terms with the half-hour period of insanity she had experienced. It hung there in her mind like a gaping hole in her previously seamless reality.

You'll look back on all this soon, she thought, *and you'll see what a dummy you were. Really you will.*

She needed to clean herself up if she was going to visit James at Cars Inc. and have the exhaust replaced. She opened her handbag and found a tissue to use on her smeared face, then used her brush to tease the tangles from her hair. After she'd cleaned mud and blood off her knees and removed her soaked and torn jacket she looked a little less like a woman who had almost lost her life and a little more like a woman who might have recently tripped up some steps. That would be far easier to explain.

She got back in the car, spotted the single shoe and told it goodbye.

Then she threw it out of the window.

Twenty minutes later, S'n'J sat in the reception area of Cars Inc. with a cup of weak tea and a pile of *Trucker* magazines to leaf through while she waited.

But S'n'J didn't read. She took an A5 size sheet of note-paper from her handbag and folded it in half across the middle.

One, she counted.

Then she folded it in half the other way. *Two*.

Then she repeated the process.

The sheet of paper now measured somewhere in the region of three inches by two inches.

S'n'J folded it again. *Four*.

Someone had once told her that it was impossible to fold a sheet of paper more than six times. No matter how big it was to start with, or how thin.

She had made quite a tight wad after five folds, and the

sixth turned it into a deep letter U rather than a neatly folded piece of paper. It *was* impossible to make another fold.

S'n'J spotted a price list on the reception area's counter, picked it up and took it back to her seat. This was A4 size. Twice the area of her notepaper. When you folded it once and the A5 size once, the resultant area was still two to one. And so it remained, right down to the sixth fold. But she was unable to make a seventh. A strong man might have managed it, almost.

S'n'J shrugged. She didn't know what she was trying to prove. Mr Winter's vanishing trick had happened to a real man, not a piece of paper.

She glanced down at her origami, feeling a little sorry for herself and began to reconstruct the afternoon.

When she thought about it with a clear mind, it became glaringly obvious what had taken place.

When she had left the car park in Falmouth after eating her lunch-time pastie, she'd had the windows up and the heater off. There had been no fresh air getting into the car. Only the dreaded CO. By the time she'd arrived at the King Arthur Hotel in Tintagel, she had been well and truly wiped out. She didn't know whether or not she had actually spoken to the builder who was working there, but she suspected she had. He hadn't necessarily said any of those things which seemed to have a dark undertone to them though. He'd probably just pointed her in the right direction for the track down to the sea.

And the twenty-four pages of manuscript that had seemed so alive inside her head had provided the rest. Sure, the rock was there and the track led to it, but S'n'J had just wanted the house to be there too. And had hallucinated it into being. Along with the fastest dog in the West and the origami man.

'All done!' James said, striding back into the office. He was smeared black from head to toe and looked more like he'd been mining coal than fitting an exhaust.

'Thanks James,' S'n'J said, searching in her bag for her credit card, 'I was beginning to feel a bit sleepy when I was driving.'

'Deadly,' he replied, glancing up from the paperwork. He looked away, then looked back. Twice.

'What?' S'n'J said.

James looked down at his paperwork. 'Nothing,' he said.

He's wondering why you're barefoot and he's too embarrassed to ask, she told herself, warming towards him. He was quite sweet really. If you liked your men a little grubby.

'My shoes?' she asked.

'What? Oh, you're not wearing any,' he said. Then hesitated, grimaced and quickly looked away.

The famous old double *entendre, she thought, smiling.*

'I broke the heel off one of them,' S'n'J said, 'and I was clomping about like a monster, so I took them off.'

'Oh,' James said, not looking up.

If you didn't have all that black muck across your face, you'd be shining like a beacon, she thought, and smiled. The dark cloud that had been casting her mind into shadow had suddenly been swept away by a summer breeze. And it wasn't just the cloud of Black Rock that had gone, but also the shit-storm cloud that Martin had left behind him.

Here, finally, and in the place she least expected to find it, was something she could understand and deal with. *Forget Mr Winter, forget the hallucinations and the bad taste Martin left in your mind because here we have a guy who's maybe twenty-five and a little bit shy and who would be quite good-looking if all the grime was cleaned off him. A good, honest working man and he may not drive a Ferrari or own a mansion and he may not have two pennies to rub together, but you never know, he might be quite fun to be with.*

For the first time in two months S'n'J felt sunny. There was no better word to describe it.

You'd better run it up the flagpole and see if it flutters, she told herself.

'Sixty-two, sixty,' James said.

At least there wasn't a sixty-nine involved, S'n'J told herself, and grinned.

'Hey James,' she said, feeling her heart begin to rattle in her chest and telling herself she was silly.

He looked up at her. 'Yeah?'

'How old are you?'

He stared at her, his mouth slightly open.

He has nice teeth, she noted, then asked, *So what happened to Miss Sophisticated then? Nice teeth? What are we looking at, a* horse?

'Twenty-three,' he said after a long pause. 'Why?'

'Well, you know when you looked up at me just now?'

'Yeah?'

S'n'J felt a treacherous hot flush rise through her. She hoped she wasn't blushing. 'Well, you were going to ask me something.'

James nodded, embarrassed.

'The answer is yes.'

There! Said it!

James frowned.

'I'm sorry?' he said.

'Yes . . .' S'n'J replied and hesitated. She had intended to say *Yes, I will go out with you*, but obviously some wires had got crossed somewhere, '. . . the question you were going to ask me,' she faltered.

He shook his head. 'It doesn't matter. Really it doesn't,' he said, glancing towards the workshop where his colleagues were wrestling with a Morgan.

'OK, let me put it like this,' S'n'J said, handing him her credit card. 'Would you consider going out with an older woman?'

James fumbled with the card and dropped it. It fell behind the counter and he dived after it.

'How much older?' his disembodied voice asked, and S'n'J didn't know whether he was being playful or not. He seemed to have missed the point totally.

Are you sure *this is a good idea?* her Girl Guide asked, but S'n'J ignored the question. She wasn't prepared to have anything else spoil her day. What harm could result from going out for a drink? If she found out later that it was a mistake, she could call it off then.

'Only two or three years,' she said. 'I'm not *that* long in the tooth.'

James took a long time to get back up to where she could

see him. When he did, he was blushing furiously. It showed through the grime on his face quite plainly.

'You mean *you*,' he stated haltingly.

'I mean me,' she said, flashing him a sunny smile.

'But ...' James said, '... you live with that rich guy,' he finished.

S'n'J shook her head. 'Not any more,' she said.

'And you want to go out with ... me?' he asked, as if looking for the catch.

S'n'J nodded. 'You were going to ask me out, and I'm saying yes, I'll go out with you.'

'*Was* I?' he asked.

'Were you what?'

'Going to ask you out?'

S'n'J could feel the first few moving stones of what promised to be a landslide. Good old Sarah-Jane, the dumb brunette, had been talking at cross-purposes for the last minute or so. 'Well, you were going to ask me something,' she said.

James nodded as though he finally understood. And grinned like a man who's lost a quid and found a tenner.

'OK,' he said. 'Yes. I'd like to go out with you. I really would. Honestly.' Then he added, 'But that wasn't what I was going to ask you.'

S'n'J felt her mouth begin to drop and snapped it shut, mentally blaming her misinterpretation on the CO still in her system.

James paused, obviously weighing up the chances of his real question terminating her offer of a date. Then he said, 'I was going to ask you how you got all that pink stuff across the front of your car.'

S'n'J felt as if someone had whacked her over the head with a big, soft hammer. 'What pink stuff?' she heard herself ask. 'Paint?'

'Not paint,' he said. 'I dunno what it is, exactly. Didn't you know it was there? It's like jelly, but it's really sticky. Gets on your fingers like glue, and goes all stringy when you pull your hand away. We thought it was some kind of adhesive or something. Hey, are you OK?'

S'n'J wasn't sure of anything any more. All she knew was that she'd imagined she'd hit a dog with the car. An imaginary dog which hadn't dented the car because things that existed only in your mind couldn't damage real vehicles. And if that dog had not dented the car, then it could hardly have left any of its innards there either.

'Not blood and guts?' she asked, distantly.

James shook his head. 'No, nothing like that. Smells like . . . I dunno, it's kind of like the way dogs smell before they get so stinky you have to put them in the bath. Come and have a look,' he added brightly.

S'n'J already knew she wasn't going to be able to see anything. Moving like a zombie, she followed James into the workshop. The other two guys were underneath the Morgan, busy with a welding torch.

Her own car was still up on the ramps. The bottom of the front spoiler, where there should have been a dent made by a dog, was at the level of her eyes. She followed James across and when he stopped, she stopped.

'Oh,' he said, a note of surprise in his voice.

When S'n'J looked up, James was running his fingers up and down the bumper and radiator grille.

The clean radiator grille.

'There *was* stuff there,' James complained.

Someone is doing this to me on purpose, S'n'J thought, and not for the first time. Earlier on she'd caught herself remembering a hamster she used to have: Snowball. A demon on the exercise wheel and a real finger-biter. Except that when she thought about it, she knew the memory was spurious. She had *never* had a hamster called Snowball. It was as if someone had placed the memory inside her head, ready-made.

James turned round. 'Don't know *what* happened to it,' he said, and S'n'J didn't know if he was referring to her hamster or the vanishing pink stuff that had surely never been on the car in the first place.

'George!' he shouted. 'Georgie!'

Underneath the Morgan the welding torch went out with a pop.

'What?' George yelled, irritated.

'That stuff. On this lady's car. What happened to it?'

'What, the Crud-u-Loathe?' the other guy called. He came out from under the Morgan. He was fair-haired, very young and dirtier than James. A pair of welder's goggles hung around his neck. There were two clean circles round his eyes where they had been. He sauntered over.

'Cleaned it up, didn't I?' he said to James, then turned to S'n'J. 'Any idea what it was? Looked like some kind of paint stripper to me; thought I'd better get it off before it did any damage. Used a bit of white spirit on a rag.'

'Where is the rag?' S'n'J heard herself ask.

'Over there. D'you wanna see?'

The boy went and got some cloth that stank of white spirit but which bore not the faintest trace of any pink substance, sticky or otherwise.

'Must have dissolved,' the boy said, shrugging. He lost interest and wandered back towards the Morgan leaving James and S'n'J.

'Don't worry about it,' James said happily. 'It's gone now, and if you pick up any more you'll know just how to get rid of it, won't you?'

S'n'J nodded.

Everything would be back to normal tomorrow, she decided. Anything strange that happened between now and then would just have to be treated as part of this same natural mental aberration.

'So what about tonight?'

S'n'J was surprised to find that she'd followed James back into the reception area and not only had he finished swiping her card in the machine, but he had also apparently been carrying on a conversation with her while he'd been doing it.

'Sorry, I was miles away,' S'n'J said, snapping herself out of her reverie. She looked up at James and felt a surge of warmth. The eighty per cent cloud-cover over her mind broke again and allowed a little sunshine through. A guy that could make that happen had potential.

'So what about coming out with me tonight?' James repeated.

And a part of her told her that it would be a very good idea indeed. She hadn't had any half-way decent male company for a long time. But she was drained, and knew she wasn't going to be a barrel of laughs this evening. When she went out with him she wanted to be on peak form. Because her libido had been getting restless for quite a time now and she thought that at the end of their first evening together, she might well end up fucking his brains out. And if that was going to happen, she wanted to be fit for it. Today she didn't feel so much a tigress as a three-toed sloth.

'How about tomorrow?' she asked. 'Give me your phone number and I'll ring you.'

James looked at her carefully – presumably for signs that she was already giving him the bum's rush – then apparently decided she was serious and wrote his number in a booklet of Cars Inc. matches and slid it across the counter to her with the bill. 'I'll look forward to it,' he added.

So will I, S'n'J thought, signing the Visa slip and pocketing the matches.

On the way home, in the Sierra which was now guaranteed safe to drive with the windows rolled up, she began to feel better. There was something to look forward to now. Something that existed in the real world. She no longer needed romantic notions of being swept off her feet by the tall dark and hallucinatory Mr Winter.

She parked outside her flat, saw the manuscript still on the passenger seat, picked it up and tossed it into the mess in the back of the car, thinking, *So long and good riddance, I don't want you any more!*

Sarah-Jane Dresden had escaped Black Rock.

Physically and mentally.

It felt very good indeed.

Chapter Nine

Another Sample for Sarah-Jane

The glowing feeling of having beaten her fantasies lasted for less than three minutes.

Which was how long it took for her to lock the car, wrinkle her nose at the smell of paint burning off the new exhaust system, walk up the steps to her first-floor flat, unlock the door and close it behind her.

She turned around, saw the A4 envelope lying on the telephone table in the hall, and her feeling of elation vaporized.

'Oh, *crikey!*' she moaned.

She had not left the envelope there, which meant only one thing. Someone had been in the house and placed it there.

Probably the holder of the only other key to this flat.

'Martin?' S'n'J called, already wishing for her rolling-pin. 'MARTIN? IF YOU'RE HERE I WANT TO KNOW ABOUT IT. NOW WOULD BE A GOOD TIME IF YOU WANT TO LEAVE ON YOUR OWN TWO FEET RATHER THAN ON A STRETCHER!' she shouted, eyeing the envelope.

There was no sound except the squeaky thud of her heart pounding blood in her ears Martin didn't appear wearing his famous sheepish grin.

If he appears at all, he's going to appear looking something like Jack Nicholson in The Shining, *and he'll be armed with the fire-axe too! You know that, don't you? Martin's gone crazy.*

But Martin couldn't have got in, she realized with a shock, because he no longer held the only other key to her flat. She had taken it from him herself. That key, as she proved to herself by moving silently to the kitchen, was hanging on its hook. S'n'J armed herself with her weapon of choice – the deadly rolling-pin – and searched the house for signs of a break-in or that someone other than her was, or had been, in the flat. There were none.

Which meant that the envelope had *magicked* itself on to the telephone table.

'How did you get there?' she asked it, vowing never to pick it up, let alone open it or read what was contained within. That would be akin to opening a jar marked with a skull and crossbones and the words: BEWARE: ZYKLON B – DEADLY POISON to sate your curiosity about how it might smell.

She stared at the envelope, imagining she could see the pages inside it pulsating with their own inner life. An inner life that involved her too, not indirectly as a reader, but as part of the story.

Martin didn't write it, she suddenly thought.

Then she asked herself what evidence she had to support this. There was enough. The story seemed too good for dull old Martin to have written it. It contained a power that Martin did not possess. He couldn't have delivered it here and left it on the telephone table because he'd still been in London when she'd spoken to him earlier.

Nothing fitted the rules of normality any more.

And she couldn't go on blaming it on the carbon monoxide for ever; she hadn't inhaled any for a good long time now.

Like a woman handling something that might just be infected, S'n'J picked up the unmarked and unaddressed envelope between finger and thumb, turned it over and put it back, face down. The bad news was that the back wasn't marked either. The good news was that no strange sensation had run up her arm when she had touched the envelope. She had not been sucked in, hypnotized or compelled to open the envelope. In a Stephen Byrne story this was exactly what you would have expected to happen.

'Oh, *Jesus*!' S'n'J suddenly gasped and felt a mixture of dizziness and fear.

She hadn't checked the lounge.

She stood just outside the lounge door, telling herself that this was her home and that she couldn't imagine why she was too scared to go into her own lounge because there couldn't be anything nasty waiting for her in there – and found the argument unconvincing.

If this was a film, you'd go in there and something would fall down and everyone would scream, but there wouldn't be anything in there, she told herself. *Or you'd go in there and Mr Winter would be waiting, which would be worse. But this isn't a film or a book, so you can just walk in and sit down and put the telly on. Nothing will happen.*

But she did not believe herself.

She disbelieved herself so strongly that she did something the tough heroine in a movie or book would never have done. Her heart clattering against her ribs, her ears singing, and her body so tense she could have screamed, S'n'J collected her keys, went out through the front door, closed it gently behind her, walked downstairs and let herself out of the building.

So what do you do now, Drezy? she asked herself ten minutes later when she had walked all round the block. She was standing on the pavement on the far side of the road, looking up at her lounge window.

She could go indoors again and try to force herself to enter the lounge. She could phone the police and tell them she thought she'd been burgled and that the culprit was still in her house, or she could visit Dave and Janet and maybe get Dave to have a look inside her house for her. She found none of these plans particularly appealing.

'Excuse me,' a voice said.

S'n'J looked away from her window at a woman with a dog whose path she was blocking. The dog was not big and black and it didn't point at her.

'Sorry,' S'n'J said and moved aside, finally realizing that the woman was looking at her askance because she still had the rolling-pin against her shoulder like a sentry on duty.

As she began to summon up the courage to go back inside, she reviewed today's conversations with Martin about *Black Rock*. At first it sounded as if he'd gone crazy, but she now understood there was another explanation. A simpler one. And the beauty of it was, it fitted like a jigsaw with the two totally different styles of handwriting that were on the manuscript.

Now she knew the truth. Martin was not suffering from a multiple personality disorder that made him write the manuscript as one person, then made him edit it as another. The manuscript was written by someone else. And S'n'J suddenly knew who he thought it was.

Martin thought *she'd* written it.

Which was why he'd said he was sorry about the book. He wasn't saying sorry because he'd written it about her, but sorry about the hatchet job he'd done on it. He'd found the manuscript and believed she'd left it there for him to find. Which was why he'd taken it to pieces when he knew it was good. Because he was upset with her. And during their conversation – when she'd pictured him in his 'doing deals' mode with that smug expression on his face – he *was* actually trying to do a deal. With her. That was why he'd expected her to be delighted, and been so miffed when she'd told him to go whistle.

And that also meant that whoever had left the second envelope in her flat (the mysterious Peter Perfect, presumably) hadn't left it there for her to read, but for Martin, not knowing that he was long gone.

Which meant it was safe for her to go home.

In spite of the fact that Peter Perfect, whoever and wherever he might be, seems to know all about you in fine detail?

This was something that wouldn't be easily rationalized away. It might be pure coincidence. Martin was always full of stories about litigation by people with strange names finding accurate versions of themselves in books written by people who couldn't have known of their existence. It did happen.

Or perhaps it was someone she'd known in her college days. S'n'J didn't recall any of her ex-boyfriends having literary pretensions, but one of them might have developed some by now. And everyone had certain things in common. There were many people who didn't believe in ghosts and who were a little bit clumsy, for example. There weren't many people who had woken up in bed naked and entwined with their best friend Ellen, of course, but this could be explained away too. Ellen knew about it and she might have a guy who was a wannabe writer.

S'n'J looked up at the window once more. Shimmering light reflected on the ceiling – presumably from the big mirror which stood in front of the fireplace during the summer months – and gave a rippling effect which reminded her of the reflections you saw when the sun caught a lake.

Never noticed that before, she told herself. But this wasn't strictly true, she had never noticed it from *outside* before, but she *had* noticed that very pattern reflected on the ceiling. The last time she'd noticed it, she was on her back on the lounge floor, lying still while Martin pleasured himself inside her.

On your bike, Martin! she told the mental image that tried to form in her mind, wondering for the *nth* time how and why she'd put up with him. If she could have done it all over again, she wouldn't have done it all over again. Not with Martin anyhow.

S'n'J took another deep breath and crossed the road. She was now cool, calm and collected.

She expected the envelope to have vanished when she got back inside the flat, just as the vision of the injured Mr Winter had done.

This time she was disappointed. The offending item was still where she'd left it, face down on the telephone table.

'Get to you later,' she told it, steeling herself to enter the lounge.

It's your own home, she reminded herself. *You don't have to be scared.*

She reached out, took the door handle, pulled it down and took a step forward as she pushed the door open.

And in the teetering moment while she fought to keep her balance and stop herself from falling, S'n'J saw what had been causing the shimmering reflections on the lounge ceiling.

It was a glimmering October sun shining on the Atlantic.

And the Atlantic was in *her* lounge.

S'n'J swayed and windmilled her arms, realizing dimly that even this wasn't true: her lounge had ceased to exist. The door now opened on to thin air about a hundred feet above the sea. Somewhere near Black Rock, judging from the scenery.

Even the sudden terror at finding herself not in her lounge at all but gazing out of her hall and down into the sea was made insignificant by the single massive survival response which jolted through her like an electric shock:

DON'T FALL!

This instruction was easier for her mind to issue than it was for her body to follow. She was already in the attitude of a woman on a high board preparing to make a dive, leaning forward at an angle of fifteen degrees or so from the vertical. Her centre of gravity was over her toes and being steadily sucked further away from the point of recovery, and towards the point of no return. The door had vanished as it opened over the sea and there was nothing to hang on to with her windmilling arms.

The two seconds it took from opening the door to realizing that she wasn't going to be able to get back to terra firma again, seemed to last an age. It was long enough for S'n'J to question her swimming ability, long enough for her to wish she'd learned to dive and long enough to curse whoever or whatever had caused this to happen.

She swayed and frantically grasped behind her while she felt her centre of gravity moving inexorably forward, milli-metre by millimetre. And knew that she was going to die.

The warm Atlantic breeze tousled her hair. The smell and taste of the ocean filled her nose and mouth. The power of its huge gravitational force was too great to overcome. It was going to suck her in. She was now leaning forward at twenty degrees and there was nothing she could do to recover her balance. She was going to fall.

Her hands froze in the air before her face and S'n'J saw the broken nails that she would never get to grow now. A small, still part of her mind told them goodbye and shut up shop. She knew she was beaten and felt the fight go out of her.

The transition from leaning forward to falling seemed to happen in slow motion. Then she was falling headlong towards the sea and the doorway was above her, a small, rapidly receding rectangle which hung in mid air showing the interior of her hallway.

S'n'J lost consciousness before she hit the water.

Chapter Ten

Black Rock, Chapter Two, Bluebeard

Snowy woke up scared.

It was dark in the room and for a few moments she didn't know where she was or what had happened. Only that she had enjoyed it a little more than she ought to have done.

When she finally realized that she was not at home, but in the master bedroom of Black Rock – and alone in the huge bed – the fear began to fade and she relaxed.

You are no longer innocent little Snow White, she told herself, grinning. *You know now. You know just what it's all about and you're a part of it, just like you always wanted to be. You wanted excitement and you got it. Boy did you get it!*

It had been a dream, of course and now she was awake she could barely remember it. Only that it – like all the other dreams she'd had since she moved in – had filled her with the perverse kind of sexual ecstasy she would only expect to encounter if Count Dracula paid her a midnight visit.

If Philip had been here beside her on the bed now, she would have made him hard again and fucked him till doomsday. But Philip wasn't here. He had put her to bed earlier (and Martin had certainly never put her to bed *that* way), and after she had been reduced to something akin to a trembling jelly, had left her and gone across the corridor to his work-room, just as he did every night. Where he was, even now, hard at it, writing his book with the computer gear she'd sold him before she jacked her job to come here and be a kept woman.

His woman.

Just as she had done on other nights when she'd woken up

from one of her jungle-steamy dreams, she listened. For the sound of keys clattering as he worked. And just as it had on those other nights, her imagination provided the sound her ears were unable to hear. That of Philip, her very own Mr Winter, hard at work.

Snowy wanted him. Something had happened to her since she moved in three weeks ago. Something in the core of her had woken up. Philip called it her female soul, the essence of her femininity, but this didn't seem to fit. It seemed too flimsy – a little like calling a bulldozer a big shovel. Her 'female soul' was a massive, ravening thing. It was as if a huge power source had suddenly revealed itself, cranked itself up and gone to work like the world's biggest dynamo. Snowy, who had previously enjoyed her sex life as well as the next woman, now had a sex-drive that was so ferocious it would have left a nymphomaniac standing in the starting blocks.

She lay there aching for him but she didn't move.

Philip, whose own libido would have kept any woman in a state of permanent tremble-legged astonishment, would not be pleased. He didn't like to be disturbed when he was working. Under any circumstances.

Snowy had learned during the early part of her life that however good things were, however perfect, there was always a caveat. Always a condition that had to be observed.

Here, there were only three rules which had to be obeyed and she'd thought about them long and hard before she'd finally moved in. Two of them had been easy enough to accept, but it was the third that had given her something to think about. And even that had seemed unimportant after one of their blistering love-making sessions.

The rules were: 1) On no account must she enter Philip's work-room or disturb him while he was in there. 2) On no account must she pass through any locked door on the ground floor. 3) On no account must she leave the house without Philip's permission.

It was the third rule which for a while had caught in Snowy's craw. She had spent a long weekend thinking about it.

The other rules were straightforward enough – writers

didn't like to be disturbed by even their nearest and dearest, and the locked door thing was of no concern to her at all. The door in question was the one which led down to the basement or cellar or whatever it was called. Philip just referred to it as 'downstairs' but the only downstairs it could be was a cellar. There certainly wasn't another lower level carved out of the solid rock on which the house stood. She had told him that if he wanted to play Bluebeard he was welcome, and had enquired as to the welfare of his six other wives. The locked door held no fascination for her whatso-ever. She already knew where the key was – hanging up by the big mirror in the hall. But if he expected her to get herself into trouble by playing the curious woman, he was going to have a long wait.

But the third rule was a horse of another colour indeed. It was the kind of rule a woman might expect to come up against in the Middle East, but not one which a female living in modern England often had to consider. It reeked of total submission.

And Snowy hadn't thought very highly of that idea.

Her resistance to it had lasted a week, until the love-making session that had awoken the dynamo lurking deep inside her.

Afterwards, he'd asked her to make these solemn promises and had refused point blank to argue about them.

'Those are the conditions,' he'd said, 'and they're not up for discussion. Accept them or reject them. It's entirely up to you.'

He was testing her intentions. She had suddenly understood this. It was a kind of modern equivalent to having to go out and slay a dragon to prove herself worthy of the prince's hand.

So Snowy had said, 'OK, I've read the contract, I've cooled off during the cooling-off period and having given it due consideration, I hereby accept the conditions.'

And even that wasn't enough. 'You have to promise on your honour to observe the rules at all times,' Philip had said.

'I promise,' Snowy had answered.

And that was that.

And each time it occurred to her that she had promised away her independence, she reminded herself that rules were made to be broken and – as Philip often said before a writing session – that 'lies were there to be told'.

Which, she supposed had been the beginning of the end of her innocence. And since Philip had more strata than a million-year-old rock face, that was probably exactly what he had been aiming at. He *wanted* her to lie. She didn't know why. Not yet. But she had the feeling she was going to find out. Sooner or later.

Snowy turned over, snuggled down in the warm bed and rejected the idea of breaking rule number one. *Let him work in peace*, she thought. *If he'd rather tell lies than make love, then that's up to him.*

She lay there in the darkness, not knowing what time it was and not caring two hoots. She was warm, cared for, happy and more relaxed than since she'd been a tiny tot.

She closed her eyes, listened for computer keys rattling under deft fingers and tried to piece together the dream she'd been having.

She couldn't recall. It had probably been another dream about the basement. The dreams she'd had about Ellen had been set in the basement. Ellen, whom she had once loved, not just as a sister, but in the full, passionate sense of the word, had been present in several of those dreams which she *could* remember. All of them had been set in the forbidden basement.

See, you don't have to ban me from there, she thought, *I already know exactly what it looks like – and some of what happens there.*

The basement of her dreams was a box-shaped chamber perhaps fifteen feet along each wall and ten feet high. The walls were unfaced, but perfectly flat granite. Except the granite wasn't grey, it was black.

And it was kitted out rather like a dungeon, or an interrogation cell. It was lit by a single vandal-proof light fitting and there was a wooden work bench along one wall, upon which sat an old-fashioned reel-to-reel tape recorder and microphone. Each wall had set into it two sets of manacles which dangled on chains, and there was an assortment of instruments of torture lying here and there. Bullwhips, thumbscrews, daggers and various small items of machinery whose purpose was not suggested by their shape.

In each of Snowy's dreams of Ellen, Ellen had been naked and manacled to the wall. She had been horribly tortured and was writhing in agony, pleading for death to end her misery. And in each dream Snowy had turned on the tape recorder, knowing she wanted to preserve these cries for posterity. She felt no sympathy for Ellen, just a strange kind of warm joy at the sounds she was making and the state she was in. She didn't know if *she* had caused Ellen the pain she was suffering, but she did know that there was a part of her that badly wanted to increase that pain and subsequently increase the level of pleasure she felt. And she also knew that there was a valid purpose for the torture. But whenever she awoke, that knowledge disappeared and was instantly replaced by guilt.

You're probably just trying to exorcize Ellen from your system, she told herself sleepily. *You aren't lesbian and you weren't then and your subconscious feels guilty about what happened with her. Or something.*

Then there were the dreams about ghosts. She had made love with ghosts, both male and female – and sometimes both at once – and she had loved their cool and silky touch, the chill of their bodies enveloping her, seeping into her.

It was like being on holiday, in a way, she supposed. When you went on holiday and got away from it all and began to relax, all the nasty stuff that had been building up inside your head came out in dreams and was then filed neatly away in the right storage compartments.

And since she'd finally moved in with Philip, it had been just like being on holiday in other ways, too. For the first time since she'd left college and found employment there was no daily grind to look forward to, just an endless succession of days in which all she had to do was please herself.

He wrote and played, and she played and slept. And there seemed to be a lot of sleeping to be caught up on.

And now, lying in a big brass bed which had to be straight

out of a fairy tale because it was warmer and cosier than any bed she'd ever slept in previously, she decided to catch up on a little more of that valuable commodity of which she previously seemed to have been so deprived.

Snowy Dresden curled up and went back to sleep to chase all her fears away.

Everything was just about as fine as fine could be.

Until one day, barely a week later, she woke up late in the morning, still alone in the bed.

This was not usual. Philip's work sessions always started at midnight and lasted until three or four in the morning when he would climb in beside her, kiss her gently, sigh and fall asleep like a contented cat. Snowy seemed to have become attuned to his presence because now, each night when he came to bed, she rose close enough to the surface of sleep to become aware of him.

But apparently the converse did not apply: his failure to come to bed at the proper time hadn't disturbed her at all.

Snowy was not a morning person – one of that bright and cheerful breed who snap awake at six or seven each day already on full power and ready to rock. To the best of her knowledge she had never woken unaided and of her own accord before ten. And when she did wake up, either because of the alarm or because she had simply finished being asleep, her mind took almost another hour to crank itself up. Consequently her first thoughts today were somewhat muddy.

It's twenty past ten, she told herself. *Late.*

It didn't feel late, it felt positively early. In the half-light of the bedroom she squinted at her watch, certain she'd read it wrongly.

Philip didn't come to bed last night, she registered. The feeling that things were not as they ought to be was steadily infiltrating its way into her brain and Snowy began to feel a certain amount of concern. She was, however, quite certain that Philip was neither dead nor vanished, as her mind was trying to suggest.

He's still working, she willed herself to believe, pushing the covers back and sitting up. *He's on a roll and didn't want to stop.*

Unconvinced, her mind proceeded directly to fantasy mode without passing Go or collecting two hundred quid. And not all Snowy's fantasies were pleasant ones. In this one she found herself standing outside Philip's work-room wondering whether she should break rule number one and enter. He was not elsewhere in the house because she'd checked, so he must be in there. But he hadn't answered when she'd knocked and she couldn't hear him inside. Which meant that he'd fallen asleep at his keyboard or that he was slumped in front of it dead, or dying, of a stroke or heart attack. While she was outside, hesitating because of rule number one.

Snowy broke herself out of the fantasy and got out of bed, now far more alert than was good for her this short distance away from sleep. She was going to pay with a headache for sure.

I shall break that rule and go inside, she told herself.

One of Philip's expensive cotton shirts lay on the floor at her feet. She snatched it up, fastened two of the middle buttons and hurried downstairs.

Black Rock was bisected by the wide hall which ran from the front door to the back of the house where the back door would have been if *Haunted House Designs Inc.* had thought such a detail necessary. The lounge, which was practically large enough for a hockey match, took up the whole left-hand side of the house and had two entrances. Snowy chose the nearest door, and hurried through checking everywhere. It didn't take very long. She then tried the kitchen. He wasn't there either. Or in the overgrown back garden visible through the windows. She went back into the hall, passed the forbidden locked door to the cellar and hurried towards the library, cursing the lack of doors that meant she couldn't get from A to B without walking what seemed like a mile.

For example, the library butted up against the dining-room, but there was no access from one to the other. To get there, she had to walk what seemed like half-way around the world.

The side hall, which served only the library, ended in a

blank wall, which would have been the obvious place to have had a door to the outside. Snowy resolved that if she stayed here very long she would talk Philip into having some alterations done – then she thought she'd better make sure that Philip was still alive and well before she did any more planning for him.

One thing that constantly amazed her was the way Black Rock conformed to the stereotypical haunted house, right down to the fact that the library came complete with cases full of leather-bound books, a roll-top desk with a quill pen, ornate brass light fittings that looked as if they ought to contain gas mantles rather than electric lamps, and a genuine musty odour.

There was no Philip in there though.

Which only left the other two upstairs bedrooms, the bathroom and his work-room. Snowy hurried back upstairs and checked. And in less than a minute found herself acting out her fantasy in real life, by lingering in front of his work-room door, unable to make herself go in.

So much for breaking the rules, she scorned herself.

She put her ear to the door and listened. Inside that room was the four thousand pounds worth of computing equipment she had sold to Philip on her first visit – the very same visit during which all her fantasies about Mr Winter being Mr Right had come true on that sheepskin rug in front of the open fire.

And although you didn't pay all that money for equipment which would be noisy when it worked, she was certain she ought to have been able to hear *something*. There was not the tiniest noise from inside.

Which doesn't mean a thing, she told herself. *The doors in this house are all very heavy. The room is probably carpeted with something that has a pile as deep as the Marianas Trench and, for all you know, could be soundproofed so that outside noises don't distract him when he's working.*

Snowy knocked on the door. It felt exceptionally solid under her knuckles and she suddenly decided that, like the front door, this one might respond only to the voice of its owner. It might not let her in even if she decided to break rule number one.

Don't be so silly, she told herself, but the fact remained that the front door was not her friend. There was a trick involved – a trick she hadn't yet worked out and which Philip had refused to show her. She had been here three weeks and she had not once opened the front door unaided.

'Philip?' she called, knocking again. 'Philip, *please*! PHILIP!'

Perhaps he just went out, she told herself. It hadn't happened before, and he hadn't left a note to say where he'd gone, but that didn't mean it wasn't possible. Snowy suddenly couldn't remember if she'd seen his car outside or not. Black Rock had no garage, so he just left the car on the forecourt. It was a new Porsche 911 twin-turbo convertible and it was worth a lot of money, but Philip didn't worry about locking it. It was safe while it was within the grounds, he said.

She rushed back into the master bedroom, drew back the curtains and looked down at the forecourt. The Porsche was there, its rag-top down. And the feeling of things being wrong increased.

He wasn't in the attic, that was a certainty. The attic was another of the house's mysteries, along with the vexing question of where the stuff you flushed down the loo went to. The house appeared to possess no drainage system at all. There were no inspection covers on the property. The stuff just went down the pipe and vanished – probably straight into the sea. The attic question was just as mysterious. There had to be a water tank up there somewhere, since water came out of the taps, but there was no way up into the attic to find out for certain.

Snowy rushed back upstairs, tripped on the top step, sprawled across the landing, cursing herself. Got up, inspected her knees which now shone red with two lovely carpet burns – as did her right hip – hurried to the door of Philip's work-room, twisted the handle and pushed.

Opening doors inside Black Rock was an entirely different process from opening doors in a normal house. In a normal house you twisted the handle, pushed and the door opened to let you into the room. Those in Black Rock would sometimes open quickly and smoothly, and other times you had to put all your weight against them to make them move at all.

And on this occasion, as soon as the handle was turned, the door began to open of its own accord. It moved smoothly and slowly as if someone on the other side of it was drawing it open. Snowy let go of the handle and took a breath, half expecting Philip to be there.

And as the door opened, she froze.

For a moment she saw nothing inside. Nothing. No light, no shade, no colour. Just a pale nothingness.

Then, way below her, she saw the sea, as if the door of the room had opened into the air above the Atlantic Ocean.

Snowy screamed as her balance deserted her and frantically wheeled her arms trying to remain upright and searching for something solid to hang on to.

There was nothing there.

Screaming at the top of her voice, she began to fall.

Chapter Eleven

Waiting for James

The real, live, walking and talking (and currently scared shitless) Sarah-Jane Dresden spun the top off the bottle of Johnny Walker Black Label and tipped the bottle towards the glass. Because the glass had mysteriously emptied itself again. So far the whisky had achieved the old vanishing trick three times. S'n'J didn't recall drinking it, because you tended to lose track of what you were doing when you were engrossed to the point of being mesmerized by what you were reading.

But, she concluded, the whisky must have somehow found its way down her throat because she was beginning to feel warm inside.

Not secure. Not safe. And certainly not stable. But perhaps those things would follow hot on the heels of the warmth.

S'n'J hoped so because she didn't much like the sensation of numb dread that was building in her. Soon – if it wasn't stopped – it would peak, and she didn't want to be there when *that* happened.

She held the bottle over the glass for a count of five glugs, then gulped down as much of the Black Label as she could manage in one mouthful. It burned. Which was something real, something she could understand.

Unlike the rest of what seemed to be happening to her.

There were some things, S'n'J knew, that you could attribute to having inhaled a great deal of carbon monoxide. But there were some other things that you could not. One that seemed to belong to this latter variety – this week's enthralling episode of *Black Rock* – lay on the coffee table next to the Black Label bottle, now safely back in its envelope where it could do no further harm.

And that's quite a joke, too, S'n'J thought. *It doesn't have to do any more harm. It's already done everything it set out to do.*

Black Rock, by Peter Perfect, mightn't have been the best horror story she'd ever read, but it was certainly the most effective. If horror stories were meant to throw a scare into you, this one deserved a gold medal. She wasn't just scared, she was terrified.

No one but S'n'J knew her lounge door had opened on to the Atlantic an hour earlier (unless you counted God and she thought He'd given up on that sort of trick after Job), so it was impossible that she had just read all about it in the pages of a manuscript which had been written earlier.

Had she read the new *Black Rock* chapter first, she could have blamed what had happened to her on the story. She could have argued that it had somehow caused her to hallucinate the long drop to the sea. But she hadn't read anything until after she'd regained consciousness and, as far as she knew, stories didn't seep out of sealed envelopes and into your mind.

After what's happened to you today, you didn't ought to be surprised if that was exactly what happened, she told herself.

The fall through her lounge door and the subsequent plunge towards the sea, still seemed just as real in her memory as it had when it happened.

Or when it didn't happen, as the case may be, she told herself.

And it hadn't happened. S'n'J had woken up on her lounge floor, a few minutes after plunging through the door into the empty air. The lounge floor had been there all the time. What she'd *seen* had not been there.

And she could have stomached this, if that was all she'd been asked to stomach. But when she'd awoken, dazed and feeling a relief so intense she thought she ought to be able to touch it with her hands, she'd made the mistake of thinking it was all over.

She'd got the whisky bottle and the glass and set to work. And when the dazed feeling left her, S'n'J had found she felt strong enough to open the envelope which had been left in her home.

Now, looking back on that moment it seemed as if she had been compelled. She was certain that she hadn't decided to open the envelope but that the decision had been taken for her. Perhaps by the story itself. It was crazy, she knew, but the story seemed to possess a life of its own.

On reaching that last section, which she had read with mouth agape and mind aghast, S'n'J had begun to feel as if she was being mentally raped. As if someone, somewhere, had a direct line to the inside of her head, and wasn't using what he found there to construct a book, but was busily pumping in his own material to replace what was there already. She didn't feel as if Peter Perfect, whoever he was, was raiding her mind in order to change Snowy Dresden into her, but rather as if he was trying to change *her* into Snowy Dresden.

She came to the conclusion that she couldn't trust anything she'd seen, heard or felt since arriving at the King Arthur Hotel in Tintagel that afternoon. From then onwards, she had no idea what was reality and what wasn't.

But she hoped that her arrangement with James at Cars Inc. turned out to be real because she didn't think she could stand to be alone for very much longer. Even if it wasn't going to be the sexual event of the year, right now she just needed someone there who would hold her if she wanted to be held.

And she did want to be held. Very badly indeed.

She fished around in her handbag, found the book of matches James had given her, with his home number written in, took it to the phone and dialled the number.

And found herself talking to a woman who sounded very old and very deaf. 'Who's that?' the woman demanded in a scratchy voice.

'I may have got the wrong number,' S'n'J said. 'I wanted James.'

'What say, dear?' the woman grated.

'James,' S'n'J said, raising her voice while her mind told

her that this was either another of Peter Perfect's mind-fuck tricks or a CO-provoked episode.

It could simply be an innocent little old deaf lady answering a wrong number of course, but she doubted it. She doubted everything now.

'I'm having trouble hearing you. Could you say that again? You're very faint you know,' the woman said.

You couldn't have spoken a truer word, S'n'J thought. *I am feeling very faint. Any more tricks and I may be on the floor unconscious again.*

'James,' S'n'J repeated, as loud and clear as she could. James hadn't mentioned a grandmother, but, she supposed, he was still living with his parents and there *was* a chance that this was the parent of one of them.

'No James here,' the old woman finally croaked. 'What a day for wrong numbers! Had someone earlier wanted the police. No police here. No James neither. Sorry love, this is Maida Vale Two Seven Five. Mrs King.'

And before S'n'J could say anything, Mrs King broke the connection.

She redialled, wondering what kind of a number 'Maida Vale 275' was.

'Hi, who's calling "Air Your Views" on Two Seven Five FM?' an enthusiastic male voice enquired.

'I'm sorry, I think I have the wrong number,' S'n'J said.

'A wrooooonnnng nuuumber!' the voice shouted in delight. 'Well, you're live on the air throughout Cornwall, my darling, and tonight we're discussing the supernatural and while you're on the line I'd like to know your views on ghosts. Tell me, my darling, have you recently had any strange and eerie experiences?'

S'n'J slammed the phone back in its cradle.

'STOP IT!' she shouted. 'I don't know who you are or why you're doing this to me, but I want you to stop it!'

And it did stop. The next time she dialled she got through to James' home and James answered the phone.

Why this simple thing should seem like a magnificent triumph to her, S'n'J didn't know. All she'd done was make a phone call, after all.

'Hello, who am I speaking to?' she asked, just to be sure that she was speaking to James and not merely someone who sounded like him.

'James,' he said. 'James Green. Who's that?'

S'n'J realized she was about to say 'Snowy' and redirected her mouth. The resultant word sounded like, 'Sneejay'.

'Sorry?'

'It's Sarah-Jane Dresden. You fixed my exhaust this afternoon. We arranged . . .' she tailed off, because she was going to sound very stupid indeed if she had only imagined fixing up a date with him.

'A date for tomorrow,' James said and there was a kind of heavy, beaten tone to his voice as if he only now saw that a cruel joke had been played upon him. 'And you're ringing to say you can't make it. Am I right?'

S'n'J shook her head, hard. Then realized that James couldn't see that and quickly said, 'No, not at all. It's just that I'm feeling a little strange and . . .'

'You don't think you'll be well enough tomorrow.'

'Listen James. I *do* want to go out with you and I *will* go out with you tomorrow. But I'm feeling a bit scared, to tell you the truth. I'm on my own and worried and if it isn't too much trouble, I'd like you to come over now.'

Silence.

He thinks you're crazy now, she assured herself. *You turn up at the garage barefoot and with pink goo across the front of your car, act dazed, then you ask him out. Tomorrow. Now you've just told him you're scared. Why don't you just tell him you're not quite all there, save him wondering.*

S'n'J spoke into the silence, 'Only I think I need to be with someone . . .' She was floundering now, running out of words. 'I'm sorry, but I thought you might, perhaps . . . look after me for a bit . . . kind of . . . sit with me and talk or . . . something.'

If that doesn't put him off, nothing will, she told herself. *Guys his age don't go anywhere unless there's a chance they're going to get laid. They certainly don't put themselves out on a Friday night to go and sit with a mad woman.*

'Can I call you Sarah-Jane?' James asked, hesitantly. His

127

tone sounded official. Not cheery like his tone at work, but more that of a nervous policeman.

'If you like,' S'n'J replied, frowning. 'Or S'n'J, or Drezy.'

'Okay,' he said, sounding relieved to have overcome what for him had apparently been a major obstacle. He took a deep breath. 'Well, I think that what you're trying to tell me is that you're insecure and you want looking after, and you want me to do it, but that I shouldn't get the idea there's going to be any funny business. Is that right?'

'Roughly,' S'n'J said.

'And you don't think I'll go for it. Right?'

'Right.'

'Why not?' he asked.

'I don't know.'

'Because of this afternoon, right? Because you think I think you're nuts. Is that about the size of it?'

'That's a perfect fit,' S'n'J said.

Somewhere during the last two or three exchanges James had suddenly gained confidence and his interrogation had become playful, coquettish even, and the effect was identical to the one he'd had on her this afternoon. The dark clouds inside her head began to break and sunbeams poured through the gaps. If James hadn't had more women than she'd had hot dinners she would have been surprised. He could charm the pants off her in no time at all. He would come over. She knew that now.

'Well, I do think you're nuts,' James said. 'I also think you're very attractive. And charming. And I'd love to come over. And don't worry, I guarantee I won't pounce on you. Not today anyway. I'll make you cups of tea instead. Deal?'

'Thanks James,' she said.

'S'OK,' he replied. 'We're not all thugs, us tyre and exhaust fitters. Some of us are a bit edu-me-cated. Some of us are quite sensitive too. Anyway, it's all part of the after-sales service.'

'I'll bet it is,' she said.

'I'll look forward to seeing you, Miss Mental,' he said. 'Be about an hour, OK?'

All she had to do now was wait. S'n'J went back into the lounge and turned on the television.

An old black and white film was showing. About a haunted house, apparently.

S'n'J was now calm enough not to believe that someone had arranged this especially for her, but nevertheless she turned the television off again. However, she wasn't quite quick enough to avoid seeing a long shot of the haunted house in question. It didn't look unlike Black Rock.

Thinking nothing, Sarah-Jane sipped at her whisky and waited for James. Within five minutes she was asleep.

S'n'J woke up smiling. As far as she could tell, her nap had been populated with only good dreams.

She was certain that a noise from out in the hall had woken her, which meant she hadn't been asleep that deeply. An explosion wouldn't have brought her out of her normal sleeping mode. As Martin would say, this girl could sleep for her country. And probably win an Olympic gold, too.

That'll be James, she told herself, sitting up and wiping her eyes. The noise had sounded like the letter-box flap being used as a knocker.

She stood up, checked her face in the mirror over the fireplace, told herself that she looked dreadful and went to answer the door, wondering why James hadn't knocked a second time.

She found out as soon as she went out into the hall. James hadn't knocked a second time because James hadn't got here yet. And the rattling sound had come from someone using the letter box for its proper purpose.

There was another buff A4 envelope on the mat.

'You *bastard*!' S'n'J hissed and ran to the door, opened it and charged outside, then down the hall to the stairs, wishing she'd picked up her rolling-pin on the way out, for use when she caught up with Mr Clever Clogs Peter Perfect or whoever the hell he was.

Getting to the bottom of the stairs at the speed she was travelling without her legs becoming entangled was something she would have bet against, but her anger had seemingly filled her with the agility and grace of a predator.

At the foot of the stairs, she grabbed hold of the banister post and swung herself round to face the building's front door, which was just swinging to a close.

Got you, you shithead! she thought, dashing outside.

It wasn't just raining like it had been earlier; water was now hammering down as if it was being blasted out of the sky with dynamite. The gutters were fast-flowing rivers and the man-hole covers spouted fountains. The road was empty of moving traffic. S'n'J squinted against the blinding rain and could see no one on foot on either side of the road.

Which meant that he'd already got into his car.

There were four parked cars besides her own Sierra. S'n'J ran to the first one – a Renault – and before she realized it was empty had already yanked on the door hard enough to set off its burglar alarm.

The next two cars were empty too.

He wouldn't have parked this far away and walked. Not in this weather! S'n'J told herself as she pelted towards the next car. This too was empty.

Fifty yards ahead of her the last car's engine started.

'Got you!' she hissed and increased her pace until her legs screamed.

The car's wipers began to work and its headlights came on.

It was going to be close.

Very close.

But she would make it. She knew without a shadow of a doubt. The game was up for Mr Peter Pisshead. He wouldn't be terrorizing her any more after this.

If, as S'n'J would tell herself later, she had felt a little less like a Terminator Unit and a little more like herself, she would doubtless have saved herself a great deal of pain. This could have been accomplished by the simple act of remembering the hole in the paving slabs. It wasn't a deep hole, just a two-inch indentation where a section had broken off, but she had turned her ankle in it twice before.

And now, as she slowed to yank open the car door before it drove away, she did it for a third time.

This time it felt as if her right leg had been removed and replaced with a bolt of lightning. She skewed sideways, fell on her right shoulder, twisted and curled, and her legs sailed over her head and flipped her over. When the blur of movement had finished, S'n'J was kneeling on the wet pavement beside the driver's door of the car, facing the direction from which she had come. Her knees had taken most of the force of the fall and they felt as if they had smashed into a thousand pieces. And as any IRA 'Correction' team would have been glad to tell her, injured kneecaps provided more agonizing pain than almost any other part of the body.

But she wasn't going to let *anything* stop her. She scrambled to her feet, yanked open the car door, flung herself inside, grabbed Peter Perfect by the throat and began to throttle him.

It was a good five seconds before she realized that Peter Perfect was not Peter Perfect at all, or even male. The person currently struggling to break the stranglehold on her neck was a middle-aged woman.

S'n'J let go. The woman cringed.

'Did you just deliver a letter for anyone?' S'n'J demanded.

The woman shook her head.

'Where have you been?'

'Visiting my daughter,' the woman said in a terrified voice. 'Let me go! I'll get the police.'

'I *am* the police,' S'n'J said quickly. 'Where does your daughter live?'

The woman pointed across the street. 'Over there,' she said.

S'n'J nodded. She doubted very much that this was her author, or his postwoman. 'OK. I'm sorry about attacking you. I thought you were someone else,' she said, thinking frantically. 'We're acting on a tip-off. We're after a drugs courier and we thought it was you. We didn't see you get in the car. Are you all right? Do you want me to take you to the hospital?'

The woman nodded then shook her head. S'n'J assumed

this meant yes she was all right and no she didn't want to be driven to the hospital.

'Can I go now?' the woman said.

'Yes,' S'n'J said. She stepped back, closed the car door and the woman drove away.

She stood watching the car for a few seconds, not believing any of this had happened. She might have run down the road and fallen, but surely you couldn't half strangle a woman then make her believe you were a cop. Not *that* easily.

Getting back wasn't easy. Her ankle was badly twisted and her kneecaps shot pain into her that reached right up to her groin and down to her toes. S'n'J limped.

The question, *How could he have got away so easily?* had an answer so simple that even through the pain, she found it and had filed it away long before she reached the top of the stairs to her flat.

He'd suckered her, that was how. He'd run downstairs, opened the front door for effect, then retreated back down the ground-floor hallway – and had probably hidden amongst the junk that was stored beneath the stairs. He'd been clever enough to realize that she would give chase and also that when she saw the door closing she would assume he'd gone through it. He'd probably gone out afterwards, seen which direction she'd gone and set off the other way.

Well then, how come he didn't leave any wet footprints on the floor? She wasn't up to figuring that out right now. She entered her flat, closed the door and picked up the new envelope. The writing on the front of it was in the same hand as the corrections on the earlier pages; it was written with an HB pencil and said: *Forgot this earlier. Sorry.*

S'n'J turned the envelope over. There was a further message written on the back: *See how easy it is to tell lies? See what power it gives?*

This might have been a reference to what was contained within the envelope – Steve Byrne often did this when he sent in his completed manuscripts to Martin. On the box, he either wrote shout-lines – the kind of thing that got put on the front of paperbacks (*Visions of blood lust danced in his head*, was S'n'J's all-time favourite) or quotes from the story.

132

This might have been a story quote, but she doubted it. It looked more like a reference to what she had just done in the street.

Telling herself that this was impossible would have seemed a little like standing on the tilting deck of the Titanic and telling it, even as it slid beneath the waves, that it was unsinkable.

It wasn't until S'n'J got into the bathroom, still carrying the envelope and it wasn't until the bath was half-full, that she discovered she intended to have a hot foamy soak while she read the next instalment of *Black Rock*.

She was disgusted with herself, but there was nothing she could do about it. The story was an itch that needed to be scratched. She *had* to know what happened next.

You fool, you don't have *to know at all*, her Girl Guide voice told her.

The voice was right. Up to a point. But no matter how disgusted she felt with herself, the urge to know what was on the pages would not go away until it got what it wanted.

So she climbed into the bath, opened the envelope, pulled out Chapter Three and lay back in the steaming water promising herself that if things got out of hand she would stop immediately. Promising herself that she would only read for ten minutes anyway in order to be dry and dressed by the time James arrived.

Twenty minutes later, she had broken both of these promises.

Chapter Twelve

More *Black Rock*

The fall towards the sea ended abruptly when something flickered inside Snowy's head. She was surprised to find that she'd neither fallen nor moved at all. She was still standing on the threshold of Philip's work-room. All that had happened was that the door had reached the boundary of its travel and had stopped moving.

You hallucinated, Snowy told herself, but the vision seemed to be removing itself from her memory so quickly that it already felt like something that had happened to someone else.

She stared into Philip Winter's work-room, which was exactly as she had envisioned it. Large and Spartan and white.

She stood on the threshold for a moment, wanting to enter this forbidden zone very badly, but her feet were evidently more faithful to the rules than she was and simply refused to move. Or perhaps they simply declined to step on to a white carpet that a moment before had been a hundred-foot drop to the Atlantic Ocean.

The important thing was that Philip was not in the room. *Which means he is not in the house. Which means you can relax, little Snowdrop.*

Actually, Snowy didn't know what *anything* meant anymore. Not for sure. She was still suffering from the feeling that things were going badly wrong and she had just seen something that any psychiatrist in the world would have termed 'hallucination'.

Once, when she was with Ellen (whom she now pictured not as the happy-go-lucky bubbly blonde she ought to have remembered, but as the defiled and ruined woman of her nightmares), they had raided Ellen's parents' drinks cupboard and held a drinking match. The result, of course, was a grand throwing-it-back-up-again contest, but there was a period in between the two when they had both been alcohol-soaked to the point at which an alternate state of consciousness was gained. It was not a very pleasant state and while she was in it, Snowy had seen the long, straight road outside the house snake about like a ribbon in a high wind. As hallucinations went, it wasn't exactly a spiritual experience (if you pardoned the pun), but it was as close as Snowy ever wanted to get to seeing impossible things happen.

And now she had seen something impossible without the aid of a mind-altering substance.

And without the aid of a safety net, either, she added.

Go back to bed, she advised herself. *All that savage sex has rattled your brains. Are you really surprised you're feeling a bit odd after three weeks or so of constant love-making? They invented the phrase 'shagged out' to describe what you're feeling.*

She would have gone back to bed, but the part of her which would forever be a wide-eyed, open-mouthed, five-year-old, eager to discover and easily delighted, now woke up and began to issue requests.

Go inside, it told her. *You've already broken the golden rule by opening the door, so you might just as well go in and have a good look round. You'll probably never get another chance, so don't just stand there, go and look. He'll never know!*

Snowy tried telling herself there was no reason to snoop. She could already see what the big white room contained and there wasn't going to be anything else to discover. But even as she argued against the little girl's request – which was quickly becoming an imperative – she knew she was sunk. Now she was here she couldn't *not* go in.

She gazed into the room and what had looked like a clean, white office underwent a transformation in her mind and suddenly became an Aladdin's Cave full of mysteries and miracles, waiting for her to discover them and bring them to life.

What other reason could he have for making you promise not to enter?

Snowy went in. The carpets in the rest of the house were cripplingly expensive, but the one in here was of an even superior quality. Its deep pile felt gorgeous under her bare feet.

And what have we here? Snowy wondered, feeling a delicious thrill at the act of having crossed the threshold.

What she actually had was a big white room which contained a large bench upon which stood the computer Snowy had sold to Philip. Before it was a high-backed office chair.

The monitor was working and was showing a screen-saver which represented a high-speed flight through space. Points of light flew at you out of a black background and whizzed off the sides of the screen as if you were gazing out of the viewing port of a rapidly travelling Starship Enterprise.

The fact that the computer was switched on meant that Philip probably hadn't gone very far away and that he intended to resume whatever work he'd been doing when he came back.

Nevertheless, Snowy walked slowly down the room towards the machine, drinking in detail. Throughout the rest of the house, which had apparently been built by eye, by the Brothers Slipshod somewhere around the turn of the century, there was no such thing as a ninety-degree angle. The walls, floors and ceilings all met more-or-less where they were supposed to, but the accent was on the more-or-less. Walking a straight line from one end of a room to the other, invariably involved your wandering off-course like a drunk. Philip said you had to get your Black Rock legs before you could feel altogether comfortable, and Snowy had soon found hers.

But this room was different. Built with the utmost precision, its lines and angles were so sharp they felt as if they might cut your eyes. And when Snowy walked, it felt as if gravity itself had somehow increased.

And magical mystery number two was that there were no

lights in the room. Snowy began to tell herself that Philip used a desk lamp for illumination, but stopped when she glanced back at the desk and saw there was no lamp there.

A room with no lights! she marvelled, and treated herself to a brief fantasy in which Philip walked into the room, snapped his fingers, and the flat white walls obediently began to glow. *That'd be worth seeing*, she decided as her feet moved her steadily towards the work-bench and the computer.

The room was peculiar, there was no doubt about that. And on top of the strong sensation of gravity, there was an equal sensation of *things missing* – of which the absence of lights was only one part.

Snowy had sold computers to writers before and although the ones she had met were a disparate bunch, they all had one thing in common. They all worked surrounded by clutter. The old saw about how computers begat paper-free offices, was a myth, an ad man's fantasy. Whatever kind of work you did you were eventually going to have to print out paper copies, and you were going to have to store incoming paper mail somewhere – and if you were a writer, your finished manuscripts and draft copies.

But there wasn't a solitary file here. Not one scrap of paper bearing notes. And it wasn't even as if Philip kept that kind of stuff anywhere else in the house.

Maybe he keeps it in the cellar, she told herself, but she doubted it. It would be too much like hard work to have to visit the cellar if he wanted to refer to a letter he received a week ago.

It's magic, the little-girl voice informed her. *Just like the front door you can't open. Magic! Philip probably snaps his fingers and his paperwork appears.*

Snowy smiled. It would be very nice if this was the case, but she doubted it. What the more grown-up part of her was beginning to suspect was that there was something going on here in the order of a confidence trick.

So far she had seen no evidence whatsoever that Philip was a writer at all. Just because he crept out of bed in the dead of night and came in here (*if* he came in here) and told her afterwards that his new book was going well, it didn't mean that it was true. Add to this the fact that there were no Philip Winter books on the shelves (although he said he'd bought the house on the money he'd made from them) no incoming mail from his publishers (Ace Publishing, he said), and none of the other trappings of literary life ... and what did you have?

You had a computer in a big empty room.

Snowy had once sold equipment to a real writer called Stephen Byrne, who really was published by Ace Books. Byrne's shelves were weighed down with paperwork and manuscripts. His desk could barely be seen for clutter.

There was nothing like that here. Philip didn't have one pencil or pen on his desk, let alone a jotter to write on. There was just the keyboard, the mouse, the computer case, the screen (surely in Alpha Centauri by now, judging by the way the stars flew by) and on a shelf at the side, the laser printer. This was not a place where fiction was written by a man who made a great deal of money doing it.

So what is it then? the petulant little girl demanded, stamping a mental foot.

Snowy didn't know. But she intended to find out.

It looked, to all intents and purposes, as if the real reason Philip had made her swear never to enter this room was because he didn't want her to discover that he wasn't a writer at all.

Your secret will be safe with me, Philip, she thought, approaching his high-backed office chair. Suddenly feeling as if she was being watched, Snowy spun around, her heartbeat jacking itself up and her body tensing as if to receive a blow.

Philip wasn't standing in the doorway but just for a moment it seemed as though he was on the point of appearing – not by walking in, but by materializing like a genie from a bottle. Had she seen a slight shimmer in the air, or was it only her vision pulsing with the rapid power-beat of her spooked heart?

No one there, she concluded and sucked in air that seemed too warm and thick.

Then she watched in sinking astonishment as the door

swung smoothly back into its place and shut with a metallic *snick!*

Now you're in the kakky stuff, she admonished herself. *That door is going to belong to the genus* exitus impossibilus *just like the front door. You ain't going to be able to get outta here, kiddo.*

God only knew what would happen when Philip got back and found her stuck in the forbidden zone. There would be no mercy. On more than one occasion he'd jokingly told her, 'Just don't get me mad. Get me horny, make me laugh, but whatever you do, don't get me mad. I lose quite a lot of my charm when I'm all riled up.'

And Philip Winter with his charm all gone and fury boiling in its place was an experience Snowy hoped never to face. She might have stopped Martin dead in his tracks with a single blow from a rolling-pin, but Philip was quite a bit fitter and likely to be a lot more of a handful.

Snowy hurried back to the door, knowing she was doomed. It wasn't going to open. Philip had known this, just as he'd known she'd break the rules and trespass in his forbidden zone as soon as his back was turned. Just as Bluebeard had known that his wives wouldn't be able to resist the temptation of the forbidden locked door.

And you know what happened to them, she reminded herself as she reached out for the door handle. *They ended up like the dodo. Extinct.*

Snowy twisted the door handle. And sent out a brief prayer which ended with the words *Open Sesame* rather than *Amen*. Then she tugged.

The door swung open, heavily and smoothly and apparently of its own accord and at its own pace.

Snowy breathed a sigh of relief.

Just an ordinary door. She peered out on to the landing in case Philip was there. The sensible thing, she knew, would be to revert to plan B, which meant going back to bed and piling up a few Zs, and doing it now, while the going was good.

But Snowy Dresden hadn't got where she was today by being sensible, and now she knew the door would open when she tried it, there was nothing to prevent her from going back to that computer and finding out exactly what Philip had been using it for.

Except that you might get caught, she told herself, hesitating.

What are you, a woman or a marshmallow? she countered.

Go on, the little girl urged. *I'm pretty sure we're going to find out something interesting.*

Snowy didn't know whether she would feel worse about being caught or about walking away and never knowing what Philip really did. If he wasn't a writer, then he was lying to her about where his money came from and that meant he might be lying to her about other things. And Snowy had a right to know.

She went straight to the work-bench, sat down in Philip's chair and glared at the space-flight screen-saver. The software that ran this particular screen-saver belonged to Windows 95 if she wasn't mistaken. The idea of having a screen-saver at all was to prevent damage. If you went away and left a stationary image showing, the stream of electrons which constantly battered the coating on the inside of the screen would eventually etch that image there permanently. When you turned the computer off, you would still be able to see what had been etched there, just as you could still read what had been showing on a bank's automatic teller after it was turned off. A screen-saver was a program that automatically put up a moving image instead of a stationary one when it detected that you hadn't touched the keyboard or mouse for a while. Moving pictures didn't stay in one place long enough to be etched into the screen. And as soon as you touched the keyboard again, the screen-saver went away and you got your original display back.

The problem, from Snowy's viewpoint, was that Philip might have set this particular one to have a security password. Which meant as soon as she touched the keyboard she would be presented with a little box requesting that she enter a password she did not know. If he'd set a password, and she failed to crack it, the evidence that she'd been meddling would be there on the screen for him to see when he got back.

Snowy took hold of the mouse which lay beside the keyboard and realized two things at once. The first was that the movement of the mouse had cleared the screen-saver away, just as it was supposed to (and there was no password box to make life difficult). The second – far more shocking – thing was that the mouse wasn't plugged into the computer and therefore should have had absolutely no effect.

Snowy ignored the page of text that had appeared before her, while she looked at the offending mouse. Some were radio-controlled and didn't need to be wired to the computer, but this wasn't one. This one had a cable which came out of it, wound beneath the keyboard, curled around the desk and stopped. And there was its plug.

Not plugged in.

You touched a key, she reasoned with herself, *that would have done it.* But she knew she had been very careful not to come in contact with the keyboard; all she had done was move the mouse, which wasn't plugged in. Just to make sure she had the right lead, she traced it from mouse to plug, lifting the keyboard to make sure she had the right wire.

When Snowy glanced up at the monitor a row of lower case z's had appended themselves to the bottom of Philip's page of writing. She could get rid of those in just a moment, she decided. The important thing was discovering how this unplugged mouse had any effect on the computer.

Magic, that's how! her little-girl voice crowed in delight. *Told you we'd find out something interesting!*

Philip had been using Microsoft's 'Words for Windows', a word-processor that made use of the mouse. There was a little arrow on the screen which moved when you rolled the mouse around the desk. You pointed the arrow at little boxes and clicked one of the buttons on the mouse to turn stuff like italics on and off again. The arrow was currently half-way up the screen in the middle of the page of text.

It can't possibly move if you move the mouse, Snowy told herself, glancing back over her shoulder just in time to see the door performing its self-closing act. *Ghosts*, she thought, *as if there were such things.* And then she shivered.

This house contained more impossible things than you

could shake a stick at. There might be a rational explanation for the door closing by itself and for her failure to master the peculiar front door, but she was going to have a taxing time explaining it to herself if that pointer moved on the screen when she moved a mouse that wasn't even plugged in.

It won't move, Snowy, she assured herself. *It won't move because it can't!*

She took hold of the mouse and moved it a fraction of an inch away from her. Up on the screen, the little arrow obediently moved towards the top of the page.

Suddenly feeling scared, Snowy picked up the mouse and turned it over. According to the label it was a standard Logitech two button serial mouse, made in Ireland and complying with part 15 of the FCC rules.

She used the mouse to move the cursor to the end of the row of z's she must have inadvertently typed herself just lifting the keyboard, and used the keyboard's backspace key to delete them.

Then she stopped and thought for a moment.

And stared suspiciously at the wire that ran across the desk from the keyboard and dangled down behind it – before, presumably, it came back up again and plugged into the back of the computer.

Except that Snowy no longer expected it to be attached.

Don't you dare take hold of that wire and pull on it! she warned herself. Her head had started to spin now, and she was beginning to feel the first effects of a fear that promised to become an all-encompassing nightmare terror if it was encouraged.

But she could not stop herself.

She watched as her right hand took hold of the cable and began to pull it back towards her. Three tugs told her the bad news. The keyboard wasn't plugged in either. In a daze, Snowy held the plug in her hand and typed the letter Y. It appeared on the screen. She typed the letter R. This too appeared.

Snowy let go of the keyboard wire, reached behind the monitor and found the cable which connected it to the computer. Surprise, surprise, it too dangled free behind the bench. As did the power cord which also should have been plugged into the back of the computer case.

By this point she knew that she was also going to discover that the computer unit itself wasn't plugged into the mains.

She pushed the chair back and bent to peer beneath the desk, where the mains sockets surely were. She already knew there were no light fittings or light switches in the room, so the chances were there wouldn't be any sockets present either.

But computers did not work without power and this computer was working.

In spite of the fact that she could see no sockets beneath the desk.

It must have a separate supply, she thought. *It must be running off a big battery pack or a fail-safe supply that stops the computer shutting off in a power cut.*

But as Snowy well knew, there was nothing on the market that would run a full-sized desktop computer for very long without a mains input. And if there had been, she ought to have been able to see it, either on the desk or beneath it.

And there was nothing there.

Just a tangle of dangling wires.

The printer wasn't attached to the computer or plugged into a mains supply either, but its ready light was showing and Snowy had no doubt that in spite of this, it would print out hard copy as soon as it was asked to.

Up on the screen, the display flickered, the page of text vanished and the star-flight screen-saver began to show her that she was, in fact, at the controls of a craft which was plunging through deep space.

Snowy stared, feeling dizzy enough to fall. Perhaps right through the screen and into the cold vacuum of space.

The fear had become a kind of numb dread. It was like a paralysing venom, which kept you still and kept you conscious so that you were able to experience every aspect of what was in store for you.

The screen was actually expanding in front of her, its seventeen-inch window on to the stars first becoming a full-sized viewing port, then turning into a wall-sized one.

In less than a second, Snowy was speeding through space

at something approaching the speed of light. A jewel-studded velvet darkness stretched out before her, above her, below her and on either side of her. Galaxies whirled past beneath her feet, constellations twinkled by her. There was no longer any room or any computer. There was just Snowy, travelling through the universe.

And what happens when you reach the end? she asked herself. *What then? Infinity? Will you be dead? Will you see God Himself?*

As she opened her mouth to protest, the air was sucked from her lungs. It didn't hurt. Snowy knew she was going to die now, but that it wasn't going to be a painful death. She would just wink out of existence like a minor star. The edge of the universe was closer than she had anticipated.

Perhaps this is how it ends for everyone, a small, clear voice said at the back of her mind. *Your essence changes back into the energy from which it was made. Your being is absorbed by the cosmos.*

'YOU'VE BEEN A VERY BAD GIRL.'

The voice was thunderous and Snowy knew with certainty that it was the voice of her maker and that He was displeased.

I've done my best, Snowy heard herself reply, and felt, somehow, as if the words had been placed in her mind for her to think. As though she was not a creature of her own free will at all, but a machine that had been programmed. A character, perhaps, who was being pushed around the stage of some playwright, or written up as a bit part in a story that a playful author was busily constructing.

'BUT YOUR BEST WAS NOT GOOD ENOUGH, SNOWDROP DRESDEN. YOU KNOW WHAT HAPPENS TO BAD GIRLS, DON'T YOU?'

No, Snowy thought. *I'm sorry, but I don't.*

'BAD GIRLS HAVE TO BE PUNISHED. BAD GIRLS HAVE TO FEEL PAIN. BAD GIRLS HAVE TO STAY IN THE HOUSE. FOR EVER.'

Don't make me stay here, Snowy pleaded. *Please! I'll be good. I promise!*

In spite of the fact that she knew her emotions were being

relentlessly manipulated, the terror she felt at having to stay indoors was real.

'IT'S TOO LATE TO REPENT. BLUEBEARD IS MY SON. AND YOU BROKE BLUEBEARD'S RULES. NOW YOU MUST PAY THE CONSEQUENCES. THE GETTING IN IS EASY, SNOWDROP DRESDEN, IT'S THE GETTING OUT AGAIN YOU HAVE TO WORRY ABOUT.'

Snowy could feel herself diminishing, shrinking steadily.

'TOUCH ME NOW,' the voice of God said. 'REACH OUT AND TOUCH ME NOW.'

And so it was that Snowy put out a dwindling arm and felt the body of God. Even though she couldn't see him, she could feel him.

God was made of cold, smooth glass.

And when her hand sank through the glass, she suddenly felt air in her lungs again and screamed. Long and hard.

The universe flickered like a fluorescent lamp and went out.

Then Snowy was once again sitting in a high-backed swivel chair in Philip's big white work-room. Her hand was against the computer screen.

Except that her hand was partially *merged* with the screen, as if the glass had liquefied, then solidified around her fingers.

'Oh *Jesus God*!' she heard herself squeal, and a distant part of her noted that the expression was far too mild to fit the circumstances and wondered if it would be fixed on the redraft.

When she tried to pull her hand away from the monitor, it simply slid towards her across the smooth desk-top. Being careful not to touch the glass, Snowy held the monitor with her other hand and tugged her trapped hand, trying to free it. It moved, but not easily. She pulled harder and her fingers began to come out of the glass, drawing it out with them like strands of clear melted toffee. When her fingers finally came away from the screen, the strands released their grip on her and snapped back into the screen, which rolled as if a wave had passed across it and settled into exactly the same shape it had been before.

Snowy looked at her fingers in total disbelief. Apart from

the fact that her hand was shaking enough to be almost waving, she seemed to have suffered no ill effects whatsoever.

The question is, she asked herself, *did any of that actually happen?*

Snowy didn't know. All she knew was that she wanted to leave the room and never visit it again. Or even think of it again. Because if she did, she was going to have to revise her views about one of two things; either her disbelief in ghosts or her opinion that she was sane. She was certain of her sanity . . . but if she was sane, the computer was haunted, which was impossible.

Either way, you should leave now, before anything else happens, she instructed herself.

All well and good, but the old legs felt rubbery and she wasn't certain she would be able to stand. Tentatively, she put her hands against the work-bench to push herself up from the chair and give her some support.

This turned out to be another mistake.

Because the fingers of her right hand touched the mouse.

And the mouse moved.

In response the flying through space screen-saver vanished and the page of text came back.

As Snowy rose, a section of this text caught her eye. It was about half-way down the screen and it was written in capitals. It said exactly what the voice of God had said to her a few moments earlier.

YOU'VE BEEN A VERY BAD GIRL.

And the text below this seemed to be an exact transcription of what had happened to her since. She read: *The voice was thunderous and Snowy knew with certainty that it was the voice of her maker and that He was displeased.*

'This can't be true,' she heard herself say and read: *I've done my best, Snowy heard herself reply, and felt, somehow, as if the words had been placed in her mind for her to think. As though she was not a creature of her own free will at all, but a machine that had been programmed. A character, perhaps, who was being pushed around the stage of some playwright, or written up as a bit part in a story that a playful author was busily constructing.*

Snowy's mind spun. She had just acted out a scene that Philip had written in his book. Acted it out exactly as it was written down on the screen, with each thought and each sensation.

Impossible as it sounded, she was sitting in a room before a computer that worked even though it wasn't plugged in, reading what had just happened to her.

He made it happen to you, Snowy told herself, and wasn't sure where that left her. It seemed to leave her not existing at all, other than as a character in a book that Philip was writing. What if he'd written her whole life? What then? Would he have given her a happy ending? Somehow, she doubted it.

The other alternative was that Philip was somehow controlling her 'real life' actions through what he was writing. This didn't sound quite so outlandish, but it did raise many questions which couldn't be answered. Like, how could Philip know what she would do or think under any given set of circumstances?

The answer lay before her on the 'Words for Windows' screen on a magic computer which she could quite easily imagine was a whole lot more than a mere pack of circuit boards and microprocessors. This computer might just turn out to be the machine which controlled reality. Her reality, anyway. Perhaps 'God for Windows' was a better way of putting it.

Snowy drew a deep breath and tried to steady herself. It wasn't easy. Not when she had a written record in front of her of what had happened to her in the past five minutes. Especially when that record had been written by someone else *before* it had happened, and even more especially when it didn't end at the bottom of the screen. There was going to be more there, if she scrolled down, she knew that. She was also certain that if she read it, it was going to turn out to be an exact copy of everything she'd seen, done and felt since she'd last looked. And, if she scrolled down enough pages, she'd read what she was *going* to see, do and feel in the future. Perhaps right up until the end of her life.

Is this the punishment Bluebeard doles out to his

disobedient women? she wondered. *To see their life and death written down ahead of time?*

Snowy fought off the urge to look through the text to find out what might happen to her next. Perhaps it would be a good idea not to know. On the other hand, she did want to know if she really was trapped here . . .

So she took hold of the disconnected mouse and scrolled down the screen to the next page, and then the page after. The book Philip had been working on (BlkRck02.DOC according to the title bar), lasted for another three pages. If it was a novel, *her* novel – the story of Snowy – there was still a lot yet to come. This was only *Black Rock* Page 48. She had another two or three hundred to go yet. Maybe more.

Snowy scrolled back to Page 45, most of which she had read. She scanned down the page, only taking in peripherally the events that had happened to her since she last looked at the piece of prose, and when she got to the point which read, '*She scanned down the page . . .*' she had to look away because it was like looking at your reflection when you had a mirror in front of you and one behind. You felt as if you might fall inside those reflections and vanish.

She skipped the next six or seven paragraphs – which seemed to deal with what was going to happen when she got up – and her eye lit on a section that contained the magic words: *But now, Snowy knew exactly what she must do.*

'What must I do?' she asked aloud and her voice seemed to be coming from miles away. She back-tracked a little and discovered that she was going to make a tour of the house, looking for ways out, and find that only the front door offered an exit. And, apparently, that was going to offer the usual resistance.

Snowy read on:

The door could not be opened by normal means, as Snowy well knew. Unless you happened to be Mr Philip Winter of course. The door would open easily and smoothly for Philip. If he was outside, all he did was take hold of the large golden door knob and push gently. The door would open. If he was inside, he would simply take hold of the knob and pull gently.

There was a trick to opening the door, and, like the most irritating stage magicians, Philip would not tell Snowy what it was.

Consequently, Snowy had never yet managed to open the door. But now, alone in the house and frightened by what she had read about Bluebeard and the revenge he might extract, opening that door had become an imperative. Previously, she had not had even the faintest idea as to how the problem could be overcome. But now, Snowy knew exactly what she must do. There was more than one way to skin a cat – or open a door – and if she couldn't do it Philip's way, she would simply do it the other way.

And that other way depended on altering the flow of power which ran through the house. It would be as simple as throwing a switch, except that in this case there were many switches that would have to be thrown. But Snowy knew exactly how to throw them.

There were thought, by certain people, to be such things as geological power networks. Some folk called them leys, others, fairy highways, others, lines of geomantic force. Whatever they were called the fact remained that they were believed to be routes through which the earth's energy travelled.

Snowdrop Dresden, who didn't believe in ghosts, didn't believe in ley lines either.

What she did know was that Cornwall was thought to be particularly well endowed with sites that marked junctions of lines of geomantic force. There was St Michael's Mount, Tresvannock, Wiscairn and dozens of others.

And according to something Philip had once mentioned in passing, one of those important places was King Arthur's Castle, through which, he said, if you were in possession of a map, you could draw a line which led directly to Glastonbury Tor and magical places beyond.

Snowy also knew that Philip had drawn such a line, and believed that it ran right through Black Rock itself.

And although Snowy did not believe in leys, she was desperate. Desperate enough to try out something that might harness or alter their power. Like throwing the switches that would alter the path of the current that flowed through the house.

All she had to do was go downstairs to the lounge and align as many movable objects as she could find so they faced in the right direction. If they all pointed towards the south wall of the house – the front wall, the front door would cease to be locked against her.

Snowy read no further. There was a large part of her that didn't just disbelieve what she had read, it poured red-hot scorn on it. But there was also a part – the little-girl part – that took the matter very seriously indeed.

And she *was* in trouble, there was no doubt about that.

The exact amount of trouble she was in didn't reveal itself to her until after she had scrolled the story back to the page she'd found it on, replaced all the leads and the mouse approximately as they'd been before, and left the room on legs which seemed to be made of rubber.

She gathered her strewn wits and decided that before she could think about anything else, she needed a good hot cup of coffee.

It was when she got to the kitchen that she discovered the exact amount of trouble she was in. It took a while for it to sink in and it dawned on her only gradually. Starting when she opened the door of the refrigerator to get the milk.

There *was* no milk in the refrigerator. In fact, Snowy was forced to admit that not only was the refrigerator out of milk, it was out of a great many other things too.

With the exception of one item, the refrigerator was empty.

And Snowy thought she knew why.

It had nothing to do with the fact that all the food had been eaten and everything to do with the story which waited upstairs, still live on a computer screen which should have been dead. This had not been in the story, but Snowy expected it would be when Philip did the redraft. He'd known all about it, but he hadn't written it down because he hadn't wanted to give away too much too early on.

Snowy stared at the single item that lay on the fridge's bottom shelf.

It was not edible.

It was a white envelope and it bore her name on the front in Philip's handwriting.

She picked it up, already knowing what the message inside would say. She opened it on remote control while she asked herself how Philip could terrorize her like this, and why he should want to. He loved her deeply – as deeply as she loved him – and these were not the kind of games ordinary people played with their loved ones.

But Philip isn't an ordinary person, she told herself. *If he was, you wouldn't be here in his kitchen holding this chilly letter. Philip is extraordinary. And you broke one of his prime rules. So you should expect the consequences to be extraordinary too.*

She tore the envelope open. There was a single sheet of white paper inside. Snowy withdrew it and unfolded it. The message was exactly the one she had expected. It said:

> You've been a very naughty girl
> And naughty girls must be severely punished
> So now you have to stay inside the house
> For ever

To Snowy, this piece of poetry looked very much like it constituted a death threat.

It's a joke, that's all, she assured herself, but the evidence seemed to disagree. She'd already read that she couldn't get out of the house, and as Philip had removed all the food from the fridge, she couldn't stay here either. Not for long.

Where did he put the food? she asked herself. When she'd gone to bed the previous evening, the fridge had been chock-full of the goodies the travelling superstore had delivered. It had looked as if Philip had been laying in siege supplies.

It was a lot of food to throw away.

Snowy went to the utility room where the freezer was. There was nothing in it at all; the frozen stuff was gone too.

Apparently Philip meant to starve her to death.

Bullshit, Snowdrop Dresden, she told herself. *You are not trapped in this house. You can leave at any time.*

She went back into the kitchen. She would just have to have her coffee black. She wasn't terribly surprised to find that the coffee (and everything else) was absent from the cupboard.

But you forgot to remove the cups and glasses, Philip, didn't you? she thought, smiling grimly. She took a tall glass from the shelf, held it under the tap and turned on the water.

Then she did curse.

Philip hadn't removed the drinking vessels because there was no need to. He'd turned off the water.

She slammed the glass down, got on her hands and knees and yanked open the door under the sink unit, intending to find the cold water cock and turn it on again. This was where it would be.

And at this point, Snowy learned another mystifying fact about Black Rock which she could add to her collection.

There was no stop-cock there.

Or any pipes.

And yet water *had* come out of the taps. Until today. Scalding hot water out of the hot tap and freezing cold from the cold. Just like a normal house.

Snowy reached to the back of the cupboard and felt up the wall to where the taps were mounted in the stainless steel unit. There should have been unions there, where the taps met the pipes, or at least a big nut where they were mounted to the unit. Snowy felt nothing but smooth steel. It seemed that the taps had simply been glued to the top of the unit.

I don't like any of this, she thought, feeling dizzy and frightened.

Plan A, she told herself. *Get on your bike and get outta here!*

Snowy left the kitchen and went upstairs to the bedroom to get dressed.

On the way, she entertained herself with a brief fantasy in which she arrived at the bedroom to discover that all her clothes had vanished. She pictured herself being astonished that they were no longer draped over the chair where she'd left them. She imagined herself frantically opening cupboards and wardrobes and discovering that they were all empty, not only of her own clothes, but of Philip's too. She visualized herself sitting down heavily on the bed and starting to cry.

This was exactly what happened.

But you still have his car keys, she remembered. *Even if you have to leave dressed only in his shirt, you can just jump in the Porsche and drive away. If you can open that bastard front door, of course . . .*

She wiped away her tears, told herself she would not be beaten, got up and went back downstairs again.

She stood before the door looking at the parquet blocks of the polished wooden floor. None of them looked as if they would move; certainly not under the pressure of your foot, and probably not under the force of an atom bomb. The floor was as solid as the rest of the house.

Snowy ran her bare toes back and forth across the floor, but it felt as smooth and flat as a recently dressed ice-rink. She took hold of the door knob – knowing that she wouldn't leave her fingerprints upon this side of it, just as she couldn't leave them on the outside half of it – and pulled gently.

Nothing happened.

Snowy peeled her hand away and looked for her finger-prints. They'd left no trace.

The only difference between the outside half of the door knob and the inside half was that this side didn't have the ugly lion embossed upon it. If it had, Snowy thought the damned thing would be grinning at her smugly.

'Come on, you shit-house door, *open up!*' she commanded, and tugged on it again while sliding her foot back and forth across the floor in case there were any hidden pressure points.

This short, one-sided parody of a ballroom dance, achieved exactly the same result as her earlier attempt.

'I can easily get out of the window,' she told the door. 'All I have to do is open the one in the lounge and climb through it and I'll be out, so you may as well open for me.'

The door, apparently, was unimpressed.

She went back into the lounge, intending to climb out through one of the windows; she'd opened them more than once, and they had not offered even a token resistance. She reached the nearest window, took hold of the catch and twisted.

Or *tried* to twist: the closure was jammed solid.

Five minutes later she had discovered that every window catch on every window in the house was just as jammed as those in the lounge.

But Snowy wasn't beaten. She fetched a wooden-handled claw-hammer from Philip's tool box, bared her teeth at the first window and said, 'Now you'll open, you fucker!'

She placed the head of the hammer against the centre bar of the window frame, hooked the clawed end under the handle of the catch and levered to her right, intending not to force the catch open, but to break it clean off its centre pivot.

When nothing happened she pulled harder.

The wood on which the hammer was resting did not dent. The slender aluminium catch did not bend or snap. When she took the hammer away to inspect it, the catch wasn't even scratched.

'It's only aluminium, for God's sake!' Snowy complained, deciding it would be easier all round if she just broke the glass.

She removed the hammer from the catch, stood back and took an almighty swing at the window pane.

When the hammer hit the window it made a sound similar to the one she would have expected to hear had she struck the hull of an aircraft carrier: a solid metallic *clunk!*

Another three strikes proved to her that the windows were made of something very much stronger than standard glass and that she didn't have a hope of even cracking one, let alone shattering it.

The effort of trying to escape was making her sweat away quite a bit of the water she had left inside her, and she'd woken up thirsty. Soon she was going to stop being thirsty and start being *very thirsty indeed*.

Telephone! she suddenly thought and was again galvanized into action and running to where the telephone sat on a table at the back of the hall – where, in her opinion, the back door *should* have been. She had never used it, and now she thought about it she'd never actually seen Philip use it either.

The telephone looked as if it had been made shortly after they'd stopped using the ones on which you had to wind a little handle. It was large and heavy and made of a substance which might have been Bakelite. It had a proper handset, but that was about as modern as it got. Its cables were covered with that old-fashioned brown braided material she had last seen when she was very young and the large chromium dial had groups of three letters printed beneath each finger hole as well as the numbers. It was probably one of those restored antiques you could buy.

She lifted the handset, held it to her ear, and punched the air in triumph when she heard the dialling tone.

Have you out of here in just a jiffy, Smiffy! she promised herself, and dialled Nine Nine Nine. If this wasn't an emergency, she didn't know what was.

The operator took an age to answer. While she was waiting, Snowy had time to wonder about the odd ringing tone she could hear. Presumably it was some super-duper new technology that the emergency services had installed.

The line clicked.

'Hello?' a faint female voice said.

It wasn't the sort of voice Snowy would have expected an emergency services operator to possess. This woman was old. Her voice almost creaked.

'Give me the police!' Snowy said.

Silence.

'The police. I want the police!' Snowy repeated, croaking herself now. Her throat felt as if it was full of dust.

'I don't know what you mean, dear,' the old woman said. 'And I'm having trouble hearing you. Could you say that again? You're very faint, you know.'

'I need the police,' Snowy said, raising the volume of her voice.

'No dear, this isn't the police,' the woman replied. 'This is Maida Vale Two Seven Five. Oh dear, I don't know what's happened. This infernal thing is playing me up again,' she added, presumably to herself.

'Who is this?' Snowy demanded. People hadn't had numbers like Maida Vale 275 since the fifties, as far as she knew.

'Mrs King,' the woman rasped. 'I'm not a policeman, dear.'

And then Mrs King rang off.

Snowy stared at the phone in disbelief.

It's not a reproduction phone, the little girl inside her quipped. *This is an original. And it's still connected to the time when it was new.*

Snowy slammed her hand down on the cut-off buttons, got a fresh dialling tone and dialled again.

'Mayfair One Nine Zero,' a younger female voice announced. 'Zara Winter speaking. Can I help you?'

'I don't think so,' Snowy said and cut the connection, the name Zara Winter ringing in her ears. She dialled again.

'Fred King!' a man's voice shouted above the background roar of what had to be a factory.

Snowy's head was spinning. 'Are you related to Mrs King?' she asked.

'Well I'd have to be really, wouldn't I?' the man asked. 'I'm only called King because my parents are called King. Yes, Mrs King is my mum. Who is this anyway?'

'My name's Snowdrop Dresden,' Snowy said. 'And I'm thinking of the Mrs King whose telephone number is Maida Vale Two Seven Five.'

'Yeah, that's my mum. What about her? She been taken bad again? This the hospital?'

'No, she's fine,' Snowy said. 'I just wanted to ask if you knew a Zara Winter.'

'Don't think so,' Fred said. 'Why?'

'Could you tell me what the date is?' Snowy asked.

'October the twenty-eighth, of course. Friday. Same as it is where you are. What is this, Twenty Questions?'

'The full date,' Snowy heard herself ask. She did not want to know this, but she couldn't stop herself asking.

'That *is* the full date,' Fred Winter yelled.

'The year,' Snowy croaked. She felt as if she was burning up inside. There *were* such things as ghosts. She was talking to one now. She was certain.

'Nineteen forty-eight, of course. What year is it where *you're* calling from?'

Snowy cut the connection again, put the phone back in its cradle and wiped her hands on the shirt she was wearing as though the handset had been tainted with something which might have stuck to her. Earlier, she had hoped she hadn't gone mad. Now she hoped she had. She felt as if she was running a high temperature and her mouth and throat were screaming for water. She attempted to switch off what her mind was trying to tell her and to return to the immediate necessity, which was no longer escape, but an overpowering urge to drink.

Snowy stared at the phone for a few moments and her mind hit pay-dirt again. She suddenly knew where there would be some water she could drink.

She might never have managed to find any water supply pipes or any for waste-disposal, but in that bathroom was a wonderful invention which was going to save her life. That thing was the toilet cistern. You pulled the handle and two gallons of water gushed down the pan. Two gallons would keep her alive for a week, easily. If Philip hadn't flushed the pan after turning off the water, she was going to be fine. If he *had*, she wasn't going to be quite as fine, but she would survive longer than he had anticipated because there would be clean water in the U-bend of the pan. If he'd flushed the toilet, then pissed in it afterwards, she was going to have to think again – about boiling it before she drank it, probably – but she was certain that problem wasn't going to arise. He couldn't have thought of *everything*.

Except Philip had thought of everything.

He had emptied the flush.

He had not pissed in the U-bend water, but he hadn't needed to. Somehow, he'd *removed* the water from there. When Snowy put her hand down to touch – and perhaps claim the last few droplets for herself – she found that the trap was bone dry.

Snowy dearly wanted to collapse and weep, but refused to let herself. If what she'd read in Philip's book was true, there was one last chance. But it was the only chance she had left.

She went back into the lounge, and just as the book had predicted she would, began to align the ornaments, chairs, cushions and almost everything else she was able to move so that they pointed at the front wall of the house.

Snowy glanced over her shoulder several times as she

worked, but Philip hadn't magically appeared, wasn't suddenly standing there smirking at her.

'I *will* get out,' she heard a voice say, and for a few moments wasn't certain that the voice belonged to her. It sounded quite a lot more like the voice of Zara Winter than the one which belonged to Snowy Dresden.

The two leather sofas were incredibly heavy and difficult to move across the deep pile of the carpet and the second one caught in the sheepskin rug on which she and Philip had sealed the deal for the computer. Then there was the question of the pile of logs on the hearth. Their hewn ends already faced the front of the house and Snowy hoped this was right. She had no idea what constituted the face of a log. A sofa was easy – its face was the front, the bit you sat in – but a log was another matter. She had already taken both the poker and the tongs and set them in what she was sure was the right direction – business ends facing the front wall – but she didn't know about the logs. If it didn't work this way, she would just have to try placing their bark-covered length forwards.

Snowy left the logs as they were, adjusted the last ornament on the mantel (a priapic Greek satyr, whose erection she neatly aligned) and went to the front door.

'Now open for me, you bastard!' she hissed at it, taking hold of the handle.

Snowy took a deep, shuddering breath and tugged.

Then she went back into the lounge and adjusted the pile of logs.

Two minutes later, she stood before the front door again. 'Open Sesame,' she breathed, and took the cool door knob in her hand again.

She pulled gently.

And almost screamed when the door swung slowly open.

The sharp tang of sea air bit her nostrils, contrasting sharply with the still, dead air she seemed to have been breathing inside the house.

The air smells alive, she thought crazily, drawing in a huge breath of cold, fresh air and exhaling it in a plume. It was cold outside. And bright. Snowy suddenly realized that she hadn't been outside the house for more than a week. Looking out of the door seemed like crashing back into reality after a bad dream.

You did it, Snowy, she congratulated herself. *Now get the hell out of here while you still can.*

It wasn't until then that she realized the keys to Philip's Porsche, which stood invitingly before her, its soft top down, were not in her hand. She had left them on the drainer in the kitchen when she'd rushed upstairs to get a drink that didn't exist.

Her toes on the threshold, Snowy rocked back and forth, wanting very badly to go out through the door whether or not she had the keys. The door was currently open and she wasn't sure it was going to stay that way if she went back through the house. It would probably close again, like the door to Philip's work-room had done. And if that happened, she doubted it would want to open a second time. But she couldn't get far without the car. The only thing she was wearing was Philip's shirt, for one thing. And the ground was rough from here right up to the village; her bare feet weren't going to stand it.

So she had to risk going back for the keys.

She took another deep breath of air, turned away from the door and sprinted down the hall to the kitchen, fully expecting that the keys would be gone.

The keys were exactly where she'd left them.

She snatched them off the drainer, turned, ran back out to the hall and stopped, her heart sinking.

The door had closed.

'*Don't do this to me!*' she yelled.

But when she held the door knob and pulled, miracle of miracles, the door slowly began to open.

This time, she paused no longer than it took for the door to swing sedately towards her. By then she'd already sprinted out, through the porch, on to the gravel forecourt . . .

And into the arms of Philip Winter.

Then she screamed, long and hard.

'Snowy?' Philip said in a concerned voice. 'Whatever's wrong?'

Chapter Thirteen

Reading Chapter Three

As stated by Alexander Graham Bell's third immutable law, the telephone had begun to ring just as S'n'J had settled into the bath and started to read. And as Pavlov would have been pleased to point out, the acquired human response to the ringing of a telephone bell while in the bath is to heave yourself out of the water and try to get to the damned thing before the ringing stops. There is another law which states that the caller will quit just as you arrive, dripping, at the phone, but this wasn't what stopped S'n'J from going to answer it.

What stopped her answering the phone was several flavours of fear concerning who might be on the other end of the line.

S'n'J stopped reading and sat there, bolt upright and quivering with tension, like a rabbit in a field upon spotting a distant dog.

It's Martin, she told herself. *Wanting to know how you like the latest chapters. Phoning to tell you that he's in the call box at the end of the street and that he wants to come up and talk to you.*

But there was another part of her that feared that it might, instead, be the mysterious person who had delivered the envelope: Mr Peter Perfect himself.

Her imagination treated her to a hackneyed fantasy of a sinister, *knowing* voice saying, 'You don't know me, but I know you . . .'

She stayed put, hoping it wasn't James calling to cancel; she sincerely doubted it was him. Eventually the caller gave up. When it rang again, S'n'J did climb out of the bath. She dripped her way down the hall, waited for the phone to stop ringing, then took it off the hook. 'Get past that then,' she challenged whoever had been trying to contact her, thankful that she'd left the ansaphone turned off.

The dialling tone ceased and the phone began to broadcast the 'Please replace the handset and try again,' message and warning tone. S'n'J hoped she wouldn't be able to hear it from the bath and went back there to her reading.

Warning bells began to ring inside her head when she got to the part which read: *'I've done my best,' Snowy heard herself reply, and felt, somehow, as if the words had been placed in her mind for her to think. As though she was not a creature of her own free will at all, but a machine that had been programmed. A character, perhaps, who was being pushed around the stage of some playwright, or written up as a bit part in a story that a playful author was busily constructing.*

Because not only did *she* have a strong sensation of being manipulated by an outside force, but like her namesake Snowy, she felt that it was the author of the work who was doing the manipulating. The nesting effect in the story was also horribly disorientating. She was reading a story about a girl (who to all intents seemed to be her) who was reading a story about herself (ditto) which had been written on an unplugged computer by a man who was going to turn out to be something more than an ordinary writer. And the story looked like a script being prepared for her.

What was even more disconcerting was the hallucination she'd had that afternoon when she'd seen the blinding light shining from an upstairs window. That window, she intuited, belonged not to one of the house's upstairs bedrooms, but to the room that was supposed to be Philip Winter's workroom.

Maida Vale 275, S'n'J thought, remembering how she thought she'd seen Mr Winter fold himself up into a tiny dot and then vanish. *Who or what is he?*

But she knew what he wanted her to believe he was.

A ghost.

And she refused to let him have his way. But that did not stop her jumping when someone rattled the letter-box flap.

She checked her watch and was amazed that more than twenty minutes had passed since she'd got into the bath. Not only had she broken her promise to read for only ten minutes, but she'd also broken her promise to be ready when James arrived.

The letter-box flap rattled again. This time it was a sharp rhythmic beat.

She cursed herself for having been carried away with the damned book, then decided that James would probably be delighted when she answered the door wrapped in only a towel. Apart from which, if she didn't hurry herself up he would soon conclude that she'd been playing him for a sucker and that she'd gone out.

S'n'J got out of the bath, wrapped herself in a big towel and padded down the hall, tracing the damp tracks her trip to the telephone had left. She pulled the door open . . .

And viola, madman! No one whatsoever is here!

There were wet footprints leading to, and from, her door, but whoever had been trying to attract her attention had gone.

You couldn't have given up that easily, James, she thought. *Surely not!*

But it might not have been him. It might have been the phantom manuscript deliverer. *Who, in which case, has very tiny feet*, she noted, looking at the footprints. S'n'J knew only one person with feet so small they looked as if they'd been subjected to the ancient Chinese art of binding, and that was Janet from the house next door.

What would Janet have wanted? She'd have rung, surely. She wouldn't have come round here in this rain.

S'n'J went back inside and realized that Janet – whose aversion to the use of her tiny feet for walking ranked up there with Jesus' aversion to temples being used as banks – might indeed have tried to ring first. If she had, she would have found that S'n'J's phone was off the hook.

S'n'J picked up the phone, joggled the cut-off buttons, got a dialling tone and rang Janet, fully expecting to get through to a number that didn't (and *couldn't*) exist. Or to a radio station.

She was relieved when neither of these things happened. Janet answered.

'Hi Janet, it's Drezy,' she said. 'You wanted me?'

'I thought you were out. Or asleep,' Janet said. 'How did you know it was me at the door anyway?'

'Call me supersleuth. You left clues. I saw the little wet footprints on the outside landing and I thought, either it had to be you or Little Red Riding Hood. And as she's not on the phone I called you. What's up?'

'*It* rang,' Janet said, and for a moment S'n'J thought she meant the *It* from the magic house in Tintagel.

'Martin?' she said, reminding herself that she wasn't the only person in the world who held Martin in exceedingly low esteem.

'The very same. He must be desperate to have rung here. He said he couldn't get through to you and that he was worried. Something to do with you needing an ambulance. He wanted me to come round and check if you were all right. I would have told him to piss off, but he got me worried too. I could see the light on from our back garden, so I thought you'd be in. But when you didn't answer and I couldn't hear anything – except the phone whining because it was off the hook – I decided you were probably lying doggo because you were expecting Mr Aren't I Wonderful to call. I went home and told him you weren't answering the door. That's it. You *are* OK, aren't you?'

'Yeah, I'm fine,' S'n'J said. 'Took a bit of a fall earlier.'

'You're hurt?'

'No. Bruised and scraped, but not hurt.'

'But you wanted an ambulance?' Janet said, in a tone which suggested both that she knew S'n'J was lying and that since she was hurt she obviously needed looking after.

S'n'J knew that if she didn't convince her nothing was wrong, Janet would insist on coming over. 'It wasn't for me,' she said. 'It was for someone who fell off a roof. I was about to ring for an ambulance on my mobile and Martin called.'

'Oh,' Janet said, and just as S'n'J knew she would, wanted to know about the person who'd taken the fall.

And for the second time that night S'n'J found out how

good the telling of lies could make you feel. She thought of the message written on the latest envelope: *See how easy it is to tell lies? See what power it gives?*

'But you are in one piece and that's the main thing,' Janet said after hearing how the falling man (falling from a ladder in front of a bookshop in Plymouth and striking S'n'J a glancing blow before hitting the deck hard enough to hospitalize him) had fared.

'I'm fine,' S'n'J said.

'Will you ring him?' Janet asked. 'I mean, I wouldn't, but he *was* very worried.'

'Did he leave a number?' S'n'J asked, distantly realizing that she'd inadvertently discovered one of the laws of fibbing: The bigger the lie, the easier it is for people to swallow. This seemed significant, but she wasn't quite sure why.

'He said he wasn't at his wife's,' Janet said, 'which means that—'

'—that's *exactly* where he is,' S'n'J finished, once again reasoning that Martin couldn't have written *Black Rock*. Anyone who told a lie so old and tired it had become a joke between S'n'J and her neighbour obviously didn't have the imagination to write the material she'd been reading.

'So will you ring him there?' Janet asked.

'I don't know, Janny. I'll think about it.'

'If he rings again, what shall I say?'

S'n'J hesitated. There was a chance that Martin was nearby. He was definitely still in London when she'd spoken to him that afternoon, but he'd had time to get here by now. Time enough to deliver a second envelope?

'If he rings again, tell him I've gone to Scarborough for the weekend,' she said to Janet. Then added, 'To stay with my sister.'

'Scarborough? That's miles away!'

'Four hundred and nine, in fact. From here, that is. Probably a bit closer to London. My sister's name and address is this. You got a pen?'

'You haven't got a sister in Scarborough, have you?'

'Got a pen?'

'Hang on . . . yeah. Ready.'

'Snowdrop Algar. Forty-two Ellenfield Road, Scarborough. Got that?'

'Got it! I didn't know you had a sister in Scarborough though,' Janet repeated.

'I haven't got a sister at all,' S'n'J said.

Janet giggled. 'But that's where he'll find you, right?'

'You can tell him I'd be pleased to see him there,' S'n'J said.

'It's a long drive,' Janet sniggered.

'Not in a Ferrari, surely?' S'n'J said, feeling good for a change.

'I can't think of anyone who deserves it more. Do you think he'll go for it?'

S'n'J didn't for a moment believe he would drive to Scarborough. But it might just make him stop and think. It might make him realize that there were some things he didn't know about his little Essenjay. And the forename she'd given . her imaginary sister might, if Martin *was* connected to the mystery author, carry the message that she intended to fight fire with fire. 'Nah,' she said aloud. 'He won't go for it.'

'Be nice if he did though, wouldn't it?' Janet said.

'Wishful thinking will get you nowhere,' S'n'J quipped.

'I can dream.'

'We both can. See you later, Janny. Gotta go. Gotta date and I'm still half-way through having a bath.'

'Who with?'

'The bath isn't big enough for two,' she said, intentionally misunderstanding.

'The date.'

'James.'

'James who?'

'Green.'

'The tall one from Cars Inc.? Good-looking but shy?'

'The very man.'

'Cradle snatcher. God, I could show him a good time. I'd fit him in *my* bath, big enough for two or not. The second he came through the front door, I'd have his clothes off, the next second I'd have him in the bath and the second after that, I'd have him.'

S'n'J didn't disbelieve this for a second. Janet's sexual appetite was legendary. She probably would have given *Black Rock*'s Snowy Dresden a run for her money.

S'n'J said goodbye to Janet, put the phone back on the base and jumped when it immediately began to ring. She waited until it had stopped, then switched on the answering machine. She paused in case the caller rang again and let her mind wander back to the subject of James. And sex.

Then she decided that she might just as well stay in the bath until he arrived. Not because she intended to drag him in there with her as Janet would have done, but because the water was soothing her hurts and because she wanted to read the rest of the book chapter.

You're not fooling anyone, my girl, she told herself in her mother's voice. *You've got the morals of an alley cat!*

S'n'J smiled and got back in the bath. After a while she picked up the finger-dampened pages and began to read.

A while after that she totally forgot about James.

Because of what was happening to Snowy.

Snowy really *was* trapped.

As she read on, S'n'J felt as if she was slowly sinking in quicksand which would soon suffocate her. She fancied she'd seen the 'electrical-items-that-work-while-unplugged' trick in other novels (including one of Steve Byrne's) and the plunge through the universe was familiar from Stephen King's *It* but other things rang with a very nasty resonance.

The mysterious Peter Perfect seemed to be aware, for instance, that S'n'J had been unable to break the windows of Black Rock that afternoon. That she'd searched for a back door which didn't exist. That one of her nightmares concerned dying of thirst in a place where you should have been able to find drinking water. That she sometimes neatly aligned household items for good luck.

And the further she read, the more convinced she became that Snowy Dresden wasn't just a coincidence, but an intentional facsimile of herself. And that *Black Rock* wasn't just an unpublished horror novel, but a malicious plan for the life of Sarah-Jane Dresden.

It was all impossible, of course, but that didn't stop S'n'J from giving it due consideration.

The phone began to ring again while Snowy was busily aligning all the things in the lounge to point at the front wall of the house.

S'n'J broke out of the story and glanced at the window-sill upon which stood perhaps fifteen or twenty bottles and packets of various sizes; everything you could ever imagine using in a bath. And all of it was neatly aligned in ranks, the labels not facing her, but pointed towards what she fondly imagined was magnetic north.

It had started with the razor, of course. She owned an ancient steel Gillette job that she'd stolen from her father, back in the dark ages. And she'd stuck with it. Those gadgets that yanked the hairs from your legs using rotating discs hurt. Anyway, she'd heard stories about lengthening the life of razor blades by aligning their cutting edges to correspond with the earth's lines of magnetic force. And somewhere along the way, it had occurred to her that if she were to line up all the things surrounding the razor, so they too faced the same way, perhaps they would act as a kind of focusing device and make the blade sharper still, or increase its longevity.

But now she'd had it pointed out to her in the story it no longer seemed to be a silly experiment she'd done for fun, but a sign of potential mental disorder. The kind of thing a crazy person might do.

The phone had rung three times by the time she'd risen from the bath once more. She'd turned on the ansaphone again; so after the fourth ring, the caller would hear the 'I'm too busy with the Chippendales,' message so S'n'J wrapped herself in her wet towel and hurried up the hall to see if whoever it was would speak.

'Look Essenjay, this is Martin, and I'm worried about you,' a peeved voice said in a tone with which she was all too familiar. S'n'J flipped him a V sign and thought, *Up your pipe!*

'Would you please call me and let me know you're OK,' he said, gave the office number and rang off.

I know you're not there, Martin, she thought.

The question was, where was he? Here in Bude? After all he *could* have been telling the truth when he'd told Janet he wasn't at his wife's house. If she rang Ace and left a voice-mail message for him, he could call in and have that message played back to him from wherever he was – be it Bude or Berlin.

S'n'J called the office, just to be sure he wasn't there after all. She got through to his voice-mail box, and told him that she was just leaving the house to go and stay with her sister in Scarborough. She omitted her 'sister's' Christian name this time, but gave the same address and extended the same invitation. Martin, if he was free, would be welcome to join her there.

Suck on that! she told him, putting the phone down again. She could play Secret Squirrel games too.

Then she dialled the number of Martin's ex-marital home. Where he used to live before she'd stolen him away from poor Angie. Where he'd been living ever since S'n'J had thrown him out if the truth were known.

Which it is, by certain people, she thought.

She felt sorry for Angie on two counts. First (albeit unknowingly since Martin had said he was separated), she'd taken away the poor woman's husband, and then, to add insult to injury, she'd given him back again. S'n'J didn't know which one she felt worse about. Angie might have been unlucky to lose her husband, but as far as S'n'J was concerned, getting him back should have made her feel as if someone up there really had it in for her.

Up in London, someone had lifted the receiver. Whoever it was didn't speak, but the breathing S'n'J could hear quite plainly belonged to Martin. It was the tight-chested, shuddering, sort of breathing you would be most likely to hear when Martin was on top of you, using you as the human equivalent of an inflatable doll.

For a moment, she couldn't comprehend the messages the breathing contained. Not only was Martin *not* here in Bude, stalking her like the madman she half-suspected he'd become, but she had interrupted him while he was fucking Angie.

This is impossible, she thought and before she could stop herself, had asked, 'Martin?'

'Essenjay?'

In a single word his breathy voice managed to contain shock, hope, delight and extreme lust. A large and awful picture of Martin formed in S'n'J's mind. He was standing in the hall of Angie's house, naked and sweating, his face reddened with exertion and his thinning blond hair plastered down and darkened with moisture. He was holding the phone to his ear with his right hand and clutching his erect penis with his left. In a moment he would leer and say, 'I've got something for you, little girl. Something nice. Something big and hard and tasty . . .'

S'n'J winced and slammed the phone back into its cradle. For a few seconds she glared at it as if it held the sole responsibility for what had just taken place. Then she shuddered in disgust and wondered how she'd ever let Martin anywhere near her.

She put the image out of her mind.

Martin was in London. That was the important thing. It meant that he wasn't going to turn up here tonight. Not if he was at home fucking poor Angie.

It did raise more questions though. Like the identity of the mystery mail-man who'd been inside the house already today, and who had returned, delivered again and vanished into thin air.

A fresh picture formed in S'n'J's mind, in the space so recently vacated by the image of Martin. This one showed her Mr Winter folding up. This time he didn't do it on the periphery of her vision, but square in the centre of her mind's eye. He flattened and folded double, across his waist first, then through the centre of his body. And as she watched, the rate at which it happened accelerated massively. The first two folds were easy to see, then he became a flickering blur of flat planes which halved and shut down like a stack of pages being riffled. It took less than a second for him to become the size of a grain of sugar. Then he simply snapped out of existence.

She forced this image off its mental canvas and filed it under 'hallucination'.

S'n'J was now no longer really certain she wanted to welcome James while dressed only in a towel, but she sat down on the toilet seat to finish the last story pages, not knowing if she was being manipulated, or how to counter it if she was. The only course of action open to her at the moment was to read what she was sent and await further developments.

Inside five minutes Peter Perfect had hooked her again. She had forgotten all her own problems and was engrossed with those of her namesake who had dutifully lined up all the objects in the lounge and who was now standing by the open front door wondering if she should go back to the kitchen for the car keys she needed.

Her heart sank when she reached the end of the page on which Snowy, having finally got the keys had fled the house and run straight into Philip Winter's arms.

She turned the page over, hoping for more, but that, apparently, that was the end of the chapter.

Chapter Fourteen

Sarah-Jane's Romantic Interlude

S'n'J was still in the bathroom when the letter-box flap rattled again.

'Oh *no*!' she moaned.

But when she got out into the hall there was no buff A4 envelope on the mat awaiting her attention. And whoever it was outside was still there because the flap rattled a second time.

S'n'J put the security chain on before she opened the door, then when she saw who it was, wished she hadn't.

'Hiya,' James said.

He looked even better clean than he'd done dirty and S'n'J felt the sun break through the clouds in her mind. Its rays scattered her thoughts about the book in every direction. They skittered away like beads of moisture dropped on a hot pan.

'Hello,' she said, through lips that had suddenly formed themselves into a big, playful grin. 'Come in,' she invited, unhooking the chain and stepping back.

Her movements had loosened the towel she'd wrapped around herself and as she stood back it started to slip. She struggled to stay inside it, then realized that if she turned round James was going to be treated to a view of her bare bottom.

She thought of what Janet had said then and found that a substantial part of her *wanted* to flash her behind at him. *It's one of your best assets, if you'll pardon the pun*, she told herself, while she wrestled with the concept.

Don't! her Girl Guide voice warned.

But Janet's words about getting him in the bath inside three seconds rang in her mind, and visions of Snowy and Philip Winter fucking like animals swarmed in her head and S'n'J suddenly felt drunk with desire and very daring indeed. Her heart whacked hard against her ribs, her blood pressure rose and she began to tremble faintly, right down to what seemed to be the core of her being. She fought it for two seconds while she stared into James' brown eyes and registered his slightly puzzled smile, then she let herself go.

'Follow me,' she said, turning, and led him into the lounge.

Where she discovered that her desire equalled that of her namesake.

Half-way across the lounge, she turned back to him, let the towel fall and took him in her arms.

James was taller than Martin, his body harder, his lips more gentle, his tongue more fervent. His hands were stronger but possessed a skill that Martin's would never have.

S'n'J took his jacket off him, tore his shirt off and found her lips against pectorals that were not empty sacks of skin, but firmly muscled. His body smelled good. S'n'J took one of his nipples between her teeth and James moaned, his hands tightening for a moment against her buttocks.

She broke away from him, shuddering, and stared into his face. 'Hello James,' she said, 'I'm glad you came.' And holding his gaze, she unbuttoned his jeans, found the zipper and lowered it. He was bigger than Martin, she knew that already, but she wanted to see. She *had* to see. She took the waistband of his jeans and dragged them down his hips, taking his shorts with them.

The sight that greeted her was perfect and it pulsed with his heartbeat.

S'n'J ran her fingertips down its length and watched the resultant muscular spasm.

'I want you,' she heard herself say and encircled his erection with her hand. It seemed almost as big as her wrist and as hard as the granite her favourite haunted house was built upon. S'n'J felt as if she was coming apart inside. As if she might soon die of desire. When she took him into her mouth James made a sound like a little boy who is close to tears and its *wanting* tone drove S'n'J over the edge. Every nerve ending she had fizzled like fireworks.

'Lie down,' she said breathlessly. 'On your back.'

James did as he was told and S'n'J straddled him, and lowered herself on to him.

During the next ten minutes she let herself turn into the same kind of insatiable animal that Snowy Dresden was supposed to be.

Only when she was worn out did she climb off James (who was apparently able to buck like the proverbial bronco, indefinitely and without coming) and worked on his cock with her hands and her mouth, hard and fast. She kept on pumping while he came and was surprised by the force of his orgasm, which shot semen with enough force to fly up the length of his body and hit him in the face.

I think I'm in love, she told herself and pressed her lips to his in a sticky kiss that she hoped would go on for ever.

Chapter Fifteen

Ellen and Snowball the Hamster

Now they were clean and dressed again (and Janet was right about the bath being big enough for two) and sitting beside each other on the sofa, a respectable distance between them. James was reading *Black Rock*.

S'n'J watched him and wondered why she didn't feel as if they were lovers. Since they had put their clothes back on they seemed to have turned into two people who barely knew one another.

Which isn't exactly surprising, considering that's exactly what you are, she informed herself. *Having sex just makes you two people who had sex.*

But they would become proper lovers, if nothing happened to prevent it, S'n'J knew that. It was what she wanted. James was sweet and he'd given her more pleasure in half an hour than Martin had managed in two years. He might be a bit younger than her, and 'only' a garage mechanic, but neither of these things entered the equation as far as she was concerned. James was like Snowy Dresden: she wanted to know more about both of them.

And anyway, she asked herself, *what do you mean 'if nothing happens to prevent it'? What are you expecting?*

But that question didn't really need answering. S'n'J might have been a little confused since arriving in Tintagel that morning, but she wasn't completely stupid. James was sitting beside her reading the story, which meant that it existed, not only in her imagination, but in real life too. And the trouble, if any, was going to be caused by *Black Rock* and its author.

Unless all this was an hallucination too, and she doubted

that. If it was, it was a pretty good one. She'd give it full marks for content and entertainment value.

The others were pretty good ones too though, weren't they? her Girl Guide asked. But if she started to consider what *that* meant, she really would go crazy. Her whole life could turn out to have been nothing more than an extended dream.

All she needed to be sure of was that James was real, and that *Black Rock*, the manuscript, was also real. And she *was* sure. Once James had offered an opinion on what was contained within the pages, she would know whether or not what she had read was real.

James' lips moved when he read, but only – she learned from cribbing over his shoulder – when he got to passages of speech. S'n'J had seen people test the words of books with their mouths before, but they usually read the whole thing that way. Seeing someone do it only when they read speech was quite amusing and she warmed to James a little more.

She reached out and put her hand on James' leg and he recoiled, yelping.

'*Christ!*' he said, clapping his hand to his heart and doing that dippy kind of half-giggle people always seem to do when you make them jump. 'I'd just got to the bit where she's in his room looking at his writing on the computer. I thought that was him for a second! I thought he'd got me!'

'Sorry,' S'n'J said. She leaned over and kissed him long and deep.

'What was that for?' he asked when she finally broke away.

S'n'J could still feel her lips smouldering. She was going to have him again before she let him go home, whatever her Girl Guide might advise to the contrary. She didn't bother explaining her relief that he'd read the same words as she had. That could come later. After he'd finished the chapters and they'd compared notes on them.

'Just to say that I like you very much,' she said.

'Thanks,' he said, 'And so do I.' He grinned and added, 'But don't worry, I like you too.'

S'n'J feigned a slap towards him. 'Just read the book,' she commanded. 'I want your opinion.'

*

'So what d'you think?' she asked, peeling her sticky body away from his for the second time that evening. They were in the bedroom now; the room where she'd so often lain beneath Martin wishing he'd do some of the things to her that she'd asked him to do.

'Twenty out of ten,' James said. 'And I hope you aren't expecting any more. I'm exhausted.'

'Just when I was getting warmed up, too,' she complained. 'But I didn't mean that, I *always* rate twenty out of ten. I meant about the book.'

James smiled and pushed her hair back from her face for her. 'What do you want me to say? Tell me and I'll say it.'

'Just tell me what you thought.'

'Fishing for *more* compliments?'

'What d'you mean?'

'I'm proud of you, Drezy. You've got talent.'

'I didn't write it, James.'

'No need to be shy. I slept with a writer. I'll tell all my friends. They won't believe me, but I'll tell 'em anyway.'

'I didn't write it. Honestly. Why do you think I did?'

James frowned. 'Because it's you in the book. You've even got the same names, practically. Snowy and S'n'J are similar and the surname is identical. And her character seems like yours too.'

'How?'

James took a deep breath and blew out his cheeks. 'Well, she's confident in a way. She's full of beans. Playful I suppose you'd say. Funny. She thinks funny things. Sexy. Clever. Just the kind of girl you'd like to meet, I s'pose. Any good?'

S'n'J got her watch from the night stand and looked at it. It was half past ten. 'Apart from my odd visit to the garage, you've known me for about two and half hours now. Is that long enough to know all those things, or is that just the way you'd like me to be?'

He thought about it. 'Half and half, I'd say. I can see the potential in you for being that way. And yes, it's how I'd like you to be. The psychology all seems tickety-boo.'

S'n'J frowned. 'Psychology?'

James nodded.

'What do you know about psychology?'

'I'm a fitter, right? Too stupid to know about psychology.' He smiled when he said it but she knew the tone of her question had been wrong. James was stung.

'Sorry, I didn't mean . . .'

James shook his head. 'Doesn't matter,' he said. 'I just get peeved when people think mechanics and fitters are all thick. I told you some of us were edu-me-cated, didn't I?'

'I didn't mean I thought you were stupid,' she said, taking his hand. 'Really.'

'Well, you're talking to James Green, practising tyre and exhaust fitter and graduate of psychology. University of East Anglia. I just don't advertise it. For the same reasons, really. They won't let you fit tyres if they think you're too clever. Having said that, most of the guys I've worked with know a lot more about practical psychology than I learned in three years. But anyway, the psychology seems about right. She's just like you. Therefore I assumed you wrote the book.'

'I didn't,' S'n'J said.

'It must have been someone who knows you pretty well then,' he said. 'What about that guy you used to live with?'

'Yeah. But he wasn't a writer, he was an editor. Still is. I did suspect him at first, but not now.'

'So who did?'

'That's the problem,' she said. 'I don't know.'

'It isn't coincidence, Drezy,' James said. 'This character hasn't been spontaneously developed. It's based on you, fair and square.'

'You don't know me very well. Yet.'

James thought about it. 'But I might be able to kind of sum up the essence of you. There'd be a lot of things which didn't mesh properly. You'd be able to look at the writing and say, "That isn't me, I'd never do that". But I'll bet they wouldn't outnumber the things that matched. How much of this matches you, Drezy?'

S'n'J found a bitter smile and showed it to him. 'You're not going to like this,' she said. 'Remember that crazy woman who came into your garage this afternoon and picked you up? Well, after I tell you this, you'll think I really am a crazy woman.'

'I already think you're a crazy woman,' James said, smiling. 'Go ahead and tell me. It won't make any difference.'

'*Everything* in the book matches me.'

Still smiling, James shook his head. If it had been Martin lying there next to her, at this point his face would have taken on that condescending look of his. He might have been smiling but the message would have been coming over loud and clear: *What do you expect? She's only a woman after all.* But there was none of this in James. All there seemed to be on his face was a gentle puzzlement.

He said, 'Perhaps you just *think* everything matches you. You've identified strongly with the Snowy character and maybe you're only recalling the parts where her character matches yours perfectly.

'I wish,' S'n'J said. 'Guess where I went today.'

James shook his head. 'I give up.'

'I went to Black Rock. Do you know where that is?'

James' face had become serious now and S'n'J knew that the thought had just occurred to him that she might be crazy after all. And that he might have landed himself with something a little more complicated than he had imagined. He covered it well.

'Tintagel, according to the address at the bottom of the pages. I thought it was a kind of joke. It doesn't really exist, does it?'

S'n'J nodded. 'Listen James, tell me how you envisage it. Think about it and tell me the image you get from the book.'

James did as he was told. His description fitted perfectly with the facts and she told him so.

'That's weird,' he said. 'I've been to the Castle there before, but I don't recall seeing an outcrop of rock with a big house on it.'

'Would you, though?'

'Would I what?'

'Remember a house across the bay. You wouldn't. Not if you'd gone to see the Castle ruins. It'd just be another house.

And guess what else? The dog is there too. Diamond Ambrose Anstey.'

'So the location is real. It doesn't have any significance. Writers often base their books on real places.'

'This *is* going to sound crazy, James, but bear with me,' she said. 'Remember what it said in the first chapter about how a different story might have been told if Snowy had turned her car round and looked at the house in the rear-view mirror. About how she would have seen it as it was rather than seeing *what might be*? Well, I did that. I turned the car round.'

'And?'

'I saw a blinding light coming from the room where Philip Winter is supposed to do his writing. Not just a bright light, but like the sun was inside.'

'Could it have been a reflection?'

S'n'J shook her head. 'It was cloudy. But listen to this: when I saw that, I'd only read the first chapter. *I didn't know it was the room where Philip's magic computer lives!* And I kind of looked away and when I looked back there was a man on the ground by the front door. He looked as if he'd fallen off the roof. I went to him and guess who it was? Mr Winter himself. It was *him*. Just as he's described in the book. He was unconscious and bleeding and my mobile phone wouldn't work, so I went round the back of the house to look for a way in so I could phone for help – but there was no back door. And hear this, James, I decided that I'd bust a window, and climb in. *But you can't break the windows.* I tried! And when I went back round the side of the house I tripped and slid down the hill towards the sea and I couldn't stop myself and I thought . . . oh God, I thought I was going to die . . .'

S'n'J was aware that tears were streaming down her face and that her voice bore a distinct note of hysteria, but she couldn't make herself stop. She didn't *want* to stop. Her mind was purging itself of the bad events the way an upset stomach will try to purge itself of bad food: spewing it back out again.

'And the mobile was sticking out of my pocket and it caught in a bush and I dragged myself back up to the top, but I lost one of my shoes and that's where I got all the cuts and bruises from and why I was barefoot this afternoon. And when I got back to the front of the house he . . . he . . .'

'He'd gone?' James asked.

'*He was still there!*' she said. 'And I went out of the dead spot to call an ambulance, then went back. And then I saw the sea come up in a huge stationary wave . . . and the clouds were sucked down from the sky . . . and as it happened, Mr Winter folded himself up as if he was a sheet of paper. Again and again until he disappeared. I ran away. I got in the car to drive up to Tintagel and the dog appeared. It just appeared out of nowhere and it was too late for me to stop and I hit it and that's where the pink stuff came from on the front of the car. Oh, James I think I've really gone mad!'

James pulled her to him and held her while she sobbed. And S'n'J sobbed for a long time.

When she had calmed a little, he asked, 'OK now?' and his tone was so much gentler, so much more understanding than anything she'd ever heard in Martin's voice, that it set her off again.

'I'm fine,' she eventually said and looked up at his face.

He wiped away the tears from her cheek and smiled. 'Ready to talk some more?'

She nodded.

'None of what happened to you, happened in the book,' he said. 'Right?'

She nodded. 'But there are direct parallels. Snowy tried to break the windows, *I* tried to break the windows.'

'What else?'

'I tried to ring my neighbour earlier – before the most recent chapter came through the door – and found I was speaking to an old woman who claimed her number was Maida Vale Two Seven Five. Then I read about Snowy using Black Rock's phone and getting the same number. It's as if someone is making this stuff happen to me as kind of bad joke.'

'And you don't think it's Martin, your ex, doing this?'

S'n'J shook her head. And so he could make up his own mind as to whether Martin was responsible or not, she told him all about their break-up, then how she'd discovered the first *Black Rock* chapter under her bed, and all her subsequent contact – and non-contact – with Martin.

'OK,' James said, when she'd finished, 'We can forget the simple answer and look for another. First, we need to establish who the guilty party is. Who do you know who doesn't like you?'

'Martin,' she replied instantly.

'He could just be holding a candle for you.'

'Martin, isn't holding a candle for me, he's holding a blow-torch. And I think he'd like to use it on me.'

'Who else?' he asked.

S'n'J shrugged. Barring a couple of bookshop managers she called on, she couldn't think of anyone else. She told him the names of the managers. Both were in Bristol and neither had any reason for a vendetta.

'Which only leaves Martin,' James said. 'Any other crossed lovers?'

S'n'J was embarrassed to say. She'd had only five relationships and with the exception of Martin, the longest had been six months. The shortest had been two days.

'Not for years. Most of them probably wouldn't even remember me if you showed them a photo.'

'I'm sure they would,' James said. 'I've remembered you since the first time you came into the garage and I didn't think I'd ever have a chance with you.'

'You're being kind.'

'I'm telling the truth. You aren't the sort of woman who leaves no impression. You're very . . . striking.'

'Ugly, you mean,' she said.

James shook his head and smiled. 'I was going to use a fitter's expression. The guys at Cars Inc. think you're dead horny. I was going to say horny too, but I thought you might be offended. Sexy, gorgeous, shaggable, tasty, mouth-watering, stiff-city. How's that?'

'I like horny,' S'n'J said.

'OK. So we're down to someone you *don't* really know . . .'

'It could be you.'

'But it isn't,' he replied. 'Now, if it's someone you don't know, it has to be someone nearby. Someone who knows a bit about you. Who else lives in these flats?'

'Downstairs there are twin sisters aged eighty, Mr Campbell who's in a wheelchair and an eighteen-year-old girl called Candy or Sandy or something. She lives on her own. She's very religious and posh. Twinset and pearls type. The first three couldn't have got up the stairs to deliver the envelope and I can't believe Candy or Sandy has even heard of ghost stories, let alone written any to me to terrorize me.'

'Who's on *this* floor then?'

'Mister and Mrs Stravinsky, who are pensioners. They're rather sweet. And the end flat was bought by a couple called Verglas. Jack and Sophie, I think. They're sort of wealthy and sun-tanned and well-spoken. He's in television apparently. But it can't be them because they went to Greece on a research trip in June and they haven't come back yet.'

'So we're left with Mr Mystery,' James said. 'And his messenger, of course.'

'Which leaves us with . . .'

S'n'J had reached this conclusion well in advance of James' spoken deduction. If she had wanted to she could have told him the identity of the author of *Black Rock* all along. But she'd wanted to hear him go down the same mental path as she had trodden earlier on today. And now here he was – he had walked that path and caught her up. Which meant that the path didn't exist only in her own mind and that it wasn't that of a woman who had been struck mad. They had both reached the same point by a logical process. The author of the book was written in the footer of each page for all the world to see.

'Peter Perfect, Black Rock, Tintagel,' she said.

James frowned at her.

'Always supposing there *is* a house called Black Rock in Tintagel. And that there *is* a man sitting inside it writing a book called *Black Rock*, then why is that man sending his chapters to you?'

'Maybe it's because he's a good researcher. He found out who the right guy was to send his story to, and the right guy turned out to be Martin. And he thinks that Martin still lives here.'

'But Snowy Dresden is based on you. Even if what you say is right, it doesn't explain why you and Snowy are so closely related.'

S'n'J offered hopefully, 'Blind chance? Synchronicity? Call it what you like.'

James shrugged. 'But the odds against it happening are about fourteen trillion to one. And even if those odds came up, it still doesn't explain why you've been experiencing things that run parallel to the book.'

'Hold on a minute. I have to make a phone call,' S'n'J said, getting up.

'What's wrong?'

'Back in a moment.'

S'n'J went to the phone and picked up the little pop-up address book from beside it. She opened it to E, found Ellen's last phone number and dialled, hoping that she didn't get through to Maida Vale again. The line clicked and popped and, when the ringing tone began, S'n'J was pleased it was the same one she knew and loved, and not something from the past.

'Hello?' a male voice said.

'Hi, this is Sarah-Jane Dresden. Can I speak to Ellen?' she asked, remembering Snowy's dream-fantasies about torturing poor Ellen.

'You'd know that better than me, wouldn't you?' the man said.

'I'm sorry?'

This, a distant voice said in the back of her mind, *with one notable exception, is not turning out to be quite the day you'd hoped for when you got out of bed this morning. Is it?*

'You heard,' he said.

'You've lost me somewhere,' S'n'J said.

'She's not coming back, right?' the man – presumably Ellen's boyfriend or husband – said. 'She didn't even have the bottle to phone me and tell me herself. So she got you to do it for her. Christ, you women make me sick! You stick together like you used superglue. Put her on the line, will you?'

S'n'J held the telephone out before her, staring at it in disbelief. She could hear the man's tinny voice still prattling away, which meant this was really happening. She put the phone back to her ear and said, 'She isn't here.'

'Do you think I came up the Tyne on a banana boat?' the man asked. 'Of course she's there. She's been there a fortnight. Don't shit me.'

Shitting you and flushing you away would be the best thing I could think of to do to you, actually, she thought and said, 'We're misunderstanding one another, I think. Are you telling me that Ellen's left home?'

'Damn right she has,' the man replied. 'She's with you. I've heard nothing but "Essenjay this" and "Essenjay that" for months. Oh she wanted to go back and visit you. Oh, she missed you. Oh, she needed to see you. What good friends you used to be and what good times you'd had together. Damned woman's turned into a lesbian, that's what I think. You're a pair of queer girls aren't you? That's what it's all about. Went off sex, then started talking about you and getting all starry eyed, that's what happened. Damned dikes!'

S'n'J was surprised by the outburst, but not terribly. She could hear Martin in this character's voice – not Martin as he spoke, but the inner Martin, which he kept carefully covered and thought no one knew about. The bigger surprise was that Ellen had landed herself a bastard who could undoubtedly rank alongside Martin. Perhaps they had more in common than they'd thought. Perhaps that was why this man wasn't the first to accuse them of being 'queer girls'.

'Listen to me,' S'n'J remonstrated. 'If you're saying that she left to visit me a fortnight ago then I think you ought to phone the police because she hasn't turned up. Nor was I expecting her. Do you understand that?'

'She's not there?' the man sounded surprised. 'Really?'

'Really,' S'n'J said and considered adding that she wasn't a lesbian either, then didn't see why she should bother. Men like this were enough to turn you gay.

'But you must have seen her. She was dead set on visiting you.'

'Well she didn't arrange it with me. What did she say before she left?'

The man sounded crestfallen now. 'Actually she didn't arrange anything. We had a spat and she walked out. Suitcase job. I asked her where she was going and she wouldn't say. I asked if she was going to visit the famous Essenjay and she said she might do. That's all I know. I just thought she'd be there.'

'Was there another guy?'

'You kidding?'

'No.'

'It's *you* she's obsessed with,' he said sourly.

'Did you check with her parents? They live in Exeter. It's nearby. She might have gone there first.'

'She hasn't been there. Not yet. I've phoned every day. Look, I'm sorry about what I said. Will you please get her to phone me if she turns up?'

'Of course,' S'n'J said as a mental picture of Ellen bloomed in her mind. 'And I think you should report her to the police as a missing person.'

In the image Ellen was manacled to the wall of Black Rock's bare cellar, her naked body stained with blood, her face swollen beyond the point of recognition. *Winter got her*, a part of her mind informed her. *She's there now.*

'She'll be back,' S'n'J said, but for some reason she didn't believe this. She said goodbye and replaced the receiver.

James was still lying on the bed when she got back, looking not unlike a slender version of one of those Chippendales she lied about on her answering machine each time it took a call.

He rolled over to face her as she approached. 'What happened?' he asked. 'Who did you phone?'

'You know Ellen in the book?'

'She's *real*?' He looked shocked.

S'n'J nodded. 'Why are you surprised? She's real but in spite of what the book says – and what her boyfriend seems to think – we never had an affair. We were just good friends.'

'As they say in the tabloids,' James added, grinning.

'It's true,' S'n'J said, crossing her heart and slashing her throat. She was beginning to get a little tired of explaining this and a little worried too. Because each time she did, she felt an odd tugging sensation in her mind. It was as if someone, somewhere (*and don't you just wonder who that someone is?*) was grabbing hold of a small section of her brain between finger and thumb, tweaking it as if it was elastic, then letting it snap back again. This peculiar sensation had happened three times so far: once when she'd read the first chapter of *Black Rock*, again when Ellen's boyfriend had maligned her and just now. *That ought to have been enough*, she decided, *the cock hasn't even crowed yet and you've already denied it three times*. But it seemed that each time she denied it, instead of becoming more certain it hadn't happened, she became *less* so. It was as if Peter Perfect so badly wanted it to have happened, he was forcing it to have happened.

'So why did you suddenly have to ring her?' James wanted to know.

'This is getting crazier by the minute,' S'n'J said. 'I rang her because I remembered Snowball.'

'Snowy?'

She shook her head. 'Like I said, it's getting crazier by the minute. I used to *call* her Snowy, but her name was Snowball, not Snowdrop. Peter Perfect has only gone and used the name of my hamster for the heroine of his book.'

James pulled a face. 'You aren't making this easy for me to understand. *Who* was called Snowball?'

'I used to have a hamster. I named her Snowball. I can remember her quite well. I loved her. She got some weird hamster infection and took sick and died and I was stricken. I was at college at the time. So Ellen would have remembered her too.'

S'n'J sat down on the bed and took James' hands. They were calloused but warm and they gave her a feeling of security. Physical security, at least.

James shook his head and squeezed her hands. 'You phoned Ellen just now to talk to her about Snowball the hamster?'

S'n'J nodded.

'But you said earlier that you hadn't spoken to her for years.'

'But I still had her number,' S'n'J said, ignoring the implied question which was: *Surely you didn't phone her after all this time just to talk about a rodent?*

'And what did she have to say?'

'She didn't say anything. She's gone. Like Snowball.'

'You spoke to her boyfriend?'

'S'n'J nodded and took a deep breath. 'He accused me of being a dike and stealing Ellen. More or less said she'd left him for me. A fortnight ago. She's vanished, James! On her way to see *me*. What do you suppose that means? It means I'm jinxed, doesn't it? He's put a spell on me, that Peter Perfect.'

'Don't be silly,' James said firmly.

S'n'J shrugged. She knew what had happened to Ellen, just as she knew what had happened to Snowball. If she got another chapter of *Black Rock* tomorrow, she would be able to read all about it. Both of them had been written out of her life.

'It's all fixed up,' she said. 'It's a multi-layered plot conceived and executed by Mr P. I first remembered the hamster, you see, when I was going towards Mr Winter's unconscious body. But the memory seemed like something I'd acquired. It suddenly felt as if it was someone else's property. That's why I rang Ellen. For a second opinion. She would have known if Snowball was mine or not. But he's edited Ellen out of my life. Or rewritten our relationship. I know he has because the more I think about it, the more certain I am that what he wrote is the truth: that I *did* have a lesbian relationship with Ellen. And you know what this is all leading up to, don't you? It doesn't take a genius to work it out.'

'I know what I think you're going to say,' James said. 'But it's utterly impossible.'

'It *isn't* impossible, and I should know because it's happening to me,' S'n'J said. 'He's changing me into Snowdrop Dresden. Into what he wants me to be. That's why when I remember Snowball it feels like a borrowed memory. It's because I'm recalling it with Snowy's mind and not my own. How about that for the mind-fuck trick to end them all?'

'Why would anyone ever *want* to?'

'I get it,' she accused. 'You're thinking that I'm so much like her already that I wouldn't take much changing.'

'Not at all. I was just saying that you're pretty good as you are. Why muck about with that?'

'Because we'd all like to be able to change each other,' S'n'J said. 'And that's the truth. Unfortunately we lack the power. Consider it; you'd make your boss a little more kindly, if you could. You'd make your partner sexier, funnier, more compassionate. You'd build your ideal people and populate your universe with them.'

'I wouldn't change you,' James said.

'Yes you *would*! You'd stop me having these silly thoughts for starters.'

James shook his head. 'I like you just as you are. Including the oddball part of you. Including the way you get mad at me when I disagree. It's all perfect.'

'It might be now, but what if we stayed together for ten years and you got sick of it? "Christ", Drezy, you'd think, "I wish you wouldn't fly off the handle like that every time I argue. I wish I could stop it happening." Or you'd find there was something about me, my nervous little giggle perhaps, that used to be engaging but just lately had begun to grate on your nerves. You'd make it stop. If you found a way, you'd use it.'

'You don't have a nervous giggle.'

'I might develop one soon, if things carry on like this,' she said ruefully.

'Yeah, well, they won't. You'll feel better tomorrow. I guarantee it. You don't have to worry about the giggle. When you look at it in the cold light of day you'll find there's a rational explanation for everything. Like, Ellen's just run off with another man and that the effect of the exhaust fumes temporarily corrupted your memory of Snowball the hamster. Meanwhile, you mustn't give the story or its author a power they don't possess.'

'And coming home and finding an envelope waiting for me on the telephone table?'

'Someone broke in.'

'Without causing any damage or leaving any trace?'

'It can be done. You've got a cheap and cheerful lock on the door. Only needs someone to slide a strip of plastic between the door and the frame and push back the lock catch. Five seconds and they'd be inside. So I advise you to double lock it in future and keep the bolt on while you're indoors.'

'In case he comes back?'

'Let's face it, Drezy, we don't know who he is or what his purpose is. Not really. He may just be one of Martin's authors wanting Martin to pay careful attention to the book he's writing. But in case it's something else, we ought to take precautions.'

'Something else?'

James bit his bottom lip and thought before he spoke. 'The guy could be a lunatic,' he said, then hastily added, 'But if so, I'd have expected him to have made his move long before now.'

'I know what he is,' S'n'J said.

'Look,' James counselled. 'There's one good way of establishing exactly how much of this you're imagining and how much is real. We both get dressed, we get in my car and drive down to Tintagel. We could be there in half an hour or so. We could see if Black Rock really does exist and if it looks how we think it looks. And then we could hammer on the door and see who comes out to play. And if it turns out to be a man fitting the description of the book's Mr Winter, we ask questions.'

'And what if he's the psycho you think he might be?'

'I can look after myself,' James said, and S'n'J got the feeling that this in itself was yet another intrusion into her life by the mystery author. It was exactly the standard banality you would expect from a hero in a shoddy horror story at a time like this.

I can look after myself.

Cut to shabby car containing frightened girl and dumb

hero driving on to Black Rock's forecourt, she thought. *It is night-time. They park and go to the door. The girl cowers behind the boy as he knocks on the door – which seems to be armour-plated. Behind them, in the bushes that form the boundary of the property, there is rustling. Somewhere off in the distance an owl hoots and the girl almost screams. She turns and does scream. Mr Winter is there, between them and the car, and he is brandishing the biggest knife the girl has ever seen. The clouds part and moonbeams catch the knife's cutting edge. Cue a one-sided fight in which the dumb guy we thought was the hero is killed and the girl, injured and bleeding, manages to scramble away.*

She shook her head. 'No one can look after themselves,' she said. 'Not these days. Not against crazies with guns and knives. In a stand-up fist-fight you might come off better. But not in the dark against a psycho on his home ground. It's a ridiculous suggestion.'

'Because you're expecting the worst, that's all. And the worst won't happen. Mr Winter, or Peter Perfect or whoever he is, won't turn out to be a raving killer. He'll be a middle-aged man who spends half his life sitting in front of a computer tapping out words and the other half being an office manager or a banker or something. He hasn't even been published.'

'Or so it says in the story,' S'n'J added. 'You're doing it too – confusing what you've read with real life. And you haven't even been breathing poison gas. The guy might have been published. He might be a very successful writer.'

'You're in the trade, have you heard of him?'

S'n'J shook her head. 'But that doesn't mean anything. All I can say is that he doesn't write for Ace.'

'Do you recognize his style?'

She shook her head.

'Which means this guy's a wannabe. If he was any good, you'd have heard of him.'

'I'd say he's a *gonnabe*,' she corrected. '*Black Rock* is one of the best manuscripts I've read in a long time. Martin wants to publish it.'

'But it doesn't follow that he's a crazy, so let's pay him a visit.'

She shook her head again. 'This lady's not for returning,' she said.

'What's the worst thing that can happen?' he asked.

'We both get killed,' she told him. 'I'm not going back there. Not now and not ever and you're to put any thought of going there alone out of your head.'

'OK, OK,' he said.

'If you go there, you're not going to come back again,' she said. 'So don't. I know what you're thinking. You're thinking that it wouldn't do any harm to sail down there after you leave here. I know that and I know *why* you're thinking it. You're thinking it because that's what you'd do if you were a character in *Black Rock*. And since you aren't a book character, don't act like one. I don't want a dead hero.'

'I won't go there. I promise. I'm not a book character, I'm real. Now, I think you ought to get some sleep,' he suggested. 'I'll make you some tea first, then I'll tuck you in until you're snug and cosy. I'll sit with you until you drop off to sleep.'

'You can stay the night,' she said. 'If you want.'

'I don't want to cramp your style,' he said. 'Not yet anyway. And there's stuff I have to do at home and I have to get up for work in the morning.'

'But what about the door?' she asked, wriggling beneath the tangled sheets. 'You said it ought to be bolted. You can't bolt it if you go home.'

'Give me your key,' he said. 'And on my way out I'll double lock the door, so no one can get in, then I'll post it back through the letter box.'

'You can take the spare,' she said. 'It's on the hook in the kitchen. And you can keep it too.'

James got off the bed and began straightening out the sheets for her. 'No, I'll only lose it if I keep it.'

S'n'J was deep in a dreamless sleep when he came back into the room. She felt his gentle touch on her face and it seemed like it was happening to someone else about a million miles away from here. 'Hmmm?' she heard herself murmur. She felt safe and secure in her bed.

'Wakey wakey. Tea and toast,' he said.

'OK Philip,' she sighed.

And inside a second she was awake and bolt upright, her heart beating out a tattoo on her rib cage, and all her muscles tensed as if to fight.

'Whatever's wrong?' James said.

Then jumped back when she screamed.

Several seconds passed before S'n'J realized she had neither woken up in Philip Winter's work-room, nor just run out of Black Rock and into his arms. The confusion she normally felt during the transition from sleep to wakefulness had turned into something akin to a nightmare. She'd heard her voice use the name Philip and it had been compounded by James' use of Philip Winter's own words, 'Whatever's wrong?'

'I'm sorry,' she panted, when she finally knew where she was. 'You made me jump. I don't normally wake up screaming.'

'I'm glad to hear *that*.'

'I didn't know where I was for a few seconds. I thought I was . . .'

'I know where you thought you were,' he said, taking her hand and squeezing it gently. 'It's only to be expected and it doesn't matter. Come here and let me cuddle you.'

When she'd calmed, she let him tear up pieces of toast and feed them to her and hold her tea mug to her lips while she sipped. The last time anyone had done that for her, she'd been a poorly little girl and the person feeding her had been her mother. S'n'J began to feel very small and very secure. And for the second time that evening she told herself she was falling in love.

'Thank you,' she said.

'All part of the service, madam,' he replied. 'Now I'll sit with you until you drop off again. Then I'll go. I presume a bedtime story is not required?'

She made a face at him.

James hauled her up to him and held her tight.

It was all too good to be true.

'You're not in on this, are you?' she murmured into his chest. 'Tell me that.'

'There isn't anything to be in to, and if there was, and I was in it, I'd be out again after tonight. I wouldn't see anyone do anything nasty to you. They'd have to kill me first.'

'Don't say that,' she said. 'Just don't say that.'

And James didn't.

After a while, S'n'J's eyes grew heavy and she allowed them to close. A while after that she became dimly aware that he was gently putting her back down on the bed. She felt his gentle hands adjusting the covers, then she felt his tender lips caress her nose and heard him whisper goodbye in a voice so soft it was barely audible. And as she sailed into the darkness, she heard the front door creak open, creak closed, a rattle of the key going into the lock and turning and the tiny metallic sound as it was deposited through the letter box.

Goodbye, James, she thought.

Chapter Sixteen

Billy-Joe's Demise

While S'n'J and James were sitting in a bedroom in Bude discussing Black Rock, Janie Sanderson was sitting in a pub called the Tinderbox in Bracknell feeling rather like a piece of tinder herself – as if the merest spark would turn her into a human torch.

Janie knew she wouldn't just be able to waltz in, say, 'Hiya Billy-Joe, just putting a few things in an overnight bag because I'm going away for a while,' collect her stuff and walk out again, because if she said something like that she would find herself *unable* to walk out again.

So when the train arrived at Bracknell station, she had gone into the pub to wait for that magic time of the evening when Billy-Joe went into the lounge, turned on the television, collapsed into his armchair and fell into a drunken sleep. This would last from around eight to about ten, when he would wake up either gloomy and despondent or hyped-up and looking for trouble. As soon as his sleeping time arrived, she would sneak in, pick up a few things, get her car keys, and sneak out again.

Except that you won't have to sneak *at all*, she told herself, bitterly. *You could go in blowing a trumpet at the head of a marching band and Billy-Joe wouldn't stir.*

Janie didn't yet know where she intended to escape to. She'd thought of phoning her parents and hadn't done it. For one reason, they were in Corby, which was a hell of drive, and for another, she didn't want to have to tell them her marriage had failed in a big way.

She'd thought of going down to Bude to stay with Drezy, but it was another very long drive and although she thought she'd be welcome and had stayed there before, she suspected that Martin would be getting in his Ferrari and going down there tonight and she'd had quite enough of him for one day.

It's that magical time, she told herself, looking at her watch and trying to pretend that the thought of going home didn't fill her with dread.

Twenty minutes later she was still trying to pretend the very same thing as she sat on the bus drawing nearer to her home every second. *Resilience, that's what you have that good old Billy-Joe doesn't,* she assured herself. *Fortitude, toughness, tenacity, courage ... Christ I'm turning into a walking Roget's Thesaurus and that's what years of being an editor does to you.*

It wasn't until the bus drew near her stop that Janie realized her wordy litany had been a simple device to keep her mind free of thoughts of what might happen when she got home.

But she had *backbone*, *mettle* and *moral fibre* and a certain amount of alcohol in her bloodstream and she wanted something similar to what the Pope said he wanted when he visited Northern Ireland: *Nohw mooore bloowd-shad.* And she was *going* to have no more blood-shed, whether Billy-Joe liked it or not. And if blood had to be spilled to achieve this seemingly impossible state, it wouldn't be just her blood. This woman was going to fight back.

Outside her front door, Janie paused and took a deep breath which made her head spin. Her VW Golf stood on the drive and if Janie's car keys had been in her handbag she might have just got in it and gone, without even collecting any of the other things she wanted. But while she was at work, Billy-Joe had the keys to the car.

Janie only hoped that the keys weren't in his trouser pocket.

Her heart racing, she found her keys and slotted the Yale into the door, trying to keep it as quiet as possible. She pushed open the door and went inside. The television was on in the lounge.

Now all you have to do is open the lounge door and see what tonight's prize is. Will it be the star prize, a sleeping

195

Billy-Joe, or will it be the booby prize, a Billy-Joe who's awake?

But as her hand hovered over the door handle, Janie had a better idea. Instead of opening the door and finding out the worst, she would first visit the kitchen. If the news was going to be bad when she went into the lounge, she intended to be prepared for it. Somewhere in the kitchen was that most clichéd of wifey weapons, the deadly rolling-pin. As endorsed by Sarah-Jane Dresden.

The wooden rolling-pin felt very light in her hand and a lot less like a weapon than she'd anticipated. *It feels just like a rolling-pin, actually*, she told herself, holding it up by the handle, waving it from side to side. You could probably hit someone quite hard with one of these and it wouldn't do as much damage as, say, a hatchet handle. And the looseness of the roller would probably absorb some of the impact.

But not too much, I hope, she thought, realizing for the first time that she really did intend to use it if necessary.

You won't have to anyway, she assured herself. *He's dead to the world in there, or he would have already been out here wanting to know where you'd been until this time of night. All you have to do is pack your bags and do as the shepherds say: get the flock out of here.*

It was going to be easy.

Except that when she reached for the key-hook where her VW keys dangled on a black leather VW fob, her fingers came away bearing nothing but the imprint of an empty hook.

'Where are they then?' she muttered darkly, knowing exactly where they would be.

In his bloody trouser pocket, of course!

Things had been going so well until now that she'd expected to make her escape without disturbing Billy-Joe. The prospect of having to use the rolling-pin on him had seemed delightful while there was almost no chance of it turning into reality. It didn't sound like quite so much fun now that it had.

You could bop him with it while he's still asleep, she thought grimly, then decided that it might only wake him up.

She had no idea how hard you had to strike someone in order to render them unconscious.

Pretty hard, she imagined, but she was equally uncertain about what might constitute the difference in force between a knockout blow and a killing blow. And she didn't particularly want to murder him.

Worry about it when it happens, she thought. *Just get on and pack your bags. Pack your bags, take 'em outside and if Billy-Joe wakes up when you go for the keys, just tell him you wanted to go to the chip-shop because you couldn't be bothered to cook tonight. He'll believe that and give you the keys, you go outside, unlock the car, put the bags in and drive off. Bob's your uncle and Fanny's your aunt. No problem, as they say in Europe.*

It only took ten minutes to gather together enough clothes to survive a nuclear winter, her lap-top computer, her bubble-jet printer, her make-up, her wash kit and the manuscripts she'd been working on at home. Ten minutes after that, it was all packed into two suitcases and two bags and five minutes later it was all outside on the drive beside her car.

And Billy-Joe hadn't stirred.

Janie punched the air in triumph as she came back inside the house and quietly closed the front door behind her. All she had to do now was to take the car keys from her husband's trouser pocket.

He'll wake up, she told herself. *You know he will.*

But things had been going so well that to admit the possibility of this happening seemed a little paranoid.

There was one more thing to do before she went in the lounge to get the keys. She had to write him a note. He didn't deserve it, but she was going to write it so that when he woke up he'd know she wanted him out of the house. Otherwise Billy-Joe would just stay there and vegetate, not knowing where she'd gone and not caring.

Dear Billy, she wrote on her notepad and then got writer's block. Cursing, she gave up trying to think in a literary fashion and quickly jotted down the words of a wronged wife, ending with, *I intend to make a complaint to the police and to have my injuries photographed. It's my mortgage, and*

*I want you out of the house by the end of the weekend.
You're no longer welcome here. You no longer have a wife
or a place to live. So get out!*

This made her feel a great deal better about herself. As if
she was reasserting her own personality after years of pretending to be the woman her husband expected her to be.
She signed the note: *Your loving ex-wifey, Janie. XX.* And
grinned fiercely to herself as she folded it. She would leave
the note on the arm of the chair in which Billy-Joe was fast
asleep.

*Now all we have to do, my fine Janie, is get the car keys
and get outta here!* she told herself as she went back up the
hall. All her troubles were going to be solved in one fell
swoop.

Clutching the rolling-pin to her she opened the lounge
door. And froze in her tracks. Anyone watching would have
seen that she was swaying slightly, like a woman who has
suddenly found herself standing on a very narrow ledge a
great distance above the ground.

And someone *was* watching.

Because Billy wasn't in his chair, sleeping peacefully.

He was sat smack in the middle of the sofa, facing the
door.

'Hiya babe,' he said, grinning. 'You looking for these?'

The cold smack of shock that stung Janie had entered her
body through her pores and was now slipping silently
through her nervous system, shutting it down. She was unable
to move.

She watched Billy-Joe's left hand as it moved from side to
side, swinging her car keys by the leather fob. He was wearing
a tee-shirt and for the first time in months, Janie became
aware of the actual size and definition of the muscles in his
forearms and biceps. Half-hypnotized, she watched those
muscles slide and bulge.

'Hey babe, what's that you're carrying?' he asked brightly.
There was no trace in his voice of the slur she knew and
loathed so well. Billy-Joe had chosen today – of all days – to
stay sober.

'What?' she heard herself say in a tiny, shocked voice.

Inwardly she was thinking: *Turn around and run for it. You're going to prove nothing by staying any longer. You can get someone else to pick up your stuff, so just get out of here. You've failed.*

But there was another part of her – the tenacious part – which had other ideas.

There are the keys, it told her. *All you have to do is whip them out of his hand and run.*

'In your hand,' Billy-Joe said. 'What's that you've got in your hand? Not the rolling-pin, I know what that is. It's the little white piece of paper in your right hand that I'm interested in. What is it, babe? Not a goodbye note, surely? You ain't intending to leave your old pot and pan, are you? Let me see it, lover.'

'Don't!' Janie heard herself warn.

'Don't what?' Billy-Joe asked, still swinging the keys. 'I asked my wife a civil question, to which I would expect a civil reply. I don't recall saying I was going to *do* anything. Show me your piece of paper, babe.'

Janie shook her head. She could almost feel the ice cracking as her muscles and tendons moved.

'Don't make me come and get it, babe,' Billy-Joe said. 'That'll only make things worse. Do you understand what I'm saying?' He frowned at her for a few seconds, in a parody of thinking. Then he added, 'I'm not sure you're currently able to speak, for some unknown reason, so just nod or shake your head in reply. That suit you?'

Janie nodded. She didn't want to, but she did it anyway.

'Is that little white piece of paper in your right hand a goodbye note?'

Janie shook her head.

'OK, babe, if it ain't a goodbye note, then why have you just spent the better part of half an hour packing your stuff and carting it outside? You know what I think? I think you were going to run out on me tonight. I've been expecting it since last night when you laughed at me. You *did* laugh at your old man last night, didn't you? Yeah, you did! No point in shaking your head like that, 'cause I have total recall. I wanted to make love and you gave me that old look of disdain and laughed at me. "Billy," you said, "You can't fuck me 'cause you can't make your Peter perk up." Ain't that what you said?'

Janie could neither speak nor move. Billy-Joe laid down the keys on the arm of the sofa now, as if challenging her to try to take them and her eyes followed his empty left hand as it moved back to his lap. You could tell how close he was to violence by keeping a careful watch on his hands. When they clenched into fists things would take a distinct turn for the worse. The hand that now fell into his lap was open and relaxed. Then, for the first time, she looked at his right hand. His business hand. The one which had skinned knuckles from hitting her. When she spotted that hand, she began to feel as if she might faint.

Because Billy-Joe was holding a pair of pliers.

Billy grinned at her. 'And you were right, my little babe. Old Billy's Peter won't perk. I've pulled him, twisted him, stroked him and prodded him and if I'd been able to bend over far enough I would have given him a nice wet kiss, but poor old Peter ain't interested. I gave due consideration to your argument about it being the booze that causes it, but it don't hang together. 'Cause I've been sober all day you see. So I've reached a conclusion and that conclusion is, *it ain't my fault*. And if it ain't my fault, it must be yours. And I think it has something to do with that better-than-thou way you've had about you ever since I gave up my job to become a professional guitarist. Y'know, that idea you got in your head that you're wearing the trousers around this house. That you're the almighty breadwinner. It just makes me mad. And it's because I'm mad with you all the time that Peter won't play. Do you get all this? Nod if you do, or I'll come over there and make you nod, rolling-pin or no rolling-pin.'

Janie nodded

Billy-Joe grinned and nodded back. 'Now, another question I have been considering is this: what should I do about it? Have you any good ideas, O talented editor?'

Janie found her voice. 'Let me go,' she managed and cursed herself for sounding so feeble and terrified.

Billy-Joe screwed up his face and knitted his brow. Then he shook his head as if he was suddenly confused. 'Go? You mean to say that you *were* lying to me earlier?'

'I want to go, Billy,' Janie said. 'Please give me the car keys. We can talk about it later, when I feel better.'

He shook his head. 'If I let you go now, you won't come back, will you? So we stay here and thrash it out. Now what bright ideas do you have?'

'Don't hit me any more!' Janie said. She'd meant her voice to sound even, but it came out of her mouth sounding like a cross between a plea and a command.

'Well it's a crying shame you think *that's* the answer, babe, because it means our views are now diametrically opposed. You see, I wasn't telling the whole truth about Peter. The fact is, that he ain't dead, just sleeping. I know that because when I reached the final solution concerning what I ought to do about you, old Peter began to perk up. And I bet you can't guess what that final solution is.'

'You're going to kill me,' Janie said with the utmost certainty. She also knew with the utmost certainty that the front door was open and only about four feet away from her and that she should put herself through it as quickly as possible. And she also knew that the moment she tried to move her iced legs, they were going to betray her and throw her to the ground.

Billy-Joe chuckled, low in his throat. 'Now what good would *that* do anyone? You're my wife, Janie, and I only want things to be back like they were before. No babe, I don't intend to kill you, all I intend to do is to get your respect. Get the head-of-the-house trousers off you and put 'em back on me where they belong. What d'you think about that?'

Janie knew *exactly* what she thought about that. She thought that Billy-Joe had consciously discovered what his subconscious knew when he was drunk. That violence wasn't just a substitute for sex, but an actual expression of it. The power bit of it anyway. Billy-Joe had discovered that the sober thought of beating up his wife gave him a hard-on.

'So, today's lessons are these: Number one, you don't think

of running out on your old man. You don't even consider it for one moment, ever. Got me?'

Janie nodded.

'And number two, men don't make passes at girls who have no front teeth. So you can think of what I'm going to do as a little favour to you. *I'll* still love you when you've got a three-quarter-inch gap between your upper front teeth and that's the important thing. Now, I'll tell you what's going to happen. There's two ways we can do it. The easy way and the hard way. The easy way is, you come over here, lie down with your head in my lap and I remove those loose teeth of yours with these pliers.' He picked up the pliers in both hands and worked them: open and shut, open and shut. Then he grinned.

Janie could barely bring herself to believe that this man – who she had once loved so deeply – expected her to lie down on his lap and allow him to yank out two of her teeth with a pair of pliers.

'So which way d'you want to do it?' he was asking. 'The easy way, or the hard way?' He paused, looking at her. 'It's not that I *want* to do it Janie – I really do love you – it's just that you have to be put in your place. Do you understand that?'

'Yeah,' she heard herself say.

'How about you come over here, lie on my lap. I read your goodbye letter, then I make you eat it, then I pull your teeth and it'll be all over and we can be friends. It won't even hurt – those top teeth are already waggling about like little doggy tails, aren't they?'

'Yeah,' Janie said. The crazy thing about it was that Billy-Joe no longer seemed to be speaking to her, but to a deeply buried part of her that she was ashamed to admit existed. This part of her was rising steadily towards the surface and it wanted to do exactly what Billy-Joe commanded.

She knew when she was beaten. 'I'll scream if it hurts,' she said quietly.

'I know you will, babe,' he said. 'You scream for your old man. Just like you used to.'

Janie's legs bore her towards him easily and smoothly. The

part of her that wanted her to be tortured gathered momentum when her feet started moving and rose up inside her like a warm well-spring. Janie began to feel very good indeed about things. She smiled and relaxed.

Billy-Joe reached out for her as she approached, the pliers still in his right hand.

Apart from the instrument of torture, Janie thought distantly, they might have been two lovers meeting after a lengthy separation. She found she wanted to giggle. Everything was going to be all right after all. Things were going to work out just fine.

'Come here, babe,' Billy-Joe murmured.

And Janie hit him with the rolling-pin, as hard as she could.

She leapt back, snarling, distantly realizing that the part of her that had taken over was something as cunning and as quick as a tigress. And it had been there all along, plotting and planning. She'd merely had to let go of her conditioned intellectual processes in order to let it take control.

The target she'd chosen hadn't been Billy-Joe's head, but his outstretched right wrist – which presumably meant the part of her that had the controls thought it was important to disarm him before finishing him off.

Billy-Joe was howling now. 'You motherfucking cow!' he screeched, spittle flying from his mouth.

In that second he became the ugliest thing that Janie had ever seen.

He put both his hands down on the sofa to push himself up and the tigress in Janie saw her chance. She leapt forward and smashed the rolling-pin down on the crown of his head.

As he sat back down again, Janie saw the rent she'd put in his scalp. Blood was already welling up in it.

I've killed him! she thought, panicking, as Billy-Joe gently collapsed into the sofa. She watched his eyes roll up, watched his neck muscles loosen and his head tilt back.

He's just knocked out, she assured herself, but it didn't look as if he *was* just KOed. Billy-Joe didn't draw a breath and she could see no pulse in his exposed throat. He was moving slightly, but it wasn't the movement of a man who'd been knocked unconscious, but that of an ancient and rickety car, settling after a long and bumpy journey.

Then Billy-Joe heaved in a breath and let it go in a long sigh.

The demon that had last popped into Janie's mind in the office where it had advised her to hit Martin over the head with her computer keyboard, now spoke up again. *Hit him again, just to make sure he isn't going to get up and cause any more trouble!* it said.

I think I'll just leave, now, she told herself, touching her loose teeth with the tip of her tongue. She snatched the car keys from the arm of the sofa, said, 'Goodbye Billy-Joe,' and went outside.

It wasn't until she was half-way through stuffing her bags and work things into the boot of the VW that she began to feel angry at having to run away from her own house.

But the sensible thing to do was forget the anger, get out of here and begin legal proceedings – and not just for the dissolution of her marriage. Assault would go down quite nicely too, she thought.

'That's what I'll do,' she said aloud. 'Get in the car and go to the police.'

She picked up the last bag, leaned forward to place it in a space in the back of the car and managed a grim smile.

Which was when Billy-Joe hit her in the back.

For a moment Janie was so surprised she didn't realize she'd been struck. Several things happened at once. Her vision flashed white, her kidneys felt as if they had spontaneously exploded and her head somehow caught the rim of the car's boot.

In that moment, the thing that Janie was most aware of was the fact that her rolling-pin, which she had held while she was loading the car, was sailing away from her, end over end, in what appeared to be slow motion.

Billy-Joe heaved her out of VW's hatchback and this time, her head struck the tailgate.

'Now what are you gonna do?' Billy-Joe wanted to know, shaking her. Her head rolled about, dizzying her. He dragged her close to him, embracing her in a hug that forced the air from her lungs and drove spikes of pain through her ribs. The sensation of something cold clamping itself around her ear lobe and starting to bite brought her senses snapping back to her.

Billy-Joe had the pliers again. And he was starting to use them.

'I love you, Billy,' she said.

He leaned back from her and the grip on her ear-lobe lessened. 'What?' he asked.

And Janie found out two things simultaneously.

The first was that her leg did come up when she asked it to, and the second was that her husband wasn't expecting a knee in the groin.

She was too close to him to get a clear shot and the blow wasn't powerful enough to put him down, but it did make him let go of her. He yelped in surprise and staggered backwards a pace.

This would have been all fine and dandy as far as Janie was concerned . . . if the pliers hadn't still been gripping her ear-lobe. But when she kneed him, Billy-Joe's reflexes made his muscles tense and the pliers snapped shut.

She was wearing a pair of twenty-four carat gold hoops in her ears, the left one of which was instantly crushed flat, pinching her flesh. The sprung steel closure which fitted through her pierced ear was a great deal more brittle than the gold, however, and snapped in two. One of the ends drove a fresh hole through her lobe and the other spiked its way up into the gristle of her ear itself.

Janie didn't realize any of this at the moment it happened – but she did know that the pliers were dragging at her flesh and that it hurt very badly. And that if she didn't want her ear torn right off her head, she had to move in the direction she was being dragged.

She took a pace towards Billy-Joe, and the tigress inside her woke up again. She grabbed the strong hand holding the pliers, held it steady, then snapped her knee up again. This time it was a good one. A corker. *Peck on that Perky Peter!* she thought.

Billy-Joe yelped, let go of the pliers and folded double.

Hissing, and bent over, he hopped towards her, looking like a great clumsy bird. Janie dodged him, turned and spotted the rolling-pin.

'Motherfucking little cow-bitch!' Billy-Joe squealed from behind her as she ran for the rolling-pin.

She distantly realized that things hadn't only got out of hand, but had gone as far as murder now. If he came out on top he wasn't just going to pull some of her teeth, he was going to kill her. She was certain of this. Since yesterday, when she'd first heard those magic words 'Black Rock' and begun to visualize what the haunted house must look like, her life seemed to have taken a distinct turn for the worse.

She snatched the rolling-pin from the ground and went back towards Billy-Joe who was birdy-hopping towards her – in agony, but not believing he was beaten, it seemed.

'Enough!' Janie said. 'Stop!'

Billy-Joe looked up at her with those dark and wild eyes and his agonized face adjusted its contours until his expression became something which wasn't quite a grin, but was very scary. 'Never!' he hissed and hopped towards her. He was still bent almost double, his arms were outstretched and his fingers were splayed as if he was an adult playing bogey-man to throw a thrill of fear into a wide-eyed child.

'Stop!' Janie shouted.

And grinning, Billy-Joe hopped another foot closer to her.

Janie hit him over the head. Very hard.

This time the thud sounded different. Previously it had sounded rather like the hollow sound a coconut made when hit with a hammer, but this time the resonance was deadened. It sounded soggy.

And when Janie looked, she saw exactly *why* it sounded like that. There was a five-or six-inch indentation across the crown of Billy-Joe's head.

You've done it now! she told herself. *You've murdered him.*

Janie wasn't sure if it was murder or not, but it had to be up there somewhere in the realms of manslaughter. She felt very sick and dizzy and the only thing she could think of was to run away.

She walked towards him, her heart hammering and the panic building in her and poked his ribs with the toe of her shoe.

He didn't move.

She squatted down beside him and felt his neck for a pulse. There wasn't one.

She looked up and down the empty street, checked the neighbours' windows she could see in case anyone was watching her – which no one was – and went back indoors, trying to summon up her fairy godmother or any passing genie. Anyone would do. Anyone who could wind back the time that had passed and undo everything that had happened. Or perhaps alter history. Until last night Billy-Joe hadn't been a maniac. He'd been pretty handy with his fists, but he hadn't wanted to pull her teeth.

Yeah, well, that's because you've been doing a Typhoid Mary impersonation. You caught the Black Rock madness-plague when Drezy told you the book's title. And you brought it home and passed it to Billy-Joe. And today you gave it to Martin too. What'll he be like the next time you see him? A drooling psycho, like Billy-Joe?

But in spite of this thought, it all had to be coincidence. She had done nothing to change Billy-Joe. He'd been on a downhill slide for a long time and the only thing that changed last night was that he'd finally hit rock-bottom. His long metamorphosis from loving husband to violent drunk to psychopath had been completed. She'd seen it coming a long way off, just hadn't done enough to prevent it.

The telephone was just inside the front door. Janie took a deep breath and lifted the receiver. Then she put it back again and went to the kitchen. She dipped her head into the sink and rinsed her mouth until the flow of blood slowed, washed her face, then got a pair of tweezers from the drawer and turned her attention to her ear.

Getting the crushed gold hoop off wasn't difficult – she simply unbent it with her fingers – but the removal of the broken closure spring was another story entirely.

She went to the freezer, got the ice tray, crushed a cube and inserted it between her fat (and still bleeding) top lip and her loose teeth, then wrapped a few more cubes in a face-cloth and held it to her ear. The ice seemed to make the damage more painful, but Janie persisted.

Holding the ice-pack to her ear, Janie went back down the hall, picked up the telephone and let the handset dangle while she used her free hand to dial the number. The emergency operator was already asking questions by the time she'd retrieved the phone.

'Ambulance, please,' she heard herself say. 'I think my husband is dead.'

And as the words left her mouth, Janie glanced out of the front door to where Billy-Joe's corpse lay.

Except that Billy-Joe's corpse no longer lay there.

'Putting you through,' the operator said.

Janie only half-heard. She was staring at the empty space where her husband had been and thinking, *This is impossible. A few minutes ago he was dead. Not breathing. Expired. There was a groove the shape of the rolling-pin in his head.*

Oblivious to the new voice bleating in her ear, Janie put the handset back in its cradle and went out into the front garden.

Gone! The word rang in her head like the sound of a great bell.

She began to panic. Billy-Joe was staggering about out there somewhere and he was going to get picked up. Even if he hadn't been found yet, he soon would be. Someone would see him wandering about badly injured and call the police or an ambulance, and when that happened, Billy-Joe was going to talk. And he was going to say something along the lines of: *My wife! My wife did this. I was just sitting watching the telly and she came in from work and tried to murder me with a rolling-pin.*

And who were the police going to believe?

There were two words that had been gliding around the periphery of Janie's mind all day, wheeling lazily like vultures. They were words that seemed like very good advice indeed:

RUN AWAY!

The urge to obey this command was overwhelming. Janie stopped thinking logically about the consequences of doing this and gave into the irrepressible urge. Things could be sorted out later.

She went to the VW, slammed down the tailgate, snatched the keys from its lock and rushed to the driver's door. For a few ugly seconds she couldn't make the key fit in the lock and her mind began to crow that it had got bent during her fight. Finally it slotted home and she got in. She glanced up and down the street while she put the key into the ignition, but Billy-Joe was nowhere to be seen.

Get outta here! she told herself and twisted the key, knowing the car wouldn't start, or that it would be out of petrol in spite of the fact that the needle was showing three-quarters of a tank.

The VW started on the first turn of the key.

Janie revved the engine, found first gear, released the handbrake and rolled out of the drive before she asked herself where she was going. To her parents she supposed. Or to Drezy's place. There weren't too many choices.

By the time she got to the dual carriageway that led towards the M3 motorway, Janie was beginning to feel a little shaky.

You can make that a lot shaky, she told herself.

There was a packet of cigarettes in the glove-box. Once upon a time, back in the days before Ace's offices were designated a 'smoke-and-we-sack-you' area, Janie had been a twenty-five a day woman. The habit was broken now, but she still had fond memories of it, and the packet in the glove-box was a souvenir; a connoisseur's brand of untipped called *Sweet Afton*.

The dual carriageway bisected a forest and Janie knew there was a picnic pull-off up ahead. She turned into it and stopped.

She undid the glove-box, found the packet of cigarettes, unwrapped the cellophane with shaking hands, waited impatiently for the car's lighter to pop out, then lit up.

The nicotine hit her like an express train.

Janie inhaled, coughed long and hard then did it again.

This time she blew out a plume of smoke. Her head began to spin.

'Smoking's bad for you, babe,' Billy-Joe said from right behind her.

Janie didn't for a moment believe she'd heard this, but she glanced in the rear-view mirror anyway. A short high-pitched yelp escaped her lips around the cigarette.

That wasn't an hallucination of Billy-Joe sitting behind her on the back seat, that was the real thing, head smashed in, blood and everything.

'Where are we goin' babe?' he asked. And grinned.

Janie had left the rolling-pin on the passenger seat. If she hadn't suddenly become paralysed, her left arm would have managed to reach it in time to kill that grin.

'To Hell, I'd say,' Billy-Joe's reflection told her. 'I'd say we were going to Hell in a hand-basket. The two of us. Hand in hand. What would you say, o wifey of mine, o one true love?'

And then his left arm was locked around her throat, pulling her back and choking her, and his right hand was waving in front of her face, snapping the pliers in her line of vision.

'I think we'd better cure you of your nic-o-tine habit first,' he said and grabbed the cigarette with the pliers. The hot end showered burning sparks over Janie. Billy-Joe yanked the cigarette from her lips and dropped it into her lap. The cigarette began to burn through her skirt. She could feel a small spot of intense heat high on her right thigh. She batted at it with her left hand, but it wouldn't go away.

'Now smile at me, Janie,' Billy-Joe hissed. 'Smile at me and show me those lovely loose gnashers you've got in your sweet little mouthy.'

Janie's fingers found the handle of the rolling-pin as Billy-Joe pushed the pliers between her tightly closed lips. She felt her upper front teeth begin to give against the steady pressure, felt the new split in her lip tear wider.

'NO!' she shouted, and the pliers were in her mouth and snapping like an enraged rat.

Janie brought the rolling-pin up in a long swiping arc. It hit the side of Billy-Joe's head. The pliers rattled against her teeth, pinched down on a small piece of skin inside her cheek and were roughly withdrawn, taking the nip of flesh with them.

Billy-Joe gasped and uttered a little curse and his grip on her neck loosened. Janie hit him again. And again. Billy-Joe went limp.

'Bastard!' she croaked and brought the rolling-pin up again. Billy-Joe fell back into the rear seat.

Squealing in rage and pain, Janie knocked the burning cigarette end off her skirt, swivelled round in her seat and whacked her husband over the head again. He didn't only have the groove in the crown of his head now, he had matching ones in three other places. His jaw was twisted so far off-centre it surely must have broken clean off its internal hinges. But the pliers were still held firmly in his hand.

'Drop them, you bastard!' she told him, not realizing he wasn't going to hear. Then she hit the hand holding the pliers. They fell, but Janie wasn't finished yet. She couldn't stop herself. She hit him again, three times, screaming at him each time the rolling-pin cracked bone. 'Come back from that, you fucker!' she challenged through clenched teeth.

Then she dropped the rolling-pin, collapsed in the front seat and began to cry. She wasn't just a carrier of the madness-plague, she had caught it herself. Billy-Joe had passed it back to her and turned her into as violent a psychopath as he had become.

Eventually the sobbing subsided. Unthinking, Janie got out of the car and unlocked the tailgate. There was a car rug in there somewhere under all the other things she had thrown in. She unpacked her things until she found it, dragged it out, put her cases and folders back, closed the hatch and got back inside the car. She wasn't going to be able to drag Billy-Joe's body out of the car and there was nowhere to hide it even if she did. She pushed him down until he was sprawled across the back seat, then covered him with the rug.

Then she lit another cigarette and smoked it, staring out at the empty parking area.

Then she started the car and began to drive.

Chapter Seventeen

The Fictional Sister

Martin Louis Dinsey didn't begin to admit that he'd allowed himself to be suckered until he ran out of petrol on the A19 just outside York. He was tired, and he was three and a half hours and two hundred and twenty miles away from London. It was one in the morning, it was raining, the road was empty and there were still forty-odd miles between him and Scarborough.

It was almost as if someone had planned it this way.

He sat in the dead Ferrari Dino and keyed the starter again, knowing that it wasn't going to do any good. Even a Ferrari wouldn't run on fresh air.

Especially a Ferrari, he told himself.

Scowling, he reached for his Vodafone, the battery of which held just enough life for it to bleep at him once in a half-hearted fashion before it became completely flat.

Well that's that then, he told himself bitterly. *It's get out and milk it time. Or get out and walk, because that's what it boils down to.*

There wasn't even a petrol can in the car. He was going to have to walk God only knew how far – in the rain – to the nearest service station or telephone box.

This is what happens when you let your AA membership expire. And when you let your brain expire too and set out to chase wild geese on a Thursday evening at half past nine. You should have realized it was one of Essenjay's stupid gags and stayed home with Angela and the kids. Essenjay isn't even going to be in Scarborough when you get there.

Until now, Martin had not let himself believe that Essenjay could be so spiteful. But when he thought about it, it was just about par for the course. Just about the right kind of childishness he should have expected from her. *Should have stayed home instead of getting soaked like this. Haven't even got a bloody umbrella!*

But the truth was, he still thought of home as Essenjay's flat in Bude, and his *real* wife as Sarah-Jane Dresden. Which was the reason he had allowed himself to fall for the message in his voice-mail at the office. The one that said she had gone to stay with her sister in Scarborough and that he was more than welcome to join her.

Which was when he ought to have seen what the game was. Because during his years with Essenjay she had never mentioned a sister. He'd called Essenjay's home again – twice – and had got the answering machine. Then he had looked at the address he'd written down – Mrs Algar, 42 Ellenfield Road, Scarborough – and he had been so sure it was a made-up name and address that he'd checked it out by calling directory enquiries and asking for the telephone number.

While he'd waited to be told there was no listing for this name and address, the ice-block in his brain had burst into life, which he thought ought to be significant. But all it showed him were various snapshot views of his least favourite haunted house. There was Black Rock brightly lit against a sky full of thunderheads and a grey sea. There was a side aspect showing the steep incline down which he'd seen Essenjay fall. There was the overgrown back lawn. The final shot – the one which occurred at precisely the same instant as the recorded voice began to speak – was another view of the front of the house. Except that in this last image, which faded almost as soon as it had formed, one of the upstairs windows was blazing with a blinding white light.

But Martin didn't think about it for more than a moment because there *was* a number for Mrs Algar living at that address in Scarborough. He'd jotted it down on a scrap of paper, and put it in his jacket pocket thinking, *Eureka!*

Looking back on it – which he was now doing as he trudged down the road, squinting against the rain which blew horizontally into his face – Martin felt as if it had been a script, written for him to play and embedded in his unconscious so that he acted it out without really knowing what he was doing or why he was doing it. But the imaginary scriptwriter had been skilful enough to make the scene closely resemble Martin's real life. So close to life, in fact, that he hadn't noticed the difference.

What a load of old cobblers, he thought, angrily wiping rainwater from his face. *The mistake you made was being too eager. Too eager to fall for Essenjay's little trick. You thought that the message in your voice-mail box was true because you so badly wanted it to be true. You went for it, hook, line and sinker, just as she expected you to.*

Now, as he walked towards a garage that might be non-existent, he wondered what had made him drive all the way up here without phoning the number to check that Essenjay wasn't playing a bad joke on him.

Probably because you knew it was a trick all along, he told himself, *and couldn't bring yourself to admit it.*

Now the car was out of it and he was reduced to walking in the pouring rain, things looked quite different. Essenjay *wasn't* going to be waiting for him at 42 Ellenfield Road, Scarborough at all.

There was certainly a Mrs Algar living at that address, but that didn't mean she was Essenjay's sister. Essenjay had probably got hold of a Scarborough telephone directory and picked the name at random. Damnit, the surname even began with an A. She hadn't even bothered to delve into the directory – she'd just opened it at the beginning and chosen the first name she saw.

The reason that Martin knew he wasn't simply going to be able to turn the car round when he'd got it going and head for Bude to give Essenjay a piece of his mind was because of the billion to one chance that she *might*, just might, have been telling the gospel truth. He'd come this far, so he may as well go and knock on the door and see for himself.

There were lights up ahead and if he squinted, Martin thought he could see a tall yellow sign about half a mile away. It looked like a hotel sign and a hotel might be a very good idea at the moment.

Here's another very good idea, a part of his mind told him.

Martin frowned because he didn't recognize this as his own inner voice, nor did it seem to emanate from his mental ice-block. In fact, it sounded rather like Essenjay herself.

You could buy her red roses, the voice continued. *You could check into a hotel, sleep till you're feeling fit, get up, get on the phone to Interflora and send her a dozen red roses. Get them to put:* I love you, M. kiss kiss, *on the card. And ps I've had you put on the insurance for the Ferrari. Send her another dozen each day for a week. She'll have softened up by then.*

The concept of putting Essenjay on his Ferrari insurance and letting her drive it offended Martin deeply. It was *his* car, and he was the only being on the planet rightfully entitled to drive it. But Martin had an understanding of tactics. Putting Essenjay on his insurance was a sure way of making her warm to him. Just because she was on the insurance, it didn't necessarily follow that she was going to get to drive the car. What harm was there in a little deceit?

I'd let her drive my *car*, the mental voice chipped in. *It's a brand-new Porsche 911 twin turbo convertible and it cost more than your second-hand Ferrari. She's already on the insurance, in fact. The car's stood here on the drive waiting for her to speed off to wherever she wants to go.*

'I'm going crazy,' Martin told himself aloud. His voice sounded hollow and frightened in his ears. Over the hours the ice-block had hung in his mind's eye he had changed his beliefs as to its cause. Earlier he believed he'd stripped a few mental cogs due to the pressure of his failed relationship with Essenjay and that he could quite possibly term himself *cracked up* from now on. Then – in an amazingly short time – he'd found that he could live with that huge cold block standing there like an empty computer screen. It didn't adversely affect his thinking, it was merely a temporary aberration and, he believed, it would probably be gone when he woke after a good night's sleep.

Now he wasn't so certain. Having a mental movie screen appear in your mind's eye was something, but starting to hear voices that spoke independently of your own mental processes was something else again. This wasn't nervous breakdown territory, this was the stuff schizophrenia was made of. Hearing voices was not something to be taken lightly. Especially when the voice seemed to speak in the tones of the woman you loved. If Martin had been able to believe in telepathy – which he didn't – he might have thought he was picking up Essenjay's thoughts. Probably not ones that she was sending directly to him, but her unconscious thoughts. But even if this had been the case there was still a problem. Whoever was sending him those thoughts spoke about Essenjay in the third person. '*She will have softened up by then,*' the voice had told him. Not, *You will have softened me up by then.* And there was one last thing that ruled out the possibility of those thoughts belonging to his own subconscious or Essenjay's: the person transmitting them claimed that he owned a brand new Porsche 911 twin turbo. Martin had never in his life given so much as a thought to the possible acquisition of any kind of a Porsche. Porsche didn't enter into his mind in any context especially that of fast cars. As far as he was concerned, there was only one race of people who made *real* sports cars and those people weren't Germans. They were Italians. He'd never had any desire to own a Porsche and he most strongly doubted that Essenjay had a yearning for one either.

Which left him with a dilemma he was quick to spot. Years of editorial practice had sharpened his mind to a point at which even a minor inconsistency in plot or motivation would leap out from a manuscript and hit him in the face as soon as his eyes lit on it. The process here was similar. It ought to be answerable to logic. And as he trudged down the road towards the yellow sign, feet squishing in his wet shoes, his mind started to work out the options.

Logically, he told himself, *if you haven't gone mad, you must have become telepathic. Your mental ice block showed you pictures of Essenjay trip and fall down a steep drop earlier today, and you didn't question that at all, did you? And since you believed what you were seeing, you must believe in telepathy.*

'There's still something wrong though,' he mused.

No there isn't, his mind told him. *So far we've established that you believe in telepathy – or at least some kind of unusual method of communication, call it what you will. cTherefore you're hearing a voice from elsewhere. The only remaining inconsistency is that Essenjay seems to refer to herself in a strange way. As if she's a different person. This is easily resolved if you quit believing you're hearing the voice of her subconscious. Or any voice of hers at all. There is only one way all this shit fits, and that is if the voice is not hers after all. Essenjay doesn't have a Porsche and as far as you know, doesn't want one. Even if she did, she wouldn't think those things. But if it was someone else thinking those things, it all fits quite neatly. So forget about believing that the voice belongs to Essenjay, because it doesn't. If you think about it, you'll realize who that voice really belongs to. And if you think about it for two seconds longer, you'll realize who would drive a Porsche 911 twin turbo.*

Martin thought about it long and hard. He knew *exactly* who would drive that make and model of car. And he also knew that this person would send Essenjay red roses every day and have her put on his car insurance so she could drive that Porsche.

That person was Peter Perfect, of Black Rock, Tintagel.

The only problem was, that person was fictitious.

What do you always tell your authors? the voice asked him, and Martin stopped dead in his tracks because he always told his authors that their characters shouldn't be cardboard cut-outs with no motivation. He said that if you wanted your readers ensnared in your characters' problems, you had to make them rise from the page, living and breathing.

'This is bullshit! That's only speaking metaphorically. They should live and breathe in the reader's *mind*. Book characters cannot live and breathe in real life.'

And if anyone presented me with a book in which a fictional character came to life, I'd say, read King's The Dark Half *because it's already been done*, he added mentally and began to walk again.

That wasn't the piece of advice to which I was referring, the voice said, no longer sounding as if it had ever belonged to Essenjay. It was a male voice for one thing.

'So what *were* you referring to?' Martin asked aloud, no longer believing he was sane. You didn't have conversations with book characters.

The piece of advice I was actually going to remind you of was this: 'In order to convince your reader, to take them with you and your characters, you have to blur the boundaries between real life and fiction, so they no longer know which is which.' Sound familiar? It should do. You've said it to hopeful writers at enough literary seminars. And I don't think I ever claimed to be a work of fiction, did I? Isn't Peter Perfect the name of the writer *of Black Rock? Isn't the lead character in* Black Rock *called Mister Winter? You see Martin, my writing's good enough to force you to blur the boundaries between reality and fiction. You no longer know what to believe and what not to believe. Which means I've succeeded in what I set out to do.*

Martin could almost read the lettering in the big yellow sign up ahead now – it was a hotel sign. For a long, shocked moment he read the words as: 'Black Rock Motel.' The voice in his head chuckled and Martin felt as if he might soon scream. It was only as he approached the glowing sign that the wording swam and resolved itself until it read 'Beech Lock Motel'.

At which point the unwanted voice said, *And here's another snippet of extremely useful information. Don't bother with the old red rose routine. You'll be wasting your money, honey. It's too late, you see, because tomorrow your little Essenjay will be mine and mine alone. For ever and ever, Amen. I claimed her long before you did – and I'm the one who will have her to love and to cherish.*

'Who the hell are you?' Martin said irritably.

Peter Perfect, Black Rock, Tintagel. Writer of stories. Writer of my own story and yours too. And most especially, writer of that lovely lead character Snowdrop Dresden. Essenjay didn't write Black Rock, *Martin, I did. Remember that. I made it real. And I'm still writing it, Martin, even as we speak. I'm writing your bit now. I bet you'd love to know what happens!*

Martin knew what was going to happen. He was going to

turn into the hotel driveway, hammer on the door until someone let him in, get a room, get a bottle of Scotch and drink it until the voices and the ice block faded into insignificance. He'd been under tremendous pressure, he'd brought himself on a huge wild-goose chase and he had thrown one or two cogs. And when he'd drunk himself to sleep those cogs would find their way back to each other and begin to mesh. And when he woke up the following morning, everything would be running smoothly again.

Yeah, so it might be, the voice told him. *But by then it'll be too late. Exactly as I've planned it to be. Think on this, Martin: what if I put the thought into Essenjay's head that she ought to trick you into going to Scarborough? Why would I do that? Ask yourself as you lay down to go to sleep.*

And the voice vanished.

The ice block, however, stayed exactly where it was.

Martin thanked God for small mercies and tried the door of the hotel.

It was open.

Twenty minutes later, as he lay naked on his bed watching his sodden clothes dripping onto the floor while he sipped the third miniature of Bells from the mini-bar, Martin began to wonder about the *what-if* the voice had mentioned.

The voice purported to be not a book character who'd come to life, but a real-life person who was, to all intents and purposes, changing him and Essenjay into fiction. It was ridiculous whichever way you looked at it, but a large part of Martin had begun to believe it was true.

Because of the *what-if*.

Martin had barely been able to believe that Essenjay would play such a spiteful joke on him, and now that he had the *what-if* to consider, it followed that it might not have been her idea. If the idea had been forced upon her, everything fitted neatly into place again if the mystery author had coerced Essenjay.

That author could be a writer whose work he'd once rejected and whose shoulder had carried a large chip ever since. It wouldn't be the first time an editor had been threatened by a disgruntled writer.

But it would be the first time an editor has been contacted telepathically by that writer, his rebelling mind added.

The biggest of his worries was that this author intended to attack – and perhaps kill – Essenjay simply because he assumed he was going to hurt Martin by doing it. And when push came to shove (tomorrow if the voice was to be believed) Martin was going to be too far away to help. He'd been tricked into leaving the battlefield.

But, Christ, I'm only in Scarborough, not the other end of the world. I can get back down to Bude before anything has time to happen, can't I? Unless it happens tonight, I can be there in time to . . . Save her?

But now he thought about it he doubted it. If there was anyone who knew how stories worked, it was Martin Louis Dinsey. It wasn't going to be as easy as that. If it was, Peter Perfect wouldn't have made himself known so early. He would have waited until it was too late for Martin to be of any use.

Which presented him with a perfect way of checking out whether or not he'd gone crazy. If everything he'd thought since the ice block had formed in his head was delusion, it had all happened *internally*. And if it had all happened internally, that meant it would have had no effect on the outside world. Which meant that if he tried he would easily be able to get the Ferrari going, get in it and drive to Bude. Nothing would happen to stop this. It might prove he'd cracked, but coming to terms with this would be easy when compared to the alternative: that Essenjay was really being stalked by a lunatic.

Whereas if he was still sane, and all this shit was *external* and consequently *real*, he wasn't going to be able to leave quite so easily.

So check it out! he told himself, and found that he didn't really want to.

He drained the remainder of the whisky, picked up the telephone, dialled nine for an outside line, then dialled Essenjay's number. While he waited, he opened a miniature of Gordon's gin and poured it down his throat.

'Sarah-Jane cannot come to the phone at this precise

moment because she is currently in her boudoir being enter-
tained by several members of the Chippendales. If you would
like to leave a message and your number, she will call you
back as soon as possible – if she isn't too tired, that is!'

'Damn and blast it!' Martin spat. He waited until the bleep
stopped and then began to shout because Essenjay always
kept the answering machine turned up loud, and if she was
awake she'd be able to hear him leaving the message. Perhaps
she would even come to the phone.

'Essy! It's Martin! Look, I need to talk to you. Now. I
think there's someone coming after you. Don't leave the
house and don't let anyone in until I get there. Phone the
police and tell them I'm in receipt of a letter threatening to
. . . threatening you. I'm on my way!'

She isn't there, he thought as he cut the connection. *Has he*
got her already? But the voice he'd heard had said, *tomorrow*
your little Essenjay will be mine. The question was, since he'd
heard the voice after midnight and it was Friday already, did
tomorrow mean during the daytime of Friday, or not until
Saturday? There was no way of telling. All Martin could do
was act now, as quickly as possible.

He went to his dripping – and ruined – Savile Row jacket
and retrieved the piece of paper on which he'd written the
number of Mrs Algar, Essenjay's fictional sister. He dialled,
chewing the insides of his cheeks in frustration, until the
connection was made.

'I need to speak to Sarah-Jane Dresden,' Martin said. 'It's
urgent!'

'Sorry dear, I can barely hear you,' a woman replied. She
sounded ancient. Much too old to be Essenjay's sister.
Perhaps it was another relative.

'Sarah-Jane. Get me SARAH-JANE!'

'You're very faint dear. Are you calling from a long way
away?' the woman asked.

'ARE YOU MRS ALGAR?' Martin asked.

'Mrs *who*?'

'*ALGAR. A-L-G-A-R!*'

'No dear, this is Mrs King. Maida Vale Two Seven Five,'
the woman rasped. 'It's raining out. I don't know *where* the

cat is. My husband is in prison, y'know. Left me high and dry. The devil got into him, I suppose. He murdered a Spanish girl. People keep on telephoning me and asking if this is the police station. Pranksters, you see. They know about my husband. A girl keeps ringing me.'

Martin cut the connection, his heart sinking. *Here we go,* he thought. *Back into the crazy hole. They haven't had numbers like that since the dark ages. You just imagined that conversation. People don't tell strangers that their husbands are in prison.*

Except that in a Davey Rosenburg novel they would be very likely to do just that.

But we're not in a Davy Rosenburg book, are we? he asked himself and dialled again.

'What's wrong?' a male voice replied, almost instantly.

'Mr Algar?'

'Yeah. What's wrong?'

'I need to speak to Sarah-Jane Dresden. Urgently.'

'Then I suggest you dial the right number next time,' the man said gruffly and rang off.

Martin dialled again. 'What now?' the same voice barked.

'Can I speak to your wife?' Martin asked.

'If your telephone can patch into the afterlife you might be able to, but otherwise you're out of luck, pal. She's been gone fifteen years.'

'I'm sorry,' Martin said.

'I'm not,' the man replied. 'I'm only sorry you're keeping me from sleeping. Some of us got work tomorrow. Anything else I can help you with before I go back to bed?'

'Could you tell me, did your wife have a sister?'

'Yeah, so what?'

'Could you tell me her name?'

'You're phoning me in the middle of the night to ask me what my sister-in-law's name was?'

'*Was?*'

'Yeah, she's dead too. Christ, she died before my wife.'

'Well, what was her name?' Martin asked.

'*Whose?* My wife was called Snowdrop and her sister was called Barley, for some unknown reason. Used to be common for girls to be named after flowers, but why they chose a cereal for poor old Barley I'll never know. That do you?'

'You don't have any friends or relatives called Sarah-Jane Dresden then?'

'You got the wrong number pal. Never heard of her. I'm going back to bed now and I won't be very happy at all if you ring me again. Bye.'

Snowdrop, Martin told himself. *This is all one big complicated joke. Either that or you have gone crazy.*

He dialled reception.

The wait was even longer this time.

'Yes?' a tired male voice eventually replied.

'I need a car. Now,' Martin said. The motel was a small, family-run place. The guy on the other end of the line was the guy who had booked him in and almost certainly the owner.

'It's almost two,' the man complained. 'Avis and everyone will be shut till morning.'

'I have to get down to Bude in a big hurry. My own car's down the road and it's run out of petrol. It's imperative that I get away as soon as possible.'

'Don't you belong to the AA or something?' the man asked.

'No,' Martin said.

There was a pause, during which Martin found himself able to imagine the unspoken words of the motel owner: *Then why don't you fucking well join?*

'Look, my car's outside. There's an all-night filling station not far away. I'll go and get you some petrol. I'll ring your room when I get back. OK?'

'You can add the cost to my bill,' Martin said.

'I was going to,' the man replied and rang off.

While he waited for the motel owner, Martin sipped his drink and thought about Essenjay's fictional sister.

Chapter Eighteen

James Pays a Call

James Green lay on the sofa in the lounge of his flat, wide awake when he should have been in bed and full speed asleep. His mind, which should have been beautifully relaxed and uncluttered as it usually was after sex, was working overtime.

The television was on and he was staring at it but he did not see the images or hear the dialogue. Earlier, he'd made himself a cup of tea, but it stood before him on the coffee table, cold and untouched.

James told himself, for what must have been the millionth time, that it was simply because his life had changed this evening. He was smitten. He'd had plenty of girlfriends and some of them had been intelligent and some had been pretty, but none of them compared favourably with Sarah-Jane Dresden, either in the sack or outside it.

For the first time James Green believed in love at first sight. Or at first date, at least. They'd *clicked*. There was no better way of describing it. He'd simply never identified this strongly with a woman before. S'n'J's effect on him was almost hypnotic. He had been enchanted, knocked out of the stadium, hit for six, bowled over – you name it, it all added up to the same thing.

James Green was in love.

This was not what was keeping him from his bed and a good long sleep. The problem he was wrestling with was an overwhelming urge to do exactly the thing S'n'J had forbidden.

That urge was to act like a character in *Black Rock*.

James, who during the course of the evening had become fiercely protective of S'n'J, was pained by the distress the book and its mysterious author was causing her. And he badly wanted to do something about it. Which meant, in the first instance, going to Tintagel and knocking on the door of the house called Black Rock.

'I know what you're thinking,' S'n'J had said earlier. 'You're thinking that it wouldn't do any harm to sail down there after you leave here. I know that and I know *why* you're thinking it. But you're not a book character, don't act like one.'

Would he be acting like a book character if he went there? James didn't know. On the surface it sounded like it – the dumb hero going to his doom – but this wasn't a book, it was real life.

Peter Perfect might have convinced S'n'J that she was being fictionalized, but S'n'J had failed to convince James that this was actually the case. The world outside was fixed and didn't change at the whim of some hack writer.

It was a nice idea – or it had been back in the fifties when sci-fi was on the up – but these days it was viewed as a cliché. The world was not a construct of someone's mind. Unless that someone was God, and as far as James knew, God just created. He didn't go back and fiddle with what he'd done. If he didn't like what he saw later, he waggled a finger, flooded the world and wiped everyone out before starting again.

James appreciated that S'n'J just *thought* she was being changed into Snowdrop, though. The trouble with fiction was that it was quite a lot closer to reality than most people gave it credit for. You could build a whole society based around, for example, the fiction that men were superior to women. All it took was enough people telling the same lie.

If he went outside, got in his car and drove to Black Rock, he would be doing it for all the same reasons as a book character would have done. During the drive there he might also feel the things a fictional character would. And he would arrive expecting to meet 'Peter Perfect', warn him off scaring S'n'J any more, and go home. In fiction the outcome would be different, of course: something dreadful would happen.

The main difference between real life and fiction was that the dreadful thing (even if you wholeheartedly expected it) almost never happened. In real life, Peter Perfect would probably turn out to be Martin, who had a score to settle. The whole thing could probably be sorted out in less than an hour.

The story of *Black Rock*, clichéd though it might be, had a certain power. He would be the first to admit that. *But it doesn't have the kind of power that could make it come true, does it?* he asked himself. What it *did* have was the power to convince S'n'J that the possibility of its coming true existed. And her mind had done the rest. That was why she was so spooked.

When you put aside all the supernatural stuff that S'n'J was frightened about, the real problem was that someone was terrorizing her. And as far as James knew, people like that didn't target complete strangers.

There was usually a reason behind any kind of vendetta. And that reason was often revenge.

Martin?

There was no Mr Winter. There was no Peter Perfect. They were both Martin.

James thought he knew what *Black Rock* was working towards; what Martin's denouement would be. He was going to *scare* S'n'J back into his arms. On his own terms. The book was a device to convince S'n'J that the only outcome to her life was to go back and let him dominate her.

Quite how it was working so well on her, James didn't know. She struck him as a woman who knew her own mind, but where *Black Rock* was concerned she seemed to be very susceptible. Martin was obviously a master of the art of suggestion.

'So he's the one I ought to go and call on,' James said aloud. 'And tell him what's what. Warn him that Snowy has a new friend and protector.'

James spent the next thirty seconds frowning. There was something wrong with that verbalized thought but he couldn't for the life of him see what it was.

When realization came, it didn't so much dawn on him as smash him in the face. What followed was a very uncomfortable sensation of having been not just suckered, but *altered* in much the same way as S'n'J had described: as if reality had changed around him, then allowed him to re-enter.

'I said Snowy,' he heard himself say in disbelief. 'I called S'n'J, *Snowy*.'

It was a slip, he decided as the odd *déjà-vu* feeling faded, that anyone could have made. To all intents, Snowy Dresden and Sarah-Jane Dresden were the same woman.

There you go again! he scolded himself, then told himself that what he'd meant was that Snowy was a fictionalized version of S'n'J.

James was beginning to feel like a puppy chasing its tail. You went round and round, faster and faster and you still didn't catch up with it.

'There's only one way to sort this out,' he said, got up, turned off the television and got his coat.

James picked up the keys to his Cadillac and went to the front door. *Sorry S'n'J*, he thought, *but someone's got to do something. And sooner rather than later.*

It was a little chilly outside, but the rain had stopped. James glared up at the sky which should have been angry with moonlit cloud, but which was clear and full of stars.

Sometimes promises had to be broken.

James climbed into the Caddy, slammed the heavy door shut and started the car, thinking, *In a book, the car wouldn't start. There'd be a mysterious force stopping it.* The Caddy's idle was a bit rough, but it had been like that for months. It needed the service he kept promising it and never giving it.

OK, S'n'J, he thought. *How about this for a compromise? At the first sign of something unnatural happening, I turn back. If I see strange lights in the sky, or glowing from the house, or if I see things that couldn't possibly be, I'll come home with my tail between my legs. Anything a little bit scary, and I'm outta there.*

James put the car into drive and moved smoothly down the road towards Bude's empty main street, telling himself that by this time tomorrow all S'n'J's problems would have been solved. There would be no more phantom mailmen delivering fresh book chapters to her.

Bude looked like an American mining town after the gold

rush was over. There wasn't a moving car or pedestrian to be seen. James turned right towards the Falcon Inn where he'd arranged to meet S'n'J tomorrow evening. They hadn't actually discussed this; he'd left a note in her kitchen saying he'd meet her there at eight – if she still respected him in the morning. There was a chance that she'd only wanted a one-nighter, but he thought it was an outside one.

James headed towards Widemouth Bay. This road followed the coast all the way down to Tintagel. It was narrow and there were some tight turns in it, but he thought he could make good time, and the chances of meeting anything coming the other way were remote at this time of night.

As he approached the bay, he had a sudden attack of the heebie jeebies concerning what might happen when he arrived at Black Rock. Its occupant might only be Martin, but Martin could have become a psychopath. And if that had happened it put a different complexion on the matter.

James pulled the Caddy into the bay's car park, and stopped to plan his tactics. He wasn't Bruce Lee or Sugar Ray Leonard but you didn't have to be to hold your own in a street-fight – you just had to be quick and mean. But being quick and mean didn't necessarily mean you were equipped to take on a lunatic who might be armed. Especially when your last fight happened three years ago.

But the idea of going home again and forgetting all about it was unthinkable.

Just like it would be for a fictional character, he admonished himself. *You'll brand yourself a coward if you give up now and you'll never be able to live with it.*

It was so excruciatingly clichéd it was unbelievable.

It was also true.

But you don't have to worry, because there won't be a crazy lying in wait for you, he told himself. The thought, which was undoubtedly a truism, didn't give him much comfort. What he thought might give him some comfort was to be as prepared for the impossible as he could.

He got out and unlocked the huge boot. Somewhere beneath all the spares and junk was a big rubber torch and a crowbar.

James felt quite a lot better when he had his right hand wrapped around the crowbar, and to his astonishment the torch didn't just glimmer, it shone like a searchlight.

That's it then, he told himself. *Peter Perfect or Martin or whoever it is, doesn't know you're coming. Or if he, she, or it does know, they can't do anything about it except wait for you.*

It wasn't until he was on the outskirts of Tintagel that the other alternative occurred to him: that whoever lived in Black Rock might not have bothered to try to stop him. James did his best to dismiss this and was surprised to find his best was good enough.

'Here I come, Martin!' he yelled as he turned into Tintagel's main street. He didn't even care if he sounded like a hack horror-story hero. 'Ready or not, I'm coming down there to get you!'

James didn't realize how dry his mouth was until he reached the turning that veered off towards the campsite. According to the book – and to S'n'J – you turned right, then hooked left again on to a steep and narrow track which led downhill through the valley to the bottom part of Barras Nose where the house was supposed to stand on a rock that was almost surrounded by sea.

His heart began to hammer as he made the turn and there it was: the infamous hoggin track.

James took the car to the start of the track and asked himself the question that was required of all visitors to Black Rock. *If I take the car down there, will I be able to get it back up again?*

James peered down into the gloom beneath his headlights. It wasn't the angle of the track which bothered him – although from here it looked as if it was a one in five descent, perhaps getting steeper later – but the width. S'n'J had said it was just about wide enough to accommodate her Sierra but the Caddy's breadth made her car look pencil-slim.

Go for it, he told himself. *Just take it slowly. You can always back up again if it starts looking a little too sticky. Or you could simply park up here and walk down.*

James Green did not now, and never had, placed a great

deal of credence in the power of pride. He had always subscribed to the belief that no matter how capable you were, it was always best to give anything that looked like trouble a very wide berth. Even if you were supremely confident. Everyone knew that pride came before a fall – or in this case, a very long drop.

So when he put the Cadillac Eldorado back into drive and began to creep forward towards the steep descent he told himself that he wasn't doing it because his pride would be wounded if he chickened out.

He knew it wasn't true, but he told himself anyway.

The drive wasn't easy. The Caddy's front wings reached either side of the track and the combination of the big bonnet and his driving position obscured his view of the way forward for a distance of about ten feet. All he could do was proceed exceptionally slowly while he tried not to think of the pink goo that had been on the front of S'n'J's car. The unidentifiable sticky substance had scared him, whether he'd admitted it to himself or not. It seemed to have spoken to a deep and primal part of him that recognized it as something to be avoided at all costs.

Because it wasn't dog guts, but something that might have been ghost-splatter? James asked himself. *The kind of thing you'd expect to see if you ran down a ghost. Ectoplasmic innards?*

The last time he'd seen anything like that was in *Poltergeist* when the woman crashed back through the ceiling carrying her daughter. They'd been covered in some yukky-looking kind of jelly. James couldn't recall whether or not it had been pink, but he *could* remember that they'd bathed it off quite easily. The stuff he'd seen on S'n'J's car clung like chewing-gum to a child's hair. It wasn't water soluble at all.

If that's the case, the dog is a ghost, he thought. And then he shook his head. None of this had anything to do with the supernatural and if he had any imaginings that leaned that way, he'd inherited (or caught them) from S'n'J.

'There aren't any such things as dog ghosts,' James said aloud and didn't much like the frightened tone of his voice.

Then he screamed.

At the big black dog that had leapt out of nowhere and landed lightly on the track about twenty feet ahead of him.

Reflexively, James hit the brakes. The wheels bit and the car stopped with a slight crunch of gravel. The bonnet dipped and bobbed level again in a meet-the-queen curtsy and James was left staring at the big black dog, who was neither dead, nor injured nor ghostly in any way.

Looking almost majestic, Diamond Ambrose Anstey, his black coat shining in the car's headlamps, turned to face James. His eyes gleamed white in the reflected light making him look a little like one of Angela Carter's wolves, but this wasn't a devil dog, or a ghost, or even a dog come back from the dead.

James could see why *Black Rock*'s author had chosen to fictionalize the dog though. It was impressive and scary, taller than a lurcher but with a thicker body and a more muscular build. It had an intelligent face – seemingly a combination of Labrador and something that might have been greyhound. Its movements were graceful and fluid. It looked as if it knew what the score was and that as far as James was concerned there was little point continuing.

James took two deep shuddering breaths and then said, 'Cripes dog, you threw a scare into me!'

He wasn't terribly surprised when the dog tilted its head up sideways as though it could hear and understand. This was impossible of course – James was fifteen feet away and sitting in a soundproofed car with the windows rolled up – but that was the impression he got.

Then Diamond Ambrose Anstey did the very thing that not three hours earlier James had read about him doing. He lowered his head, raised a paw and began to point. Directly at James.

He's telling me to get the fuck out of here and he's pointing the way, James thought and was instantly ashamed that he'd entertained this piece of fancy. Dogs – even intelligent dogs – were not renowned for their power of precognition.

'Get out of the way, Diamond!' James yelled.

The dog stayed where it was. Pointing the way out.

Perhaps – in spite of what the book had said – the dog

actually belonged to the house and guarded it. Perhaps it was trying to let him know that if he insisted on continuing, he was going to have it to contend with when he got out of the car.

Now he'd reached this conclusion and he'd recovered from the shock of the animal's appearance, the only problem that remained was that Diamond was blocking the way. He couldn't treat the dog to a blast on the horn because that would merely announce his impending arrival to whoever was inside the house.

Still not entirely happy with the way the dog was pointing at him like he meant business, James waited a few seconds, then let his foot off the brake.

The Eldorado rolled slowly forwards.

Diamond Ambrose Anstey remained as motionless as a statue, eyes glittering white in the moving headlight beams.

'Get out of the way, dog!' James yelled as the car drew nearer.

When there was still ten feet between his bonnet and the dog, James saw Diamond's posture change slightly – as though the animal had tensed his muscles.

He's going now, he told himself. *He'll probably run back down the track and bark until he alerts his owner to the fact that someone is approaching. There goes the surprise entrance.*

The car rolled steadily closer.

He isn't going to move, James finally realized.

At the exact moment that James finished telling himself this, Diamond Ambrose Anstey *did* move.

But not the way James had expected.

Diamond came straight at the car.

James hit the brakes again.

The dog took two great ground-eating bounds and sprang on to the Eldorado's bonnet. The deep *crump!* registered the impact of what couldn't possibly be anything other than a live animal and the front of the car dipped under the weight.

Diamond stood on the front of the bonnet like an oversized hood ornament, head dipped as he peered across the expanse of metalwork to where James sat.

James was riveted to his seat, his eyes locked in the dark gleam of the dog's. He knew with the utmost certainty that the dog intended to come in through the windscreen after him. And not only that, he suddenly believed that the dog could actually do it. This windscreen, which had once stopped half a housebrick without taking damage, would shatter into a million pieces when Diamond hit it.

With this prediction came the astonishing realization that the animal had somehow known on which side of the car James would be sitting. Even though it was left-hand drive. The dog, who couldn't have seen where he sat from the wrong side of the headlights hadn't had to search for him. It had located him instantly. Even if this astonishing fact could be attributed to chance, what was happening to the car's bonnet where the dog's paws were in contact with it could not.

Frost was blooming there.

It was spreading rapidly in twinkling crystalline tracers as though the dog's paws were freezing it.

Can't be! James thought, but there wasn't time to consider it because the dog was communicating with him in some peculiar fashion. There were no words and no images, just a deep, aching sensation of loneliness and despair. It only lasted a moment, but in that moment James knew how it must feel to be damned.

Then Diamond was crouching as if to pounce and James understood what the transference had been about. He was the one who was damned, not the dog. The dog was the one who was going to send him to Hell.

The following second seemed to James to last almost eternally.

Diamond drew back, his muscles tensed. James saw them bunch and stand out in rippling cables. Then the creature sprang forwards at him, all its paws leaving the car's bonnet at the same instant. In the coating of frost left behind there were four unfrozen spots which perfectly outlined the shape of the dog's paws and claws.

Diamond flew through the air towards the windscreen in a

perfect, graceful arc, mouth closed, front legs outstretched, sad eyes gleaming.

James tried to bring his hands up to protect himself when the animal missile burst through the windscreen but his limbs moved in real-time and were only half-way up from the steering wheel at the crucial moment.

Just before the dog hit, James distantly noted that Diamond was penetrating the glass without damaging it – the screen was still whole and unbroken.

The dog's full weight connected with him in the centre of his chest.

If there had been time, James would have screamed, but there were too many other things happening at once.

The creature was passing through him, in much the same way as it had done with the windscreen, but seemingly more slowly, as if it were sinking into him.

And it hurt. Where it made contact it froze like ice and burned like a welder's torch. It seemed to be melting its way through his body. There was a moment when the dog's head and front legs were inside his chest and its back and hind-quarters were standing on his thighs and pushing. Then its back was entering him too. It felt like someone was pushing a blazing telegraph pole through his flesh. James had no breath, his heart had cramped to a tiny cube of ice and his mind had hidden itself away in a tiny corner of his head.

All he knew from then on was pain.

It seemed to go on for ever.

Chapter Nineteen

A Message from God

Twenty-five minutes later, Martin was sitting in his Ferrari getting his proof. It was the proof he didn't want – the proof that everything he'd experienced so far consisted *not* of his fevered imaginings, but of reality. He really *had* held a telepathic conversation with a maniac author who called himself Peter Perfect and, so far, everything Peter Perfect had said was holding up to scrutiny. The man (or whatever he was, and the word god – with a small 'g' – kept creeping into Martin's mind) had intimated that he'd arranged for Martin to go to Scarborough in order to keep him away from Bude until it was too late for him to save Essenjay. And now it looked as if this was indeed the case.

Because although the Ferrari now contained two gallons of petrol, it still wouldn't start.

'You're just going to flatten the battery,' the motel manager said from outside the open car window. 'I don't think it *was* lack of petrol that made it stop. I think something else is wrong with it. Did you check the H.T. system to see if it got wet? Probably picked up some rain-water. Open the back up and I'll have a look. I've got a torch somewhere. I'll get it.'

Martin pulled the release for the engine bay and started to get out of the car.

And his mental ice block chose this moment to light up.

Martin paused, his legs out in the driving rain and his body still in the car. Rain blew into his face, but he was barely aware of it; his attention had been forcefully grabbed by the three-dimensional mental movie-screen.

The honed edges of the crystal flickered like a slow-to-start fluorescent tube, except that the colour was a deep, fiery red.

Then it caught and for a few seconds, the ice block's edges shone with a blinding red light. Martin could feel the frame of light etching itself into his brain. If the light went out and the ice block vanished now, he knew, he would still be able to see its outline. Very probably he would still be able to see it a month later. That shape would scar his mind.

Then the light vanished and a fresh image of his favourite haunted house appeared. The house didn't fill the block this time though – he was seeing it from what seemed to be about a hundred yards away and from a viewpoint that had to be ten or fifteen feet in the air. He could see the hoggin drive that led down to Black Rock's forecourt. A stunted hedge bordered the drive, ran in a straight line to either edge of the rock on which the house stood, and quit, as though it was too tired to curve any further around the rock.

Martin had not seen Black Rock from this angle before. Neither had he known there was a hedge along this aspect of it. But none of this new information came as a surprise to him. It exactly fitted the image he would have if he'd been asked to visualize the place from this angle.

He knew now why he and Janie had shared such similar mental pictures of Black Rock. It wasn't because the book's author was extremely skilled at drawing a picture, but because the place was *real*.

And now he'd realized this, he understood something else that had been bothering him. The reason the mysterious Peter Perfect had, at the bottom of each manuscript page, given his address as 'Black Rock, Tintagel' was because that *really was* his address. The only fictional thing about the book's footers was the author's name. Those pages had come from a man who had used his own home as his imaginary haunted house.

Which means that you don't have to rush back to Bude after all. You have the guy's address. All you have to do is ring the police.

Then he realized that he had nothing to tell them. *What are you going to say? That there's a man calling himself Peter Perfect living in a house called Black Rock in Tintagel and you want them to stop him harming the woman you love? We haven't even got a threat, except a telepathic one, and even if it was written down, it wouldn't constitute a threat. Your average policeman would simply believe that Peter Perfect is your rival in love.*

'Shit!' he said aloud.

And the vision cleared.

'You OK?' the motel owner asked, coming back towards Martin with his torch. He was dressed in a yellow waterproof cape, sou'wester and rubber boots, and looked like a lost lifeboat man. His name was Harold, he'd said earlier, but Martin could call him Harry. But he was one of those slow and pedantic people who did everything so methodically and calmly that however grateful you were, you ended up wanting to strangle them. Out of spite, Martin called him Harold.

'Of course I'm all right, *Harold*,' he snapped. 'What did you think? That I was soaked to the skin and pissed off with being stuck here in the middle of nowhere?' He bit his lip before he could add, *with only an arsehole like you for company.*

'You just looked a bit peaky,' Harold said. 'Glazed over.'

'I'm fine,' Martin said, getting out and standing up in the full force of the driving rain. 'I'm just agitated about being stuck.'

'We'll get you going in a jiffy,' Harold said. 'Don't worry.'

Martin followed him to the back of the Ferrari, hoping Harold knew more about car engines than he did.

This hope was dashed within two seconds.

'Jesus H. Christ on a cross,' Harold said mildly, peering into the depths of the engine. 'I've never seen anything like *this* before. I can't even *see* the distributor. It's all belts and pulleys.' He leaned in and searched with his torch. 'Ah, here we go. Just as I thought. You've been hammering through deep puddles. Wires are all wet. Got a tissue?'

Martin hadn't. 'Haven't you?' he snapped.

Harold searched beneath his cape and found a handkerchief. He leaned beneath the shelter of the bonnet and began to fold it neatly. Martin found himself wanting to bellow at the man to hurry up, or to shake him until he woke himself up and started *doing* something, but he restrained himself.

Harold wasn't happy with his work until five long minutes later.

During this time, the ice block in Martin's brain lit up twice. The first time, the vision of Black Rock was a little further away and he could see the sea raging around the outcrop on which it stood; the second time, night had fallen. It was dark but, surprise, surprise, Martin could plainly perceive every detail. It was as if the house was lit by the light of the brightest full moon ever.

Well it would be, wouldn't it? Martin thought bitterly. It's a fucking haunted house, after all. What good would it be if you couldn't see what was going to happen there?

What happened next, however, could have been seen in total darkness. The upstairs window of the house which had earlier let out a blinding flash of light, now emitted another.

At exactly the same time as good old Harold began to say, 'There you go. It'll start now.'

He turned to look at Martin, squinted, then shone his torch directly into Martin's face. 'Are you *sure* you're feeling OK?' he asked.

Martin batted the torch away from his face. 'I'd be a damned sight better if you wouldn't keep blinding me like that,' he snarled.

'You can leave now,' Harold said in a wounded tone. 'Your car will start on the first turn of the key.'

'No it won't,' Martin said. He understood it all now. He didn't have the faintest idea how it worked, but he knew what was happening.

Down in Cornwall, on a rock which was almost surrounded by the Atlantic, sat a *real* house called Black Rock. Inside that house, was someone who might or might not have been called Peter Perfect. Peter Perfect might be a writer, and a good one at that, but writing well was no longer his main talent. He'd progressed several steps beyond that. He no longer manipulated fictitious characters through his stories, he now manipulated reality itself. He might be doing it the way a novelist would – constructing a reality that suited his purposes – but his characters were *real* people and his world was the *real* world.

Which makes him . . . what? A god? A ghost?

Martin didn't know. But he *did* know that Peter Perfect was in Black Rock, and which room he was in. The upstairs room on the left-hand side of the house. The writer's workroom. The one which emitted blasts of blinding white light each time Peter Perfect changed reality.

Martin had seen one of those lightning-like emissions the moment before directory enquiries had informed him that there really was a Mrs Algar living at the Scarborough address he'd been given and he'd just seen another. If those pulses came when Peter Perfect changed reality so that it contained, not only the usual things, but also those things that he desired, the latest one was going to have something to do with the car. If Peter Perfect *could* change reality and he really did want to keep Martin away, he wasn't going to allow the car to start.

'The car won't start,' Martin told Harold. 'I'll try it, but I don't expect it to go.'

He climbed back into the Ferrari thinking, *Why should he be frightened of me turning up? Why doesn't he just roll back his cosmic word-processor – or whatever he uses to edit reality – to the point where I enter, and erase me; just delete me so that I never existed at all?*

The answer, Martin assumed, was because he could not. Reality, presumably, had been up and rolling for a good long time before Peter Perfect arrived on the scene, and it had achieved a momentum which he could not overcome. He might be able to patch into reality as it arrived and alter bits of it before it went by, but he surely wasn't powerful enough to, say, completely remove a person. Or even to rewrite them so that they acted as he wished. If he could have, he would have. That much was obvious.

It didn't explain why he was so determined to keep Martin away though. *Surely not because you're an editor?* Martin wondered as he put the key into the ignition. *He can't possibly be frightened of you because of that! Does he think that you're going to tell him his plotting is faulty and his characterization is weak?*

He doubted it. It was going to turn out to be a lot more

complicated than that, and something to do with Essenjay, whom Peter Perfect had apparently earmarked as his perfect woman.

Or his perfect sacrifice, Martin thought, and twisted the ignition key.

The Dino burst into life and idled roughly, missing a little on one cylinder.

Put that in your pipe and suck on it, Peter Perfect! he thought defiantly. *Martin Louis Dinsey is coming to get you and he's real pissed off!*

And the Dino cut out.

'You *shithouse*!' he yelled.

'Try it again,' Harold advised from outside.

Martin keyed the ignition. The Dino fired up . . . and died before the engine caught. When he looked out again, Harold was shaking his head. 'It isn't going to go,' Harold predicted.

Martin turned the key again. This time nothing happened at all. No warning lights lit, no starter motor turned, no dials moved.

'The battery *cannot* have gone dead that quickly!' he shouted.

'Wasn't my fault,' Harold said, backing off a pace.

Martin got out of the car. 'Who said it was?' he demanded, advancing on Harold. 'WHO SAID IT WAS?'

Harold held up his hands. They were trembling. 'Steady on,' he said mildly. 'I'm on your side.'

'I've got to get back down to Bude,' Martin moaned, 'it's a matter of life and death. Literally.' His eyes lit on Harold's car. It was a worn-out powder-blue Vauxhall Victor. Ancient and rusting.

'Lend me your car,' he said. He had aimed the tone of his voice towards a request and missed by a mile. Even to his own ears, he sounded more like the school bully demanding the little kid's packed lunch. To Harold, he apparently sounded demented.

Harold shook his head. 'Can't,' he said, looking ready to take a speedy hike in the opposite direction. 'The car's not taxed. The two back tyres are bald and there's a big oil leak.

It'd die before it got back to York. Or you'd kill yourself. And anyway, it's all the transport I've got.'

'I'll buy it!' Martin informed him. 'You've got my Visa number. Put it on my bill. I'll pay whatever you ask. It can't be worth more than two hundred, but I'm stuck and I'll pay over the odds. A grand. Let me buy it for a thousand pounds!'

Harold shook his head once more.

'Two grand!' Martin shouted.

'No,' Harold said in a small voice.

Martin suddenly found himself with two handfuls of yellow rubber cape. He yanked them towards him and snarled into Harold's face. 'I'm getting sick of this. Can't you understand me, you stupid little man? I'm offering you two thousand pounds for a pile of junk on four wheels. *How much more can you possibly want?*'

'Let me go!' Harold pleaded, presumably wondering how his quiet night had degenerated into a face-to-face confrontation with a maniac. He looked as if he expected to die.

Martin did something he'd been wanting to do since he'd first climbed into the man's clapped-out car. He shook him, hard. Harold's teeth clattered together. 'Listen-to-me-close-ly,' Martin hissed, rattling Harold with each syllable. 'My-wife-is-in-dan-ger. She-needs-me-to-help-her-and-I-need-your-car-to-get-me-back-to-Cornwall. Un-der-stand?'

He gave Harold one last shake and let go of him.

Harold tottered backwards, tripped and sprawled into the road. He didn't try to get up.

'Put two thousand pounds on to my bill,' Martin said, walking away. He climbed into the Vauxhall, sat down and felt for the keys.

They were not present.

Martin's temper reached boiling point and he began to scream.

Chapter Twenty

James at Black Rock

'KEYS!' someone who sounded vaguely familiar shouted. 'GIVE ME THE KEYS!'

They're in the ignition, for God's sake, just take the damned things and leave me alone, I'm hurt! I cannot give them to you because I cannot move.

'Please!' a stranger replied in a tiny, terrified voice. 'Leave me alone. The car won't go anyway. We both have to walk back to the motel from here. Don't you see?'

Motel? What motel?

'Just give me the keys!' the familiar voice shouted.

Told you where they are. Just take them. I'm broke and I'm probably dead by now. The big black dog got me. He burnt me to death and I can't pick up anything solid any more because I'm a ghost.

The snatches of conversation he seemed to have been hearing for the past billion years faded and James Green's eyes popped open.

For a few moments he knew neither where he was nor what he was doing there. This agreeable state of existence didn't last for long enough, because when James finally remembered he began to feel very uncomfortable indeed.

He had recently been killed by a dog which had dived through his chest and, apparently set him on fire.

This piece of information didn't sound at all right, but he could remember it happening – and in fine detail.

James was no longer certain if he was alive, or if he'd become the ghost he'd been busily claiming to be when he woke up. He was still sitting in the Caddy and he could still feel its seat beneath him – which was a good sign, he thought

– but there surely had to be a dog-sized hole in the centre of his chest.

He was frightened to look.

It took all the courage he had, and some borrowed from thin air, to make himself raise his hands and touch his ribcage, but when he'd done it he was glad he had. Not only was it whole and undamaged, but he had a good solid heartbeat too. It was a little fast, admittedly, but that was hardly surprising after what had happened.

James felt the Cadillac's ignition just in case he really had invited that strange voice to take the keys. He seemed to remember the ignition being on, and the car's engine running when the dog had come through the window, but both were off now.

The keys were present, which was another good thing. James turned them and the car started immediately, which was surely the third and last good thing. He had to be running out of good luck by now. He turned the lights on, half expecting the big black dog to be out there glaring at him and pointing, but the way ahead – as far as he could see – was empty.

He took the torch from the seat beside him and shone it out of the back window. The dog wasn't out there.

Good thing number four, he thought. *Keep it up!*

James shone the torch at the front of his tee-shirt and discovered something else he could add to his collection of ideal happenings: the shirt did not bear the ragged hole he had so fondly imagined was burned through it. It wasn't even scorched.

The result of the equation he'd been running through his head since he'd woken up, now appeared: a black dog had *not* burned its way through his body.

Now he was forced to consider the bad news, first and foremost of which was the item marked: *Then why did I think it had?*

There was no good answer to this question. He'd had an experience that *couldn't* have happened.

You've been acting like a book character, and now you've had a fictitious experience. That isn't very surprising, is it?

But it was surprising. James had, for a few moments back there, lost his grip on reality and finished with a flourish by losing his grip on consciousness too. But it was the reality thing that concerned him; he'd lost consciousness before, but he'd never experienced unreal things.

Unless what happened was *real*, he told himself.

'I think we ought to get ourselves out of here,' he told the car. 'We did promise we'd retreat at the first sign of anything being awry. And I think that first sign has presented itself.'

Reversing back up the steep hill was going to be a bastard but it looked like a better option than continuing. Perhaps S'n'J was right and there *was* some weird connection between the book and this place. It no longer looked as if his mission was going to be quite as simple turning up at Black Rock and threatening S'n'J's ex.

James froze for a moment because now he'd brought Martin to mind, his memory had woken up and gone to work. The familiar voice that had demanded the car keys through his unconsciousness had belonged to Martin. The man had once thrown a fit at Cars Inc. when his Ferrari's new exhaust hadn't arrived on time. And he'd sounded just as irate and unreasonable back then.

Whether that meant that the magic man behind all this was Martin or not, James didn't like to judge. All he knew was that in the garage he'd seemed an inconsequential little man, full of his own importance; but when James had heard him just now his voice had sounded a lot more scary.

Work it all out later, he told himself, looking over his shoulder at the steep hill. *S'n'J wants a live boyfriend not a dead hero. We'll get the police in on it or something. Let's just get out of here.*

He put the Caddy into reverse, put his foot on the brake, released the handbrake and twisted round to look out of the back window.

The reversing lights were not on.

'I don't fucking believe it,' he swore. But as the words left his lips, he already knew he *could* reverse up the track with no lights. It wasn't going to be easy, but it was possible.

James let his foot off the brake. The car's automatic

gearbox held the Cadillac in position just as it was supposed to. James gently applied his foot to the accelerator pedal. And felt a moment of pure terror when what happened next turned out to be the exact opposite of what he had anticipated.

The car, even though it was in reverse, rolled slowly forwards.

James hit the brake, moved the shift into park then put it back into reverse again.

He took his foot off the brake and touched the accelerator.

The car rolled forward.

What made it worse was that this was a physical impossibility. He could live with it if the gearbox had broken. If that had happened the car would naturally roll down the hill when he let the brake off. But the gearbox *wasn't* broken and neither was reverse gear. Somehow it had turned into a forward gear.

He even thought he knew why, but he kept this one at bay. It was impossible and if he allowed himself to voice it, he thought he might go mad. All that mattered was that if the gearbox had magically transposed itself then reverse gear had to be where drive usually was.

James selected drive.

The car, when he let off the brake, went forwards.

He repeated the performance, selecting the gearbox's low gear options – first and second. Both these took the car forwards too.

James' head spun. Nothing had been transposed. What had happened was that reverse had independently turned itself into a forward gear. It defied the laws of physics, but it had happened.

The only way you're going to get out of here is to go right down to the house and turn round on its forecourt. Whatever's inside that house knows that. It made this happen, for God's sake. It knows you're here and it wants you down there. So badly that it's somehow fucked up your gearbox so you can't leave. It's waiting for you down there.

Suddenly James was more frightened than he had ever been

since he was a child. The fear was black and all-consuming. It seemed to be turning his body to jelly.

'What are we going to do?' he asked the car and his voice sounded as if it ought to belong to a frightened four-year-old.

The answer was obvious and it was just as scary as the thought of driving down to the house. He could abandon the car and walk back up the hill.

James found that he didn't particularly want to get out of the car.

The big black dog might be out there lurking somewhere, off the edge of the track. Waiting for him. This time it might kill him. James looked at the crowbar, doubted it would provide any measure of protection at all, then decided he would take it with him anyway.

As he was reaching for the door handle the car began to roll.

James hit the brake pedal.

Which sank gracefully – all the way to the floor – and provided no braking effect whatsoever.

The Caddy was heading towards the edge of the track and picking up speed. His foot still pumping at the dead brake pedal, James grabbed the steering wheel and straightened the car. When it was back on course he yanked the handbrake on.

Nothing happened.

'Bastard!' he shouted, steering the car with one hand while he groped for the gear shift with the other. His hand found the lever and he yanked the car out of drive and forced it into park. This should have been impossible to achieve but it wasn't. It should also have locked up the transmission and stalled the car's engine. Neither of these things happened either.

What did happen was that way off in front and below him – probably at sea level – something flashed. It was white and bright, as if someone had just taken a photograph of him using a powerful flashgun for illumination. James was blinded for a moment, unable to see where he was steering. His reflexes made him hit the brake pedal which sank to the floor again and just as he thought, *We're going off the edge now!* the second thing happened.

The car stopped.

It started again before the after-images of the light had cleared from his vision. This time the car maintained a steady speed of about three miles an hour in spite of the fact that it was going downhill and should have been accelerating.

You aren't driving this car any more, he told himself and touched the accelerator and brake to check this theory. Neither pedal had any effect on the steady speed of the Cadillac.

The car is moving in accordance with someone else's rules. Whoever it is heard you think you were going off the edge and it stopped the car. The flash of light you saw didn't come from a lighthouse or a ship out at sea, it came from the house. S'n'J was right in thinking there was something supernatural going on. The house is haunted.

James let go of the steering wheel and shut his eyes.

He saw the following flash through his eyelids and when he opened them again, the steering wheel was moving of its own accord.

There was now a choice of two from which he had to select. He either stayed right here in the car and let it drive him down to what looked as though it was going to be his death, or he jumped out.

It wasn't difficult to make the choice. If the ghost – or perhaps, the house itself – could wrest control of the car away from him as easily as this, then James and his crowbar were going to be no match for it. He would jump and take his chances.

He picked up the crowbar again and reached for the door handle. This time there was no flash of light and nothing happened to stop him. Inside five seconds he realized why. The thing had foreseen this and had already taken the necessary steps to prevent it happening.

The Caddy's driver's door wouldn't open.

And neither would the passenger door.

James didn't think there was any point in climbing over the seats and trying the back doors.

But there was another way. All he had to do was break the windscreen and climb out through it.

It won't break, he told himself. *You've been sucked into the book just like S'n'J was. You've been sucked in and the story has started to write itself around you just like it did to her. When S'n'J gets her fresh chapter tomorrow she'll be able to read all about what's happening to you now. She'll probably read how you acted like a dumb novel character and got yourself killed like one, too.*

In spite of knowing it wouldn't work, James took the crowbar in both hands, twisted himself away from the windscreen, gritted his teeth and summoned up all the strength he had left.

As he was about to make the swing, the car stopped. James, still tensed and ready to strike, looked around him. The house was now about a hundred yards ahead of him. There was a light burning in one of the upstairs windows – the window where Peter Perfect wove his tales and rewrote reality.

Half-way between the house and the Caddy, something was happening in the air. It looked as if a cloud was spontaneously forming there.

What now? James wondered.

The Cadillac's engine died and the lights went out. James saw the ignition key turn and the light switch move as though he was sharing the car with an invisible driver. He glanced at the door beside him just in time to see the handle move as if that invisible driver was intending to get out of the car. A moment later the door swung open.

If you think I'm getting out now, you're crazy! James thought. He reached for the keys, meaning to start the car again but the moment before his hand made contact, they were snatched from the ignition. For a second they danced in the air in front of his face, jingling. James grabbed at them, missed and followed them with his eyes as they moved towards the open door and then vanished – as if into an invisible pocket.

'*Shit!*' he heard himself protest. At the far edge of his distant mind he realized that all the clichéd reactions to fear he could think of were now taking place within his body: his heart was hammering fit to burst, his limbs were shaking with adrenaline, his bladder and bowels were threatening to purge themselves and his hair was trying hard to stand on end – and probably turning white as it did so.

If he'd somehow walked into a story, he thought, he should soon reach one of those points where all his negative emotions would suddenly become positive ones. He should soon start to feel invincible and charged.

James waited for it to happen.

Unfortunately, in this particular story it seemed the author was giving the good guys no quarter, no helping hand and no special powers. It was just going to be the hero against the house and Peter Perfect.

In other words it's fixed, he thought. *The outcome is known from the start.*

These were not the words he wanted to be ringing in his head when he climbed out of the car and went to meet his doom, but they were the only ones that would come to him. His mind had blanked as far as words of hope went.

James picked up the torch, climbed out of the car, found the edge of the track and carefully made his way along it to the front of the Cadillac where he stopped and looked up at the rapidly coalescing cloud.

There was no reason for a cloud to be there at all – no *natural* reason – which obviously meant that Martin or Peter Perfect or whoever had placed it there. It was too low to be a normal cloud, it was the wrong colour and it seemed to be folding in on itself, getting larger by drawing wisps from its underside and piling them on the top.

James began to walk towards it, recognizing the shape it was taking on. This, when it was finished, was going to be a thundercloud. And he was going to have to pass under it before he could approach the house and whatever lay in wait for him.

He didn't need to wonder what was going to happen to him when he got beneath that cloud. He was going to be struck by lightning.

James took a few more paces towards the cloud – which seemed to be turning brown rather than the black he would have expected for a thunderhead – and then put the crowbar down. Walking underneath it with what amounted to a lightning conductor in his hand didn't seem like a terribly good idea. There was no point in making things any easier for the house and its occupant.

James considered trying to retreat but dismissed the idea. He wouldn't be allowed to go back, that much was certain.

Besides, if he was going to be killed – and he thought there was a very good chance of it – he wanted to be killed going towards the problem, not running away from it. If he was going to die, he was going to die fighting, not running.

There you go, he scorned himself. *You thought the tough words at last. He's probably only just got around to writing them for you!*

'If I get my hands on you, Martin, or Peter Perfect or whoever you are, I'm going to make you regret what you've done,' he said aloud and began to walk towards Black Rock.

The cloud flashed, not with searing lightning light, but with an angry red colour that looked like molten metal.

James stopped and stared up at it. *What the fuck is that?* he asked himself.

Whatever it was, it didn't look very inviting.

It didn't look terribly large either, which gave him a little more hope than he'd anticipated. It wasn't going to take very long to pass beneath it if he ran.

That's what it wants you to think, he told himself. *That's exactly what S'n'J meant about not acting like a book hero. You can't run faster than lightning, can you?*

But he might not *have* to run that fast. He thought there was a pretty good chance that whoever was controlling this cloud would have to target him first, and as everyone knew, a rapidly moving target was a lot harder to hit than a static one.

I've got rubber soled shoes on anyway! he thought, grinning bitterly.

James took a deep breath, glanced around him and then went for broke.

The cloud didn't burst until James was exactly half-way under it.

And when the storm began James realized what the ghost dog had been doing when it had jumped through him. It hadn't been trying to kill him, it had been trying to *warn* him.

Because what happened in the sky above James was not the thunderstorm he had anticipated.

It was something much worse.

Chapter Twenty-one

Hijacking Harold

Screaming, Martin got out of Harold's car again. 'KEYS!' he shouted. 'GIVE ME THE KEYS!'

Harold was on his feet by now. '*Please!*' he said in a tiny, terrified voice. 'Leave me alone. The car won't go anyway. We both have to walk back to the motel from here. Don't you see?'

'Just give me the keys!' Martin shouted.

Harold took the keys from his pocket and held them out at arm's length, shaking his head. 'It won't work,' he said as Martin snatched them away from him. 'There's something going on.'

'Do you think I don't *know* there's something going on?' Martin yelled, not yet wondering how Harold had reached this odd conclusion.

He threw himself back into the Vauxhall, put the keys in, twisted them and when nothing happened, suddenly remembered what Harold had just said: *We both have to walk back to the motel from here.*

He flew out of the car, grabbed hold of Harold and demanded that he tell him everything he knew about this.

'Words,' Harold said. 'A string of words just lit up in my mind. They said, "The car won't start and now you're both going to have to walk back to the motel." That's it. I don't know any more. It was like being spoken to by God. I think I ought to go back to the motel and just stay there. That's what it wants, I think. I'm frightened now. I don't really want you to come. That thing might come back with you. I don't want it indoors.'

'Thing?' Martin asked. 'What *thing*?'

'The voice. It isn't God though, is it?' Harold added in a voice that was verging on the hysterical. 'I think you know what it is, and it isn't God. It's a *ghost*, isn't it? You're being haunted by a *ghost*.'

'Don't be silly,' Martin replied and was surprised by the amount of disdain he'd managed to work into his reply. 'There are no such things as ghosts.'

'How do you explain all this then?' Harold asked petulantly, waving at the two dead cars.

'Bad luck, that's all,' Martin said. 'Nothing's haunting me. Or you. You're just stressed. I'm sorry I got so upset with you. It looks like I'm stuck here, whatever the reason. I'd like to come back with you, but I'll understand if you'd rather I didn't.'

Harold shook his head. 'I don't like it,' he said. 'I don't know whether it will be worse if I let you come back, or if I tell you not to. It wants you back in the motel. I *felt* that. But if you come back it might come too. And if you don't, it might be upset with me. I don't want any ghosts under my roof.'

'Don't be stupid, Harold,' Martin said, 'there's nothing here for me to bring back with me. There isn't a ghost.'

Harold nodded. 'There is,' he said. 'It might not be here now, but it was a few moments ago. There was something going on just now. I could feel it in the air. It was like there was a struggle. It's stopped now and I'm glad about that, but it might start again. And if it starts in the motel, it might decide it likes it there. For all I know you might be trying to pass it off on me. Y'know, give me your ghost. Do you know what I mean?'

Martin nodded. 'Yeah, I do, but you're barking up the wrong tree. I don't have a ghost to give away. Or even one to keep. I just got a little frazzled. I've been on the go since early yesterday and I get up here for an appointment, phone the wife, and she's in trouble. She wants me back in Bude. Pronto. And the car won't start. I just threw a cog. I'm desperate to get back to her, that's all. There are no ghosts involved.'

Harold nodded. 'Fair enough,' he said and tailed off.

Martin found a smile for him. It hurt him to arrange his face in this way for the motel owner, but he managed it.

Harold grimaced in return. He looked as if he was trying hard to summon the courage to say something else. Finally he spoke. 'As I said, fair enough. Except that you don't have a wife, do you?'

'Yes I *do*!' Martin snapped.

Harold shook his head. 'Divorced. Or nearly. And she lives in London, not Bude. You don't have anyone down in Bude.'

Martin gritted his teeth. 'OK, what else did this voice tell you about me?'

'Nothing,' Harold said quickly.

'It said I was dangerous, didn't it?' Martin said. 'It said I had to be kept away from Bude, didn't it?'

Harold's face took on an agonized expression. He suddenly looked like a man suffering from a terrible toothache.

Or as if someone somewhere is drilling into his brain, Martin thought. Impossible as it seemed, Peter Perfect had located Harold and was manipulating his mind, even as Martin waited for a reply.

Harold sobbed. 'I-I don't know what's happening. Everything keeps ch-ch-ch-changing ... and it's like the whole world keeps sweeping through me. As if it's drawing to a point, puh-passing th-through my body and expanding again be-hind me. And every time it happens I can remember stuff that I shouldn't be able tuh-to. Stuff I know that I never knew before. It's like someone is filling me up with a lot of memories. I know they're not mine, but they seem as if they ought to buh-be.'

Martin thought that down in Tintagel light was probably flashing from a certain upstairs window of a certain house each time Harold received a fresh set of spurious memories.

That's what happens when you rewrite a character carelessly, Martin realized.

It was a bad joke. And the joke wasn't being played on Harold to benefit the perpetrator, it was being done to frighten Martin. Because, as Martin well knew, certain things often happened when he sent a writer away to revise a book. The hurried reconstruction of a character would often lead to that character knowing things that he or she could no longer know. A careless author might well remove the passages where their character found out certain pieces of information, but inadvertently leave those snippets of knowledge in the character's mind. Or that author might equally inadvertently put memories *into* a character's mind without showing they belonged there.

And since Peter Perfect didn't strike Martin as an author who would be the least bit careless, he had to be doing this to Harold as a demonstration of the extent of his own power. Not to Harold, but to Martin.

'Forget all the shit you think you know,' Martin advised the man. 'None of it adds up and none of it is worth a wank on a wet Sunday. Just keep your mind empty. This'll stop happening to you as soon as I'm out of your hair. We'll walk back to the motel and I'll get on the phone, get myself a taxi and leave. You'll go to sleep and when you wake up in the morning you'll wonder what all the fuss was about.'

'There *is* a ghost, isn't there?' Harold insisted.

Martin nodded. Peter Perfect was either going to turn out to be a ghost, or a minor god. It didn't really matter *what* you called him. All that mattered was his weak point.

And like almost every author Martin had met in all his years as an editor, Peter Perfect's Achilles heel was going to turn out to be his ego. The pen-name he'd chosen summed it up quite succinctly.

The trouble with many fiction writers, Martin knew, was that they got so used to playing God and presiding over their imaginary universes, that they eventually began to believe they had god-like qualities. Hubris was the magic word. Arrogant pride in themselves and their infallibility. Pride, as any old Joe Soap would be pleased to tell you, comes before a fall.

Like many writers before him, Peter Perfect wasn't quite as perfect as he believed. All it took to prove that, was one sharp-eyed editor: Martin Louis Dinsey.

Who had already spotted some gaping holes in the Peter Perfect's plot.

The first was that Mr Perfect could not alter the past and

edit Martin out of his story. And the second – the most glaring gap in the seamless picture Perfect was trying to present – was that he couldn't even directly affect Martin. If he'd been able to, he would have done so. Mr Perfect might be able to stop the car running, and he might be able to change Harold's memories, but there was something that prevented his doing this to Martin.

And Martin thought he knew what this might be.

'She used to be your lover,' Harold suddenly said.

Martin looked up from the wet pavement. 'Yep. You hit the nail right on the head that time,' he said, and looked away again.

'You call her Essenjay, and her friends call her Drezy, but her real name is Sarah-Jane Dresden.'

'Right,' Martin said. He glanced up again, but Harold was staring into the distance, his eyes wide open, his expression rapt. A watery smile twitched at the edges of his mouth. It looked as if there was a part of Harold that was actually enjoying this.

You should understand how that could happen, Martin told himself. *You should understand that better than most people. People love fiction – they enjoy falling into stories and that's exactly what Harold is doing – falling into the story that's being delivered to him. And the best part about it is, that he isn't even having to bother to read the words. It's coming to him effortlessly. Harold's actually having a story woven around him.*

And that was the key, Martin thought, to why Peter Perfect couldn't directly affect Martin Louis Dinsey. He had long since lost his capacity to be unreservedly suckered by a story. These days a story had to prove itself to him before he found himself drawn into it. And any little flaw in it would throw him back out again, scowling. Unlike Essenjay, who only had to read about two sentences before she was sucked right in and who would stay locked there until the end, not worrying about any inconsistencies, Martin read like an aeronautical engineer: carefully looking for hairline cracks in the structure.

Even authors who committed the sin of hubris realized that no matter how hard they tried, some people would pigheadedly refuse to be drawn in, and Martin thought that Peter Perfect had him down as one of this type.

He also thought that Mr Perfect had correctly estimated that Essenjay (and Harold, too, by the look of him) belonged to that group of readers who would be captivated by even the flimsiest rendering of a story.

This wasn't much help as far as discovering what Peter Perfect intended to do to Essenjay, but it did give Martin a little more confidence. He *would* get back to Bude before it got too late to save Essenjay and he *would* prevail. And if it came down to violence, Martin knew he could handle that too. 'I'm no pushover,' he muttered darkly.

'It's going to be too late,' Harold muttered. 'By the time you get there, *if* you get there – and I don't think you will – she'll be long gone. He'll have her by then.'

'I don't think so,' Martin said, squinting through the rain at Harold. 'I don't think he can put every taxi and train in York out of commission, or even latch himself on their drivers. He has limitations and I know what they are.'

'You won't stop him taking her though,' Harold said, 'because he won't actually *be* taking her. She'll be invited to go and she'll go of her own accord.' Harold stopped talking and walked away, splashing through the rain like a competition walker, his hips wiggling, his elbows working furiously.

Martin ran a few paces, caught him up and half-walked, half-jogged along beside him. 'You sound a little concerned,' he said.

Harold didn't reply.

'You listening, Harold? Well it doesn't matter if you aren't, I suppose, because you're not here, are you? I haven't been talking to Harold, whatever-his-name-is for some time now, have I? Fe, fi, fo, fum, I smell a case of author intrusion here.

'Don't you know, Mister Perfect, that you're supposed to let your characters speak for themselves? It is *you* out there somewhere having this conversation with me, Peter, isn't it? You just couldn't resist stepping into your story to straighten things out a bit, could you? To lay down the law. I wouldn't let one of *my* authors do that, but then, *my* authors get to see their books in print. Is that what this is all about, Peter? Did

I once turn down one of your books and get you mad at me? Is it revenge? You're going to hurt Essenjay to get at me, aren't you? Because you haven't the courage to get at me direct.'

Harold didn't reply, but the edges of the ice block in Martin's brain flickered with red light.

'Yeah, yeah, you're going to show me a picture now, to frighten me away. It won't work, Peter Whoever-you-are. Whatever you are. I'm coming to take Essenjay away from you, and you know you can't stop me.'

'Then come,' Harold said.

And in Martin's mind's eye, the ice block flared with a brilliant red light.

It hurt. Badly. Spikes of ice-cream pain drove down his optic nerves and into his brain. The blinding light only lasted for a few seconds but it left him feeling as though he'd spent the last ten minutes staring at the business end of an arc-welder. Huge puce and purple after-images flared across his retinas.

'If that's the best you can do, you're in trouble, you bastard!' he called after Harold who was striding ahead.

Harold, apparently surrounded by swathes of bursting maroon light, stopped and turned. 'Try this then,' he called. 'This is what happens to unwelcome visitors.'

Afterwards Martin would never be sure whether he'd actually heard the sound that followed this statement or if he'd just imagined it. It seemed to be an introductory flourish and it sounded like someone running their fingers across the strings of a harp. It was the kind of noise you would expect to hear from a magic wand used to enchant someone.

It lasted for less than a second and as soon as it ceased, the ice block in Martin's head lit up and began to show him the image of Black Rock he'd seen earlier. The front aspect of the building. Seen by moonlight from a distance. There was no light from the upstairs window, but there was a double pool of illumination shining on the track that ran down the hill to the rock.

Headlights, Martin thought, and watched as they drew slowly closer to Black Rock's entrance.

The scene looked as though it was happening in real-time. It was like watching a live broadcast. For a few seconds Martin couldn't see the car itself because it was out of shot. Whoever was behind the wheel was a stranger to the house because he or she was driving very carefully. Martin thought that the car's driver might just turn out to be Essenjay, dressed in a transparent white dress. She was going to be naked beneath it, he knew, and when she got out of her car and the breeze flattened that dress against her body, he would catch glimpses of the milky-white, marble-smooth flesh that lay beneath.

What are you, a fucking Mills & Boon editor? he asked himself.

Then he forgot the thought because the car that rolled into view was not Essenjay's, it was a big beaten-up American thing that might well have started its days as a Cadillac Eldorado. It had squishy suspension and its wings bounced gracefully as the wheels found each indentation in the track.

The image was unbelievably crisp. As the car rolled slowly towards the house, Martin had time to take in the fine detail. Moonlight shimmered on the dark flat sea that surrounded the rock on which the house stood; there were a few traceries of high cirrus cloud in the sky – the kind called 'mare's-tails' – and the stunted hedge that marked the house's border leaned spiny wooden fingers out towards the land, as if grasping for it.

While this went on inside Martin's viewfinder, Harold stood facing him, about a hundred yards ahead. Harold wasn't moving, so Martin ignored him. The outside world now seemed much less substantial than what he could see in his head.

As Martin watched the Cadillac creep forward, there was a disturbance in the air about fifty feet ahead of it, and thirty or forty feet above it. There was barely anything to see: whatever was taking place was visible only because it somehow distorted the night sky behind it. It was similar to looking through a heat-haze except the stars above and behind the disturbance shone purple and seemed to be moving like fireflies.

The car stopped almost immediately, so Martin assumed the driver had also seen what was happening. Either that, or the car's engine had cut out – it was impossible to tell without sound. Martin thought it probably *was* the engine. Peter Perfect seemed to have a way with cars.

He watched the odd patch of air as he waited for the car's driver to get out. It was expanding. Martin was pretty certain it had been almost spherical when it had appeared, but now it was flattening and spreading, moving very slowly.

The car's headlights went out.

Even before it began to take on colour, Martin was almost sure what the disturbance would turn out to be. He could tell by the way it was spreading and building up in the middle.

It was going to be a thundercloud.

Peter Perfect was going to subject the occupant of the car to a lightning strike.

The cloud began to show its colours even as Martin realized this. It was not the dark and angry hue of a thundercloud at all, but an ugly shade of dirty brown, like smoke from a chemical fire. Around its edges, wisps swirled outwards and were drawn up and back in, folding themselves over and becoming more dense as they moved. The cloud seemed to be making itself bigger by stealing streams from the bottom of itself and piling them back on the top. And impossible as it looked, it was working. The cloud was soon almost the same size as the house and so dense that Martin could no longer see through it. The top of it coalesced into the anvil shape normally seen on a thunder cloud, and then, just as Martin expected to see the first strike of lightning, the movement ceased. The brown cloud hung in the sky like a solid object. No stray wisps of vapour trailed away from it and it didn't float towards the car or the house but stayed exactly where it was, as though waiting.

The door of the Cadillac finally opened.

Martin was relieved to see that it was a man who got out, rather than Essenjay. He looked vaguely familiar, and Martin thought that he ought to recognize him: mid-twenties, tall and good-looking. He moved like someone who kept fit, and his bare arms were muscular and sinewy.

And judging from what he has in his hand, he's going to die, Martin noted.

That much was obvious. It wasn't the heavy-duty torch in his left hand that was going to kill him, it was the jemmy he held in his right.

If Martin was correct in his assumption about the cloud being a thunderhead, and the reason for it being there, this kid was going to wake up on a mortuary slab, fried to a crisp.

Put the fucking crowbar down, Martin thought. *Don't you know a thundercloud when you see one? Don't make it easy for him, you drip!*

Judging from the jemmy, it looked as if the guy had come with a score to settle. And by the look of the weather conditions, Peter Perfect had been expecting him.

Who the hell are you? Martin wondered looking at the man's moonlit face as he glanced back towards his car. His features looked very familiar indeed. *I know you, don't I?* Martin asked the image.

The man turned back to face the house and looked up at the cloud.

Leave it! Martin thought. *Just get outta there. He knows you're coming and he intends to kill you!* He tried telepathically to broadcast this to the man. If this scene was really happening, he ought to be able to do that. Peter Perfect had contacted *him* telepathically, and if he was able to see a real-life image of what was happening now, he was doing so by telepathy. And if it worked one way, it ought to work the other way too.

Except that it didn't.

Martin thought the words to the man again, half expecting to see the guy's head tilt to one side in response. This did not happen.

Go away, he's getting ready to zap you! Martin mentally shouted.

The man gave a little shrug, shook his head as if he'd imagined something and began to walk towards the dark brown thunderhead.

I can't believe this, Martin told himself. *I'm standing here in the pouring rain staring at Harold while I visualize a man*

*doing something hundreds of miles away and . . . and I can't
intervene!*

'We'd better get going,' Harold announced in a worried
voice.

He let go of you then, Harry, did he? Martin thought. *He
finally gave you your mind back.*

'I'll catch you up!' he called aloud.

Martin watched Harold turn and hurry away through the
rain while, in his mind's eye he simultaneously watched the
other man walking slowly towards Black Rock.

And suddenly he remembered where he knew him from. It
was the guy from Cars Inc., the tyre and exhaust centre in
Bude. Martin had been there on several occasions to get tyres
for the Dino. They'd had to order them specially. The guy
down there about to get zapped by a bolt of lightning was
one of the fitters who drooled over the Ferrari each time he
took it in. Martin felt his name on the tip of his tongue.

James, he told himself. That's it. *What the fuck is* he *doing
there?*

James looked up at the cloud, then at the crowbar. Then
he set the crowbar down on the ground. Apparently he'd just
had the thought that Martin had been having for him for the
last couple of minutes.

Good boy! Martin thought. *But it can still get you. You're
going to be the tallest thing passing under that cloud when
the lightning strikes and you'll be the easiest path to earth.
What you don't know about lightning that I do, is that it
isn't as simple as a flash of power hacking down from the
sky. The earth acts as one potential electrical pole and the
cloud acts as its opposite. And even if Peter Perfect isn't
guiding the outcome, you're going to be putting the earth's
pole about six feet closer to the cloud. If there is a lightning
strike it cannot miss you. So don't fucking well walk anywhere near that cloud!*

James hesitated for a few moments.

And then, to Martin's dismay, he marched towards Black
Rock.

Goodbye, James, Martin thought.

When James got to the cloud's perimeter, light flashed, but

it was an undefined light within the cloud rather than a bolt of raw power, and instead of being white like lightning, it was the deep angry red of molten metal.

It lit again, and this time the red glow moved, slowly at first. It began to expand as if it was seeping into every molecule of the brown cloud that contained it. The movement quickly accelerated. Within two seconds the cloud was seething with something that looked very hot and very angry and extremely anxious to escape.

I don't know what the fuck it is but that's not lightning waiting to happen! Martin thought. *For Christ's sake James, move it!*

And as James began to run, not back towards his car, but towards the entrance of Black Rock, the boiling cloud began to rain.

Except that what fell from it was not droplets of water.

It was fire.

It fell in hundreds of bright red, fist-sized clumps that spiralled down slowly on whickering tails of flame. When the clumps hit the ground they burst like balloons and sprayed out fire which ran as if it was liquid.

It's like napalm! Martin thought crazily. *It's a rain of fucking fire! Give that ghost a medal for inventiveness!*

James was serpentining now. So far nothing had hit him, but it soon would. He wasn't going to stay alive long in that lot. It must be like trying to dodge hailstones. Except that if a hailstone hit you, it wasn't going to burst and shower you with burning liquid. Any second now, one of those parcels of fire was going to hit James on the head or shoulder and then it'd be *Game Over*.

Martin knew that it wouldn't be long. James was rapidly running out of places to go. Most of the ground beneath the cloud was ablaze and there seemed to be a solid wall of fire between him and Black Rock's gate. What air there was left had to be hot enough to scald his lungs.

Any second now, Martin predicted, *James is going to keel over into one of those burning pools and you'll have the pleasure of watching his flesh peel away from his bones like melting plastic.*

James glanced up, saw a huge teardrop of fire spiralling down towards him and leapt from his tiny island of safety to another, close by. But Martin concluded that this clump of flame apparently had James' full name, and probably his address too, written on it because when James jumped from beneath it, it winked out of existence and winked back in again over the spot James had moved to.

It looked as if someone had suddenly rubbed it out and re-drawn it again in a better position. Or they'd crossed it out and rewritten it.

'That isn't fair!' Martin complained aloud. 'That's fucking *cheating*!'

But cheating or not, it had happened.

James watched the fireball descending, waited until the last second, and leapt back to where he had been before.

This time, Peter Perfect wasn't quick enough to rewrite the scene to suit himself. The fire hit the empty ground and exploded into a shower of bead-sized fragments . . . some of which headed directly towards James.

He saw them coming and leapt again, but not quite quickly enough. Two tiny beads fell on the right shoulder of his tee-shirt.

As James spun around, mouth open in a scream of agony, Martin was glad that there was no sound accompanying the images.

James batted at his shoulder sending sparks flying, realized it wasn't going to work and tore the shirt right off. The flame seemed to be confined to the material. James had a large burn on his shoulder, but at least his skin wasn't on fire.

For all the difference that's *going to make*, Martin thought bitterly as James began to leap again – towards Black Rock. *At best, James has five minutes to live.*

Ten seconds later, Martin realized he'd been wildly opti-mistic in his estimate of how long James would last.

Behind the dirty brown fire-cloud, Peter Perfect sat in his haunted house clattering the keys of his computer (or perhaps waving a wand) in order to alter reality. And he did this,

Martin would later acknowledge, by making a single simple addition to the storyline.

He wrote in an obstacle that James couldn't see.

Martin didn't see it either. What happened was that the beleaguered James leapt towards a clear spot just ahead of the unbroken wall of fire between him and the house and, although there was nothing on the ground which could have tripped him, suddenly he was falling forwards. Towards that wall of fire.

Martin could barely believe it. Although his chosen patch of ground was clear, James appeared to land right in front of something the size of a steamer trunk. After each previous jump it had taken him a single forwards pace to check his momentum. This time, the pace couldn't be taken because both his feet had jammed against that invisible thing. The result was that James flew over the top of the obstruction and shot straight into the wall of fire.

Martin looked at the spot where James had vanished, half expecting him to dart back out of the flame looking pretty much like the human torch he'd read about in American comics when he was a kid.

This did not happen.

A few moments later, the vision began to fade.

Finally there was just the huge empty ice block floating in his mind's eye, and good old Harold standing a hundred yards ahead of him in the centre of the road.

'What happened?' Harold called in a shaky voice. 'I could smell burning!'

'Nothing to worry you,' Martin said bitterly.

'You aren't going to bring that *thing* back to the motel with you, are you?' Harold shouted, 'Because if you are, I'm not letting you come.'

I've just watched someone burn to death and here's Harold laying down conditions, Martin thought.

He gritted his teeth. 'How many times do I have to tell you?' he shouted back. 'None of this has anything to do with you. You're safe.'

'Promise?'

'Don't be childish, Harold.'

'Do you *promise*?'

'Cross my heart and hope to fucking well die!' Martin seethed, wishing the man was nearer so he could take him by the neck and shake him gently until he stopped bleating.

That's a wish I can grant you, the voice said inside his mind. *Just come on down to Black Rock and I'll show you a real good time.*

'What?' Harold said. 'What was that? I heard *it* again.' He turned and began speed-walking again. He got so far ahead that he could no longer be seen and when Martin turned into the drive, he fully expected the door to be closed and locked against him.

But there was Harold, standing just inside the open reception door, waiting.

There is *a God, after all*, Martin thought bemusedly.

'My wife has a car too,' Harold said as Martin entered. 'If it starts you can borrow it. It's only an old Mini, but it's never failed us yet. If you wait here, I'll get the keys.'

He wants you out of here as soon as possible, Martin told himself and then added, *You and me both, Harold*. During the walk back from the Dino he'd had thoughts about James' presence at Black Rock, and they worried him. Had he gone there at the behest of Essenjay? Was he, too, trying to rescue her?

Martin thought that Peter Perfect wanted him to believe the latter scenario, so he refused to do it. Perfect didn't have Essenjay yet. If he did, there wouldn't be any point in his keeping Martin away. So James had probably gone there because Essenjay had been worried about the place and had asked him to.

How James and Essenjay were connected was patently obvious. They were connected by the genitalia. Essenjay evidently hadn't wasted any time missing her old lover, she'd gone straight out and got a new one. Martin might have felt a very large measure of jealousy if it hadn't been for the fact that he'd just watched James die. For which reason, all he felt towards the man was pity.

His feelings towards Essenjay, however, were ambivalent. James had admittedly had quite a physique, but Martin would have expected more from Essenjay. She had apparently lowered her sights since his day. It hurt him to imagine her riding this tyre and exhaust fitter like a racehorse and he wanted to punish her for that, but he still felt an oddly aching kind of love. It was as if he wanted to hold her tenderly and beat her black and blue at the same time.

How he felt, however, was not the important thing. That could be worked out later. The important thing was that Essenjay needed rescuing and her chosen rescuer had fallen at the first fence. Which meant that Martin was now her only hope.

And if he got to her before Peter Perfect, everything was going to be plain sailing.

'Here we go,' Harold said, dripping his way back across the lobby and dangling a set of keys. 'If this doesn't get you out of here, then . . . then . . .'

'Nothing will?' Martin suggested.

Harold shrugged, 'Whatever,' he said, opening the front door.

Mrs Harold's Mini turned out to be exactly as Martin had anticipated: unroadworthy. He didn't care a great deal. If, at that moment, someone had offered him a rusty bicycle with flat tyres he would have accepted it gladly.

As long as it runs . . . he thought.

Harold opened the driver's door of the Mini and got in.

Martin noticed the – fairly deep – pool of water Harold's feet were now resting in and didn't care about this either. He had a good feeling about this car. This car was going to start. And it would continue to run. Martin *knew* this. Like a character from a book, he could *feel* it, in his very bones.

Harold turned the ignition on. Warning lights lit. He twisted the key. The engine didn't so much burst into life, it woke up; smoothly and gradually.

'Sounds OK,' Martin said.

'Been looked after,' Harold replied. 'Mechanically, anyway.'

He gunned the engine, let it settle, then climbed out. The Mini idled away happily.

'All yours,' Harold said, looking very relieved indeed. He

motioned towards the driver's seat, an eager expression on his face.

Anything to get me out of here, Martin thought. He thanked Harold, assured him that the car would be returned undamaged and got in.

The engine didn't fail until he'd selected first gear and let out the clutch.

'Not enough revs,' Harold advised. 'Put your foot down harder.'

Martin turned the key.

The engine didn't start.

Martin suddenly reached the end of his tether. 'Oh *fuck this*!' he screamed.

Harold leaned in through the open window. 'Let me try,' he said.

Martin climbed out, and while Harold got back into the Mini, he searched his right-hand trouser pocket. He'd had an idea. *A very good idea it is too*, he told himself, but this congratulatory statement lacked any conviction at all. It was an exceedingly *lousy* idea, but it was all he had so he clung to it.

Amongst all the junk in that right-hand trouser pocket was a weapon with which, if he could find it, he could put things back on the right track.

Harold turned the key and the car started.

'Open the passenger door,' Martin said. 'I want to see if the car stops when I'm in it.'

Martin went to the far side of the car, frantically searching his pocket. And there it was, underneath the Colibri lighter he'd stolen from Lulu Kaminsky to teach her a lesson. Kaminsky had gone down the tube – literally – without ever knowing what had happened to the gem-encrusted lighter.

The weapon – also stolen, but from Essenjay this time and unintentionally – was a Swiss Army knife. Except that it wasn't what most people envisaged when they thought of a Swiss Army knife. This wasn't one of those great fat things with a blade for every purpose but one of the tiny ones people sometimes put on their key-rings. It had a nail-file in it and a knife blade which was barely an inch and a half long. There was a minute pair of scissors mounted in the other side, but it was the knife blade Martin was interested in.

He didn't think that it was going to look very convincing at all, but he was desperate and he didn't think Harold would need too much convincing.

Martin opened the tiny knife blade and got into the car.

The engine didn't stop.

That's something, Martin told himself.

'It's going to be OK now,' Harold said, as though desperately trying to convince himself. 'It's warmed up a bit. It *didn't* stop because you got in it.'

Yeah, but it'll stop when I get behind the wheel, Martin thought. *And I'm not going to allow that to happen.*

'Just put her in gear and ease her forward a little way,' he said, 'so that we can prove she doesn't stop when you try to drive her.'

Harold glanced over at him, questioningly. The word *suspicion* might as well have been written all over his face. 'You try it,' he said, and reached for the door handle.

Martin grabbed his left arm and pulled him back. 'You try it first,' he said, trying to summon up a smile that would look a little like a shark that's just spotted its dinner.

The expression he attained felt as if it ought to look hilarious, but it worked on Harold anyway.

'OK,' Harold said and sighed.

When he put the Mini in gear and let out the clutch, the car rolled forward exactly as cars should. Harold brought it to a standstill, took it out of gear, turned to Martin, and asked, 'How's that?'

'Not out, I'd say,' Martin said, still trying to grin his horrible grin.

Harold now began to look extremely worried. Martin knew why. He was sitting less than a foot away from a man he'd first thought was haunted, and now thought to be deranged as well. He thought that he was about to be murdered so the madman wouldn't have to bother returning his wife's car.

And like almost no one in real life did when presented with something that bothered them, Harold performed a literary cliché. Like Billy Bunter before him, he blinked. Several times. In quick succession.

'What?' he said when he'd finished blinking.

'Gosh! Not out, old bean, as they say in jolly old cricket,' Martin said pointedly in case he was talking to Peter Perfect again. He didn't think so, but Harold hadn't acted like this before.

'I'm going,' Harold said as though he'd suddenly made up his mind and there wasn't a second to lose. 'Take the car.'

'That's what I meant,' Martin said, laying a restraining hand on his arm. 'Not out. You. You're not out.'

'I don't quite understand you,' Harold said with a distinct trace of hysteria in his voice.

Martin nodded. 'Yes, you do,' he said. 'When I try to drive the car, it stops. When you drive it, it doesn't. Therefore, you are going to drive me back to Bude.'

'I can't,' Harold said.

'Why not?'

'My motel.'

'It'll wait until tomorrow. You'll be back by lunchtime if we leave now. Your wife will look after things, I'm sure.'

'But I don't want to go,' he complained.

'Nothing will happen to you. I'll pay you. Handsomely.'

Harold shook his head. 'No, I'm getting out now,' he said. He tore his arm away from Martin's grasp and snatched at the door handle. The door began to open and Harold moved towards it, seemingly pouring out of the opening while it was still only a few inches wide.

Martin saw red. He was very accomplished at losing his temper, but this time he surprised himself by acting violently.

The tiny Swiss Army knife was clutched in the hand Harold had just shaken away from his arm. Harold hadn't noticed the blade protruding from between Martin's forefinger and thumb and Martin hadn't yet been ready to threaten him with it.

But suddenly his hand was holding the knife in the right position to strike and Martin lashed out with it.

The tiny blade caught the back of Harold's left hand and skated across it. It all happened in a blur, and afterwards

Martin had the feeling that Peter Perfect wasn't the only one who could change reality at a stroke. He seemed to have accomplished much the same thing.

Harold was now sitting upright in his seat staring in horror at the wound on the back of his hand. Blood was welling up from it and dripping off its edges into his lap.

A part of Martin (the civilized part, he assumed) was horrified at what he'd done and another part was grinning wildly. The second part apparently had control of his facial muscles because that inner grin had communicated itself to his face. The sum total of the feeling was power. Martin had wielded quite a lot of power for a long time now, but intellectually rather than physically. Physical power had quite a lot going for it, he distantly decided.

'Shut the door,' he told Harold and was delighted when the man complied.

'You cut me,' Harold said in a small voice.

'And I'll cut you again if you don't start driving me towards Cornwall,' Martin said.

'But I'm hurt! I'm bleeding!' Harold whined.

'It's just a small cut,' Martin said. 'You're not going to die. Your tendons aren't severed and your veins and arteries are intact. Give me your hand.'

'What are you going to do?' Harold cried.

'Look at it and see how bad it is, for Christ's sake!' Martin spat. 'Now give it to me or I'll make it worse!'

Harold reluctantly gave his left hand to Martin who dabbed at it with his handkerchief. The cut, Martin was distantly disappointed to discover, was little more than a scratch. The army knife evidently hadn't been as sharp as he'd thought. There wasn't any real damage. Martin bound his handkerchief around Harold's hand and told Harold that he could expect to live.

'Can I go now?' Harold asked, sounding as if he expected the answer to be negative.

Martin didn't disappoint him. He shook his head.

'But I can't drive the car like this,' Harold said, holding up his hand like a dog would give its paw.

'You'd better be able to,' Martin said. He waved the blade

of the Swiss Army knife in front of Harold's face and added, 'Or I'll kill you.'

Martin privately doubted that it would be possible to kill someone with a knife blade the size of the one he was waving, short of putting it through an eye socket and pushing into the brain. And even that sounded unlikely. You could probably stab someone all day with the knife and they'd survive.

This thought didn't seem to occur to Harold, however, but there was no good reason for it to. Harold might not have been in fear for his life, but he certainly didn't want any knife blade, no matter how tiny, inserted into any part of his body.

Martin reached over and squeezed Harold's left bicep, digging his fingers into the inside of the man's arm. 'There's an artery that runs down here,' he explained, 'It's called the brachial artery and right where I'm squeezing it's close to the surface. Now I might not be able to hit any of your vital organs with a knife this small, and I might not even be able to hit your brachial artery, but I'll certainly be able to take out your eyes. So don't cause me any trouble. OK?'

Harold nodded.

'Then drive us away.'

'I don't think I can. I'm shaking.'

'Your eyes, Harold,' Martin said, making carving motions with the knife.

Harold drove.

Chapter Twenty-two

An Editor Calls

During the night things changed for Sarah-Jane Dresden.

She was aware of this when she awoke the following morning with a filthy grin fixed to her face. Things *had* changed – and for once in her life she felt as if they had done so for the better.

S'n'J lay in bed stretching and yawning and feeling very pleased with herself indeed. And very horny too.

She lay in bed for a while remembering last evening and planning what would take place when she dragged James back here tonight. During her relationship with Martin she'd developed a lengthy list of sexual fantasies that'd had to remain fantasies because Martin wasn't receptive to them. James, she thought, would be a lot more interested . . .

I think you'd better go and throw yourself into a cold shower, my girl! she told herself, giggling. *If you lie here playing with yourself you're going to be late for your first appointment at the Barnstaple Bookshop and then you'll be late all day.*

Friday wasn't a particularly taxing day – S'n'J had arranged it that way because in the summer on a Friday the traffic was normally pretty heavy. She only had another three calls to make after Barnstaple: the Ilfracombe Bookshop, the Mole and Haggis in Torrington and Mackenzie Dye Booksellers in Bideford. She was usually back here by five-thirty on Fridays – which was a distinct improvement on the six or even seven o'clock she got home on other days.

S'n'J threw the sheets off her and padded to the bathroom, the big sappy grin still affixed to her face. This morning, it didn't seem to want to go away.

You're smitten, she told herself, grinning. *You've fallen in love!*

It wasn't until she was in the shower – under a hot jet of water rather than cold because she liked the warm, randy feeling she'd woken up with and didn't want to kill it off – that she remembered *Black Rock*.

She thought of it the moment someone outside began to hammer on the front door as though their life depended on it. A stiletto of fear pricked the pit of her stomach.

Don't let it be a fresh chapter! she thought, turning off the shower and stepping dripping on to the bathroom carpet. *I don't want my day ruined this early on.*

She wrapped herself in a big towel and promised herself that if she found another buff A4 envelope on the mat she would bin it without opening it. Tonight she intended to turn one or two of her fantasies into reality and she wasn't going to let anything stop her.

There was no envelope waiting for her, only the key that James had posted back through the letter box when he'd locked her in last night. Whatever *was* waiting for her was still on the far side of the door, but if she didn't hurry up and open it, this wasn't going to remain the case for very long. Whoever it was out there had begun to hammer on the door again and they wanted to be let in in a hurry.

'Let me in, Drezy! For Christ's sake! I'm in big trouble. Quick, open the door!'

In total disbelief, S'n'J unlocked the door and stood back.

The door flew open and banged on the wall.

And Janie Sanderson ran in and threw herself into S'n'J's arms, sobbing. Her face was barely recognizable. Both her lips were fat and split, her right eye was swollen shut and one of her ears was inflamed and burning traffic-light red.

'What happened?' S'n'J whispered when Janie's breathing had steadied a little. 'For God's sake what happened to you?'

'He huh-hurt me, Drezy. He tried to kuh-kill me.'

'Billy-Joe?'

Janie nodded. 'Last night.'

'Christ,' S'n'J whispered.

'He just went buh-berserk. He was going to puh-pull my

front teeth out with a pair of pliers.' Janie sobbed for a while. 'I fought him. I got a ruh-rolling-pin and hit him with it.'

'Good for you,' S'n'J said, taking Janie into her arms. 'I hope you hurt him.'

Janie nodded into S'n'J's shoulder. 'I *did* huh-hurt him. I hurt him badly but he kept getting up again. It was huh-horrible. It was like suh-something out of one of those books that Martin edits. He wouldn't go unconscious when I hit him. I had to bash his head right in to make him stop. I killed him. He didn't have a pulse. Then I ran away.'

'And came here,' S'n'J said, not liking the turn this was taking. It wasn't so much the fact that Janie had hit Billy-Joe over the head, the really shocking thing was that Billy-Joe had suddenly *gone berserk* ... and *kept on getting up again like something out of one of those books that Martin edited.* The circle, apparently, was spreading. The arrival of *Black Rock* was the stone falling into the centre of the calm waters of a pond and the subsequent ripples were still flowing outwards.

'What happened next?' S'n'J asked, wondering if this story-addict's line was what Peter Perfect would have (or perhaps already *had*) scripted for her.

'I went indoors and pulled the bent hoop out of my ear. Then I cleaned up a bit and went to phone the police. The front door was open and when I looked out Billy-Joe's body was gone. Drezy, he was dead but he'd gone.'

'He *wasn't* dead then.'

'But I'd checked his pulse and his breathing and none of it was present. He *was* dead. I flipped. I got in the car and drove away. When I was half-way to the motorway, I pulled over to smoke a cigarette and calm myself and ... and ...'

S'n'J knew exactly what Janie was going to say next. This too fitted like a piece of a jigsaw puzzle. This had to be Peter Perfect's work because he knew what S'n'J's innermost fears were and her largest one was finding someone waiting for her in the back of her car. Not only that but it was also a real old-fashioned and hackneyed horror-story cliché of exactly the type that *Black Rock*'s author favoured.

' ... and Billy-Joe popped up from the back seat and got

me round the neck and put the pliers in my mouth and, well ... I still had the rolling-pin. And I made sure he wasn't going to wake up again, Drezy. I'm sorry but I couldn't help myself.'

'And then?' S'n'J asked.

Janie's reply was ominous. 'I drove here. I don't know why.'

No, but I think I might have a fairly good idea, S'n'J thought and said, 'And his body's still in the car?'

Janie nodded. 'What will we do?' she moaned. 'I murdered him.'

S'n'J guided her friend into the lounge and sat her down on the sofa. 'You stay there. I'll get you a drink, put on some clothes, and go down and look at Billy-Joe. Then we'll work out what to do.'

S'n'J went to the kitchen, found a bottle of Remy and poured stiff slugs into two glasses. It didn't look as if she was going to get any work done on this particular Friday. *It isn't even eight-thirty yet and the day's already been fucked up by that bastard down in Black Rock*, she told herself as she carried the drinks back. However, there was always a chance that Billy-Joe wasn't dead, but in a coma.

Janie sipped her drink and winced. 'Stings,' she said sadly.

'Keep at it,' S'n'J said. 'It'll relax you. Just stay there and rest. You're safe now. I'll get some duds on and go down and look in the car.'

'Be careful,' Janie said in a dull voice.

'Don't worry,' S'n'J said. 'I will.'

Chapter Twenty-three

Three Missing Men

Janie had parked the VW about a hundred yards away in the exact spot where last night S'n'J had pulled an innocent woman from her car and almost punched her. This 'coincidence' was not lost on her.

If what Janie had said was true then it looked rather like the mysterious Peter Perfect had been stage-managing Janie and Billy-Joe as well as attempting to manipulate her. And S'n'J thought she knew how the other two had been drawn into what, after all, was *her* story and *her* problem.

She had met Billy-Joe only once – at Ace's Christmas party at the Groucho last year – and once had been enough. Billy-Joe was drunk and offensive and S'n'J had begun to dislike him. Shortly afterwards Martin asked her, 'How's Janie's old man?' Now she thought about it she could clearly recall her reply: 'About two drinks away from becoming psychopathic, I'd say.'

Until now, she had believed that Martin was the only person who knew she'd said this. But this evidently wasn't true. Peter Perfect knew it too. Just as he knew everything else about her. Like an arresting officer, he was busily taking down everything she said so that it could be used against her.

If Billy-Joe had gone crazy and tried to kill Janie, it hadn't happened naturally. It had been forced on him by the man at Black Rock. It all fitted so horribly well. Janie had even killed him with a rolling-pin, for God's sake. And if that wasn't a barb that was supposed to hook her and tell her what was *really* going on, she didn't know what was.

S'n'J walked up to the VW slowly, not really wanting to see Billy-Joe's corpse and half believing that if she did lay eyes upon it, it would come back to life and come after her like Arnold Schwarzenegger's Terminator unit.

Her heart got busy in her chest as she drew closer to the car, and her mouth suddenly felt dry. The driver's door was closest to the kerb and it wasn't quite shut. Which meant one of two things: either Janie had neglected to lock it in her panic, or that Billy-Joe was coiled up in there like a snake, ready to strike the moment she drew level.

She walked past the car, keeping a good three feet between her and the door as she went by. The back seat had a rug thrown over it and there was something bulky beneath that rug. As far as S'n'J could make out, the thing wasn't moving.

She walked back the other way again.

The thing under the rug stayed put.

On her third pass, she worked up the courage to stop.

There was blood on the car's door handle.

Janie's, she told herself, seeing more blood down the edge of the door.

Feeling that odd intensified déjà vu sensation as though the world was shifting around her again, S'n'J took hold of the door handle.

I will not be fictionalized, she thought distantly. *You cannot rewrite my life.*

As she pulled the door open she felt the remnants of Snowball the hamster vanish from her past. A part of her mind's eye watched the memory fold itself up and disappear in the same way she'd watched Mr Winter vanish. She was left with only the memory that the hamster had belonged to the girl in Black Rock.

Trying to dispel the dizziness that was speeding her towards the edge of collapse, S'n'J yanked the car door open. There was blood smeared down the inner door panel and down the edge of the driver's seat.

Which ought to mean something very important, she thought, not yet knowing what. She tipped the seat forward and reached out for the blanket. Billy-Joe didn't leap up and grab her when she pulled the blanket away . . . because Billy-Joe was just about as dead as a dodo.

'*Jesus!*' S'n'J whispered, looking at the series of deep dents in his head and the way the blood had run from those wounds. Billy-Joe might have been dead, but something was still happening to him.

A few seconds after S'n'J removed the rug, Billy-Joe began to fade. As she watched, Billy-Joe began to lose what little colour was left in his skin. After a moment, the colour of his clothes also began to seep away.

You're hallucinating this, she told herself when he had faded so much he was almost transparent. Inside five seconds Billy-Joe had become clear. She could see the material the back seat was made of through his body, as if she was looking at it through thick glass. In another five seconds Billy-Joe had stopped looking like glass and started looking like he was no more than a heat-haze. And five seconds after that he'd vanished completely.

S'n'J stared at the space he'd occupied, unable to believe she'd seen him vanish. She put out a hand but her fingers met no resistance until they touched the stained fabric of the seat.

S'n'J put the blanket back and edged out of the car, her mind spinning. It looked very much as if Billy-Joe hadn't been there at all.

'But I just saw him!' she complained. *He was lying there under that blanket, dead.*

She was no longer able to distinguish what was real and what was not. For all she knew, Janie might not even be in her lounge waiting for her to come back.

'You'd better leave me alone,' she whispered, looking towards the sky. 'Snowy Dresden will no longer stand for this interference in her life!'

Oh Drezy, she moaned, suddenly wanting to sit down on the pavement and cry, *you said 'Snowy'. You did! Don't let this happen because if it does you won't be able to bring yourself back. If he gets you, you'll end up being Snowy for all time!*

S'n'J slammed the car door and hurried back to the flat.

'He's gone, isn't he?' Janie said when S'n'J entered the room.

'How did you know?'

Janie shook her head. 'It's like a bad joke,' she said. 'It's

279

that story. It's alive in some way. Like a disease. Once you catch it, it takes you over. You don't even need to read it. Ever since I heard about it my life's got crazier and crazier. As if the story's drawing me in, or writing itself around me. I keep seeing pictures in my head of that haunted house. Black Rock. It just hangs there in my mind calling to me, and it won't give up until I go to it. I suppose that's how I found myself here this morning. It's *your* story, isn't it, Drezy?'

S'n'J sat down beside Janie and put her arm around her shoulder. 'How do you mean?'

Janie sighed. 'At first, when Martin told me about it, I thought you'd written it. Then I thought he had. But it's bigger than that. It's as if it's God's work. As if he's writing a new draft of the Drezy story. And he's in a bad mood. And as he does it, he alters all the surrounding characters, too. That's the only explanation I can think of. After Martin read it, he could see images from it in his head. He saw you falling over the side of a steep drop.'

'Martin saw me fall?' S'n'J asked.

Janie nodded. 'We both knew you'd fallen. And *I* hadn't even read any of the story. Then he phoned you and you told him to ring off because you needed an ambulance. I could actually picture your fall, Drezy. And at the same time, I was having to think about Billy-Joe because the night before he'd beaten me up really badly and I was in the throes of deciding to leave him. So what happened was that everything started to get all mangled up together. All the while the book was seeping into me, and the bits I knew about it were eating into my life. And all the stuff about Billy-Joe got entangled with this Black Rock stuff and . . .'

'What?'

Janie began to cry.

'Oh Drezy, I knew what would happen,' Janie moaned. 'When you've been in contact with Black Rock, it gets into you, and all the bad things you imagine come true. It should have been easy for me to leave Billy-Joe. He's usually sleeping at the time I got home and even if he wasn't I didn't expect him to flip out and try to kill me. I may have let myself think it *once* during the day – y'know, worst-case scenario – but the author of *Black Rock* latched on to the thought and *made* it happen. Next thing I knew I was in a bad horror story. It was so *clichéd*! I kept hitting Billy and he kept on getting up again. It was like it had been fixed to happen that way. Like it had been fictionalized. Billy-Joe wasn't a good man. He was a grim bastard most of the time, but he wasn't a homicidal maniac. If I'd really believed that, I wouldn't have gone home at all. *Black Rock* did that for him. Like I say, it grabs the worst things you can imagine and makes them real. That's how I knew Billy would be gone when you looked for him ... because the worst thing I can imagine is his coming back from the dead to pay me back. And now he's out there somewhere, stalking me. This story's walking and talking, Drezy. It's not your normal safe-as-houses horror-romp. It's alive and it's writing itself around us. Writing us into it.'

S'n'J nodded. 'It's my fault,' she said.

Janie looked up at her, her tear-stained face a study of anguish. 'You *did* write it?'

S'n'J shook her head. 'No, I didn't write it, but it's my book. It's about me. The author is trying to fictionalize me. Change me. You and Martin have only been drawn in because you know me. Because you're closely connected with me. I'm the prime target. It's me that he wants.'

'Who *is* he?'

S'n'J shrugged. 'That remains to be seen. All I know is that Black Rock is a real place. I was there yesterday and I *did* fall off the side of the rock it stands on.'

Janie gave S'n'J a sad smile. 'We're in it together,' she said. 'It isn't your fault, you didn't make it happen. The blame rests with Peter bloody Perfect, whoever he is. What frightens me most is this: I no longer know what's real and what's fiction. When the story ends, do you think everything will go back to the way it was before?'

S'n'J quashed that one. 'Everything that happens, happens for real. That's the only way to treat it. Things aren't going back. Peter Perfect is altering reality. Black Rock is a real place and there *are* such things as ghosts and haunted houses and they *can* have an effect on real life. A very profound effect.'

'There's magic down there at Black Rock, isn't there?' Janie said.

S'n'J sighed. 'If there is, it's bad magic.'

'It's one of those special places,' Janie said. 'It's near Tintagel Castle isn't it?'

'Yeah, but it doesn't feel particularly special. It just looks like a big house on a rock. There's no atmosphere or anything.' She left out the information that whenever you looked at the house it seemed poised like a great animal, ready to spring at you. That kind of fancy wasn't going to do anyone any good.

Janie took a deep breath. '"Hard by was great Tintagel's table round and there of old the flower of Arthur's knights made fair beginning of a nobler time,"' she quoted.

'What's that?' S'n'J asked. 'It sounds familiar.'

'Those words have been running through my head all night,' Janie said. 'They arrived of their own accord. I know where they come from too. They come from a plaque that's mounted on a piece of Barras Nose which sticks out into the sea between Tintagel Castle and Black Rock.

'Arthur chose the place because of its magical qualities. But he didn't stay there. He pissed off somewhere else and left his knights to it. And while he was gone, his knights didn't make fair beginning of a nobler time, they did bad stuff. It's obvious. The Castle was built on a ley and they tapped its energy and used and abused it. And the bad ley runs through Black Rock house. There's a cave under Black Rock – a kind of cellar because the house was built on top of it. That's where the knights used to do their stuff.'

'What kind of stuff?' S'n'J asked carefully. A fresh picture of Ellen was blooming in her mind and there was something horribly erotic about that bloodstained and pain-racked naked body.

Janie shuddered. 'You know,' she said.

S'n'J nodded. She *did* know. She also knew that Janie had got the information from their friendly neighbourhood teller of tall tales, Mr Peter Perfect, which explained why it contained that subtle reek of bullshit.

'What happened there long ago doesn't matter at all,' S'n'J said thoughtfully and as she spoke, a fantasy image began to form in her imagination. It wasn't an image of Black Rock or Peter Perfect though, it was an alternative explanation. One that her own mind was constructing from the fragments of information it possessed. 'It's what's happening there *now* that's important,' she added, hearing her voice tail off as her mind plunged her into fantasy mode.

The fantasy – the first period fantasy S'n'J's mind had ever attempted – constructed itself effortlessly. The date was 1948, three years after the Second World War. It was dusk in Hyde Park on a summer's evening: a handsome young man wearing his Sunday best suit and a pretty woman in a flowery dress were walking slowly across the grass towards a thicket of trees. The man, S'n'J knew, was Fred King, the factory worker that Snowy had spoken to on the back-in-time telephone within the pages of *Black Rock*. The one whose elderly mother Sarah-Jane herself seemed to have contacted yesterday. The woman, walking arm-in-arm beside him and smiling like that cat who got the cream, was undoubtedly Zara Winter, the *other* wrong number Snowy had got connected to.

'But what *is* happening now?' Janie asked.

I know where they're going and what they're going to do, S'n'J thought as she pictured the couple walking towards the trees. *They're going to wait beneath those trees until it's dark and then they're going to make love. And Zara will become pregnant and they'll marry and the baby will be a boy. When the boy grows up he'll be a writer. A very special kind of writer. One who can actually unweave the threads of reality and reconstruct them to suit himself. And the boy will call himself Peter Perfect.*

'Drezy? Are you okay?'

But what will happen to the boy to give him the power of a god?

S'n'J didn't know. What she *did* know, was that the construction of this period piece was taxing her imagination so much that it hadn't done a perfect job. Because when the couple drew close enough for her to see their features, Fred King looked like a younger version of the Mr Winter she had seen lying bleeding on the forecourt of Black Rock and Zara's face belonged to her. Zara Winter, to all intents and purposes, *was* Sarah-Jane Dresden.

'Drezy! For God's sake!' Janie's voice called.

The fantasy exploded into a billion coloured dots. 'I'm fine!' S'n'J said. 'Really.'

'I thought you'd gone into a trance or something,' Janie said worriedly. 'You didn't seem to hear me. Oh God, Drezy, what are we going to do?'

'Get another large brandy,' S'n'J said. She felt very weak, as if she'd discovered something that was going to be *extremely important*. She got up, took the glasses back to the kitchen and filled them again, wondering if Peter Perfect had homed in on her because he wanted his mother back again and Sarah-Jane bore a close physical resemblance to her.

'*I* think we ought to phone the police,' Janie said, sipping her drink.

'And tell them what, exactly? That you killed your husband and he came back to life and ran off? That there's a guy – or a ghost – down in Tintagel and that he, or *it*, is writing a book and not only are we in it, but we're also being forced to act out the scenes he writes for us? We'd be in hospital under sedation in half an hour.'

'But Billy-Joe *did* get up and walk away,' Janie said. 'And he did do this while he was in the car,' she added opening her mouth and showing S'n'J the inside of her cheek. There was a circular piece of skin missing. The torn part was about the size of a five pence piece. 'I don't know about the ghost stuff, but I do know that happened. Some of my teeth are chipped too.'

'So we phone the police and tell them your husband attacked you and you knocked him out and drove all the way to Bude before he came round, and then he got out of the car and wandered off?'

Janie nodded.

'And what good will that do?'

'They might find him. They might be able to stop him coming back here for me.'

'But he won't know which flat you're in. If he starts hammering on doors we're going to know about it long before he works his way up here to the first floor. And I don't think he's hanging around in the street anyway. I would have seen him when I went out. I think I know where he's gone and I think you know that too.'

Janie nodded. 'He's gone to Tintagel,' she said. 'To Black Rock.'

'That sounds right to me, Janie,' S'n'J said. 'If we inform the police, they won't find him. He's gone to Black Rock to wait there for us. Peter Perfect knows that we're going to go there eventually. He's writing our story and making it inevitable that we do. And we've got nothing in our arsenal to fight back with until we know what he wants from us. And we've got no way of finding out. I think we just have to sit tight, nurse your wounds and wait and see what develops.'

Janie shook her head. 'I can't stand it much longer,' she said. 'It's like waiting to be hung. There must be *something* we can do. Can't we just ask him to stop it?'

'If you were writing a book, Janie, and you were having a good time putting your characters through the mill and one of them suddenly began to speak to you and said, "Won't you please stop this? It's doing me in!" what would *your* reply be? Would you say, "Okey dokey, I'll only make good things happen to you from now on,"? No you wouldn't. I wouldn't, and Peter Perfect wouldn't either. We'd all reply, "And *what* kind of a story would that leave me with? One with no tension or drama." We'd say, "You get on and do as you're told and if you're good maybe things will work out for you. But I'm not promising anything because I'm the author and I damn well do as I please. If it pleases me to then kill you then hey presto, you'll die."'

'But we're not fictional characters, we're *real*,' Janie pleaded.

'Are we? Or are we just Peter Perfect's pawns? You were

right about the bad magic, Janie. He's worked some of it on us.'

'But surely we can fight back?'

'Yeah, but on whose terms? Ours or his? Neither of us knows how much of what's happened has *really* happened.'

'Look at me,' Janie said. '*That* happened. And I don't want anything like it happening again. Can't we just go over there and bust his head open with a rolling-pin?' she added hopefully.

'I wish I could believe something that simple would sort it out,' S'n'J said sadly. She sipped at her brandy. 'I'm going to run you a bath now. You're going to sit in it until you feel a little better, then I'm going to put you to bed. While you're in the bath I'm going to phone my calls for today and tell them I won't be coming. When you've slept we'll talk about what we can do. If we're going to go down to Black Rock, I think we're going to need to take some things with us. Something a little heftier than a rolling-pin. Like a couple of priests ... and a barrel of holy water and half a dozen crucifixes.'

'And silver bullets and garlic,' Janie added, finding a smile.

Sometimes the only defence you had when the cards were stacked against you was humour, even if it was bitter humour. Sometimes it proved you weren't as beaten as you'd thought. Sometimes it merely kept you going. On this occasion it seemed to prove to her that Peter Perfect had yet to dominate them totally.

S'n'J didn't notice the answering machine light flashing until she'd put Janie in a warm bath and gone to the phone to cancel her appointments for the day.

I got a call, she thought in surprise. *When did that happen? I didn't hear the phone ring.*

She rewound the tape, almost certain that when she played it back she was going to hear a list of instructions from Peter Perfect concerning what she and Janie had to do next. Or perhaps he'd read out the next chapter of his book for her. The tape was taking quite a while to wind back, so it was a possibility.

Are you sure you want to do this? her Girl Guide voice asked her as her finger hovered over the play button. S'n'J wasn't at all sure. But she couldn't simply ignore it in case it was a message from James.

Holding her breath, she hit the play button.

'Damn and blast it! Essy!'

Martin, S'n'J acknowledged during the pause. *What does he want now?*

'It's Martin!' Martin's voice shouted. He sounded angry and frightened. 'Look, I need to talk to you. Now. I think there's someone . . .'

As his voice reached the word 'someone', the answering machine began to screech in a high-pitched electrical buzz. It only lasted a second, but it was enough to blot out the following few words.

'. . . you,' Martin said, 'Don't leave . . .'

The screech began again and stopped as Martin said, '. . . get there. Phone . . . tell them . . . receipt of . . . to . . . threatening . . . way!'

Then the message ceased. And was replaced with an electronic version of 'Frosty the Snowman'. The tinny tune sounded like one of those things the switchboard of a large company forced you to listen to when you were on hold around this time of year. Late October was pretty early for anyone to be playing Christmas tunes, but what worried S'n'J most was that this particular version of 'Frosty the Snowman' didn't sound the least bit seasonal or cheery. It sounded downright sinister. What was worse, it didn't just loop around and begin again like these things normally did, it kept going, growing as it played. Inside thirty seconds, what had started out as an electronic tune turned into something being played by a full orchestra. Thirty seconds after *that* it began to sound as if Richard Wagner had got his hands on it and was changing it into something that wouldn't have sounded out of place in one of the more threatening sections of the Ring cycle.

S'n'J let it play in case Martin was going to make another appearance with something new to say. 'Frosty the Snowman' lasted for ten minutes, grew to a crescendo and stopped with the sound of crashing cymbals still hanging in the air.

S'n'J waited, now expecting to hear Peter Perfect's laughter. What she actually got was a voice she didn't recognize saying, with feeling, 'Baby it's *cold* outside. Do you think it'll snow?'

And that was it.

She wound the tape back again and hit the play button once more, trying to fill in the blanks where Martin's voice had been bleeped out.

He had presumably spoken the words 'damn and blast it' when he'd realized he had the answering machine rather than S'n'J herself. The introduction to the message was unharmed. Martin needed to talk to her urgently and he thought there was someone . . . S'n'J hit the pause button, wondering.

What *does he think? There's someone, blank blank blank, you. Trying to get you? Coming after you?*

She strongly suspected that Martin had reached the same conclusion as she and Janie had. That Peter Perfect was real and dangerous. She had no idea how he'd arrived at that conclusion, but for once in her life she congratulated him. He might have been a bastard, but he was a *sharp* bastard.

She hit play again. *Don't leave, blank-blank-blank-blank-blank-blank-blank-blank-blank-blank get there. That's going to be a tough one*, she told herself, hitting pause again. *Don't leave home? It has to be home. Don't leave home until he gets here? There's a bit missing, Dropsy. What's the other bit?*

'Don't leave home and don't let anyone in, until I get there,' seemed too easy though and S'n'J spent ten minutes trying to work in other patterns of words before she finally accepted the obvious option.

The rest of the message was going to be harder to work out. Martin apparently wanted her to phone someone and tell them something about a receipt. The word 'way' might have suggested he was on his way here.

S'n'J told herself that this hung together. Janie was already here, and Martin was the only other person who knew about *Black Rock,* so it seemed fitting that he was on his way too.

It all hung together a bit *too* nicely for her liking. Peter

Perfect, son of Fred and Zara King, was obviously responsible for the distortion which had blocked most of Martin's message. He'd wiped just enough to enable her to reconstruct the important parts; presumably so that she would feel very clever – as if she'd won a small battle.

S'n'J only wished Martin had stated the time of his call. If he'd made it last night, he should be here by now. If he'd made it this morning, he would be here soon. *If nothing happens to him on the way*, she thought.

She yelped when the telephone rang.

She looked at the receiver for a moment and then snatched it up. 'Yes?' she said.

'Baby, it's *cold* outside,' Peter Perfect said, 'Do you think it'll snow, Snowy?'

For a moment S'n'J's muscles all locked solid. Then she slammed the phone into its cradle.

You've never heard Peter Perfect speak, she admonished herself. *How can you recognize his voice?*

But if it wasn't him, she didn't know *who* it was. Who else could it have been? The voice had sounded a little like Fred King's, but less working-class, more well-spoken. The kind of voice she would have expected Black Rock's Mr Winter to have.

Drezy, you called yourself Dropsy again, a few moments ago! she suddenly remembered. Then she remembered something else. There weren't just three people who knew about *Black Rock*, there were four.

The fourth person who was going to get drawn into the story was James.

Nothing can have happened to him since last night, she told herself, but her hands were already dialling his number. She didn't care what he was doing, he could just stop doing it and get over here where she could see him.

'James Green can't come to the phone at the moment, but if you'd like to give him money, leave the time, the date and your message, he'll ring you back.'

Oh, James, she thought and after the tone said. 'It's Dro . . . Drezy. Get over here. Now. I'm frightened.'

She replaced the receiver and dialled Cars Inc. And learned that James hadn't turned up for work this morning.

She put the phone back, her heart hammering in her ears.

'You better not have got him already!' she hissed towards the front door, which she thought faced west towards Tinta-gel. 'You're really starting to piss me off!'

The question was, was her failure to reach James a trick of Peter Perfect's or merely bad luck? It looked like the writer's work to her. He would have known that she would want to immediately drop everything and go over to James' flat, *and* he would have known that she'd realize that no matter how much she wanted to, she wouldn't allow herself to. For one thing she had a message from Martin telling her to stay home until he got there because it was going to be dangerous for her to leave the house.

Damn you to hell! she thought. *Damn your eyes!*

She snatched up the phone, made three quick calls cancel-ling her appointments and making fresh ones for next week.

This seems a bit like booking tickets to Mars, she thought, dutifully writing down her new appointments in her diary. *When the time finally rolls around, there's a pretty good chance you'll be too dead to go.*

She gave a bitter laugh, and went to the bathroom to make sure Janie was still living and breathing.

Janie was sound asleep, her right-hand loosely holding a brandy glass upright on her chest between her breasts. Her rib cage looked as if a karate expert had spent a busy fortnight using it to perfect his roundhouse kick, there were friction burns around her neck, and her lips were swollen and split.

How could he do this to you, Janie? S'n'J thought, remem-bering times when Janie had spoken of him and her face had taken on the kind of soppy, dreamy look that you only ever saw in films when people were hypnotized.

Janie's eyes opened and she smiled. Her expression made S'n'J want to cry.

'I fell asleep,' she said. 'Tired.'

'I think we'd better get you out of this water and tuck you up in bed,' S'n'J said. 'How do you feel?'

'Like I was run down by a truck,' Janie said.

'Martin's on his way,' S'n'J said, thinking, *We don't need Martin; what we need is a flame-thrower or some incendiary devices. What you do with haunted houses is burn them down.*

'Is he?' Janie said, uninterestedly. 'You'll have to help me get out of this bath, I think. I'm all shaky.' She reached out and took S'n'J's arm. 'I'm glad I came here,' she said. 'I knew you'd be able to look after me. Thanks for everything you've done, Drezy. I appreciate it.'

'I hope you didn't mean that as a goodbye statement,' S'n'J said, *because that's what it sounded like.*

Wincing, Janie used S'n'J's arm to pull herself up to crouch. 'It won't be so bad,' she said.

'What won't?'

'You know.'

S'n'J shook her head. 'No I don't,' she said.

'It can't hurt any more than I hurt now,' Janie said. 'It won't be so bad.'

'Janie, nothing is going to happen to you!' S'n'J said. 'I won't let it. You are *not* going to die!'

Janie heaved herself to a standing position, grabbed S'n'J's shoulders with both hands to steady herself and said, 'Would you say we look a bit like one another?'

S'n'J shook her head. 'You're a bit tipsy,' S'n'J said. 'The drink got to you.'

'We wouldn't be mistaken for sisters then?'

'We don't look that much alike, Janie,' S'n'J said. 'Why do you ask?'

Janie shrugged. 'Just something I dreamed.'

'What was it?'

'Something to do with a girl getting killed because she looked like you. It doesn't matter. If I don't look like you, it doesn't matter.'

'It might,' S'n'J said. Janie might not resemble her, but she knew someone who did. Someone she'd been very close to. Someone who had been mistaken for her twin sister on more than one occasion. Someone who had run away from home in Newcastle on the pretext of coming down here and visiting her.

Ellen!

'Tell me more about it, Janie,' S'n'J said.

Janie yawned. 'I've forgotten most of it now. You know how it is with dreams. It was something to do with him having to kill your lookalike in order to do something to you. Change you or something. That's all I know.'

S'n'J remembered how she'd told Ellen's boyfriend that his missing lover had probably gone to visit her parents. It ought to have been obvious that Ellen had gone to Black Rock. *In the book she's hanging naked and half-flayed in the basement, for God's sake, Drezy!* she told herself. *And that's what's happened in real life too. That's why she's missing. He got her!*

'We don't look like sisters, Janie,' S'n'J told her friend. 'So don't worry, you aren't going to die.'

Janie stepped out of the bath, still using S'n'J to support herself. 'But it's your story, Drezy,' she said, 'and I'm only a bit part in it. We all know what happens to bit-part players, don't we? They get written into books just so they can be killed off and give the reader a few thrills. Cannon fodder people. As soon as they're introduced you know they're going to come to a sticky end. Martin calls them *shreddies*. I'm in your story as a shreddie.'

'Rubbish!' S'n'J said, thinking of James who suddenly seemed to be an archetypal *shreddie*. 'I'm not going to let anything happen to you.'

She led Janie to the bedroom, put her in bed, tucked her up like a child, then sat with her and held her hand until she fell asleep.

It didn't take long.

Now we wait, S'n'J thought. She got herself a fresh drink, went back to the lounge, turned on the television and settled down.

She was still awake when the weather forecast came on, but only just. The brandy had finally found its way to her brain and she was beginning to feel sleepy. The weather currently on its way in from the Atlantic was going to bring rain, the forecaster was saying. And temperatures were going to be above normal for the time of year.

So, Peter, she thought dreamily, *I don't think we're going to get any of that snow you were wondering about. I don't think it's time for Frosty the Snowman yet. And everyone knows it never snows in Cornwall, anyway. One big fall every four or five years, they reckon round here, and then only in January or February. Never in October. I think you're going to be out of luck with that there snow, my good friend. Still, we can always keep our fingers crossed . . .*

S'n'J's head toppled forward and the last thing she thought before sleep finally took her was, *Martin should be here by now, surely. Where the bloody hell has he got to?*

Chapter Twenty-four

Dawn

Where Martin had got to was a service area on the M5. He and Harold had arrived less than ten minutes ago and, it now appeared, he was stuck.

Martin, the keys to Mrs Harold's Mini dangling from his right hand, stood staring in disbelief at the space where he'd last seen his lift. The word, *GONE!* in italicized capitals flashed on and off across the ice block in his mind.

'This is not possible,' he told himself, his voice simmering with rage. 'Harold cannot have moved the car. I have the keys here in my hand. I can see them. This key here, with the blue bit of rubber around the top of it, is the ignition key. I took it out with my own hands. HAROLD CANNOT HAVE GONE!'

It should have been a straightforward fuel and toilet stop, and he had been sure that nothing bad could happen.

And he had been wrong.

They had pulled in, filled the Mini on Martin's credit card, then driven to the space in the car park where Martin now stood, fuming.

After Harold had parked, Martin had had a heart to heart with him, waving the tiny knife blade under his nose as he laid down the rules: no trying to escape; no yelling that he'd been kidnapped. 'Think about your brachial artery, Harold,' Martin had finished. Then he leaned across the man, took the keys out of the ignition and ordered him out of the car. Harold got out and obediently waited for Martin to lock the Mini. 'Stay beside me,' Martin told him and began to walk towards the service area.

Everything went according to plan until they got inside the

building and entered the toilets. As Martin marched towards the urinals, Harold peeled off, skipped into one of the toilet cubicles, slammed the door and bolted it.

Martin banged on the door. 'Harold! Your eyes!'

Harold didn't reply. Inside the cubicle, the toilet seat banged down.

Martin ground his teeth for a few seconds, then gave up and went to the urinal. And the moment he began to piss, the bolt on Harold's cubicle door snapped back and Harold shot across the tiled floor like a greyhound leaving its trap. By the time Martin had squeezed off his flow and got his dick back inside his trousers Harold was gone.

He won't get far, Martin told himself as he rushed out into the corridor. Harold wasn't at the AA counter, or in the shop, or in the restaurant, which meant he'd gone outside.

Martin ran to the car park, failed to see Harold and realized he'd gone out of the other entrance at the far side of the building. 'You fuckhouse!' he snarled and turned back. He ran down the length of the corridor towards the far exit and skidded to a halt outside the truckers' cafe. No Harold. He pushed his way through a coach party who were coming in through the door and ran out into the lorry park.

Harold, damn him, was not there.

Cursing, Martin sprinted back to where the car was.

Then he performed his pointless soliloquy, telling himself he had the car keys in his hand.

Finally he began to admit the terrible truth to himself. Harold had been able to leave without him because the bastard had been in possession of a second set of keys for the car.

'Fuck him!' Martin spat. He was now faced with trying to hijack some other poor mug – in broad daylight and with only a tiny knife to use as a threatening weapon – or simply standing on the exit ramp with his thumb up and hoping that some good Samaritan would take pity on him. Or calling a taxi which wouldn't come.

Martin walked slowly back towards the service area, grinding his teeth. Then he smiled. There was another option.

He strode into the self-service restaurant, stationed himself beside the counter and addressed the breakfasters the way he would address a sales conference.

He clapped his hands and then said, 'Can I have your attention, please, ladies and gentlemen?' in a booming, confident voice.

Apart from a few nervous voices who presumably anticipated the announcement that a suspect package had been discovered in the building, the restaurant fell silent. Everyone turned to see what he had to say.

'I'm in a bit of bother,' Martin said. 'My wife is seriously ill in Bude, Cornwall and I'm on my way to her. I pulled in here to freshen up and during the five minutes I was away from my car, someone stole it. As you'll appreciate I'm rather stuck. I was wondering if there was anyone who would be willing to drive me home. I'll make it worth their while. I'd be willing to pay two hundred pounds.'

The room responded to this offer with total silence.

Martin waited.

The breakfasters all looked at him, presumably awaiting the punch-line.

'I'm serious,' he added, sounding a little too much like John Cleese for his own liking. Just as he was wondering how Peter Perfect could possibly manage to control this many people at once, something finally happened.

At the back of the room a girl raised her hand. 'I'll take you,' she said, getting up.

Everyone turned to look at her. She was a mousy girl, maybe twenty or twenty-one. She wore a Clint Eastwood poncho, scruffy jeans, cowboy boots and steel-rimmed glasses. She carried a string bag, inside which was a very large Jiffy bag.

When she reached Martin, she put out her hand. 'Dawn Tauber,' she said.

'Martin Dinsey,' Martin said, and if the girl hadn't cut in on him he would have told her how relieved he was that she'd decided to help him.

'I know,' the girl said. 'Snips.'

Martin's heart hit his boots. He felt his mouth drop and couldn't make it rise again.

'I also happen to know you aren't married,' the girl said.

'Do I know you?' Martin asked, his sunken heart finding a few more inches to descend. Suddenly he realized what he'd done. He'd made a very big mistake indeed.

The girl smiled. It was a cold smile. 'Probably not. But I know you.'

Martin let go of her cold hand. 'You're it, aren't you?' he said.

'Are we playing tag?' the girl asked.

So you had razor-blades for breakfast, Martin thought. *Ha ha very funny, get a needle and thread, quick because I've just split my sides laughing.*

'You know what I mean,' he said sullenly.

The girl frowned. 'Nope,' she said, 'I don't think I do.'

'*Black Rock*,' Martin said. '*You* wrote it, didn't you? That's it in that padded envelope in your bag, isn't it?'

'Are you OK . . . Snips?' the girl asked. 'I mean mentally. I've wondered before, but you're giving me fresh cause for concern. Are you *compos mentis*?'

'Of course I am!' Martin said, loudly enough to attract the attention of some of the nearer tables.

'Then why are you talking in riddles?' she asked mildly.

'Look Dawn, I've already gathered that you're a writer, I know that you've got a manuscript in your bag and a chip on your shoulder, now would you please just answer this question. Did you write something called *Black Rock* or didn't you?'

The girl thought about it. 'Nope,' she said eventually, 'I can't say I did. I imagine that one was written by someone else who wants to string you up by the balls,' she added.

Martin shook his head. 'I've been up since yesterday morning. Twenty-five hours now. I'm tired out and I have to get back to Bude in a hurry . . .'

'To your wife that doesn't exist.'

'. . . and you've lost me. A moment ago I'd never met you, then you offer to drive me home, now you want to string me up by the balls.'

'Right, wrong, right, right,' Dawn Tauber said. 'University of East Anglia, ninety-one. University of Southampton,

297

ninety-two. University College London, ninety-three. Mean anything?'

Martin shook his head.

'You haven't got Alzheimer's, have you? You've got a very shaky memory,' Dawn said.

'Remind me,' Martin said.

'You did courses. Creative Writing. Science Fiction and Fantasy. How to Succeed in Cyberpunk.'

Martin nodded.

'I was on all three. You asked me out after one of them when you were drunk. I refused. You invited me to send you my manuscript. I did. You rejected it, probably because I rejected you. Then you rejected another. Then another. Do these words mean anything to you? "I cannot see a place in today's market for something as hackneyed as *Slick City Blues*. The style is stilted, the delivery is hesitant, the characterization and motivation are ill-judged. In ninety-five thousand words all you've succeeded in doing is confusing me beyond measure."'

'I didn't write that,' Martin lied. He remembered the submission as soon as he heard the title. He wondered briefly what kind of world it was that sent him a rejected author as his saviour, then cancelled the query. It was obvious what kind of world it was: one that – as far as he was concerned anyway – Peter Perfect was running.

'You signed it,' Dawn said. 'I got the manuscript back this morning.'

Martin shrugged. 'Sorry,' he said, 'I just didn't like it.'

'So I gathered,' Dawn replied tartly. 'Now, I'm willing to take you to Bude, if that's where you want to go, but it's going to cost you more than two hundred pounds. Quite a lot more, in fact.'

Martin knew what was coming. 'I'll walk,' he said, and turned away.

'No one else here will take you,' Dawn said. 'You know that, don't you? Anyone you approach now is going to think I changed my mind and they'll wonder why.'

Martin ignored her and began to walk off. Peter Perfect had arranged events so that Dawn would show up – which meant that he expected Martin to accept her offer. Which, in turn, meant that if he did he would be travelling at Peter Perfect's mercy. *Which means that you won't get very far*, he told himself. *She'll probably crash the car within two miles.*

'It's going to cost you two grand,' Dawn said from behind him, keeping pace. 'But the two grand won't be for the lift, it'll be for this manuscript. Listen to me. "*Slick City Blues* shows that you have a sharp eye for a fast-paced story." Hodder Headline said that. "Excellent characterization and a stunning ability to evoke a fully-realized parallel world." Richard Evans at Gollancz wrote that.'

Yeah, but talk's cheap when you're rejecting a story, Martin thought. *Neither of those publishers wanted the book, did they?*

'I think two thousand is nothing for a first novel by an exciting new talent, don't you?' Dawn asked.

Martin stopped and turned to her. 'OK,' he said. 'Done!' Two miles down the road would be two miles closer to Essenjay. He put out his hand to shake on the deal. Handshakes were cheap too, when it came down to it. Who was going to believe a rejected writer with a chip on her shoulder when she started yelling that he'd reneged on a deal? No one, that was who. She had his original rejection letter and he had a copy of it, so making this promise now wasn't going to mean a thing when it was all over.

Dawn glared at his hand. 'I'm not such a poor judge of character as you think,' she said. 'I wouldn't clinch a deal with someone like you on a handshake. You're gonna have to write all this down and date it and sign it. Then, before anything else happens, I want to know why you're in such a hurry to get back to Cornwall where you don't have a wife.' She ferreted about inside her string bag and brought out the title page of *Slick City Blues* and a pen. 'Take this,' she told Martin, 'and write the date on the top of the page then write this: "Ace Publishing hereby undertake to license British and Commonwealth volume publishing rights in *Slick City Blues* by Dawn S. Tauber for a period of ten years at the sum of two thousand pounds sterling to be paid within one calendar month of this agreement. Publication will follow within twelve calendar months of the above date. Should Ace Publishing decide not to undertake to print and publish twenty thousand copies as agreed above, the rights will revert to the author and a cancellation fee of twenty-five thousand pounds will become payable."'

Martin looked at her.

'Go on,' she said. 'And sign it legibly. Please note that there'll be a witness, added by the next time you see this piece of paper. It doesn't cover everything but it'll do for now.'

Martin wrote and signed. It didn't matter whether or not the contract was legal – it wouldn't be acted upon.

Dawn S. Tauber snatched the sheet from his hands when he had finished, folded it and stashed it away beneath her poncho, saying with a cold smile, 'OK, now we can go.'

As they walked across the car park, where not ten minutes ago Martin had looked in horror at the empty space where Harold and his wife's car should have been, Dawn said, 'Tell me why you have to get back to Cornwall in such a hurry. You're divorced, apparently and your ex-wife lives in *London*. She didn't understand you, did she?'

'How do you know all this?'

'You were drunk, weren't you, when you tried to pick me up that time? You told me all this in the Students' Union bar at the University of East Anglia. You also said you wanted to fuck me into oblivion. Except you were so drunk you said you wanted to fuck me into a Bolivian. I told you what you could do with your dick – stick it up your arse if it would reach – and you asked me if I'd ever heard of the Publishers' Blacklist, upon which my name would be going. "You'll never get published in this country," you said, "I'll make sure of it", and I didn't believe there was such a thing as a blacklist until my submissions collected three hundred rejections. Then I thought, *please God, let me meet Martin Dinsey again and let him need my help* and now my prayers have been answered. It's a funny old world, isn't it?'

'Hilarious,' Martin replied sourly.

'And now I've got me a publishing deal.'

Or so you think, Martin thought and said, 'Yeah, I think you're gonna do well, too.'

'So why *are* you in such a hurry to get down to Bude?'

'My girlfriend,' Martin said. 'She's in a fix.'

Dawn nodded. 'Something to do with this *Black Rock* thing you're so frightened of, I take it.'

'Yeah,' Martin said. 'There's a guy down there in a house called Black Rock and he's crazy.'

'And he's threatened to get your girlfriend because you rejected him, right?'

Martin stopped and turned to Dawn. 'Are you real?' he asked.

'Of course I am. Why?'

'Because you sound like one of those story characters who happen by and just *know* all about what's going on. You've been having visions, haven't you?'

Dawn smiled. 'You *have* gone crazy, Snips. The pressure got to you did it? You always used to say that publishing had a high rate of nervous breakdowns and that you had to be tough to survive. You weren't tough enough, were you?'

Martin glared at her. 'What do you know about Black Rock?' he demanded.

'It was a film starring Spencer Tracy. Only it was *Bad Day at Black Rock*. It was a good film too. Then there was the Dicky Attenborough film, only that was *Brighton* Rock. I once read a short-story called Straker's Island which was about a writer named James Green who'd written a book called *Black Rock* but that book was only alluded to. I don't know what happened in it.'

'There's more, isn't there?' Martin said.

Dawn grinned. This time it was a sunny grin that wouldn't have looked out of place on the face of Essenjay herself. 'There's a certain magic in writing that you must have come across yourself,' she said. 'Sometimes it's like . . . Serendipity, they call it, don't they? Like a great big fat coincidence that makes you wonder if you've actually predicted something. A guy called William Gerhardie did it with a book about an unsinkable ship. The book was called *Futility*. The boat was called *Titan*, and guess what?'

Martin already knew *what*. The story was legendary.

Dawn's grin got wider. 'Titan hit an iceberg and sunk. That was published ages before the Titanic thing. It was like reality was mimicking fiction. Sometimes that *does* happen. It's like reality doesn't have enough ideas of its own to go round, so it borrows some of the good ones from literature. There was a woman called Judith Wax who wrote a book called *Starting in the Middle*. On page 696 of the book she said she was convinced she would die in a plane crash. She *did* die in a plane crash and the flight number was 696. That's real life for you. Stranger than fiction.'

'And?' Martin asked. There was more – it was written all over her smug face.

'And, after my first rejection from you, I wrote a venomous short story called *Black Rock* in which an editor's girlfriend was attacked by a rejected writer as revenge. The message was: "You don't publish my book, you suffer." Does that just about sum up what's happening to you?'

'What do you think?' Martin asked.

Dawn nodded and grinned.

Martin felt a very strong urge to plant his fist in the centre of that *serves-you-right* smile. He did not do this. Dawn had a car and the car probably wouldn't start for him. The only way he was going to get back to Bude was by hitch-hiking, that much was certain. He shrugged in an OK-you've-got-me-now-what look and said, 'Let me take a guess at what your middle name might be. The initial is "S" isn't it?'

Dawn nodded.

'Snowdrop, right?'

Dawn looked amazed. 'How did you know?'

'Like we agreed, truth is stranger than fiction. Except that sometimes it *is* fiction. Now how about taking me to your car and fulfilling your side of the bargain?'

Dawn Snowdrop Tauber's car turned out to be an ancient Fiat 500. It was about as far away from the Ferrari as the Earth was from Alpha Centauri. *Two cylinders and five hundred cubic centimetres of raw power*, Martin thought bitterly. *Flat out, it probably goes about forty*.

Then he stopped being bitter and started wondering if he

ought to run because in the clear blue sky a hundred feet above the car, a very familiar brown cloud was forming.

'What's *that*?' Dawn said, looking up.

Martin began to back away. There were two reasons why he didn't answer Dawn's question, and the first was because he could barely believe what was happening. The second reason was that if there was anyone who more deserved to be engulfed in a rain of fire at this particular moment than Dawn S. Tauber, he didn't know who it was.

Dawn didn't notice that Martin was no longer beside her. She stayed where she was, her key in the door of the Fiat while she stared up at the coalescing cloud. Martin backed into a car and slid down its length, his eyes flicking from the cloud to Dawn and back again. He gave Dawn about another thirty seconds on the planet Earth.

The cloud built up and darkened, the brown coloration fading.

Not fire then, Martin thought moving steadily away from the Fiat. *He's done a proper lightning cloud this time.*

There was about ten seconds left now. 'It looks like a little thundercloud,' Dawn said, suddenly looking round for him. She did a double take at the empty space beside her, then spotted Martin fifty feet away, facing her but walking backwards.

'Where are you going?' she asked in a surprised voice.

Martin fought a brief battle with himself. Half of him wanted to see dear little Dawn turned to a pile of ashes, and the other half wanted to warn her.

'Get out of the way!' he shouted, hating himself for it. 'Lightning! You'll be struck!'

Dawn smiled at him as though she'd seen the joke he was playing on her. 'Oh,' she said and nodded. She glanced back at the cloud, then looked round again. 'You're joking,' she called. 'Aren't you?'

Go on then, get it over with! Martin thought. Dawn was down to be hit, apparently. Above her head the cloud rolled and thickened.

'Should I run?' Dawn asked, confused now.

'I would if I were you,' Martin called back. *But I think it's probably too late for you even if you can run as fast as a Russian sprinter.*

Dawn shrugged her bag off her shoulder and began to prove that she could indeed run as fast as a Russian sprinter – if not faster.

The trouble was, Martin realized, as soon as she'd begun, that she was running *towards* him. Which meant that if she got zapped, he would get zapped too.

He turned away from her and dodged through a series of parked cars.

As he glanced over to see where she was, a double bolt of lightning flashed from the cloud and thunder rocked the parking area.

The twin strike – as far as Martin could discern before the flash blinded him – hit the Fiat *and* Dawn. In the seconds it took for his vision to recover, he was showered with thousands of pieces of burning ash, which he took to be the remains of the girl.

'Fucking hell,' a voice exclaimed from beside him. Someone took his arm in what felt like a cast-iron grip. Martin turned and was both relieved and disappointed to discover that the voice belonged to Dawn. She hadn't only *not* been hit, she hadn't suffered any damage at all.

Martin blinked away the after-images of the lightning and when he realized what the burning ash was, he giggled.

The lightning had blasted Dawn's manuscript out of existence.

And that, as they say in the trade, is a deus-ex-machina, he told himself. *A ghost from the machine. A direct intervention by God. Peter Perfect is a jealous god, apparently. He doesn't much care for other writers' work.*

'That was the only frigging copy I had of that, too,' Dawn protested in a voice that bore so much shock and horror it was comical. 'The disks I saved it on were in the bloody envelope. I was taking them over to my boyfriend to have them printed out.'

'That's show business,' Martin said, grinning at her.

Dawn slapped him. Hard.

'Don't worry,' he chortled, 'I'll publish your *other* books. If you can get them to me in one piece that is.'

Dawn slapped him again.

'I just saved your life,' Martin reminded her, trying to get a grip on his hysterical giggling. 'That could have been you raining down on the car park!' he added, stifling the remainder of the giggles to chest-juddering hiccoughs.

The cloud above the car had gone now.

'Come on, we'd better see if your Fiat's OK,' Martin said.

Dawn didn't look even the teeniest bit self-satisfied any more. She looked frightened. She took Martin's arm. 'I'm sorry,' she said.

'For hitting me? Don't be.'

'For thinking you were crazy. The story I wrote came true. I can't believe that it's happened! It's like I'm responsible.'

'Don't think that,' Martin replied. 'You're no more responsible for this than Gerhardie was for the *Titanic* disaster. It's just coincidence.'

She shook her head. 'No, it's more than that. I can *feel* it.'

'You're still going to take me to Cornwall?'

Dawn nodded. 'You're in trouble. I don't know what kind and I don't *want* to know. I'll take you there and I'll drive away again and try to forget about it. And you can forget about the contract too. I'll tear it up.'

'If you can get me where I want to go,' Martin said, 'I'll publish everything you can damned well write. And that's a promise.'

Apart from a star-shaped pattern of ash on the melted tarmac where Dawn's manuscript had fallen and a few scraps of string from the bag it was in, there was no sign that anything untoward had happened.

'One of those bolts hit the car,' Martin said, inspecting the roof and finding nothing.

'It didn't hurt if it did,' Dawn said. 'The keys aren't melted or anything.' She opened the door and got inside.

Martin climbed into the other side of the tiny car and tried to make himself comfortable. 'It smells of petrol,' he said, envisaging an explosion when Dawn turned the ignition key.

'I've just filled it. It always smells a bit after you top up the tank,' she replied. 'Don't worry, it won't catch fire.'

Martin tensed as she turned the key, but the Fiat didn't explode. All that happened was that the little two-cylinder engine started.

'Dawn, there's something I should explain,' Martin began.

Dawn shook her head. 'Don't!' she interrupted. 'Don't say anything because I keep thinking of ghosts and gods and a haunted house and I don't want to know any more. I've had my warning. All that's happened so far is I've lost a manuscript. I don't want to lose anything else.'

Martin nodded and didn't say anything else.

'It doesn't look as if the lightning strike had any effect on the car,' Dawn said as they reached the car's top cruising speed on the motorway – a speed which the Ferrari would have happily doubled in second gear.

It certainly didn't make it go any faster, Martin thought. *You could get out and run alongside if you wanted a bit of exercise.* 'Seems fine,' he replied.

Dawn checked the wipers and lights and indicators and concluded that the Fiat (which she had christened Looby Lou, for God's sake!) was unhurt. Those were her actual words: 'Looby Lou didn't get hurt by the look of it!'

Martin only hoped that Looby fucking Lou didn't suddenly turn into Poison Percy or Asphyxiation Alec. Or Road-Death Reggie. He opened his window and took a deep breath of motorway air while he wondered what Peter Perfect had been trying to achieve back there at the service station.

Evidently he had not wanted to kill either of them, or to incapacitate the car. The burning of the manuscript had to be some kind of warped literary joke, and if there had been only one bolt of lightning, Martin would have left it at that. But there had been *two*.

And one of them struck the car! So what's going on?

Martin didn't discover what was going on until they had been travelling for more than half an hour. Then he realized. Peter Perfect didn't do the same things in his story as Davy Rosenburg would have done. Rosenburg was pretty straight. He gave his characters a problem you couldn't miss and let them deal with it. Peter Perfect was more like Stephen Byrne in that his characters had to figure out what the problem was before they could deal with it. Sometimes the problem was vague and difficult to discover and sometimes you didn't spot it until it was too late.

And this, to Martin, looked like one of those times.

From this point, the nature of the problem took less than ten seconds to uncover. All he had to do was wonder what Peter Perfect wanted to do. That was easy: he wanted to prevent Martin getting to Bude in time to save Essenjay. Why had he struck the car? That was easy too. So it would break down on the motorway, miles from the nearest help.

Unfortunately Martin discovered this when the Fiat was less than fifty feet from an exit ramp.

'Turn off!' he shouted, too late. 'Take this junction! Here! Quick! Turn off!'

'Can't! No room!' Dawn yelled.

If Martin had been driving, he would have thrown the car towards the queue on the ramp and a space would have magically opened to accept him, but Dawn either didn't know this chicken-out trick or she didn't want to try it. As it was, Martin had already forgotten the missed chance and was now wrestling with his seatbelt, trying to get the two buckle sections apart. When the seatbelt finally let him go, he twisted round in his seat, peered out of the car's back window and saw exactly what he had expected to see.

The Fiat was leaving a trail. The thin black line of moisture coming from beneath the car and which Martin knew he would be able to follow all the way back to the service station if he cared to, was some – probably most by now – of the four star Dawn had just bought. Peter Perfect hadn't fouled up at all. The lightning had achieved exactly what he had planned. It had punched a hole in the petrol tank.

That was why he'd smelled petrol. It wasn't because Dawn had just filled the tank at all. It was because it was busily pouring out again.

'What's wrong?' Dawn asked.

'Petrol's leaking. We're leaving a nice trail of it behind us,' he said, and wondered if some bright spark back at the service station was dropping a lit match on it. He could quite easily imagine a streak of fire hammering down the motorway after him like it would in a cartoon.

'The gauge still says the tank's full,' Dawn protested.

'Well, it would say that, wouldn't it?' Martin countered.

'We should get all the way to Bude before it runs out,' Dawn said.

'They sound like famous last words, if I ever heard any,' Martin said.

He waited and the car didn't cough and judder to a halt. He waited a little while longer and concluded that Peter Perfect was going to keep him guessing. 'How far is it to the next junction?' he asked.

'About fifteen miles,' Dawn replied.

'Then I know exactly where we'll run out,' Martin said, 'and it won't be Bude. It'll be half-way between the junction we just passed and the next one. And do you know what else?'

'Nope.'

'When this car dies, we'll be about as far from a help phone as it's possible to get. And when we walk to the nearest one it'll be out of service. And so will the one after that. We'll hope for a police car we can flag down but there won't be one. We'll get to the phone that works and ask for an AA van or something and then we'll walk back to the car and sit on the bank and wait for two or three hours.'

'On the bank?'

'Yeah, on the bank because if there's one thing I know about cars parked on a motorway hard shoulder it is this: they become magnets for large lorries. If we sit in the car something will crash into us and kill us. So we'll sit on the bank and wait. Until it's too late.'

'For what?'

'For me to be in Bude in time to save my girlfriend from Black Rock and the man inside it.'

Ten minutes later, when the Fiat was exactly half-way between the two motorway junctions, Martin's predictions began to come true.

Dawn parked the Fiat on the hard shoulder, they got out

and began to walk, knowing that the first telephone they got to wasn't going to work.

When they were five hundred yards away from the Fiat the ground seemed to shudder beneath their feet and way behind them, a long, low rumbling sound began.

Martin and Dawn glanced at one another and turned around.

The Fiat was gone.

Where it had stood was a very badly damaged articulated lorry. The truck had jack-knifed. Its trailer had swung across the road, blocking it, and its twisted cab was partially embedded in the bank that ran up from the hard shoulder.

The Fiat, presumably, was somewhere underneath it.

'That's Peter Perfect for you,' Martin growled, staring back up the road. 'Always full of surprises.'

Chapter Twenty-five

Looking for James

On two occasions since she had moved into her flat in Bude, Sarah-Jane had booked alarm calls with Telecom. Both times she'd had to rise well before her usual waking-up hour in order to get to the airport.

On neither occasion had the ringing of the telephone awoken her. As Martin had quite rightly claimed, Sarah-Jane Dresden could sleep for her country.

The answering machine attached to her telephone allowed the telephone to ring four times before it cut in, played its message and invited the caller to leave a message of their own.

Four rings didn't take very long to happen and even if she hadn't been fast asleep in front of the television, it would have been hit and miss as to whether S'n'J got to the phone before the answering machine cut in. As it was, she didn't hear the ringing at all. What finally penetrated the wall of sleep behind which she was sheltering, was the voice of James being broadcast from the machine as he left his message for her.

S'n'J's eyes blinked open, she shook her head and listened, wondering whether the sound she could still hear was something to do with what she had been dreaming. A second later she was charging across the room towards the hall where the ansaphone was recording James' voice.

'... hope you get this message. I love you,' she heard as she snatched the phone off the hook and began to babble.

To a dialling tone. James had rung off.

'Damn and blast!' she said and slammed the phone back into its cradle. The answering machine's light lit and flashed on and off, informing her that there was a message for her to hear.

It'll be tampered with, she thought. *When I play it back,* he'll *have got to it.*

But he might not have had time yet. James had only just finished making the call and if she played it back quickly, she might be able to listen to it before Peter Perfect had time to operate on it and leave another rendition of 'Frosty the Snowman'.

She rolled the tape back then pressed play.

'Drezy!' James said. He sounded breathless and worried. 'Where the hell are you? Surely you haven't gone to work yet? What's the time? Oh, it's almost eleven so you probably have. Look, I need your help. I hope you'll forgive me, but I broke my promise to you last night and acted like a story hero. I went over to Black Rock during the night and I got myself into a little trouble. I'm OK, but something's happened to the car. I've managed to get as far as Widemouth Bay and now she's gone out of commission. I'm parked in the car park by the beach, the battery's flat, the engine won't run and I need you to pick me up. You said you only had a small round today, so I'm hoping you'll be back soon. Everything's going to be all right, Drezy. I hope you get this message. I love you.'

Fighting off the urge to pick up her keys and hammer down to Widemouth Bay, S'n'J rolled back the tape and played it again because the Girl Guide part of her told her it needed checking out.

James sounded like James. His voice was his voice, not the voice of someone pretending to be him. His speech patterns were right. The content of his message was right.

But something is wrong.

She rolled back the tape again.

This time parts of it were blanked and her current least-favourite tune was stuck on the end of it. She listened to a few bars of 'Frosty' and turned off the machine defiantly, thinking, *You weren't quite quick enough this time, Mr Perfect, were you!*

She picked up her car keys, checked on Janie, who was still

snoring gently, then she hesitated. If she went out she would be leaving Janie on her own.

The question was: did it matter?

It mattered if Billy-Joe was out there somewhere watching and waiting. But logic said that Billy-Joe was finished off. S'n'J didn't particularly like the idea of leaving Janie, but she liked the idea of leaving James where he was even less. She left Janie and closed the bedroom door. Widemouth Bay was not a long haul. She could easily get there, and back with James, in twenty minutes.

Less if possible. So quit stalling. That call from James had to be real. If it wasn't, Peter Perfect wouldn't have had any reason to ruin the tape, would he?

'Unless it was a double bluff,' she said aloud.

But she didn't think it was. When you got down to it, you sometimes had to trust your instincts. And on this occasion she was pretty sure her instincts were right. It *was* James on the phone.

It wasn't until she was approaching Widemouth Bay that she realized what had been bothering her. Then her heart began to sink. James was a competent mechanic. And he worked at a garage. Admittedly it was a tyre and exhaust centre, but it was full of his buddies who had cars of their own and mechanical knowledge. Surely he would have got someone from there to pick him up. Or maybe even tow him home. Why call her?

'It'll be Peter Perfect in the car park waiting for me,' she murmured. 'Not James.'

And another thing, her Girl Guide voice chipped in, *do you remember telling him how many calls you had to do today?*

Now she thought of it, she *didn't* recall telling him what her Friday round involved. It was too late now anyway; she was almost there.

The road that skirted the bay was long and open and gently curved and S'n'J could see the beach car park as she approached it. Six or seven empty cars were parked there.

'Shit!' she said as she drove into the car park. She wasn't even sure what kind of car James drove. She fancied it was a big American thing, but there wasn't one of those here.

Neither was there a Porsche, so Peter Perfect evidently wasn't present either.

S'n'J got out and toured the parked cars, keeping well away from the doors and peering in through the back windows for any sign that one of them belonged to James.

There were no clues.

She looked down on the beach. The tide was out. There were three people down there, two of them walking dogs and another, right down at the water's edge, skimming stones.

None of them could be mistaken for James.

Go home right now! her inner voice suddenly demanded. *It wasn't James's voice at all, it was Peter Perfect mimicking him. It was a trick to get you out of the house. That's why you got to listen to the whole message. He blocked the words* after *you convinced yourself that it was James on the tape. It was a double bluff. You fell for it because you wanted it to be a message from James.*

S'n'J ran back to her car.

You haven't been gone long, she told herself as she did a gravel-churning about-turn across the car park. *And what about Martin? He should be there by now. He'll have turned up in time to stop anything happening to Janie.*

She hit the main road, did a skidding left turn and floored the accelerator, realizing she did not believe this and feeling very much at Peter Perfect's mercy.

'But,' she told herself, braking for a bend, 'if it was that easy for him he would have already taken you and done whatever he wanted with you. It's been . . .'

She tailed off. It might have been weeks since she'd found the first manuscript sample beneath her bed, but it was only two days ago that she'd read it and somehow pressed its start button. And forty-eight hours had not yet passed since she'd made that first phone call to Janie. It was less than twenty-four since she'd decided to visit the location of Black Rock and had really got things moving. A lot had happened since yesterday morning.

Peter Perfect could in no way be described as a slow worker.

It's almost as if it's been happening for . . .

S'n'J cut the thought off, but not quickly enough. She had been going to tell herself that it was almost as if it had been happening for ever, but that thought would indicate that she was looking back with the mind of Snowdrop, not with her own. The line between fact and fiction was getting completely blurred.

And what happens when that line no longer exists? she asked herself. *Will you remember ever having been Drezy? Or will you always have been Dropsy? Will you cease to exist in this universe and appear only as a book character?*

She thought she knew the answer to this question too. There was a fate that was worse than death and this was it. Being an immortal book character in Peter Perfect's story.

Won't happen, she told herself. *Real people cannot be turned into fiction. And even if they can, it won't happen because I'm pretty handy with a rolling-pin. Soon as I set eyes on the bastard, I'm going to let him have it.*

Five minutes later she drew up outside her flat, got out of the car, locked it, and went in through the building's front door.

There was no trail of bloody footsteps leading up the stairs, no sign of a struggle.

Nothing's happened, Drezy! she assured herself. But this thought didn't push her heart back down from her throat to its rightful position though. It didn't produce saliva in her arid mouth or stop her hand from shaking when she held out the key for the front door lock.

She let herself in, checked the answering machine for more messages and went to her bedroom – the door of which was still closed. *If someone had come in and killed Janie, they wouldn't have closed the door behind them, would they?*

S'n'J took a deep breath and went into the bedroom.

The bed's covers were thrown back.

Janie was gone.

In her place was a brown A4 envelope.

Chapter Twenty-six

Flashback

A strange kind of somnolence settled over S'n'J as she leaned forward and picked up the latest *Black Rock* sample. There was an inevitability about it all. It was as if she knew this scene by heart and had played it out more times than *The Mousetrap* had been performed. She already knew that when she touched the sheets where Janie had been, they would still be warm. And she already knew that running outside to search for her would be pointless. All that mattered was what was written in the book.

She picked up the envelope and carried it back to the lounge, moving like a sleepwalker. The battle was lost. She would read this latest chapter and it would work its bad magic on her. And afterwards she would no longer be Sarah-Jane Dresden. Afterwards there never would have been a Sarah-Jane. Only a Snowy Dresden.

S'n'J sat down on the sofa and took out the pages. There were six of them which meant, she realized ruefully, that it was going to take no more than two or three thousand words to complete her transformation from fact to fiction.

Will I still be me? she wondered. The answer was obvious. Of course she would still be herself. In the pages of *Black Rock* she always *had* been herself. Only the job and the name and some of the historical details had been changed. *To protect the innocent, I s'pose*, she thought.

She would retain some of her memories, too, she assumed. Not enough for her to recall who she used to be, but a few. Those which Peter Perfect allowed her to keep.

She looked at the first page. It was headed: 'Flashback'. S'n'J assumed that it followed on from the last sample she'd read where Snowy had finally escaped the house only to run straight into the arms of Philip Winter. It probably detailed a part of Snowy's previous life. The one she'd had before her favourite author had fictionalized her and captured her in his haunted house.

This turned out not to be the case. This piece of *Black Rock* didn't follow on from the last chapter – or have anything to do with previous sections of the book at all, as far as she could make out.

It began:

One

S'n'J had to read the first sentence three times before she was able to take in what was written there.

The effect this simple sentence had on S'n'J was colossal. And not just because she had to read the sentence three times before she could take in what was written there, either. It was like reading about what was happening to you *while* you were reading about what was happening to you. It made your brain want to collapse.

Me? S'n'J thought. *It can't be me. I'm not in it. I'm not in* Black Rock *under my own name. He can't do it. If he swaps tracks like that, the story won't hang together!*

But whether the story would hang together or not, Peter Perfect *had* swapped tracks and *had* written her into the book.

It continued:

She sat there with the pages in her hands, not wanting to read on and not able to stop herself from doing so. The book was talking directly to her now. She knew that its author had already won. There had been no battle fought. Or thought. Peter Perfect had simply arranged things so there could be no other outcome.

James had been captured or killed, that much was certain. And so, probably, had Martin, who hadn't yet turned up and didn't look likely to. What kept S'n'J reading was the niggling thought that if she could discover how it had all been accomplished, there might still be a chance for her. So she read on, rediscovering things she already knew.

For example: that Billy-Joe was indeed dead. And while a dead body would be of no further use to a writer of general fiction, the same rule did not apply to a writer of ghost stories. Or a writer of biographies, come to that. To these people, being dead was only the first step. After that, things started to get very interesting indeed.

One of the interesting things that involved Billy-Joe had happened in S'n'J's flat shortly after she'd left on her fool's errand.

Billy-Joe's body, which had been waiting round the corner, its head wounds covered by a ski hat left in the back of Janie's VW, had walked to S'n'J's block of flats concealing a weapon beneath his shirt. The weapon, ironically enough, was the very same rolling-pin with which his wife had killed him. When she had fled the car and run up to S'n'J's flat, she had left the murder weapon behind her.

Billy-Joe's body, which, S'n'J thought, had been animated by the willpower of Peter Perfect, followed in Janie's foot-steps. He reached the front door, chose a bell at random and pressed it.

As S'n'J well knew, the entry-phone system which con-nected each flat with the front entrance did not work. This, accompanied by the fact that visitors often pressed the wrong bell, was enough to trigger an acquired response in the owner of the flat whose bell had been rung. In this particular case, the owner, a Christian girl called Candy, did what any other resident would under the circumstances: she automatically pushed the button which opened the front door. If the visitor was for her, he or she would eventually find their way to the right door and begin to hammer on it. If it was for someone else, the same thing would happen.

Getting inside the building was easy.

Billy-Joe knew exactly where to go after that, which wasn't terribly surprising since he was being driven by someone who had done this several times before. He went straight up the stairs to S'n'J's flat and hammered on the door.

It took quite a while for Janie to wake up and when she finally regained consciousness she called for S'n'J who didn't answer. This didn't surprise her because the chances were that S'n'J had fallen asleep in one of her famous comas.

Janie got up and pulled on Drezy's bathrobe, wondering if she could escape via the fire escape which led down from the kitchen. But, she realized, it was unlikely to be Billy-Joe or the police out there, looking for a murderess – it might be Drezy herself, if she'd gone out, or Martin, who was on his way here.

She went to the front door, waited for the next bout of hammering to stop and said, 'Drezy? Is that you?'

'I forgot my key,' S'n'J's muffled voice said. 'I went out for a newspaper and forgot to take the bloody key. Let me in will you? I thought you were never going to wake up!'

You've got a very powerful knock there, Drezy, Janie thought as she fought with the lock. *Sounded almost as if you were knocking the door with a piece of wood or something.*

The following three things happened simultaneously. Janie added the words: *Like a rolling-pin, perhaps*, to the end of her previous thought, the front door was thrust open, pushing her back into the hall and Billy-Joe appeared before her brandishing the very rolling-pin she'd just thought of.

'Hiya babe,' he said.

Janie screamed.

Until Billy-Joe prodded her in her cracked ribs with the handle of the rolling-pin. When this happened she stopped screaming instantly because the air in her lungs vanished and was replaced with something that felt like fire.

Janie dropped to her knees, clutching her chest. Through eyes that were blurred with tears of agony, she looked up at her husband, unable to make any sound at all.

Billy-Joe's skull was in ruins and his face was covered in a cracked sheet of drying blood. His eyes were misted and vacant like those of a fish three days dead. The only thing that looked alive about him was his mouth which twitched and grimaced as though someone was working it with invisible strings.

'Hell in a hand-basket,' Billy-Joe said, his voice bubbling as if his throat was full of phlegm. ''Cept we'll actually be going in your Volkswagen. Hell in a VW doesn't have quite the same ring to it though, does it?'

I'm going to die, Janie thought.

'We're going now, O love of my life. I'm going to take you for a rest cure in the Black Rock emporium of health and vitality. Poor old Ellen's starting to run down now, like a used-up battery, and we need some fresh blood to boost her up a bit. I'm sure she'll be pleased to see you.'

Janie squinted up at him. She managed to shake her head a little, but that was all.

'Now, I don't want you fighting or resisting, so I'm going to have to whack your head in a little. Don't worry, you won't die.'

The last thing she saw was a foot of cylindrical beech sweeping down between her wide-open arms towards her face.

A moment later, a bomb exploded inside her skull.

Then there was nothing.

Two

'I had a strange dream last night,' Snowy said, smiling. Philip had just kissed her awake and presented her with a breakfast tray on which stood a china bowl containing sugared grapefruit, a cup of black coffee, a rack of toast, a plate of tiny butter pats and a selection of jams. Now he was drawing back the curtains. It was sunny outside and the light seemed to drip into the room like honey.

'You did?' he said turning back to her. For the thousandth time she told herself how gorgeous he was and how lucky she was to have him.

You've fallen right on your feet this time, Dropsy, she told herself.

Philip sat on the edge of the bed, smiling at her as she sipped the coffee.

'How did you get on with your book last night?' Snowy asked.

Philip nodded. 'Fine,' he said. 'Going great guns. But I'd rather hear all about your dream.'

Snowy shook her head. 'It's silly,' she said, feeling a little embarrassed. Now that she was awake, the dream had lost all its power. It no longer seemed significant. Except as a crazy, disjointed nightmare.

'Tell me about it anyway. I might be able to pick up something I can use.'

'Are you running short of ideas?' Snowy asked, frowning. 'You haven't got writer's block, have you?'

Philip slowly shook his head. He looked incredibly pleased with himself. His expression struck Snowy as amazingly sexual – but then, practically everything about him struck her that way. She would have him before half an hour had passed. She promised herself that.

'You know me,' Philip said. 'Cornwall's number one liar. I've got enough lies in me to last throughout eternity. I don't get writer's block. It's not getting on with a story that worries me. The problem I have is stopping. I always want my books to go on for ever. Now how about telling me about this dream?'

'Only if you promise me two things. The first is that you won't laugh at me.'

Philip put his hand beneath the duvet and laid it high on her thigh. It was cool and it sent a thrill through her. 'I promise,' he said, solemnly.

'And the second thing is that afterwards you'll let me read one of your books.'

Philip frowned. 'I don't think you'd like them. They're pretty horrible.'

'I don't care. I just want to read one.'

'Why?'

'Let me tell you about the dream, then you'll understand. I dreamed I woke up in the night and you weren't here.'

'That's possible. I would have been working.'

'And I got worried about you for some reason, so I went to look for you. I stood in front of your work-room and listened and I couldn't hear any keys clattering or anything. I knocked. You didn't reply. I got the feeling that something bad had happened to you. Guess what I did?'

'You broke the rules and went inside,' Philip said.

Snowy looked carefully at him, but she couldn't tell whether or not he was angry about her even *dreaming* of breaking the rule. 'I wouldn't do it in real life,' she added quickly.

Philip smiled and moved his cool hand higher up her leg. 'I'm sure you wouldn't,' he said. 'This is different. You don't have to apologize for what you do in dreams. What did you find inside?'

'A computer which worked even though it wasn't plugged in. There was writing on the screen. Stuff you'd written. About me. I read it, and then something happened ... the computer sucked me in and threw me through space ... and I spoke to God ... and he told me I had to stay in the house for ever. Then I got back into the room and I read some more – stuff about how to open the front door by aligning all the things in the lounge and diverting the power that ran through the house. I went to look for you ... and you weren't in the house ... and all the food had gone and there was no water ... and I thought you wanted to kill me for breaking the no entry rule. There was a note in the fridge saying that I had to be punished and that I had to stay in the house for ever. I couldn't open the front door to get out, and I couldn't break any of the windows. Eventually I went into the lounge and lined up all the things in there and got the front door open. And when I ran outside, I ran straight into your arms.'

'And then you woke up?' Philip asked.

Snowy shook her head. 'Then everything changed.'

'How do you mean?'

'The world blew up. Or something. I don't know. Everything flew apart in a billion tiny sparks of light like those simulations of what the Big Bang was like. Except that it didn't just all fly away and keep going. After a second or so it all came back in towards me. It was as if I'd suddenly expanded to twice the size of the universe, and everything came back at me and passed through me. In through the front of me – through my stomach – and out of the back. And when it had finished I was someone else.'

'How do you mean?' Philip asked. There was a playful smile on his face but Snowy didn't know whether it was because his hand was slowly moving closer towards the hot spot that most desired his touch, or because he was playing a game with her. It amounted to the same thing, really, she decided. Everything was a game to Philip.

'I wasn't me any more. Except I was me, but my name was different and I was no longer in this house with you and I had a different set of memories. I could remember things I knew I didn't know. And things that were untrue. For instance, remember I told you how I had an affair with Ellen?'

Philip nodded. 'I remember it in fine detail,' he said.

'Well, in my dream, all that I remembered happening between us was that we woke up in bed in one another's arms and we were dead embarrassed. Each of us thought we'd been seduced by the other one. But nothing had happened. We just went to bed drunk and held each other while we slept. There *was* no affair.'

'Wishful thinking?' Philip asked.

Snowy shrugged. 'I don't regret what happened.'

'You told me you dreamed of torturing her.'

'I also dreamed she was a ghost and she came to my bed. That isn't wishful thinking, is it? Even if I hated her, which I don't, I wouldn't wish harm on her. Anyway, as I was saying, I had all these memories that didn't quite ring true – except that they did, because I was this new person. My name was Sarah-Jane Dresden, not Snowy. And I wasn't a computer saleswoman, but a publisher's rep. Anyway, I was sitting in my flat – I don't know where it was, but I could hear seagulls, so it was somewhere near the sea, and I was reading a chapter of a book called *Black Rock*. And the book was trying to take me over. The more I read of it, the less certain I became about who I really was. The character in the book was me. The *real* me. I was called Sarah-Jane but the more I read, the more I felt I was her. It was like someone had changed me into Sarah-Jane. It was a weird sensation. I was losing my identity.'

'So what happened?'

'I read this chapter about what had happened to my friend. I had this friend called Janie, who was an editor. She was supposed to be in my flat asleep. She told me she'd killed her husband and she'd run away. Well, somehow she'd gone. Her dead husband came and took her away, or something. I don't really remember that bit. But the upshot of it was that I was frightened about being turned back into Snowy. I was scared because my universe seemed to be unravelling. I had this other friend called Martin, I think, and a boyfriend called Jim or something and I was waiting for them to come and help. But as I read the chapter I had in my hands, I found out that both of them had come here to Black Rock and that *you'd* captured them. So I realized that the only way I could save myself was to come here. But I was terrified of being turned into Snowy, because I thought that Snowy was a ghost or something. I can remember the last bit I dreamed before I woke up. Most of it's still in my head.'

'Tell me,' Philip said.

Snowy searched for words, then began. She recited the passage she had read.

'Sarah-Jane Dresden pulled up and got out of her car. She walked towards the house with the sound of Diamond Ambrose Anstey's howling ringing in her ears. The dog, apparently, was trying to tell her something she already knew. That it was dangerous for her to come here. Sarah-Jane did not allow herself to think about this.'

'Very good,' Philip said. 'Perhaps you ought to become a writer too.'

Snowy nodded, barely hearing him. She found the next section and said it:

'Her heart in her mouth, she walked towards the huge black door she knew so well. A part of her remembered touching that golden door knob, remembered how it had eaten her fingerprints before they'd formed. All of this had happened to someone else, but the memories now belonged to Sarah-Jane. The metamorphosis had come on in leaps and bounds during the drive here. The change from being Sarah-Jane to being Snowy Dresden had completed itself. It had begun, she realized, the moment she read the first chapter of Peter Perfect's book, and it had been working at her ever since: eating her away piece by piece. Now it was done and she was totally Snowy.

'Sarah-Jane, finally, had gone.'

Philip nodded sagely. 'Anything else?'

'Some more stuff,' Snowy said. 'But I must have been getting close to waking up by then. It's all fuzzy. Something about striding up to the door not knowing anything except that I had to fight, that I had to cling to the memories that were flooding away from me. "Once upon a time," I was telling myself, "there was a girl called Sarah-Jane who had a boyfriend called James and . . ." that's all I can remember. What do you think it means?'

Philip shrugged and smiled enigmatically. 'Haven't a clue,' he said. 'But I'm sure someone, somewhere, will be able to make sense of it all. Maybe Carl Jung would have if he'd still been around. Or maybe there's a real Sarah-Jane Dresden out there somewhere reading that story at this very moment and feeling the things you felt in your dream. That would be spooky wouldn't it?'

Snowy shuddered, but the spookiness of the issue was not the prime reason for this response. The prime reason was that Philip's gentle fingers had finally hit the spot and gone to work.

'It isn't so bad being Snowy, is it?' he asked as Snowy pushed her hips up towards the fingers that had suddenly moved away from her.

She shook her head. 'No,' she gasped.

Philip touched her. 'Even with the rules?'

'Stuff . . . uh . . . uh . . . the ruh-hooools!'

'Would you like a surprise?'

'Ooooh . . . yessss!'

'We have visitors.'

Snowy didn't care about visitors at that moment. The visitors could damned well entertain themselves. All she cared about was the oncoming orgasm that was rushing towards her like an express train. It would measure about nine on the Richter scale when it hit her. The earth would move. And then some.

'Ellen's here,' Philip said, pushing back the duvet and

lowering his head towards his busy fingers. 'And James and Janie and Martin and Billy-Joe. The gang's all here. And you want to stay here with them and with me, don't you?'

'Mmmm!'

'And be mine for ever?'

'Yours!'

'Here in my universe?'

His fingers left her clitoris and stretched her wide and his hot tongue began to flick at her. 'Fuck me!' she moaned.

'You have to promise to be whatever I want you to be.'

'I promise!' Snowy groaned, shuddering with uncontrollable muscle spasms.

The orgasm that followed was better than nine on the Richter Scale. It was apocalyptic.

'I want you to be someone else,' Philip's voice said out there in the distance.

Three

Sarah-Jane finished the last page and put the latest sample of *Black Rock* down thinking that her only option was to go to the house in Tintagel to try to rectify things.

Whereupon, she understood, she would lose her sense of being Sarah-Jane, become Snowy Dresden and live happily ever after as a gasping nymphomaniac who would do whatever her master required of her. And that, she thought, would probably include torturing poor Ellen and her other friends too.

I won't go, S'n'J thought defiantly. *I'll run away.*

But deep down inside, she knew that this option did not exist. Peter Perfect was more than human. He might have been an ordinary mortal once, but he belonged to that genus no longer. Somehow – presumably from living in Black Rock – he had elevated himself to the position of mortal god. And gods could find you wherever you ran. Even if they were only half-gods. And no matter how long the chase lasted, it could only end one way. The way the god intended it to end.

Sarah-Jane felt incredibly weary. She couldn't fight a battle because she had nothing to use as a weapon except her faithful rolling-pin or a selection of kitchen cutlery. Attacking Peter Perfect with a weapon of this type would be akin to making an assault on a battle tank with a banana. It wouldn't work. Neither could she out-think or out-manoeuvre him. Nothing could be done.

It was all over.

Whatever Peter Perfect wants, Peter Perfect gets, S'n'J thought bitterly. *And he wants me. God only knows why. Perhaps I can make a deal with him. Perhaps I can get him to release Ellen and James and the others in return for his having me. That would be the least I could do. That would save some of us. Maybe he'll listen to reason.*

And hoping that Peter Perfect would listen to reason, S'n'J got her jacket and her car keys.

Do you think it'll snow? she thought as she went out of the front door.

'You mother-fucker!' S'n'J spat, standing up. She threw the pages across the room with all the force she could muster. The pages separated and swayed down towards the carpet like huge discoloured snowflakes. 'You arrogant bastard! I'll show you who's giving in and coming to you begging for a deal. I'll show you!'

She sat down again, shaking with fury. If she'd thought *Martin* was the world's biggest and most egotistical shit, she had been very wrong indeed. He didn't even make the minor league in comparison with Peter Bastard.

'Fuck me, *indeed*!' she hissed. 'You could torture me until doomsday, you fuckhead and I'd never say that to you. I'd rather be burned alive at the stake.'

The nerve of the bastard! she thought, glaring at the scattered pages. *He not only had Snowy dream she was me, but he also predicted my reaction to reading about it!*

The thing that irritated her most of all, however, was the fact that Peter Perfect knew exactly how she had felt when she'd sat down to read his latest chapter. S'n'J refused to consider this and let her fury ramble on for a while.

S'n'J got up, intending to get her coat and her car keys, then she sat down again. It was no good going blazing down there to tear him off a strip. This, presumably, was what he had intended. That last section had been written with the sole intention of inflaming her. Which meant that if she went there when she was cool, calm and collected, she might well have a better chance. Folks who rushed into dangerous situations without considering what might happen often got themselves hurt.

There's got to be something you can do! she told herself. *Despite what he claims in his bloody book, there's got to be!*

But if Peter Perfect had a weak spot, she didn't know what it was. If only he'd been Superman, she could order a chunk of green Kryptonite; if he'd been a vampire she could take garlic and crosses and Holy water. What did you take to ward off a writer? The only thing S'n'J could think of was an editor. Those were the only thorns you could insert into the sides of writers. And according to what she'd just read, he already had two of those.

'Unless what's written there is all lies,' she said. But she doubted this. Martin wasn't around, and neither was James. And Janie had vanished. The only place they could all have gone was to Black Rock.

Which meant that Peter Perfect was impervious to editors.

Maybe they're in awe of him, like you would be if you met God Himself, she thought. *Maybe he gave them demonstrations of miracles to stun them. Perhaps that's the problem. Perhaps Martin can't treat him to any of that editorial derision he's so fond of because Martin's terrified. But Janie once said that all writers have egos the size of China with a black strip of paranoia a hundred miles wide running through them, so perhaps a little derision is the thing that'll bring him down a peg or two.*

But derision didn't sound like much of a weapon to use against someone who could make your lounge floor turn into a hundred-foot drop into the Atlantic Ocean; against someone who was getting stronger with each passing second.

Or that's what he'd like you to think, she told herself. She emptied her mind – or got rid of as much of the crap as she could – and took deep and steady breaths.

She *was* going to have to go down there, she knew. If she

wanted to see James and the others again she was going to have to break her promise to herself, go to Black Rock and fight for them.

All you have to do, she told herself, *is hang on to your own identity.*

If she was going, she realized, she needed a God on *her* side. But S'n'J didn't have a proper bible to take with her. All she owned in the way of religious literature was a yellowing copy of *The Watchtower* she had once bought from a Jehovah's Witness who expected to go to heaven if she made enough converts, and a tiny copy of the *Illustrated New Testament* that they had given her at Sunday school when she was little.

She found the little half-bible in a cupboard, took it to the kitchen, found the rolling-pin she'd hit Martin with the last time she'd seen him, waved the bible over it and said, 'Bless you, weapon of righteousness,' feeling supremely stupid as she did it. She filled an empty plastic Panda Cola bottle with tap-water and blessed it in the same way. The rolling-pin ought to have momentarily gleamed with light and the bottle of water ought to have sparkled for a second (and would have done in a decent horror novel, she thought) but neither of these things happened. In a Stephen Byrne book, this action, even performed without faith, would have guaranteed that both objects would be endowed with a certain power, but in real life this wasn't the case.

Did you expect it to be? she asked herself.

She hadn't expected it, but the wide-eyed little girl who lived inside her (as Peter Perfect had so accurately portrayed) had hoped it would happen and would have been delighted if it had.

You'd better keep on hoping for a miracle, S'n'J told the little girl inside her, *because we're going to need one if we're going to get out of this the same way we got in!*

She took the bible, the rolling-pin and the bottle of water back to the lounge, set them down on the table, looked at them for a while, then shook her head. None of them looked remotely convincing. A Remington pump-action shotgun lying there might have given her a little more confidence, but these little things were not going to work.

S'n'J put on her jacket, put the bible in its inside pocket, picked up the bottle of water, fumbled and watched it fall.

Dropsy! she admonished herself as she stooped to pick it up.

When she'd put the bottle in her pocket, she picked up her car keys and the rolling-pin and headed for the door, her heart in her mouth.

Look out, Peter Perfect, she thought. *Snowdrop's coming home, and she is one extremely angry woman!*

Chapter Twenty-seven

Meeting Mr Winter

The journey to Tintagel and Black Rock did not take the shape that S'n'J had expected. The car didn't play up, no other drivers came at her like madmen and no black dogs attempted suicide at the wheels of her car.

She did not arrive at Tintagel hanging on to her identity with only a tenuous grasp, and no one had sent any hallucinations to frighten her.

It stood to reason, she supposed. She was doing exactly what Peter Perfect wanted her to do. He was confident that things would happen exactly as he had written them: she would get out of her car with the sound of Diamond Ambrose Anstey's howling ringing in her ears. She would walk towards the house with its golden door knob, recalling how it had misted beneath her fingers and how it had eaten her prints. She would no longer know who she was: she would be more Snowdrop than Sarah-Jane.

Get out of it, Drezy, she told herself, *according to the book, the metamorphosis is supposed to be coming on in leaps and bounds as you get closer to the house. That isn't happening, is it?*

She thought about it and decided it wasn't. She was still pretty clear about who she was and who she had to stay.

Put that in your pipe and puff on it, Mister Perfect, she thought defiantly. *I may end up going out like a lamb, but I'm coming in like a lion!*

But, beneath the wafer-thin coating of bluster she was more frightened than she could ever remember being in her whole life. If the resident of Black Rock had already captured (or even killed) Janie, Martin and James, there was no good reason why he shouldn't do exactly as he wanted with her.

Except for the fact that you are special to him, she told herself. If there was any saving grace to the story, this was it. She was the author's main character, and as such, he couldn't let her die before the end. The problem, she realized, was not knowing how far ahead the end lay.

I'll give him a run for his money, whatever happens, she resolved and managed a grim smile.

She drove slowly along Tintagel's main street, followed it round the sharp right-handed bend by the King Arthur's Castle bookshop and on to the caravan park, glancing to her left from time to time, looking out to sea. The sea was flat and slate-grey. Above it, the sky was black and angry as if a storm had been commissioned for her arrival.

That's about what you'd expect on your way to a haunted house to meet your fate, she told herself. *I expect the thunder and lightning will start as soon as I go down the track and can see the house waiting for me at the bottom. Maybe I went to sleep and woke up in a low-budget film . . .*

She made the tight turn at the end of the road and paused at the top of the steep track, her already hammering heart whacking up its work-rate a few more beats-per-minute. She now thought she knew how novice parachutists felt the first time they stared out of the open hatch of an aeroplane. Once the threshold was crossed there was no turning back.

Except that parachutists expect to be still in one piece after they reach the ground, she told herself. *This is like jumping out without a parachute and hoping that you'll get down safely by flapping your arms.*

She found first gear and rolled slowly towards the track.

From about half-way down she could see the huge American saloon blocking the track ahead of her. It stood there on the track with the driver's door wide open as though someone had left it in a hurry. Probably, S'n'J surmised, something to do with the fact that the car looked as if someone had doused it in petrol and put a lit match to it.

It wasn't just burned, it was totally annihilated.

As she drew closer to it, S'n'J realized that the piles of

black ash that lay beside the car's wheels had once been its tyres. The vehicle's paintwork no longer existed. There was no glass in any of the windows, but she could see a pool of what might have been melted plastic lying on the boot lid.

It burned hot enough to melt the glass, S'n'J told herself, and before she could cut off the thought, her mind added, *and you know who was driving it, don't you?*

S'n'J felt tears well up in her eyes. James. He had come here last night, exactly like a paperback hero. He'd broken his promise to her, not knowing how dangerous it was.

And this is what happened, she told herself, rolling to a halt behind the car.

She turned off the Sierra's engine, picked up her rolling-pin and got out, willing herself to believe that James had escaped unharmed.

Ahead of her, the house looked hunched and tense, as if it was a wild animal waiting to pounce the moment she went in through the entrance where the front gate should have been.

Here I am walking towards my death, or eternal damnation, S'n'J thought, fingering the bottle of tap-water in her jacket pocket, *and what am I carrying? A rolling-pin, a bottle of water, and a picture bible, that's what. I would have been carrying a tiny Swiss Army knife with a two-inch blade too, if I'd been able to find it. This is exactly the kind of thing that people in horror stories do. Why do they never phone the police? That's what you should do.*

But in her case, it was too late. The police would find nothing untoward going on at Black Rock. There was another fiction convention that would come into play if she called the police: *Squad cars arrive, lights flashing. Police look suspiciously at burned-out hulk of American Car. Policeman #1 turns to partner and says, 'That car wasn't just burned, Dick, the bastard has been cremated!' The police walk down to the house and hammer on the door. A charming and handsome man answers their knocking, invites them in and speaks to them in soothing tones. 'Yes,' he says, 'I saw the car after it caught fire. I thought I saw someone behind it, hurrying back up the track. I went up to it, but couldn't get close because* of the tremendous heat. I went back indoors and called you guys. I thought I'd better let you deal with it.'

'We have no record of that call,' Policeman #1 says.

Policeman #2 gets on the horn to base. Call has indeed been placed, but for some strange reason, not acted on. 'Sorry to have bothered you,' Policeman #1 says.

They leave, frowning. Something is wrong but they have no evidence.

'And meanwhile something like this happens,' S'n'J muttered. *Girl goes to haunted house because that's the only place her missing friends could be. Pan up track from crouched house to frightened girl. She is holding a rolling-pin. In her pockets are other useless items. Cue music of the 'Going to her death' variety.*

She was acting like someone from a lousy book simply because there was no other alternative. If she'd stayed home cowering behind her door, Peter would simply delete a few paragraphs from his magical word-processor and rewrite. When you had control of reality it didn't matter what people did: you could still get them.

S'n'J walked slowly towards Black Rock, wishing for Diamond Ambrose Anstey, who was not in position on his trailer pointing down at her, nor in the road in front of her. Diamond would help her. Diamond was trapped, just as she would end up being. He was a ghost dog, she knew that now. He was a spirit entrapped by *Black Rock* in exactly the same way she was. Peter Perfect had probably spotted him and written him into the story. After all, when you suddenly became a new god, you didn't just rush in and start changing the world, did you? You started small – with something like a dog – and worked your way up.

Diamond wasn't a demon dog at all, but a poor trapped soul. And he'd known that S'n'J was getting into trouble. He'd tried to warn her off, in the only way he could.

Maybe, if only he would turn up, he could still help her somehow.

But Diamond was nowhere to be seen.

That doesn't fit in with what you wrote, S'n'J thought. *According to the book, he should be howling like a banshee by now. And I should already be more Snowdrop than Sarah-Jane.*

'He's rewriting,' she whispered to herself as she stared down at the house. 'He's up there in his work-room at this very moment, deleting lines and replacing them with fresh ones. He has to catch reality and alter it and that's what he's doing now. In real life things don't work out exactly as they do in the book, so he has to alter the book to suit. And he's got to a complex part now. The part when fantasy wrests control from reality. Permanently as far as I'm concerned.'

Unbidden, S'n'J's mind lit up with a fantasy of its own. In it she was in the originator's work-room staring at the screen of his word-processor. It was no ordinary IBM compatible: it was a terminal that connected directly to the force that shaped reality. He'd hacked into reality's program and was altering it. She knew this as she stood there in front of it, watching words scroll up the screen. The words of *her* story. And Peter Perfect's and Janie's and Martin's and James's. The words of *Black Rock*. She also knew that there was a very simple way of breaking that link and destroying the fiction that had been woven around her and her friends – and probably destroying Peter Perfect too. All she had to do was smash the computer with the rolling-pin that was currently clutched in her right hand. Just put it through the screen, then attack the plastic case in which the computer's guts resided.

The only question she had was whether doing this would short-circuit all reality too. If this thing really was connected to God or whatever drove the universe and everything in it, its removal by force might send out shock-waves. *It might be the end of everything,* she told herself solemnly. *Not just me and Peter Perfect and my friends, but everything that ever existed. All life. All history. All possible futures.* Then she decided that if it was, it wasn't her fault, and swung the rolling-pin at the screen.

S'n'J grimaced as the fantasy itself exploded in her head. If she could get to his work-room, she would give it a go. As battle-plans went, it rated about 0.00001 on a scale of nought to ten, but at least it gave her something which might, if she could make herself believe in it, be construed as hope.

'Smash the bastard,' she whispered. 'That's what I'll do!'

Ahead of her Black Rock lit up.

Or rather, *transformed* itself.

Suddenly it was the brightest thing on the landscape. It looked artificial, as if it had been re-painted in brighter colours than normal. Or as if there was a row of spotlights in front of it, shining on it. The windows bore the sparkling traceries of the frost she'd seen before through her car's rear-view mirror, and the window on the right-hand side – the bedroom in which Snowy slept – was black and empty. The ebony front door reflected almost no light and looked as if it had opened on to the darkest night ever witnessed. Its shining door knob glinted like a single gold tooth in an empty mouth.

Around the rock on which the house stood, the sea looked dull and flat and lifeless. The greenery which edged the property looked as if it had been coloured with thousand-year-old paint. The only thing which looked real and vibrant and alive was the house itself.

Above it, the sky was dark and restless. An invisible hand stirred the clouds into restless towering shapes like huge battle-cruisers.

S'n'J paused for a moment, staring open-mouthed at the transformation. The thing that horrified her most was that there was a large part of her which rejoiced at the change she was witnessing. This part – her wide-eyed little girl – was watching a miracle taking place and badly wanted to be a part of it.

That's why he wants you! she scolded herself. *Because there's a part of you that wants to live in a magical world!* But the feeling of joy didn't go away. *If it can be as good as this . . .* the little girl thought, *what's wrong? If it can be this brilliant, this magical, why don't we just accept it, go down there and go inside. It'll be wonderful!*

And looking at the house, S'n'J could see what this part of her meant. There was Black Rock, a mere hair's breadth away from twinkling like a star. Set against the backdrop of the mundane real world, it looked very inviting indeed.

If she had just been able to forget that behind its front door lay eternal damnation, she might have skipped all the way down there like a little schoolgirl looking forward to a half-day holiday.

Black Rock *was* magical. It *was* beautiful.

And it had no right to exist.

If there's a way of getting rid of it, I'll find it! S'n'J told herself.

But Mr Winter was in there. The man of her dreams. Her ideal. Her Mister Right. *Things could be perfect!* the little girl said, and showed her a fleeting image of just how perfect the love-making – on that sheepskin rug in front of the open fire – was going to be.

S'n'J thrust the image away and replaced it with one of her own: the image of her and James last night, consuming one another's bodies with a passion so intense it had made them both scream. But standing here in front of the house, the image of her and James was the thing that seemed unreal. The other picture seemed very real indeed.

She shook her head. Way out at sea, a huge wave was forming, piling itself up into a foaming wedge.

You can't frighten me with that old trick, S'n'J thought. *I've seen it all before!*

She glanced back at the house – upon the roof of which no mysterious writer was balanced – and told herself that no matter how much she ached to be a part of it, she was here to destroy it and she mustn't forget that. She feared that she *was* changing into Snowy after all, and reminded herself that this was what the writer wanted her to think. It wasn't going to be that easy for him to accomplish or it would have happened already.

She looked back at the sea, which was now flat again, and congratulated herself. She seemed to have achieved at least some progress. Perhaps there was a chance for her after all.

The whole sky was now looking disturbed though, and the angry area of cloud above the house was performing some kind of trick where vapour streamed off from the bottom of it towards the top and piled up there, forming a tall, ugly shape. It looked rather like it might be a thundercloud.

But it won't strike you, even if it is, she assured herself. *He isn't going to hurt you. He wants you to be his Snowdrop.*

She moved slowly towards the house, trying not to look up at the strange shapes that swirled in the sky. To her left King Arthur's Castle stood on its 'figure eight' shaped pair of rocks. A mist was rising from the sea at their foot and tendrils were flowing up towards the Castle. S'n'J looked at it once, saw the slender line of mist that ran directly from the Castle's rocks across the bay to the rock on which the house stood, and told herself that Janie was right. The site of the Castle – and of Black Rock – had been chosen because the place had some kind of power. Arthur's knights probably *hadn't* made fair beginning of a nobler time at all. Or if they had used the power in a positive way, whoever had placed Black Rock here since had corrupted that power.

She resolved not to look over there again. She didn't want to know what was happening over at the Castle; her imagination could quite happily conjure up pictures of dead knights coming back to life and marching on Tintagel with blazing banners. They would be unstoppable and they would show no mercy.

She gazed down at the ground as she walked because she could no longer bear to look at the beautiful icy thing the house had become, either. It was too *wrong.* And a part of her was too impressed with it.

But after she'd taken two more steps, S'n'J noticed something wonderful. Spring had come.

She knew this because in the places where she had trodden, vegetation had sprung up in the shape of her shoes. For a moment she thought she was imagining it, then she turned and looked back at the way she'd come. She had left tracks. Each of her steps was outlined with tiny blades of grass and filled in with purple flowers.

Frowning – and fighting off the part of her that wanted to be delighted and charmed – S'n'J peered at the last two footsteps she had taken. The flowers there weren't just tiny, they were minute. Each had four flat petals and a little black centre part that looked furry. None of the flowers had a diameter of more than four millimetres. There had to be thousands of them in each footprint. S'n'J knelt down and sniffed at the nearest one. It smelled vaguely like honeysuckle and hit her olfactory nerves in much the same way as a bottle of smelling-salts. One inhalation was enough to make her feel as if her brain had expanded inside her head.

S'n'J inspected the soles of her shoes, which were unchanged. Experimentally, she placed one foot on the ground ahead of her, then withdrew it. The flowers were already there when she took it away. She put the foot back into the print, expecting it to sink into the earth. Nothing happened at all. The flowers weren't even crushed.

What does it mean? the little girl part of her asked enthusiastically.

S'n'J snapped her mind down on the voice of the little girl and put the question out of her mind. What it meant was that Peter Perfect was trying to bring out that willing part of her and make it take over. If she could keep it at bay, she had a chance. If she let herself be seduced by this magic, she was sunk.

Don't you remember? the little girl asked plaintively. *At Tintagel Castle, where Arthur's knights made fair beginning of a nobler time? Don't you remember what happened then? When we went there? Don't you remember the magic he showed us?*

S'n'J shook her head. The last time she'd gone there she'd just seen a ruin of a well-placed castle.

You're just shutting it out because you're frightened! the little girl complained. *You could remember if you wanted to!*

But S'n'J didn't want to, because there *was* a memory there. A deeply buried one which threatened to surface soon. She frantically piled things on top of the place in her head where the memory seemed to be located, because she didn't believe it was one of hers. It was *his*, a made-up, false one.

Looking at the track ahead of her, and never up at the building itself, S'n'J went towards the enchanted house.

She was aware that she'd passed through the entrance to Black Rock's grounds when the light changed. It became brighter. Much brighter. At her feet, the shingle shone like jewels, each stone glinting and winking.

Can't take much more of this! a dizzy part of her mind warned as she struggled to keep her balance in the shifting sea of light.

The print her right foot had just left was neither filled with tiny flowers nor edged with grass. Nor were there twinkling shingles where she had trodden. Her foot had left a print which was dead flat and totally black . . . except for a circular spot in the heel which shone golden and on which was printed an exact facsimile of the were-lion gargoyle which was embossed upon the house's door knob.

S'n'J's left foot came up leaving an identical print beneath it.

And suddenly she realized the mistake she'd made. She was already dizzy, and now she was leaning too far back to hold her balance. And wasn't the world's most elegant mover at the best of times.

S'n'J's left foot came down on its outer edge, her weight shifted forwards and as her ankle began to complain, her right foot stove into her left ankle.

Which tensed, twisted . . . and gave way.

For a moment S'n'J felt as if someone had just blasted that ankle with a rifle and then the bejewelled surface of the drive rushed up to meet her.

Her elbows took most of the force of the fall, but they didn't stop her face from hitting the ground. S'n'J rolled over to her back, spitting gravel and blood and cursing her ankle which felt as if it was ablaze.

It isn't broken! she told herself as she pushed herself up to her hands and knees. *It's just twisted, that's all. Only sprained!*

But sprained or not, the ankle shot arrows of agony up her leg when she tried to put her weight on it. She sat down again and inspected the damage. She couldn't feel anything that was snapped, which was a good thing, but the ankle hurt when she touched it, which was a very bad thing indeed. She glared up towards the front door, tears of pain and anger and fear in her eyes. 'You *bastard!*' she spat.

Then she stood and dragged herself the rest of the way to

the front door, where she glared at the smirking were-lion or whatever the thing was and whacked it with the rolling-pin.

Hope that wipes the stupid grin off your face! she told it, and hit it again, a little harder.

The gargoyle's smile seemed to have increased. S'n'J was furious. She considered whacking it again, a lot harder, but reasoned that her only weapon would break if she did that and that was probably what Peter Perfect wanted. That was why he hadn't opened the door yet. He must know she was there, waiting for him, but he hadn't made a move.

You can wait inside as long as you like, el bastardo, but Drezy here isn't going to ruin her rolling-pin on your door knob. She's knocked for entry and now it's up to you.

S'n'J propped herself up beside the door, one foot off the ground, and waited.

Eventually the black door began to move, opening as smoothly and as quietly as it had done in the pages of *Black Rock*.

S'n'J stood up straight, planted both her feet squarely on the ground, got the bottle of holy tap-water from her pocket and spun the lid off.

The door opened on to an empty hall.   .

For a split second, S'n'J saw the stairs up which she'd run 'with' Snowy during the story; the long hall that led to the back of the house where there should have been a door, but wasn't; the door that led into the dining-room and the one that led into the lounge. She knew this house like the back of her hand. Every detail, imagined, alluded to, or described, was exactly as she'd known it would be.

The worst thing about it was that it felt like home.

And then there was a blur of movement, the source of which could not be discerned, and Peter Perfect stood in front of her, smiling.

And as S'n'J had imagined, Peter Perfect was not some wizened-up little old man who lived his life in lands created by himself on a word-processor, nor was he a bright young university educated hack.

Peter Perfect was Mr Winter.

He was achingly handsome.

'Hello Snowdrop,' he said. His ice-blue eyes seemed to be drinking in every detail of her and his expression told her that he was pleased with what he saw. His voice was soft and well-spoken. Musical even.

Good material, she thought. *That's what I am to him. Malleable. Changeable.*

But in spite of this she could feel herself warming to him – presumably in the same way that the Count's victims did when he fluttered in through their windows and changed back from being a bat.

'I've waited so long for this moment to arrive, my Snowdrop,' he said. 'You have no idea.'

S'n'J felt the universe start to change behind her. She also knew exactly how she could stop it. She shifted her weight on to her hurt leg. She managed to keep her face expressionless when the jolt of pain shot through her and was pleased with herself. She was even more pleased that the sensation of *things changing* ceased almost immediately.

Mr Winter frowned.

'I'm not your Snowdrop,' S'n'J said, smiling back at him. 'I'm someone else's Sarah-Jane.' Then, inspired, she added, 'And you're not Mister Philip Winter, are you? You're not Peter Perfect either, you're Fred King. Fred King who killed his wife Zara and who wants Zara back again. Am I right?'

Mr Winter shook his head very slightly. 'I'll be whoever you want me to be,' he said mildly.

'I want you to be gone, spirit!' S'n'J said, feeling even more foolish than she had when she'd blessed the tap-water.

He frowned. 'I'm not a spirit,' he said, 'I'm Philip Winter and I'm a writer. And, as it happens, I'm also your husband. You only became Snowy Dresden again when you ran away. You're Snowy Winter really.'

S'n'J shifted her weight on to her bad leg again. It didn't seem to hurt so much now. She shook her head. 'I'm not your Snowy. I'm Sarah-Jane and you've been writing about me, haven't you?' she said. 'Trying to change me.'

Philip Winter looked mystified. And intrigued. 'Would you like to come in and talk about it?' he asked.

S'n'J shook her head so violently she almost fell over.

'Nope!' she said. 'I would not. What I would like is for you to tell me what you've done with my friends. The ones you've captured.'

Philip Winter looked at her, long and hard. 'Who are you, Snowy?' he asked quietly. 'Who are you really?'

The question fell on her like a thick blanket. She knew *exactly* who she was. She just couldn't say, because it would sound supremely stupid. Not just silly like it had done when she'd accused him of being a spirit, but stupid enough to qualify as an entry for the *Guinness Book of Records*. She was someone who didn't exist. She was Sarah-Jane Dresden, a woman who no longer had a past or a future, only a present. In a moment even that would be extinguished.

Fight! she told herself and stamped her bad leg on the ground. This time the pain made her gasp.

'Are you hurt, my Snowy?' he asked. 'Would you like to come in and sit down?'

The voice was soothing. His very presence was soothing. It would be so easy. All she had to say was 'yes'.

'Come on,' he soothed. 'You're just distressed. You've had a breakdown. You can expect periods of confusion. They'll pass.'

'No breakdown!' she hissed. 'Not in the book!'

'Which book?' Philip asked.

'You know!'

'I don't. Please tell me which book! Have you been reading my books?'

'*Black Rock*,' she gasped. She could only just recall it now. Just being close to him was enough to sap what little of her personality remained.

Philip reached out for her and took her hand. His own was cool and dry and hard and comforting. Like the hand of the lover she knew so well and had never had. She wanted to be his. It would be so easy.

'I haven't written a book called *Black Rock*, Snowy. There isn't one.'

Tears were rolling down S'n'J's face. 'Stop confusing me!' she said.

'It's OK, you're home now. Come in. Please. It's so good

to have you back. I've been worried about you. Where have you been?'

'I've *been* home!' she sobbed, stamping her bad leg again. Even the pain didn't cut through her confusion.

He shook his head. 'This is your home, Snowy. You haven't been here for a long while.'

'This house is *haunted*!' she moaned.

'The only thing that's been haunting this house since you've been gone, is me, love,' he told her.

'That's what I mean!' she sobbed.

'Shh,' he soothed. 'It's going to be just fine. You ran away, but you've come back to me at long last. Come indoors.'

S'n'J drew back. 'Not with a ghost!' she said.

'Can you feel my hand on your arm?' he asked gently.

She nodded.

'Then I'm not a ghost, am I?'

S'n'J despaired. 'Help me,' she said.

'I'm trying to. I love you, Snowy. I've missed you.'

'But I haven't been here before. Not until yesterday.'

'Yes you have. We've lived here for years.'

'What have you done to Ellen?'

'Ellen?'

'She's in the basement, isn't she? Dead or dying. And so is Janie and James and Martin.'

Philip studied her benignly. 'I don't know any of these people and they aren't in the basement. They can't be because we don't have a basement, or a cellar. You'll remember when you come in and look around. I'll get in the Porsche and drive up to the village while you do so if it'd make you feel more comfortable.'

'There isn't a Porsche out there,' S'n'J said, 'and there are two cars blocking the road. One of them is mine and the other belongs to James. You killed him. He was trying to help me and you killed him.'

'Breathe deeply, Snowy. The Porsche is out there on the drive. The track is not blocked and never has been since the last fall of snow we had four years ago. Don't you remember how we joked about it? We used to look out at the clouds massing over the sea and I used to say, "Do you think it'll snow, Snowy?"'

'It's all a trick,' she insisted. 'You're trying to confuse me. That was just something you said on my answering machine.'

As she spoke she turned away from him and looked out into the forecourt. The Porsche was there, shining red, its convertible top lowered. Up on the empty track, Diamond Ambrose Anstey stood, pointing down at her.

S'n'J turned back. 'I saw it flicker!' she said.

'I don't think anything flickered, Snowy,' he said. There was a tone to his voice that sounded odd.

'I'm losing and you're winning,' she said in a voice that sounded tired and defeated.

Philip disagreed. 'No one's winning or losing. Your true personality is surfacing, that's all. Don't you remember what the doctors said after your breakdown? About how you could expect periods when you didn't know what was real and what wasn't? About how you had to relax and let things take care of themselves rather than try to reconstruct yourself to a set pattern? What you've done, Snowy, is, you've created yourself a spurious personality. One that isn't you and never was you. You're Snowdrop, you always have been and you always will be, no matter how much you try to convince yourself that you're someone else.'

'Liar!' she said. The terrible thing was that she could indeed remember what the doctors had said. She remembered her breakdown (or at least the after-effects of it) quite clearly. She recalled a time when she'd been Snowy, then something had happened (she couldn't recall what that something was), and then she'd been no one. Then came the doctors and the white pills that stuck in her throat. And after that the smell of the leather couch beneath her as a man called De Witt encouraged her to talk about a past which featured a lover called Ellen, a hamster called Snowball and herself as a sales engineer for a computer firm. That particular past seemed a great deal more real than the one in which she'd lived with an editor called Martin and then had a lover called James.

'Liar!' she said again, but her voice lacked conviction. S'n'J stamped her leg. The pain was white-hot. There was a shaft

344

of wood in one of her hands, cool glass in the other and a bible in her pocket. These things seemed significant. 'Get thee behind me, Satan!' she shouted.

Philip backed away a pace.

'Begone, demon!' she yelled and struck out at him with the rolling-pin. It was a clumsy blow and missed Philip's head by a foot. As she struck, he leapt back and brought his arms up to defend himself. The rolling-pin whacked into Philip's moving elbow and clattered to the floor.

'Don't, Snowy,' Philip said sadly, and she thought she heard a note of fear in his voice.

Holy water! she thought. *Let him have it right between the eyes! You've got him now!*

'Get thee hence, foul spirit!' she thundered, groping in her pocket for her Illustrated New Testament with pictures by E.S. Hardy. Her fingers found it and dragged it out. She brandished it, showing Philip its pretty cover depicting Jesus on a riverbank, preaching. Jesus wore robes and head dress and a goatee beard and held yellow flowers in his left hand.

'Flee from this place!' she said, thrusting the bible towards Philip.

He took another step back. 'Don't!' he said.

She threw the water at him before she even realized she was going to do it. The neck of the bottle was too narrow for much of the contents to come out with a single shake, but some of the liquid hit Philip in the face.

Although it was only tap-water, and it had been blessed by someone who wouldn't have described herself as the least bit religious, it worked.

The water steamed and hissed as though it had been dropped on to a hotplate. And Philip actually began to burn away.

He didn't scream, he didn't turn and run, he just stood there, his dark eyes glowering while the water ran down his face, etching deep, smoking runnels into his flesh.

'I win!' she shouted. 'I win and you lose, demon! Get thee hence!'

She shook more water from the bottle. One of Philip's

glowering eyes dissolved and ran down his face like smouldering jelly.

'Where's Ellen?' she demanded.

And when Philip spoke it was with the voice of the demon he really was.

'Gone,' he grated. 'Used up. Drained. Flat, like a battery.'

'What did you do to her?'

'What did *we* do to her,' Philip corrected from behind the stinking steam that was covering his face. 'We used her, Snowy. Me and you. We chained her to the house and let the house take her power. Like feeding the furnace. Everything needs fuel to work. Black Rock runs on pain and fear, and on life and soul. Ellen is gone, in spirit and in body. Used up.'

'What about Janie and Martin and James?'

'All dead.'

She shook more water over him. 'Liar!'

'Janie's in the basement screaming in agony. Can't you hear the echoes? Martin and James are both gone, too.'

Snarling, she threw the remainder of the water over him.

Philip's body suddenly looked as if all the bones and organs had been removed; his skin collapsed inside his suit and his suit folded to the ground, steaming.

S'n'J gazed down at the clothes and saw Philip's boneless wrists and hands hanging out of his sleeves like a set of deflated party balloons. A bag of hair stuck out of the neck of his shirt.

As she watched, the empty skin withdrew into the suit as if it was shrinking.

'Begone!' she shouted and shook the last few drips of water from the bottle.

'Have you finished?' a voice said from beside her.

She spun round, and there was Philip, soaked in water, but not even slightly damaged. She turned back to the place where his empty suit was – except that it *wasn't* and probably never had been. She had just hallucinated all of that.

Philip plucked the empty bottle and the bible from her hands. He didn't smoulder. His hand didn't catch fire where it held the bible. 'Enough, Snowy,' he said. 'I am not a demon or a ghost.'

'I'm not Snowy!' she wailed, backing away.

'Look at your driving licence, Snowy,' he said gently.

She took the wallet out of her pocket and opened it. There was her licence and her insurance certificate. Both gave her name as Mrs Snowdrop Winter.

'*Now* do you believe me?' Philip asked.

'I lost, didn't I?' she said thickly.

Philip shook his head. 'No one lost,' he said gently. 'Do you want to come in? We'll both have won if you want to come in.'

And she *did* want to go in. She wanted to be home again and whole again.

'Yes,' she said in a small voice, 'I want to come in.'

You shouldn't have said that! a mental voice she no longer recognized snapped, and she paused on the threshold for a moment, wondering if she had made the wrong response.

And then it didn't matter one way or the other because she was inside, feeling dizzy because all the flat surfaces in the house seemed wrong and she hadn't yet rediscovered her Black Rock legs and Philip was supporting her, holding her upright. By the time the next doubtful thought surfaced, Philip had taken her into his strong arms and was holding her, comforting her as she sobbed, and his warm lips were pecking tiny homecoming kisses all over her face and telling her how much he'd missed her.

In seconds, the remnants of Sarah-Jane Dresden were gone.

Chapter Twenty-eight

Snowy, Unravelling

Snowy awoke from an uneasy sleep in which she had heard the screaming of the damned battery-girls, the ones that Philip kept in the cellar so that the house could feed on their pain.

She lay there in the big bed, echoes still resounding while she tried to piece together the shattered fragments of the dreams she'd had.

The curtains were closed and it was gloomy inside, but Snowy got the distinct impression that it was daytime beyond the window. She didn't recall going to bed – only that there had been frantic passion at some point beforehand. Then Philip had gone into his work-room to catch up on some of that writing he was supposed to be doing.

He's probably actually rewriting, she thought, and didn't quite know why the voice of her imagination sounded so snappy. She didn't think he'd finished the book he was working on, so there shouldn't be any need to redraft yet.

Remembering the dream, she began to picture some unfortunate in the cellar, manacled to the wall. She could also remember Philip explaining to her that the house – like any half-way decent haunted house, she supposed – needed pain and suffering in order to exist. Except that he hadn't said that, exactly. It had sounded a lot more mystical than that. Something to do with God wanting to rebuild reality in his own image. The battery-girls who died in the cellar had been something to do with feeding the fire that forged the new reality.

It all sounded like Japanese to her, especially now that she couldn't remember half of it.

But the fire allegory had stuck. She visualized the house connected in some mysterious way to a roaring power source that sounded like a furnace and looked like blazing Armageddon.

Snowy could clearly remember looking at it in her dream. She'd found the source by opening a door in Philip's work-room – a door that she knew did not exist in real life. The door – although it should have been on the other side of the house in her dream because it was in real life – opened back into this bedroom. Except that when you came into this room from the work-room, everything was different. When you came in here from there, you walked in on the source of the power that ran the house. The power with which God could re-shape reality.

And if that isn't heavy going, I don't know what is! she told herself.

But there were other snippets of dream-memory that were also pretty heavy going. You didn't just take those girls to the basement and leave them there, she knew, you had to do things to them, too. She could remember a pretty girl called Janie who was manacled to the wall where a girl called Ellen had once been. Nothing remained of Ellen to mark her passing but a patch of dried blood on the cellar floor. Ellen had taken some heavy-duty usage.

Snowy didn't want to think about it anymore. Sometimes you were better off leaving things alone. Like the fact that she had two different memories of a girl called Ellen; one in which she'd been her lover and one in which she hadn't. Or the memory of having had an argument with Philip, in spite of the fact that they hadn't had a disagreement.

'Something's *wrong*,' she said and got out of bed. The spike of pain that shot up her right leg cleared her head. She sat down and examined her ankle, frowning. She'd twisted it quite badly, apparently. The problem was that she couldn't recall having done this.

You did it this morning, her mind told her and treated her to a fantasy in which she was walking across Black Rock's forecourt carrying a rolling-pin and a plastic bottle of water. She watched as her legs became entangled and she stumbled.

Snowy suddenly knew that if she hobbled to the window and opened the curtains she would see a burned-out American car blocking the track about a hundred yards away. There would be another car behind it. The one she had arrived in. A Ford Sierra.

The car you had when you worked for the computer company, she told herself. *The car you no longer have because you left your job years ago when you moved in here. We've been married for four years. He told you that earlier.*

'Then why can't I remember the wedding?' she wondered.

There was no burned-out American car on the track, or red Sierra like the one she had once driven. What there was appeared to have been stolen from the special effects department of a low-budget film. There were two patches of shimmering heat-haze in the position where she could almost recall the cars being. If what she could see up there was supposed to be a mask, it wasn't a good one. You couldn't see either of the cars, admittedly, but you *could* see that something was covering them. He might as well have thrown a tarpaulin over them.

A picture of a sandy-haired man flickered into life in her mind. He looked absolutely astonished and terrified and there was blood running down his face from his scalp.

Where you hit him with the rolling-pin! she told herself.

The problem was, there wasn't a Martin and there never had been.

Think! Try to remember! If there's no Martin to recall, then how about thinking back on what happened to you during those four years you've lived here!

Snowy tried. It was like falling into a pit. There were no memories of the past four years of her marriage to Philip. There were snippets of other memories though, of things that had nothing to do with Philip. But nothing was complete. It was as if something had erased these from her mind. But the erasing hadn't been done successfully. Bits were still there, lurking beneath new memories which only went back as far as the nervous breakdown she'd had. The old memories were disjointed and broken but even in this condition they felt more real than the ones she had.

Well, they couldn't feel any less real than four years of emptiness, could they? she asked herself as she gazed out of the window at the wavering shrouds around the cars.

There's something peculiar going on here and I think I know what it is.

But Snowy didn't allow herself to voice the thought because she had the distinct feeling that she would instantaneously vanish if she did. Her whole personality felt about as thick as a rainbow of oil on the surface of a puddle.

Out on the track, the heat-haze wavered as if a wind had pushed against it and for a moment Snowy saw the front corner of the car beneath it. The car was red and the wing looked distinctly Sierra-shaped.

If this was a spurious reality and Philip was orchestrating it, then he had bitten off more than he could chew. Like a juggler with too many balls, he was being sorely taxed trying to keep everything in the air at once.

She was Philip's creation, she was sure of that, and she wouldn't be able to act against him. He would have built that rule in, like one of Asimov's Laws of Robotics.

She just wished that she could reject the silly notion that Philip had created her. Then she could do something. But the message – whether or not he had planted it in her mind – was big and bold. She was his and his alone. She belonged to him, heart and soul, for better or for worse. And if she did anything to him – even a small thing, like remembering one of those things she oughtn't remember – he could and would make her wink out of existence in the twinkling of an eye.

Come on, Snowy, you're made of tougher stuff than that! she told herself. *What are you, a woman or a marshmallow? There must be something you can do, even if it's only to get to the bottom of this! Answer this simple question and win yourself a prize: Why did you wake up thinking Philip was busy rewriting?*

The answer, of course, was because she'd dreamed he'd created her as a character in a book. He was rewriting, because of the holes in the plot – one of which she could see quite clearly, if she cared to stare at the twin patches of heat-haze a hundred yards up the track.

He made me on his magical computer, she thought. *He made me. Magical computer. Magic. Made me.*

There was something there, buried deep. But if she kept at it, she was sure it would surface.

The answer, when it came, was absurd. The answer was 'God for Windows', a computer joke she had once cracked in a time of stress. Windows was the Microsoft answer to tricky computing. Your programs were represented on your computer screen as little picture icons in little windows. You simply pointed at the program you wanted to use, clicked a button on your mouse, and you were in business. And all the programmes that worked for Windows were called 'Something-or-other for Windows'. 'God for Windows' was the term Snowy had used when she'd ... and here came the memory, not popping up like a jack-in-the-box or rising from the depths like a cinema organ, but flickering like a faulty fluorescent tube trying to light.

Suddenly the light was on and Snowy could remember what had happened all that time ago. She'd woken up worrying about Philip and had gone to his work-room thinking about what had happened to Bluebeard's wives when they had disobeyed him by entering the place that was forbidden to them. And then she'd opened the door and gone in.

And she'd fallen two hundred feet into the Atlantic Ocean.

But that had been an hallucination. When her vision had cleared she had discovered that although there was no power source in the room, the computer that stood on Philip's big clean desk was working. She had gone to it, marvelling at how it could work without being plugged in.

And the computer monitor had expanded around her and sucked her in, then flung her through space where the voice of God had told her that it was too late to repent because Bluebeard was his son and she'd broken Bluebeard's rules and must pay the consequences. 'The getting in is easy, Snowdrop Dresden,' the voice of God had said, 'It's the getting out again you have to worry about.'

Then both the voice of God and the computer screen had told her that she would have to stay in the house for ever.

That was when she'd read the text that Philip had been working on before he left the house. It was called *Black Rock* and it was about her. About what had happened to her in real life and what was *going* to happen to her too.

And then, in a panic, she'd tried to escape.

Because I discovered the truth. The truth is that Philip wrote my story, and brought me to life, not in his own mind, or in the mind of a reader, but properly to life. He made me exist. Using the magic computer and the god behind it, he brought me to life, straight from his imagination.

Snowy shifted her weight to her bad right foot because there was still something that wasn't quite right and she knew that in the aftermath of the pain, her head would be crystal clear for a few seconds.

She clenched her teeth as the lightning-conductor leg shot tracers of agony right up to her shoulder.

During the moment of clarity between the pain and the dull ache which followed, Snowy corrected herself. He *hadn't* created her solely from his own imagination, but from another person. This was why she had conflicting memories. He'd shaped her from a woman called Sarah-Jane. A woman whom she had fleeting memories of having been. He had sat at his magical word-processor – which was somehow linked to reality – and had changed that reality for Sarah-Jane Dresden until she became what he wanted her to be. Snowy Dresden.

And now he's rewriting me to fix the mistakes he made during the transition. You are Snowdrop Dresden in Sarah-Jane's body. There is no such person as Snowdrop Dresden.

The thought left behind it a nasty after-taste of madness. Here she was, living and breathing and thinking, and she didn't exist. Except as Sarah-Jane.

And for a few minutes she didn't know what the hell she could do about it.

You could creep across to his work-room, start up his computer and delete him from his own story, a sly mental voice eventually suggested.

She doubted that she would be able to do anything approaching a creep with her right leg in its current condition, and she didn't know what good it would do, but she would try.

And what if Philip is outside the door, waiting for you? He must know what you're going to do. If you're a story character he must have already written all this.

But she didn't think Philip would be awaiting her. The shielding he'd arranged around the two cars was proof enough of this. The heat-haze covering was growing thinner as she watched. She could almost discern the shapes of the two cars beneath it. Philip was struggling to keep everything in its place. His furnace was running low. He would not be at his keyboard rewriting her because if he was she would not be having these thoughts. Philip would be down in the cellar feeding the house on someone's pain.

And when he's stoked up the fire, I'll be the one sitting in front of the screen ready to take advantage of it. I'll be there unwriting him and editing out everything he's done. I'll make it so that none of this has happened, so that no one has suffered. I'll unwrite the bloody house itself if I can! Two can play at being God.

Snowy turned away from the window and limped across the thick bedroom carpet to the door, knowing it was going to be locked. Any half-way decent captor would have done this.

But the door wasn't locked and Philip wasn't waiting for her outside.

Snowy was half-way down the stairs when she spotted an empty plastic Panda Cola bottle upright in the corner beside the front door. Next to it was a rolling-pin and a little copy of the Illustrated New Testament – *with colour illustrations by E.S. Hardy*, Snowy told herself. *That bible is mine! I brought it with me. I tried to exorcize Philip with it. I remember. The bottle contained tap-water that I had blessed and I threw it on him. Those aren't Snowy's memories, they're Sarah-Jane's. You are Sarah-Jane!*

She picked up the rolling-pin – which felt good in her hand but a little too light to make a really effective weapon – then she looked at the front door. The were-lion embossed into the big gold knob seemed to be grinning at her.

This house is haunted, she told herself. *Philip Winter is a ghost.*

She took hold of the cold gold door knob. It would not turn. There was no catch on the door and no letter box. She shoved the knob, then pulled it, then spoke several magic words, but the door would neither open nor even move.

Which means you are a prisoner. So get up those stairs, get in that forbidden room and get to work on that word-processor. We'll see who's God!

The sigh that Snowy heard the moment she'd finished thinking this thought seemed to come from right beside her. She hopped around, the hairs in the nape of her neck prickling and the rolling-pin raised to strike.

Nobody there! she told herself madly.

'I'm right beside you, Snowdrop,' Philip's voice whispered. She felt his breath against her ear. Reflexively she hopped away.

'It won't work, Snowy,' he said into her other ear. 'You can't run away because you can't get out, and you can't fight me because you can't find me. That's what it means to be a god. I'm omnipotent.'

'*Impotent*, more likely,' Snowy replied in a high-pitched squeak as she hopped away again. This time she saw the shimmering in the air as it vanished.

'You won't edit me out of my own story,' the voice said from behind her and she felt a cool hand slide up under the tails of the shirt she was wearing and trail across her bottom. She stumbled away, hating him for being able to do this to her and hating him even more because the mere touch of his ghostly hand inflamed her with passion. Presumably he had written this into his story. She was being ruthlessly manipulated.

The air began to shimmer about three feet in front of her. 'Janie's downstairs,' Philip's voice said from inside the disturbance. 'Why don't you come down and see what I'm doing to her? Why don't you help me hurt her? Janie's strong, Snowy. You'd like her. She's a long-life battery. Listen.'

Snowy heard a woman's scream. It was dreadful and it sounded as if it would go on for ever.

'How much pain would it take to make *you* scream like that?' Philip's voice asked from beside her left ear.

'You won't hurt me,' she said.

'Unless you misbehave. I can always write myself another Snowy. You know that, don't you?'

Snowy believed him. 'Yes,' she said obediently.

'Then go upstairs, get back in bed and wait for me.'

'Yes,' she said and began to shuffle towards the stairs.

Janie began to scream again, louder this time.

I'm sorry Janie, Snowdrop thought. *I'll make it better for you again. I promise.*

Snowy paused at the foot of the stairs then walked past them down the hall to where the second forbidden entrance was. Philip's voice didn't speak to her again so she assumed that he was busy. Judging from the continuing screams of agony he was very busy indeed.

For once, the door to the cellar was open. Steep steps led down into darkness. They appeared to be hewn from the black stone of the rock on which the house stood and they were worn concave in the centre. They looked as if they might lead down to the very bowels of the earth.

For an agonized moment, Snowy considered going down there. She thought she could see the faintest tinge of green light at the bottom as she approached the first step.

'*Sarah-Jane!*'

Snowy heard the sibilant whisper from behind her. The voice was female, and familiar. Even though it was compressed and hissing, she knew that voice as well as she knew her own.

She turned round.

'Ellen? Is that you?'

'*Here*,' the voice whispered from down the hall.

Snowy walked towards it and away from the screaming.

'*Here I am Drezy. Here!*'

As she moved, the voice moved away from her. The next time it spoke it seemed to be coming from the stairs.

And there was Ellen, perched on the steps, smiling, her chin cupped in her hands. She was real and whole and substantial. She was not dead and her body and face did not bear the marks of torture. 'You know who you are, Drez,' she said. 'And you know what you've got to do. Don't make the same mistake that me and the others made. Don't believe. Get up them there stairs, and rewrite the book, Drez, then follow the dog.'

And then Ellen was gone as if she had never been there.

That didn't happen, Snowy told herself. But *something* had happened because she could now quite clearly remember being Sarah-Jane. Snowdrop was beginning to come unstitched.

She started up the stairs towards Philip's work-room, unsure if the vision of Ellen had been shown to her by Philip to entice her to his room or if she had just seen Ellen's ghost.

The work-room door was not locked as she had so fondly imagined it would be during her hike up the stairs. Snowy paused outside for a moment, taking deep breaths. This was either going to be the end for her, or a new beginning.

All you have to do is unwrite him and your problems are all over, she told herself. *It's going to be easy.*

She pulled the door handle down and pushed.

Like a bank-vault door, it swung slowly open.

And there was Philip's work-room, blindingly white and sparse.

And Philip was not there.

At the far end of the room, on a white table that was set against a white wall, the unplugged computer was running, showing the 'Space Journey' screen-saver.

Snowy limped down towards it, each step sending a jolt of agony up her leg and through her body. *Get the bastard!* she told herself. *Teach him to make me into someone else!* She reached the high-backed chair in which Philip wove his lies and threw herself into it.

I'll unplug you, Philip Winter, she thought, being careful not to look at the screen-saver in case she got sucked through it like she had done last time. She moved the mouse and the screen-saver cleared. What now lay in front of her was not a screenful of the latest instalment of her own life, but a blank screen ready to be written on. According to the title bar at the top of the screen this was *Document1* and that was it.

Her heart hammering hard, she moved the pointer to the file menu and clicked a button. A list of Philip's documents was presented to her. There was BLACK ROCK01.DOC to BLACK ROCK09.DOC, which she presumed were the nine chapters he'd written so far and another file called ROCK NOTES.DOC which presumably contained the notes he'd jotted down before starting work.

That stuff could wait. Time was short. She didn't have long before Philip realized what she was up to and came hot-footing it up here to stop here. What she had to do first was delete any reference to him. She selected the last chapter, got it on screen, scrolled down to the first mention of Philip Winter, put the cursor after the words, then used the back-space key to delete them.

Which was when she realized it wasn't going to be as easy as she had imagined.

The backspace key didn't work.

Neither did the delete key.

Neither did the cut function.

Whatever she did, she couldn't remove any words.

'You *bastard*!' Snowy hissed, glancing nervously over her shoulder in case the bastard was already here and observing her.

What do I do? For God's sake, what do I do?

The obvious answer was to do what Ellen had advised her. She was going to have to alter the story, but not by cutting things out of it. She was going to have to put something in.

She moved to the end of the chapter and read the last four lines:

The backspace key didn't work.

Neither did the delete key.

Neither did the cut function.

Whatever she did, she couldn't remove any words.

'He hasn't written up the bit after that, when I hissed and asked myself what I should do,' Snowy said aloud. 'Which means that I'm on my own.'

'But Snowy was not beaten', she typed, hunting and pecking at the keys like someone who had never before used a keyboard. Philip had evidently removed her keyboard skills for his own safety.

When she looked up at the screen she immediately saw the error she'd made and cursed. She tried to delete the misspelt word, tried to overstrike it, then she tried to change it with the spell-checker. None of this worked. This magical word-processor was of the one-time-only variety, apparently. If you didn't get it right first time, tough shit.

Which is why there are holes in the plot of Black Rock, she told herself. He's had to tailor his material to fit in with what happens outside in the real world and doing that has left him with inconsistencies that cannot be corrected. That's why you can almost remember being Sarah-Jane.

Glancing nervously around the room she began to create her own version of events. 'Snowy stayed in the writing-room for three hours, and Philip did not turn up,' she typed.

'When she went to look for him, Snowy found that Philip had suffered a massive coronary at the foot of the stairs and was well and truly dead,' she added. 'The spell that Philip and his haunted house had woven over Snowy and her friends broke when he died. Now there was nothing to keep Snowy imprisoned there. The three hours passed in a twinkling. She then went downstairs and found her friends, all alive and well, if a little confused. "Is it over?" they asked her.

'Snowy nodded. "We'd better get out of here because you know what happens in the end of ghost stories, don't you?" she said. "The haunted house burns down. And this one is about to go that way," she said, smiling. "There is going to be an electrical fault. Or that's what the investigators will say. We've got five minutes, now let's hoof it!"

'Snowy and her friends were half-way up the track when the fire started. They turned back and watched it for a while. None of them spoke.

'When they were sure that nothing would remain of the house, they turned, as one person, and walked away.

'They all lived long, happy and healthy lives.

'The end.'

*

It seemed to take for ever to type all this. By the time she'd finished, the inside of Snowy's bottom lip was raw where she'd been chewing it in concentration. She read back what she'd written and scowled. It didn't look as if she would ever make a writer.

But at least she wasn't even going to have to wait for three hours. She'd written that the time passed in a twinkling, therefore it had already passed. That was the beauty of fiction – you could manipulate things to suit yourself.

There was only one way to find out if her strategy had worked and that was to go to the top of the stairs and see if Philip was at the bottom, dead of a heart attack.

And why shouldn't he be?

Snowy got up and wished she'd remembered to add a line concerning the injury to her leg. Would the machine allow an inserted line? It was worth a go.

She sat down again, moved the cursor to the end of the line where Snowy had found her friends alive and well, and added the words, 'And now she thought about it, Snowy's leg didn't even hurt any more.'

The words went in easily and stayed there. You could insert extra lines apparently, even if you couldn't take any out again.

It wasn't really early enough in the story for Snowy's liking – she wasn't going to find out if her leg was better until everything else had happened – but it was the only place the added line seemed to fit. It would do.

She got up and limped towards the door, hoping that three hours had really passed in a twinkling, that Philip really was dead and that she was free.

Chapter Twenty-nine

A Conversation with Peter Perfect

The sound behind Snowy stopped her in her tracks.

It was the crisp *flap flap!* of paper being rapidly unfolded.

She turned round slowly, remembering – with Sarah-Jane's memory – how Philip had once seemed to fold himself up until he vanished.

Over in his high-backed chair, the opposite thing was currently happening.

Philip Winter was *unfolding* himself.

Heart sinking, Snowy watched what appeared to be nothing more substantial than a flat piece of black paper double its size with the following movement. Within a second the unfolding had speeded to a blur.

A second later the movement snapped to a stop, and there was Philip, large as life and twice as handsome. He did not appear to be in any distress at all, let alone look like a candidate for a fatal heart attack. He looked relaxed and happy.

He smiled. 'Sorry to disappoint you, Snowy, but I'm not dead or dying. Or even feeling poorly. The trouble with novels, as I'm sure you know, is that although they don't have to be terribly logical, they have to be *convincing*. Your little addition doesn't make sense, you see, so it can't work. If you'd been thorough, you'd have scanned the text for important plot-points and worked round them. You missed one, you see.'

Snowy glared at him. She didn't care about plot-points or anything else any more. All she knew was that she had failed; she didn't need to know why.

'Chapter five,' Philip said, grinning. 'Chapter five, page

one-twenty, lines thirty-two to thirty-nine. Let me quote: "Philip knew that Snowy would try to use the computer to change reality and he also knew she would fail. She would fail because she had not read chapter five. Where she would have learned that nothing she wrote could become reality until she'd saved it to disk. Until the words had been saved in the computer, they merely hung there on screen, existing only in electronic limbo. All Philip had to do to kill Snowy's own additions was to quit the document that was currently being displayed without saving what she'd appended." Which is exactly what I'm going to do now,' he told her.

Two seconds later, all Snowy's hard work was gone.

'You should have read chapter five,' he said, turning back to her, 'then you would have found answers to the questions that have been bothering you lately. Let me elaborate: you would have discovered that in my story – as in real life – this house was designed by a man called William Copplethwaite. Mister Copplethwaite knew his onions, not just about house design, but about geomancy too. He understood the principles and rules concerning the dimensions of buildings and the placement of those buildings. Do you understand what I'm getting at?'

Snowy was too dazed to speak.

'I'm talking about making magic by harnessing potential power sources. Certain physical objects of the right shape, and arranged in the proper way, may tap and amplify the latent power of the earth's energy. Or even cosmic energy. I know it comes across as a bit New Age, but the fact is it works. What the New Agers will forget to tell you though, is that everything has a price. We know what the price is, me and you, don't we? You have to pay in blood and pain. No pain, no gain, I think the keep-fit industry says. Whatever, it's true. Our man Copplethwaite knew all this and he knew all about this site. They used to bring prisoners from the Castle over here in the olden days. I don't have to tell you what they did to them. A woman with your imagination can picture it quite well.'

Snowy tried *not* to picture it and failed. Her imagination showed her the rock before the house was built on it. There was a fissure in the centre which opened on to a tiny cave nestling half-way between the top of the hill and the sea. A neat opening had been hewn from the fissure and steep steps had been carved out, leading down to that small cave. The cave was now Black Rock's cellar. This was where they had brought people and chained them to the walls in order to pay the price. They'd made blood music here. Plenty of it. They'd ruined people's bodies, slowly and agonizingly.

'And during the late eighteen eighties and early nineties, Copplethwaite drew up the plans for the present house. According to the records he left, the construction wasn't completed until the year nineteen hundred. This was because the land put up a resistance. The upshot of it all was that Copplethwaite's project, Black Rock, was already ... *haunted* ... by the time it was completed. It was designed to be. The house is placed so that parts of it are windows into another realm. Not large parts, but the corner of a room here, and a section of wall there. These windows look into the place where reality is born. Except that it's not really a place, it's more like a sea of raw power. With me so far?'

Snowy nodded. She was more concerned with what was going on inside her own head. As he spoke, all her memories were coming back. She was now more Sarah-Jane than Snowy and trying to keep up with the fresh changes.

Philip smiled. 'Do you remember having a dream in which there was a door behind this computer which opened out into our bedroom?'

'Yes,' Snowy said. Her voice sounded different, a little less bemused and a little more frightened. Inside her a little girl had suddenly woken up and the little girl was dangerous because she thought the idea of being able to open a window on to God or on to the power source that made reality, or whatever it was, was an amazingly good one. This little girl marvelled at what you could do with such power and badly wanted to hold it in her hands.

In pretty much the same way as Philip Winter does, Snowy thought bitterly. *Apparently it's true about power corrupting.*

Philip was talking again. 'You should remember that

dream, because I wrote the entire sequence for you. It was a playful little hint. And it's true. It's one of the effects of the placement of the house, you see. This wall, against which my table and word-processor stand, is the rear wall of the house, isn't it? So what should be directly behind the computer?'

Snowy suddenly knew what he meant. There should have been a window there. The one behind her – from which blasts of brilliant light sometimes shone – was there, but the other was missing.

Philip nodded. 'You've got it. This window exists only on the outside. It's one of the countless things that gives the house its charm. If you were to climb a ladder up to it you'd be able to see into this room through it. I think that's rather sweet.'

Snowy gazed at Philip in awe, distantly telling herself that it must have been like this watching Jesus speak. It was difficult not to become enchanted. It wasn't the sum of his features that made him beautiful; it was his charisma. He seemed to shine with a golden inner light. The power in him drew her like a magnet and his voice was like the song of the Sirens: if she didn't give in and go to him, she was going to end up with a brain like scrambled eggs.

Philip smiled again, as if he knew exactly what effect his presence was having on her. 'The reason there is no window on the inside of the house is the same reason that there are no back or side doors at the far end of either of the corridors. All these places meet the power source. If there were doors there and a window here, and you opened them, you'd be consumed in what would seem like hell-fire. Your dream that you could open a door in this wall and walk through it to our bedroom doesn't make sense because beyond this wall is the back garden. The delightful thing is this . . . watch!'

Philip swung his seat round until he was facing the computer screen. He leaned to the side of it and placed his fingertips on the wall behind it. 'Don't do this at home, boys and girls,' he said, glancing at her over his shoulder. 'Uncle Phil knows what he's doing, but you little folk will get your fingers singed if you try it.'

He turned back and walked his fingertips closer to the back

of the computer screen. Then he nodded. 'The window's open a crack just here,' he said. 'This is where I access it with the computer. Here goes!'

He pressed against the wall. Snowy could see little circular indentations around his fingertips as the wall gave beneath them. His fingers penetrated it and his hand slid in up to his wrist. The plaster puckered around his skin, reminding Snowy of those veterinary programmes where they were always putting their arms into cows. But the wide-eyed little girl inside her was delighted.

Snowy suddenly understood why Sarah-Jane's mother had always tried to kill off that part of her personality. It wasn't because the little girl wanted magic more than anything else in the world, it was because she would be prepared to accept any amount of chaos in order to achieve it. The little girl didn't care about the consequences. The little girl was bad.

The little girl was also in the ascendancy.

Philip knew this. This was what it was all about. He knew his graft of Snowy on to Sarah-Jane hadn't taken, so now he was trying to seduce Sarah-Jane herself.

And Sarah-Jane *wanted* to be seduced.

'If you were to go into the bedroom, you'd find that my hand is waving at you from the wall,' Philip said.

In that moment, the remnants of Snowy curled up like burning cellophane and fell away in ashes.

And Sarah-Jane found herself with a big grin on her face, her rolling-pin tucked under her arm, and her hands poised ready to provide the applause that was surely necessary.

She glared at her hands and put them down to her sides, where they refused to feel comfortable. She crossed her arms and trapped her twitching hands beneath her armpits.

It's wrong! she admonished herself. *He wants you to want to stay with him. Don't let it happen! Remember what he's doing to Janie to achieve this, and what he did to Ellen.*

Philip drew his hand back, twisted round in his chair and held out his arm for her inspection.

S'n'J knew that it wasn't possible for a man's fingers, hand and wrist to glow red-hot like metal, but this was exactly what she saw. Philip's hand was almost molten and tendrils of stinking smoke were curling away from it. She could feel the radiant heat even from ten feet away. There was a thick gold ring around his middle finger and it was melting.

'See what I mean about hell-fire?' Philip asked, inspecting his hand. He took the melting metal of the ring between the forefinger and thumb of his other hand, seemingly oblivious of the sudden pall of grey smoke and the smell of charring flesh that arose, and picked the gold away. He dropped the soft blob of hot metal into the palm of his good hand and closed his fingers around it. His hand sizzled and steam shot out from the sides of his fist.

'I know you think I'm a ghost, Snowy, but I'm real flesh and blood. It's simply that my flesh and blood is no longer ordinary. I'm an incarnation. A new god. I found the house, I found out how to use it and now I've bumped myself up the scale from man to superman to mortal god. The next step is immortal god. That's where we're going, you and me. We're going to be up there playing with the big boys. Come on! Look! Magic!'

He suddenly threw the melted blob of gold at her.

S'n'J reflexively put out her hand and caught it. The ring was whole again. It was still hot – almost hot enough to burn – but it was as perfect as a new one.

'If that's a proposal, I'm afraid I'll have to turn it down,' she said, and threw the ring back.

Philip waved his hand like the queen might have done from the royal carriage, in a short semi-circular motion.

Half-way across the room the ring turned to gold dust which glittered to the floor.

'You don't understand, do you, Snowy?'

'There is no Snowy,' S'n'J said, glancing behind her. The door was still open.

'Snowy, I know what you're thinking. I wrote all this, remember? You're wondering if you could get out of the room before I have time to close the door. You're forgetting that I already know the outcome.'

S'n'J shook her head. 'This part isn't written yet.'

'You look so confused and sweet, standing there in my shirt with your little rolling-pin tucked under your arm. Just like a sexy little toy soldier,' Philip said. 'You aren't sure if this part is written or not, are you? You think you've escaped Snowy and that you're Sarah-Jane again, but you don't know if it's only temporary. You're wondering what's in that file you didn't have time to look at, aren't you? The one that contains the outline notes for *Black Rock*. Well, my pretty little Snowdrop, I'll tell you what's in that file. It's our history. I haven't included it in the main text yet because it isn't finished. But it goes further than you think. Backwards and forwards from this point.'

'Liar!'

Philip looked pleased. 'Lying is what I'm best at,' he said. 'Lying is what writers live for. To be gods and to tell lies. The difference between me and all the others is that when I tell a lie it becomes reality.'

S'n'J deliberately shifted her weight to her bad leg. His honey-sweet voice ceased to have its magnetic effect. He was talking again now, but she ignored the words and cut in over them. 'What did you do to Zara?' she asked through teeth that were clenched with the pain. 'She was your wife, wasn't she? The original Mrs Winter.'

Philip fell silent and stayed that way for a long time.

'Well?' she prompted, feeling there was a chance for her after all. She'd hit a raw nerve.

'This is something else I knew would happen,' he said. 'Like I said, the ghosts are a side-effect of the house. The house is a bit of a maze. Some of the windows open on to themselves. Some of the tracks between here and there are convoluted and lead to other places. Copplethwaite built in a few traps he didn't know about. There *are* ghosts in this house. Not only ghosts of humans, but ghosts of the past. But you know this already. You've spoken to some of those ghosts on the telephone. And from what they've told you, you've drawn conclusions, just as I anticipated.'

'You knew I'd work out that you were once Fred King?'

Philip nodded. 'Guilty as charged,' he said. 'After my wife died, I took her surname so that every time I wrote my name I would commemorate her. I dropped the Fred when it became unfashionable and became Philip instead. Philip Winter is the result.

'I used the pen name Peter Perfect because I knew that it would appeal to the little girl inside you, Snowy. The children inside us all want things back as they used to be, long ago. They remember a young world greener than green and bluer than blue, a sea that was colder than dry ice and a sun that really *could* shrivel your skin. They remember how good it was to live in a big friendly world where dew glistened like jewels on early morning cobwebs and the days lasted forever. But most of all, they remember the potential for magic. They yearn for the days when *anything* seemed possible; when the very air seemed to shimmer with power.

'And inside Sarah-Jane there is a little girl who truly believed in magic. This little girl believed – and still does believe – because she saw real magic happening. Saw it with her own eyes. Saw it dancing in the palm of a man's hand. And that little girl wants real magic back again.'

S'n'J squeezed her eyes shut again. She knew he was referring to her first ever visit to Tintagel Castle and now the submerged memory was sweeping towards the surface, huge and dark . . . but she fought to keep it down. She had to keep her head clear and get things back on track. She lifted her foot from the floor and let it fall.

'How did Zara die?' she persisted.

'Ahh, those telephone ghosts of the past!' he replied. 'I didn't think they would tell you enough for you to work out that I was once Fred King, but I should have known you would find out. You're bright, Snowy. I'm proud of you.'

'Don't patronize me, just tell me about Zara!' S'n'J said from behind her closed eyelids.

'She was the love of a poor factory hand's life. A greater love no man has ever known. I love you as I loved her, Snowy because you and she are identical. Two peas from the same pod.'

S'n'J opened her eyes and shook her head. 'Nope!' she said. 'If we were identical you wouldn't want to turn me into Snowy, and then from Snowy into Zara. If we resemble one another in any way it must be purely physical.'

'Wrong. Your personalities are identical. All you need is her history. I can do that in easy stages. She was called Snowy, too. A silly nickname because of her surname: Snowy Winter. I knew she would come back. I always knew that, right from the start. I waited for her. I lived in this house and learned how to use it, and I stayed young and waited for her.'

'But she never came,' S'n'J said.

'She's here now. Standing in front of me. A reincarnation. You are Snowy, Sarah-Jane.'

S'n'J shook her head. 'You don't get two chances at it, Philip. You ought to know that. Think of your bloody computer. Once and once only, that's the size of it.'

Philip's expression had hardened. 'Don't get me mad, Snowy! You won't like it!'

'Is that what *she* did? Got you mad? So mad you killed her?'

'I sacrificed her,' he said.

'*Murdered* her, you mean. She upset you and you murdered her.'

Philip's face cleared. S'n'J watched the transformation and was stunned. One moment he'd looked like the psychopath he was, the next every trace of that expression had been wiped from his face.

He smiled. 'Just hear me out. We married, Zara and I. We were blissfully happy, working all day and loving all night. Then one of her relatives died. Left her a great deal of money. We came to Cornwall and found this house standing empty. We made enquiries and bought it. It had a reputation, but we didn't care. We moved in and marvelled at the strange front door and the way you always felt as if you were walking up or downhill – sometimes across the same piece of floor – until you got your Black Rock legs. We lived and loved here, too. You know how it went. You've read about it and you've lived it out. We were blissfully happy.

'And then I made a discovery. It was the dog, you see. Diamond Ambrose Anstey. He was alive then, not just a dead dog who won't go away. I noticed that he could get into the house even though all the doors and windows were shut. He would just turn up as he chose. I began to research. And I discovered that we were living in a very special place. A dormant place that could be put into action, if I could somehow power it up.

'You see, Zara and I used to hold one another and say, "What more could we ask for?" the answer to which is obvious. It's the answer which any happy person would give: "I wish it could go on forever." And I began to believe it *could*.

'From Copplethwaite's copious notes left in the library, I discovered how to make the house *work*. I was going to have to make blood music. Perform a sacrifice. Of course, I didn't do it. But there are some ideas which, when they've occurred to you, just won't go away. I became obsessed. Eventually I began to experiment. I took small animals to the basement and slaughtered them. Nothing happened. I captured larger animals – cats and dogs – and tortured and killed those too. Then, one day when Zara was away visiting her parents, and my mother was here, I took her downstairs and killed her. It's in the blood you see, killing. My father murdered an Italian girl. He was hung for it.

'But still nothing happened. It wasn't until I realized the true nature of sacrifice that I discovered where I was going wrong. It's no good sacrificing something you don't care about, and that's what I'd been doing all along. Just killing. A true sacrifice means giving up something you care deeply about. Something that it will hurt you to lose. Something you love. And the only thing I had that I loved was Zara. My Snowy Winter.'

Philip's eyes filled with tears. 'I'm sorry my love,' he said to S'n'J. 'I'm so sorry for what I did to you. But I kept my promise. I brought you back and now we can be together for ever. We'll never die. We will be immortal.'

S'n'J's head was spinning. She was ahead of him now, way ahead. 'I'm not your Snowy,' she said. 'I'm not her reincarnation. She didn't come back. They don't. It's one time only.'

Philip nodded. 'I know,' he said.

'But you waited for her. You checked out all the little girls who came by in case one of them was Snowy. Born to different parents but the same little girl. You waited and watched and she didn't come. And in the early seventies you decided to do something constructive. Am I right?'

The memory she'd been keeping at bay was surfacing now. It had been buried in her mind for a very long time indeed. Since she was six. Since her first and only visit to King Arthur's Castle. She *had* seen magic that day.

'Yes, I was able to do it, by then. I'd learned about altering reality. I knew that I wasn't going to get Snowy back by natural means, but I also knew I didn't need to. I could *write* Snowy back into life. I could recreate her. You *are* mine, Sarah-Jane Dresden. I wrote you into existence. To become Snowy. It's downstairs in the library. A thousand-page type-script that I wrote sitting up here against this wall on an old Royal manual typewriter. From your very beginning to the day we first met, a few hundred yards away from here. You were conceived – literally, not literarily – on the little curve of beach down in the bay between Black Rock and Tintagel Castle. The manuscript opens with your parents' visit to the Castle. Go and look if you don't believe me, it's downstairs on the third shelf up, about half-way along. I had them linger long after everyone else had gone. It was a warm evening for late October and darkness fell quickly. Your parents – Josie and Victor – were feeling particularly amorous. For the one and only time in their lives, they stripped naked and made love on the beach. And for the one and only time in her life, Josie became pregnant.'

He smiled. 'It's today, Snowy. Today is your birthday. The day I brought you from fiction to fact. The day you were conceived. I wrote it all. Even down to how the baby would look. I had pictures, you see, of Zara when she was a baby. She was an only child, you were an only child. Everything matched.

'Now let yourself remember this,' he said. 'The day we met at Tintagel. You can access it now. You haven't before, because I disallowed it. But let it come out now. *Remember.*'

And suddenly S'n'J *was* remembering. She seemed to have no control over the process at all.

He's right! she told herself as the image began to form in her mind, *The bastard is right! He did conceal the memory and now he's let me have it back!*

She wanted to scream, she wanted to lash out and call him a liar and kill him and stamp on him and grind the pieces into the lush carpet, but she couldn't.

She couldn't because the house and Philip were both gone now and she was a six-year old child in a short yellow dress. She had a fringe that hung in her eyes and she was sweaty and tired of walking up steep hills to look at piles of old rocks. When they'd told her she was going to see King Arthur's Castle, she'd expected to see tall towers and a moat and drawbridge, and the slots through which archers had once fired arrows into the eyes of bad kings.

Her daddy kept promising to show her where those slots were, but instead he and mummy were walking round all gooey-eyed, saying that they wanted to walk down to the little beach.

So Sarah-Jane wandered off to explore.

Up ahead of her, at the top of a steep climb was the ruin of what had once been a tower and she ran towards it, hoping for archer's slots.

And suddenly she had run out of the sunlight into the cool shade at the foot of a tall wall. It smelled of moss and grass here. She looked up the wall and didn't see any slots, just the blue sky above. There was a seagull up there, wheeling gracefully.

'Are you lost?' a man's voice asked.

Sarah-Jane gasped in surprise and turned towards the voice. There, in the shadows where two walls met, stood a man. He was old – about as old as her daddy – and very tall and strong looking. He was smiling at her.

'Nope,' Sarah-Jane said, shaking her head. 'I'm not lost, I'm exploring.'

The man nodded. 'Good,' he said. 'What did you find?'

Sarah-Jane shrugged. 'Not much,' she said. 'I wanted to see where the archers shot arrows from.'

'I can show you,' the man said.

'Can you lift me up so I can see?' Sarah-Jane asked. She wasn't supposed to talk to strangers, she knew, but this man looked nice. And he sounded friendly too. And her mummy and daddy were nearby.

'I can do better,' he said. 'I can show you the whole castle. As it was before. When it was brand new.'

Sarah-Jane grinned at him. 'No you can't!' she said. 'They didn't have pictures then.'

The man shook his head. 'But they did have magic,' he said. 'And so do I, Sarah-Jane.'

She frowned at him. 'How do you know my name?' she asked suspiciously. 'Do you know my mummy and daddy?'

He nodded. 'And I know all about you too. They told me. I've got it written down in a big book. I've got a book of you.'

'Why?'

'Because one day, when you're grown up, we'll meet again and I'll tell you about my book of you and you won't believe me because you'll have forgotten today. But I'll remind you. I'll say don't you remember the day we met at King Arthur's Castle and I showed you magic? And you will remember.'

'You haven't showed me any magic.'

'Do you want to see some?'

'Yes please,' she replied, expecting the kind of trick her grandfather did for her. He could make a knotted hanky dance on his hand and make you think the tip of one of his thumbs came away in the fingers of his other hand.

'Then come here,' the man said, 'and kneel down in front of me.'

She walked towards him, ready to turn and run if she needed to, but she didn't think she would need to.

'Kneel down here, just at my feet,' he said. 'Shuffle a bit closer or you won't see.'

Sarah-Jane moved a little closer, but the man wasn't happy until she was so close she could feel the heat of his body through his trousers. She suddenly felt all trembly and shy and didn't know why.

The man cupped his hands and put them down between her face and his trousers. She was so close that his fingertips touched her chin. They were cool and soothing.

'Put your hands under mine,' he said softly, 'and watch closely.'

The feel of his skin made her hands tingle.

And as Sarah-Jane watched, a ball of shimmering air formed in the man's hands. It was a little like the heat-haze you saw on roads when the weather was hot, but this one contained golden twinkling specks that shone like fairy dust. Sarah-Jane was delighted.

'What is it?' she asked breathlessly.

'Shoosh,' he whispered. 'Just watch.'

And the heat-haze and twinkling cleared and suddenly the man was cupping a tiny castle in his hands. *This* castle, in olden days. It was whole and it was perfect. It stood on the pair of big rocks and the sparkling blue sea shimmered at the bottom, lapping at the shore formed by the flesh of the man's hands. There was a little wooden boat sailing across the sea, propelled by a breeze in a big red sail.

And there were guards at the castle gates. And a pair of knights in armour were riding beautifully bedecked horses up the steep hill to the castle. Thin plumes of black smoke were rising from two or three places inside the castle and Sarah-Jane imagined blacksmiths in there somewhere, heating iron and steel and beating out new horseshoes and swords. She could almost hear the sounds of hammers on anvils.

'It's beautiful,' she heard herself say.

'It's magic,' the man said softly. 'Remember that, Sarah-Jane. Only gods can do this.'

She nodded, watching one of the horsemen flip up the visor of his helmet to speak to the guards. The knight looked just like the man who was showing her the vision.

'WHAT THE DEVIL DO YOU THINK YOU'RE DOING?'

The magic vision ceased instantly.

Sarah-Jane recognized the voice of her father and looked over her shoulder at him as he stormed towards her, his face dark with anger.

'STOP THAT YOU PERVERTED BASTARD!' her father shouted, and suddenly, the man was pushing her away from him as he moved. Sarah-Jane fell over.

'Sarah-Jane, come here at once!' her father yelled. For some

374

reason he had stopped about twenty feet away from her. He looked very angry and very frightened. The man – who was supposed to be her daddy's friend – was standing against the wall in the shade, glaring at her father.

'Get up, Sarah-Jane, and come here at once!' her daddy shouted.

She scrambled to her feet and ran to him.

'Don't you ever do anything like that again!' he yelled at her, raising his hand. He wouldn't hit her. She knew that. Her father had never struck her. Ever. But his anger at her was enough to make her eyes fill with tears.

'He was only showing me a magic trick, daddy,' she wept, looking up at that hand which seemed as high above her as the sky.

'NEVER AGAIN YOU BAD GIRL!' her father yelled, and his hand swept down towards her. There was a flash of light and pain, then darkness.

And S'n'J came back to herself, dizzy and shocked.

'He hit *me*,' she heard herself say in a small, astonished voice. Her face was wet with tears and she felt as if she could curl up and die. She felt filthy. 'You fixed it so he thought you'd made me give you a blow-job and he hit *me*,' she repeated.

'He was frightened, Snowy,' Philip smiled. 'And there were a lot of things running through his head when he saw you knelt there in front of me. You licked your lips when you turned round.'

'But I wasn't doing anything!' she heard herself complain.

'I had to fix it so it appeared there was. So you would be too frightened to remember anything about what had happened. So that you would believe me now, when I made you remember. Do you believe me?'

S'n'J shook her head. It wasn't just her mind that had been raped, it was her whole existence. 'I don't know *what* I believe any more,' she said, tearfully.

'You can believe this quite safely: I *am* a god and you cannot harm me. I created you.'

'What now?' she asked, stunned.

'You may as well forget about ever having been Sarah-Jane

375

because by tomorrow morning she will never have existed. You'll be Snowy and I shall sit here and alter the story so that you've *always* been Snowy. At dawn tomorrow, none of this will have happened. Not even the little glitch where I sacrificed you, my darling. Our histories will be seamless. You and I will live here for ever, in perfect happiness. What more could a woman ask for?'

'Her own life,' S'n'J said, dully.

'But Sarah-Jane never did have her own life,' Philip replied. 'You owe your very existence to me. It belongs to me.'

S'n'J simply looked at him. The tears in her eyes blurred his image so that he appeared dark and terrible. In that moment she hated him more than she'd ever hated anything in her life. It gave her a little strength. 'Then you'd better make a good job of getting rid of my memories,' she said venomously. 'And you'd better hide the finished book away somewhere I'll never see it, because I swear that if I ever remember even so much as a minute of being Sarah-Jane, I'll kill you, god or not. Immortal or not. If I remember, I'll find a way.'

Philip smiled his melting smile. 'Very eloquent, Snowy,' he said. 'A fitting speech for the end of a woman's existence. Now, if you'd just like to go back to bed and try to sleep, you'll find that things will look very different in the morning. You'll feel much better.'

Sarah-Jane stayed where she was, no longer knowing what to do

Philip began to frown. 'I didn't expect that to happen so quickly,' he said to himself. He seemed to be peering past her to the window behind her.

'What?' S'n'J asked, glancing over her shoulder.

A heavy curtain hung over the window blocking her view of the outside. There was no curtain rail to hold it up, but it hung there anyway, moving slightly as though in a draught. And as she watched, the reality of the curtain began to falter. The pattern on it faded and the material it was made of became transparent.

He doesn't have enough power to do it all! S'n'J's mind cawed in triumph. *He isn't damned well invincible at all!*

Outside, up on the track, the shielding over the cars had gone completely. Beyond them, way up the track, another car was coming down. A Cavalier, if she wasn't mistaken.

'Who's that?' she asked, turning back.

But Philip wasn't about to tell her. He had other fish to fry, apparently. He waved, said, 'Ciao!' and folded up.

Inside a second he was gone.

Chapter Thirty

Fighting Fiction with Fiction

S'n'J did a quick limping shuffle to the window. The Cavalier had now stopped behind her Sierra and the door was opening.

Martin got out, looking very small and frightened. He was carrying what appeared to be the handle of a pickaxe.

She had never thought she would be so pleased to see him.

'Be careful!' she yelled as Martin looked all around him, his head bobbing from side to side as if he was a bird that had just landed in a cat pound.

Evidently things weren't quite as cut and dried as Philip made out. If they had been, he wouldn't have disappeared so quickly when he'd seen Martin coming. Apparently, Martin was a force to be reckoned with. S'n'J had no idea why this should be.

If Philip's weak and losing his grip, you might be able to smash the window. You could at least let Martin know you're alive!

She whacked the window with the rolling-pin.

It bounced off with the *chink!* noise of a hammer hitting a ship's hull.

Up on the track, Martin was less than ten feet away from the car he had come in. He had gone to the side of the track and was peering down into the valley.

The computer! S'n'J thought and shuffled back to where its display was still working, now showing a blank page.

I'll write on this one, she told herself. *And this time I'll remember to save what I've written. Philip shouldn't have told me the secret, because now I know how make things come true, too.*

She flung herself down into the chair, already reaching for the keyboard.

And before her fingers had touched a single key, words began to appear on the screen.

Seventeen

Martin arrived at the track leading down to Black Rock with the mother of all battles already going on inside his head, she read as the words formed themselves on the screen.

'You bastard!' she shouted at Philip, wherever he was. This was another talent he'd kept quiet. He didn't even have to sit at the bloody computer to write; he could do it remotely. It quite neatly explained Snowy's suspicions that Philip never actually went into the room to write; explained why she had not heard the rattle of the keyboard while he worked. It was another of his horrible literary jokes.

'It had started at the car-rental office, as soon as he'd put his name on the agreement. The ice block in his brain had suddenly lit up and begun to send out spiked pulses of red light which seemed to scorch the very meat of his brain. Each pulse struck in a different place and each left a deep, dull ache behind it when the searing agony stopped. Martin suspected that his brain was haemorrhaging; that he was suffering multiple strokes that would leave him crippled and mentally disabled. He could live with being crippled, he knew, and function almost as well at what he did best; it was the prospect of losing his mind that frightened him.'

The writing paused here, as if Philip – blast his eyes – had stopped for inspiration. The 'save' menu appeared on the screen, the option selected itself and the computer's hard-disk light lit as the writing was saved.

No more words appeared on screen. S'n'J saw her chance.

'But this wasn't happening', she wrote, carefully hunting down the keys and pecking at them with two fingers. It took her nearly thirty seconds to type and save the words.

It took Philip less than five seconds to alter it to suit himself.

'But although this wasn't yet happening, Martin knew it

soon would. His fingers had begun to tingle and his mental vocabulary seemed to be diminishing.'

Cursing, S'n'J acknowledged that she'd just made things worse for Martin, rather than better.

The writing continued: 'He picked up the pickaxe handle and looked nervously around him. Somewhere inside that house which looked as if it was hunched ready to pounce, was his Essenjay. And he would either get her back or die trying.

'*Die trying, probably*, he told himself cynically.'

The machine saved, then paused again. Tears of gratitude stung S'n'J's eyes. She hated the bastard. She'd sent him to Scarborough on a wild goose chase because he deserved nothing better. But here he was ready to die for her.

'Martin will not die!' she typed and saved it.

And watched it grow to read: 'Martin will not die! he told himself, and this thought provided him with the exact amount of comfort he'd expected to derive from it. Absolutely none at all.'

S'n'J picked up her rolling-pin and weighed it in her hand as she read that Martin could hear faint noises from off the side of the bank and that he was going to go over there to see what was making them.

Philip had told her that he'd created her on an old Royal typewriter, on this desk against this very wall. Now he did it with a computer. But the important point was that his musings had to become permanent in order to become reality. If it was typed, it was permanent. If it was written on paper or saved on disk, it was permanent. It was *not* permanent while it only existed in the computer's memory: if you turned off the word-processing program before you'd saved your writing, what you'd written vanished.

His thoughts didn't count until they were outside his head and stored somewhere else.

S'n'J hit the computer screen.

She may as well have hit a wall.

I'll stop you, you wait and see! she thought, placing the rolling-pin down on the desk. She picked up the keyboard and set it down on top of the computer screen, then dragged out the unplugged case which housed the computer's works and its hard disk.

She could still remember things from when she was Snowy – who had once sold computers – and one of those things was that hard-disk drives did not like to be handled roughly. A gentle bump was sometimes enough to lose you everything that was stored there.

We'll see about a gentle bump! she thought, and hefted the plastic case off the desk and stood up with it. She turned away from the table, lifted the computer case above her head and flung it at the wall as hard as she could.

She watched the case sail gracefully through the air as if it was moving in slow motion. On its way to the wall, it twice turned end over end.

It hit the wall about three feet off the ground.

The case exploded into spiky fragments.

It hit the floor, damaged beyond repair. The plastic was shattered into five or six large pieces and many more smaller ones. Green circuit boards had spilled from inside it. They lay there gleaming dully, cracked and bent, their collections of chips and resistors and God knew what else no longer fit for use.

S'n'J saw what she had done and was pleased. *Put that in your pipe and suck on it, Peter bloody Perfect!* she thought.

Somewhere inside the broken electronics, the hard-disk light winked on – she saw the reflection of its light in a corner of the case – heard the quiet tinkling of the disk as it saved a new piece of writing.

'It *can't* still *work*!' she shouted. 'It cannot! It is broken beyond repair!'

She turned back to the screen where another paragraph had appeared.

' "Who's that?" Martin demanded, peering into the bushes that grew down the steep side of the track. He clasped his pickaxe handle between both hands and raised it, ready to strike if it was necessary.

' "It's me," a vaguely familiar voice replied. "I fell and hit my head. Knocked myself out. Christ almighty, I've got the granddaddy of all headaches."

'"James?" Martin asked in astonishment.'

S'n'J felt a huge wave of relief wash over her. Followed by a fresh wave of hatred towards Philip for lying about James, and telling her he was dead.

The next burst of writing went on for a minute or so.

'"You're dead. I saw you fall into a wall of fire," Martin said suspiciously.

'"Dead but I won't lie down," James said from somewhere about ten feet away. "Hang on. You'll have to give me a hand up when I crawl out of here."

'James, when he finally appeared, looked as if he had indeed been through a wall of fire. His clothes were blackened and scorched. His arms were red and badly blistered and all that remained of his hair was a few singed fragments that lay close to his scalp. His eyebrows and eyelashes were gone. He crawled up the bank towards Martin, then reached out a hand.

'Martin took it, braced himself and heaved James up on to the track.

'James picked himself up from the ground, tested his limbs and then turned to Martin, grinning. His face was so sooty he looked like a failed Al Jolson impersonator.

'"James Green, slightly singed, but otherwise alive and well," he said breathlessly. "And you're Martin. We'd better do something pretty damned quick, Martin, because very soon, someone's going to start trying to kill us."

'Martin said, "I can't believe it. I saw what happened to you. I had a vision and saw it all. The cloud and everything. I can't believe you're alive."

'"They don't call me Mister Nifty Footwork for nothing," James said.

'"You know what's happening here, don't you?"

'James nodded. "The house is haunted, just like it says in the book. Drezy's inside. We have to get her out. The trouble is, the guy who wrote the book is in there and he doesn't want us to."

'"Have we gone crazy, or what?" Martin asked, glancing up at the overcast sky in case any brown clouds were forming between here and the house.

'James shook his head. "I don't know. What I do know is that I'm going to give getting into the house a bloody good try. I brought a crowbar. Did you see it?"

'"Just back there," Martin said, pointing. "And you needn't worry about getting in. Getting out again is supposed to be the hard part."'

'Very heroic,' S'n'J said bitterly. She knew exactly what Philip was doing. He was building them up in order to knock them down again in a few moments. You had to make your customers think the good guys had a chance; had to make them hope your heroes would prevail. This would make it hurt the reader more when you killed them off.

In retaliation, S'n'J took the computer's mouse in her hand, moved the pointer to the file menu, got a list of options to show and selected the line which said, 'NEW'.

I'll make you sorry you made Snowy a computer sales-woman, S'n'J thought. If you hadn't done that I wouldn't know how to work this damned machinery!

Under normal circumstances, clicking on 'NEW', would bring up a fresh blank page on top of the current one. With this program you could compose two separate letters or manuscript chapters simultaneously, switching between one and the other whenever you wanted.

It worked. The words DOCUMENT2 showed in the title bar.

'Chapter Seventeen – Additions' S'n'J typed, knowing Philip was still working on this chapter. She would steal a march on the bastard. If she couldn't ruin it for him directly, by typing into his chapter, she could spoil it indirectly by writing some inserts that reality would have to slot in – whether reality (and Philip) liked it or not.

Beneath the heading she began: 'Things were beginning to go seriously wrong for Philip now. There wasn't enough power available to keep everything rolling because upstairs, Snowy was somehow siphoning it off for herself. Philip didn't know what she was doing up there.'

She saved what she'd written to the mangled remains of the computer across the room and snarled, 'Got you, you shithead!'

At which point the screen flickered and Chapter Seventeen

reappeared on the screen: 'Snowy was doing something. Philip knew this and he knew why. She was trying to siphon off his power to weaken him. "It won't work, Snowy," he said, and she heard his voice as if he was standing behind her.'

The save menu flicked down and vanished.

'It won't work, Snowy,' Philip's voice said from behind her and S'n'J wheeled around. Philip wasn't there. She turned back to the screen where Philip was busily adding more text:

'"Whatever you're doing, it won't work," he said. "Stop being bad, Snowdrop, because if you don't I'll kill you. And your agony won't even end with your death. I'll keep your tortured soul in the house throughout eternity. I can get another Snowy. You're not the only one. There are more. You may have wondered why I stopped manipulating your life after the incident at Tintagel. So here's the reason: I was too busy to continue. I was writing more little girls into existence. You're not the only one. Why would I risk everything on one girl when I could just as easily write another one? You were my first, Snowy, and my best, but you were not the last. I can do without you. There are more."'

The machine saved the text and S'n'J heard the words from behind her. She didn't even bother turning around this time. The important thing was that he really *didn't* know what she was doing. He could feel the power draining, but had no idea she was writing a fresh chapter for him.

Some god you turned out to be! she told herself, suddenly feeling dizzy because of the power at her fingertips. The enchanted little girl inside her who had once seen real magic up there in King Arthur's Castle was crowing with delight. *Do some more! Quick, do some more!* she chanted.

Before she could begin to type, the computer switched back to Philip's chapter.

'Up in Philip's work-room, Snowy was still being a bad girl. It didn't matter. Her only chance was for Martin and James to save her and she could not influence what was going to happen to them. No matter how much power she drained off from the house it wouldn't be enough to halt their story.

'"We'd better go quickly," James said. "It's starting. There's a cloud forming. Look!"

'Martin had spotted the condensing vapour the moment the first strand of it had appeared. "It's gonna be a thundercloud this time," Martin said, watching the cloud. It was darkening quickly. "Put the crowbar down," he advised.

'"I might need it."

'"Yeah, you really do need a lightning conductor, don't you?" Martin said. "Don't let's make it easy for him. Or it. Or whatever it is."

'As he spoke, the cloud darkened until it was black and began to . . .'

This time the sentence ended part way through. S'n'J watched the machine save it and the room suddenly darkened. She turned to the window, already knowing why the light had been reduced. Outside the house the cloud had come into existence. It hung there, dark and angry. It was low enough to block her view of the track on which Martin and James stood.

Whatever was to come for them, she could not influence it. Philip had stated this and saved it. But she could still influence Philip, before he prevented it. She switched the computer back to her own piece of writing and began to type: 'He was just a man wearing the garments of a god. An ordinary man who had found the power of the gods in a haunted house and who had wrapped it around himself like a cloak,' she wrote. 'And now that power was draining away. There wasn't enough of it to hold everything in place. Philip had created reality for others but he had failed to create it for himself.'

S'n'J found her fingers becoming nimble, her touch, sure. It was almost as if her hands had become enchanted. Without having to even look at the keys she typed: 'Without the power the house tapped he would become mortal once more. And that power was peeling away like the layers of an onion. There was nothing he could do to stop it. In a matter of minutes it would be all over.'

But as she saved what she had written, her hands tingling and her mind surging with the power of composition, S'n'J had the strong sensation that something was in the room with her. She spun around.

Curled up on the floor next to the ruins of the computer case, was Diamond Ambrose Anstey. His eyes held S'n'J's.

Follow the dog, the ghost of Ellen had said. *Write the book . . . then follow the dog.*

'OK, Diamond,' she said, pushing herself up to a standing position. Her bad leg hurt like hell. 'I'm ready to leave now,' she said and added, 'I think,' as she tested her leg.

The dog didn't move.

'Good boy. Take me out!' S'n'J encouraged.

Diamond blinked at her.

'Isn't it time?' she asked, worriedly glancing back at the computer screen, which still hadn't switched back to Philip's page of writing. 'My mind's gone blank. I don't have to write any more, do I? Please!'

Apparently she had to.

She sat back down again, now very close to the point of screaming with frustration and panic. Her mind wouldn't clear. There were hundreds of things she could be writing, she knew. But they were all floating around on the periphery of her mind and outside her reach. She tried to apprehend at least one of them and failed miserably.

Then Diamond barked. A single deep *wooof!*

And S'n'J's block broke.

What always happens to haunted houses? she asked herself and found that she knew the answer.

Her fingers were suddenly energized and poised over the keyboard ready to describe the demise of Black Rock. She held down the shift button and reached for the 'T' to type 'The house was already on fire,' when the screen flickered and her page vanished.

A new text appeared.

BITCH!
IT WON'T WORK
IF YOU THINK IT WILL YOU MUST BE CRAZY
THERE CAN BE ONLY ONE GOD HERE
AND IT ISN'T YOU

YOU'RE DEAD, SNOWY
DEAD
I DON'T NEED THE COMPUTER ANY MORE
THE STORY IS FINISHED AND STORED
I HAVE BECOME A TRUE GOD
TRY ALTERING THIS REALITY!

The computer screen then flicked back to a completed page of text and began to scroll. Thousands of words went past, so quickly she could barely see them, let alone *read* them.

He did them instantaneously, she told herself in dismay.

The blur of moving words ceased only at the end and S'n'J had time to read the last line before the screen faded to grey. It said: 'The story was complete. Peter Perfect had prevailed.'

'No!' S'n'J shouted. Her fingers found the keys and hit them. Nothing happened.

Downstairs in the basement, Janie began to scream, a thin, high, strangled note.

S'n'J clapped her hands to her ears and could still hear it.

'Stop it!' she screeched, squeezing her eyes shut.

When she opened them again, the computer's screen was cracked into a crazed pattern of glass and the plastic that surrounded it was smouldering and melting, dripping strands of burning plastic on to the desk.

'Write on *that*! Bitch!' Philip said from behind her.

S'n'J spun around just in time to see him fold up and vanish.

Outside the window the black cloud roiled and thunder cracked, the noise shaking the house to its foundations.

Diamond lay on the floor, glaring at her.

'Get up dog!' she screamed. 'Get up and take me out of here! Help me get away!'

But the dog didn't move.

Chapter Thirty-one

Martin to the Rescue

Martin only arrived at the track that led down to Black Rock after an uphill struggle.

Which was what he'd thought was going to happen.

When Dawn S. Tauber's car had been crushed to pulp beneath a juggernaut they'd given up on the idea of walking to the emergency phone. It hardly seemed worth it since every emergency vehicle within miles was going to be heading for the scene of the accident.

When Dawn had dried her eyes and demisted her little round glasses, they'd climbed the bank beside the motorway, walked across a couple of muddy fields to the nearest road and had begun to hitch.

Martin didn't even know what town they'd been dropped in. The important thing was that it had an Avis office. Martin had headed for this, and Dawn – who wanted to get away from him as quickly as possible – had gone to the police station to report what had happened to her car. She would make her own travel arrangements from here, she'd told him, thank you.

Things took a turn for the worse while he was still in the Avis office. Just as he'd signed his name on the rental agreement, the ice block inside his brain lit up again.

Except that this time it didn't show him any pictures.

This time it began to shoot out spiked bolts of red light that seemed to burn their way through the matter of his brain. The ice block pulsed in time with his heart; each beat causing a fresh blast of light.

Which was a very good joke on the part of Peter Perfect, because the agonizing pain of the light-blasts (and the deep, dull ache that was left behind them) was causing his heart-rate to increase. It was a closed loop. The more it hurt, the faster his heart pounded, making it hurt even more.

Martin took deep breaths and tried to keep calm. The Avis girl began to look at him askance – which, he supposed distantly, wasn't surprising since each blast of pain made his facial muscles twitch in a gymnastic grimace of agony.

He made it to the car – a Vauxhall Cavalier, which was no Ferrari but infinitely better than a Fiat 500 – and collapsed into it, no longer sure that he was going to be able to drive it anywhere.

But the Avis girl was out there, carefully watching his facial churning and waiting to see what he would do next, so he started the car and gave her what he hoped was a cheery wave.

The girl didn't go back inside the office, just stood there watching.

'You little shit bag!' Martin hissed at her, grinning sweetly.

He put the car into gear and drove away.

Two hundred yards away from the office, he parked the car, put his head in his hands and cried with the pain.

Which didn't go away.

When he finally looked up, a spot in the centre of his vision was blurred and pulsing. Martin tried not to think about how high his blood pressure must be and what it must be doing to his kidneys and his heart. A stroke which paralysed him, he could live with, he knew. What he was frightened of was suffering a stroke that would wipe his memory or disable his sharp mind.

He searched his jacket pockets and eventually came up with a single grubby and misshapen Co-Proximal. It had half dissolved in his pocket. Martin dry-swallowed the mashed remains.

Eventually the pain subsided to a bearable degree and Martin began to drive.

When he arrived at Tintagel he could not recall most of the drive. This suited him just fine. At some point he'd broken his journey and found his way to an ironmonger's. He knew this because there was now a brand new pickaxe handle on the passenger seat and it hadn't been there earlier. He knew why he'd chosen it, too. Because unlike James Green's crowbar, it wouldn't act as a lightning conductor.

Now, here he was at the top of the track to Black Rock, asking himself the question everyone asked: *If I go down here, will I be able to get back up again?* But this particular man was asking himself this question for a different reason entirely.

His heart in his mouth and his brain-haemorrhage headache returning, Martin began the descent. There were two cars a hundred yards ahead of him: the Cadillac that James had come in last night and Essenjay's Sierra. The Caddy was burnt to a crisp.

Martin wondered how Peter Perfect had tricked Essenjay into asking to be admitted to the house. That was pivotal, apparently. She'd had to enter of her own accord.

All that matters now is getting her out, he thought as he brought the car to a standstill behind hers.

The pain in his head increased. He suspected that his brain was now haemorrhaging; that he would be left crippled and mentally disabled.

But this wasn't happening, he thought as he turned off the car's engine. Then he wondered why he'd just spoken to himself as though he were the narrator of a story stating a fact. Either someone had just committed this sentence to paper or disk, or his mind was going.

But although this wasn't yet happening, Martin knew it soon would. His fingers had begun to tingle and his mental vocabulary seemed to be diminishing.

Get her out, that's all you have to remember, he told himself, flexing his tingling fingers and trying – and failing – to collect his scattered thoughts. He picked up the pickaxe handle, got out of the car and looked nervously around him.

Somewhere inside that house is S'n'J, he thought, *and I'll get her back or die trying.*

Die trying, probably, he added cynically.

He could hear something moving, off the side of the track, about ten feet ahead of him. *The dog?* He walked towards the source of the noise, peering around, his head bobbing from side to side like a boxer on the defensive.

Martin will not die! his mind thought, apparently on his behalf. It felt just as if someone had just planted the idea there for him to think. The thought provided him with the exact amount of comfort he'd expected to derive from it. Absolutely none at all.

He went to the side of the bank and peered down into bushy undergrowth. There was something there crawling slowly through the bushes.

'Who's that?' he demanded, poised and ready to strike if necessary.

There was a pause in which time seemed to come to a standstill.

During this moment all sound ceased: the gentle breeze stopped blowing, the noise of the sea faded, the solitary wheeling gull that had been cawing fell silent and the thing under the bushes seemed to have vanished.

Martin waited, as tense as a bowstring.

To the side of him – down towards the house – a noise began. It was a kind of slow, swishing noise which reminded Martin of the way the huge axe had swung in the film of Poe's *The Pit and the Pendulum*. It sounded like a huge, well-oiled machine beginning to run.

Martin didn't turn to look at it because he had a pretty good idea of what was making that steadily speeding *swoosh-swoosh* sound.

'Who's down there?' he demanded again and was relieved when he heard a cough that sounded distinctly human. The undergrowth began to move again.

'It's me,' a voice croaked. 'I fell and hit my head. Knocked myself out. Christ almighty, I've got the granddaddy of all headaches.'

'James?' Martin heard himself asking in astonishment. He didn't know why he'd said it with a question mark – he already knew that the voice belonged to James.

Except that you do know why, he told himself. *Because down there in Black Rock, Peter Perfect wrote it for you like that. And since you're aware of that, he must be losing his*

*grip. He's trying to take over your mind and he's failing.
That's why he wanted to keep you away. He's frightened of
you because you know fiction when you see it. You can see
joins where other people wouldn't.*

'You're dead. I saw you fall into a wall of fire,' Martin said
suspiciously.

And knew that these words had been scripted for him too.
What he'd really wanted was to ask how close to death James
was and whether he was going to be of any use in rescuing
Essenjay.

'Dead, but I won't lie down,' James said from somewhere
about ten feet away. 'Hang on. You'll have to give me a hand
up when I crawl out of here.'

Martin's mouth dropped a little further when James finally
appeared. No one could possibly look that badly burnt and
live.

Outside fiction, that is, he reminded himself. James *could*
have survived a searing this intense if he was a character in a
novel.

James crawled up the bank towards Martin and reached
out a hand.

In close-up he didn't actually seem to be so damaged. His
hands and arms were reddened and blistered, he'd lost a lot
of his hair and his eyebrows, but everything else looked like
window dressing. As if an astounding make-up job had been
done on him.

Trickster! Martin thought at Peter Perfect, as he grabbed a
sweaty hand, braced himself and heaved James up on to the
track.

James picked himself up from the ground, tested his limbs
and then turned to Martin, grinning. His face was so sooty
he looked like a failed Al Jolson impersonator.

'James Green, slightly singed, but otherwise alive and well,'
he said breathlessly. 'And you're Martin. We'd better do
something pretty damned quick, Martin, because very soon,
someone's going to start trying to kill us.'

Martin was shaking his head. There were words in his
mouth, just ready to tumble out, but they felt like the careless
and clumsy dialogue of a writer in a rush. He knew he was

supposed to say that he couldn't believe it and that he'd seen what had happened to James and so on, *ad nauseam*, so he resisted.

'Someone is putting words into your mouth for you to say,' he warned.

'They don't call me Mister Nifty Footwork for nothing,' James responded, as if Martin had spoken the words that Peter Perfect had written for him.

'Think man! Start speaking for yourself!' Martin barked. 'Resist. Don't take the easy path. It's fiction. You have to think your own thoughts. If you think *his* we're sunk.'

James frowned. Then his face cleared and he nodded. 'The house is haunted, just like it says in the book. Drezy's inside. We have to get her out. The trouble is, the guy who wrote the book is in there and he doesn't want us to.'

Martin fought off the ready-made sentence that appeared in his mind for him to say: 'Have we gone crazy, or what?' and actually said, 'If you don't assert your own mind, I'm going to hit you over the head with this pick handle. I don't need any more hindrances.'

James nodded and responded to the question Martin *should* have asked but didn't: 'You know what's going on here, don't you?' he said, then repeated, 'The house is haunted, just like it says in the book. Drezy's inside. We have to get her out. The trouble is, the guy who wrote the book is in there and he doesn't want us to.'

His voice was starting to sound very wooden now, and his expression suggested he was trapped. He knew what was happening to him and could do nothing to prevent it.

'Fight it!' Martin shouted. The swishing noise was growing louder now and for the first time Martin glanced down towards the house.

Where a white cloud had formed at roof-level. It was huge and misshapen and revolving like a centrifuge. The swishing noise happened each time a protruding arm of vapour passed.

James was still being fictionalized, still acting out his script even though he was getting none of the necessary responses. His face was a picture of supreme confusion. He looked like an actor who has learned the lines for *Macbeth* and half-way through finds himself in the middle of *The Tempest*.

He shook his head. 'I don't know. What I *do* know is that I'm going to give it a bloody good try. I brought a crowbar. Did you see it?'

'One last chance, James,' Martin said to this latest *non sequitur*. 'Snap out of it!'

'Just back there, where you dropped it last night,' James prompted and nodded at Martin knowingly.

'I'm not saying it,' Martin hissed. 'Break out of it!'

James nodded frantically. 'Just back there,' he said, glancing at where his crowbar lay.

Hit him! Martin told himself. There was a fifty-fifty chance he'd be doing the right thing. *No there isn't*, he realized. *Peter Perfect really has sucked James and Essenjay into his story. They don't have to suspend their disbelief to appreciate fiction. They don't have any disbelief to suspend. They may get sucked into a good book, but it doesn't happen to Martin Dinsey because you don't get fooled by fancy footwork. That's what makes you such a good editor. He might be able to do the magical effects for real, but he knows I can see how he's putting it all together. He knows that if there's a little flaw in his story, I'll find it and work on it.*

Suddenly Martin understood exactly what that flaw was. It was being acted out in front of him, by James. If Martin hadn't arrived, James would have gone down to the house and been killed. After which things would have been past the point of no return. Fiction would have turned to fact.

Which meant, Martin realized, that he was here only to bring James out of the web of lies that was being woven around him. James was the one who would get Essenjay out, not Martin Snips Dinsey. The story was rolling and couldn't be stopped and there wasn't a place in its finale for him. All he existed for was to free James from the enchantment he was under. And having done this he would bow out.

This wasn't good news. Not merely because it relegated him from hero to bit part, but because being a bit part meant one of two things. Either he was going to die, or he was going to go home without the girl. But the circle around him was now closed. Whatever he did from here onwards was going to be bad for him.

'Just back there,' Martin said, speaking the words that James (and Peter Perfect) so badly wanted him to say. 'Where you dropped it last night.' He pointed at where the crowbar lay on the track.

James went and retrieved the tool.

Martin watched him, thinking, *Well this is it, Dinsey. You've been well and truly stitched up. If you let it carry on, you'll lose Essenjay to Peter Perfect, and if you interfere with the story, you'll lose her to James. And you may well die, too. What's it gonna be, big boy?*

James came back, looking for all the world like a story-book hero. He was tall and muscular and determined. Martin felt it was a bit like watching Clint Eastwood stride towards you. He could suddenly see what it was Essenjay saw in this manual labourer. And something extraordinary happened.

For the first time in his whole life, Martin Dinsey acted altruistically. For the first time in his life he did something without wanting a reward. He did it for the love of Essenjay and in spite of knowing that it was likely to be the last important thing he ever did.

He spoke the words he knew Peter Perfect had scripted. 'Ready?' he asked.

'As I'll ever be,' James said, giving the required response. His look of confusion had faded now that things had got back to the script. 'We'd better go quickly,' he added. 'It's starting. There's a cloud forming. Look!' He pointed up above the forecourt of Black Rock.

Martin didn't need to turn. He already knew the score.

'I warned you, James,' he said, lifting the pickaxe handle from his shoulder and raising it into the air. 'This is what you get for stealing my woman. And for not listening to me. I hope it hurts, you shithouse and I want you to know something. If I get through this alive, I'll win her back from you.'

James heard none of this. He was staring at the revolving cloud waiting for Martin to say that this time it was a thundercloud.

After a short pause, James said, 'Can it strike us from there?'

Martin shook his head. 'No, but this can,' he said, and brought the pick handle down.

It was a single-handed blow, but it landed true and made James drop to his knees, a strange, far-away look in his eyes and blood blooming from the crown of his head.

'That fucking *hurt*!' he said in a small voice.

Martin stepped forward and slapped his face. Hard.

And suddenly James was back.

He was in pain, but he was back.

Did it! Martin congratulated himself. 'Let's see what you can do about *that* Mister Fucking Perfect!' he added aloud. 'Your nemesis is here. The eagle-eyed editor has arrived and boy is he pissed off with you!'

'Martin?' James said in astonishment. 'What happened?' He touched his head and looked vacantly at the blood on his fingers.

'You were hypnotized and I got you out of it,' Martin snarled. 'Now for fuck's sake get with it because we've busted the story wide open and now we have to zap the writer before he recovers.'

'Too late,' James said, pointing at the cloud. It was spinning like a top now and the lower part of it was snaking down towards the ground in a point.

'Twister!' James said.

Christ, Martin thought to himself. *I thought twister, and he fucking well made one. This isn't a thundercloud at all, it's a bloody whirlwind.*

And even as he had the thought, the tip of the cloud touched the ground. Martin watched, amazed, expecting the whole revolving mass to start moving up the track towards them now that it had made contact with the ground, but a piece of it seemed to break off, still spinning.

This piece was a six-foot-high column that snaked across the forecourt of Black Rock, picking up gravel and dust as it reeled back and forth. Beside it, another part of the cloud snaked down and made another little twister.

But Martin was watching the first one. It seemed to have

found a track to follow, and it was serpentining towards them.

'Here it comes,' James yelled.

'It's an hallucination,' Martin shouted, hopefully. 'It isn't real.'

He had half expected his disbelief to make the twisters vanish, but this did not happen. There were four now, lining up in single file and heading towards the gate in huge sweeping curves. Another was being formed every five seconds or so.

'What do we do?' James yelled over the increasing noise of the revolving cloud.

'We go down there,' Martin said. 'Come on!' The wind was already tearing at his hair and clothes and most of the twisters weren't even out of the gate yet. 'We'll have to dodge 'em,' he said. 'You ready?'

He looked over at James and saw that he was. Just standing beside the tyre-fitter gave him confidence. If James had survived a wall of fire, a few tornadoes weren't going to be much problem.

Get thee behind me, Peter Perfect, Martin thought and found that his headache had gone. And it had taken the ice block with it. During the last two seconds, his face had lit with a big, stupid grin of the kind you saw in kids' war-hero comics. *What a wanker you are!* he told himself and didn't care. If he was going to go, he couldn't imagine a better way of doing it than fighting for something he loved.

'Let's go!' James yelled at him and Martin saw that his face also bore the same crazy comic-book hero expression.

And side by side, they walked towards the house.

The first twister had wandered off the track and wound its way down the bank, picking up stones and dirt and throwing them out again in a circular hail. The second one did a kind of stall between the gate posts. It remained where it was, debris falling out of it as its spinning slowed. It petered out entirely before the third twister reached it.

'They're not very strong!' James shouted over the roaring *swoosh* of the big cloud.

'He's losing power for some reason,' Martin yelled back,

eyeing the revolving vapour in front of the house. The author wasn't losing enough power for Martin's liking. That big disc of cloud was forty feet across and twenty or thirty feet deep. It looked as if it could muster plenty more whirlwinds.

The third twister came out through the gates, in a dead straight line towards them, the fourth close behind it. The fifth stalled and vanished, and the next peeled away and headed for the side of the house.

He can't control them, Martin realized. *He's just making them and throwing them in our general direction. He can't steer them.*

'Look out!' James yelled as the one approaching grew close. The lowering air pressure made Martin's ears pop. 'Just leap aside when it gets here!' James advised, running forwards. He dodged to the side of the twister and was obscured from Martin's vision by the cloud of vapour and debris.

Gravel whipped out from the whirlwind into Martin's face and he brought his arms up to shield his eyes. He was ready to leap when the twister veered away from him, leaving a clear passage through to where James was crouched ready to leap away from the next little tornado.

And Martin began to run.

And as if it had been waiting for him to do this, the wind whipped back across towards him.

Missed me, you bastard! Martin crowed as the twister whipped at his heels.

And then he was in the air being pelted with stones and grit and twigs and leaves. For a moment there was no world, no up or down, just an ear-tearing shriek of wind, a face-stinging shower of missiles and a vast centrifugal force.

And then he was slammed face first into the track.

Martin's body felt as if it had been hit by a truck. There seemed to be no air out there to breathe.

'Come on!' James was screaming from above him. 'There's another one coming. GET UP!'

Martin raised his head far enough to see the next whirlwind cruising towards him but that was as much as he could do. Suddenly, James was dragging him out of the twister's path.

The following tornado danced in front of them and left the track. The one behind it spun into streams of vapour and vanished, throwing droplets of stinging water into their faces.

'Nearly finished!' James shouted and pointed up at the mother cloud.

With stinging eyes, Martin peered up at the huge revolving disturbance and saw that it was thinning.

James pulled him to his feet, propelled him forwards, yanked him out of the way of the next twister, and suddenly they were passing through the Black Rock gateposts.

The last of the whirlwinds danced towards them.

James stayed where he was, holding Martin up. 'It's gonna miss us!' he said.

'No it isn't!' Martin screamed. And closed his eyes.

There was a noise which sounded like a cannon firing and suddenly the air seemed too thick to breathe.

'It went!' James said as Martin opened his eyes. The forecourt was clear. The big cloud had gone. Apart from the channels the twisters had dug into the gravel forecourt there was no sign that they had ever existed.

'You OK?' James asked, scanning the area.

Martin nodded. He'd lost a shoe back there somewhere and he was bruised, but otherwise all right. 'He's exhausted himself,' he muttered. 'I can't believe it. No good book finishes that quickly. There has to be more.'

'And there it is,' James said, stabbing a finger at the sky. 'The cloud cover. It's getting lower. More puffy. He's bringing the real weather down. Come on!' He started towards the front door and Martin followed, ignoring the pain where sharp stones bit his shoeless foot.

They stood outside the big, black, impenetrable front door, gazing at it. There really was no lock or letter box. Just a gold knob.

James looked at Martin. 'How do we get in?' he asked.

'You should know this,' Martin said. 'The getting in is easy. It's the getting out again you have to worry about.'

And the door began to move, opening slowly and soundlessly.

Martin shuffled backwards, pushing James away from the threshold.

And there was Janie.

Or at least a wet red thing with her head on top of it.

Something that didn't quite become a scream gurgled in Martin's throat.

Janie advanced from behind the door, as though propelled on rollers. There was no body movement that might suggest she was walking.

Which wasn't so surprising since she *couldn't* be walking.

Janie had no feet.

Martin glanced at her and his mind did a double-take. Even on the second try, it still didn't believe what Martin's eyes had shown it.

Janie, Martin's stunned mind informed him, was just about as naked as it was possible for a woman to get.

From her neck down to her ankles, Janie's skin had been removed.

'I was . . . a . . . shreddie, Martin,' Janie's face said in a tiny pained voice. 'A bit part player. It hurts.'

Impossible as it seemed, Janie was alive. Her face had expression, her eyes moved.

But she can't be alive! Martin's mind protested. *Her hands and feet are not present and the only reason she is upright at all is because there is a wooden post stuck through her chest at an angle of thirty odd degrees.*

'Kill . . . me,' Janie implored. 'Get me out . . . of . . . here. Kill . . . me! *Please.*'

'Don't you touch her, she's mine!' a voice said from the shadows.

And Janie's body did a horrible little dance as whoever was holding her up on the wooden stake worked his way up towards her.

If it was possible for Martin to have felt any more shock, he would have felt it now. The man who was holding Janie up on this stake was not Peter Perfect at all, but good old Billy-Joe, Janie's husband.

Janie might still be alive, but Billy-Joe was surely dead. His head was smashed in like the shell of a hard-boiled egg. His eyes were filmed and all the blood that had ever been in his body was soaked and dried into his clothes.

Billy-Joe reached his wife, put his arm around her back and heaved her towards him with one arm so that he was supporting her at his side.

Janie made a tiny squeal like that of a kitten being tortured.

'She's mine,' Billy-Joe said proudly. 'We had a reconciliation. We're going to Hell in a hand-basket.'

'Oh,' Martin heard himself say. His mind had just noted that the ends of Janie's handless arms had been cauterized by burning. He was trying not to look at her ankles.

'And guess who's coming with us,' Billy-Joe said. His hand and wrist protruded from beneath her armpit and now his fingers began to move, tearing parts off her.

'Let her go, Billy-Joe,' Martin said and was distantly aware that he'd spoken a little rhyme. It didn't sound even a bit like a magic one.

Billy-Joe shook his head. 'Like I say, we're going to hell, my old story-book editor. Not just me and Janie girl, but you and Drezy too. And the fuckhead behind you. We're all going.'

'Is this real?' James said from behind Martin. He sounded like a five-year-old at a showing of *The Exorcist*.

Martin nodded.

'We *are* pleased you've come,' Billy-Joe said. 'Aren't we, Janie?' he added and shook her.

Janie squeaked. Blood dripped from her mouth.

Billy-Joe nodded at his wife. 'Cry baby,' he said, rolling his eyes. He dug his fingers into Janie's rib cage and she produced a scream which made Martin want to die.

Then Martin was yanked aside and a blur of metal passed his head. James had come to the end of his tether and struck out. But Billy-Joe and Janie both vanished instantly beneath the blow.

'Oh *Jesus*!' James cried.

'A trick,' Martin squeaked. 'That's all. A pretty picture to fool us!'

Black Rock's interior did not look as it did in Martin's imagination, or as it had been described in the pages he'd read of Peter Perfect's book. Where it should have been carpeted and decorated, it was bare and empty. There was nothing here to suggest the house was inhabited at all.

'What do we do?' James asked.

'We go in and look for your girlfriend, of course,' Martin replied.

And there she was, at the far end of the hall: Martin's little Essenjay, dressed in a man's white shirt and nothing else. A distant part of Martin noted what fabulous legs she had. She was looking directly towards him, but didn't seem to be able to see him. It was something to do with the haze in front of her, Martin knew. Peter Perfect had placed it there to confuse her.

'Essy!' he shouted.

'That's not her!' James said, placing his hand on Martin's shoulder. 'It isn't her, Martin. It's . . . something else.'

'This way!' Martin yelled, ignoring him. 'This way, Essy! We've got her, Jimmy boy. We've got her!'

Martin started forwards and felt James tug him back. He spun round. 'What the fuck are you doing?' he screamed and knocked James' hand away from him.

'Don't, Martin. That isn't her. I don't know what it is, but it isn't her. Don't go down there. Don't!'

Martin glared at him and turned away. His little Essenjay was there and she was stuck behind something that looked like a heat-haze, but he would have her out of here in two shakes of a lamb's tail. No problem.

'I'm coming Essy!' Martin yelled, and as he started down the hall, James grabbed his shoulder again and shouted something at him.

Martin didn't hear it. He shrugged James' hand away from him and sprinted down the hall.

Chapter Thirty-two

Retreat from Black Rock

Martin had a weak point and Peter Perfect knew exactly what it was and had gone to work on it. Martin had seen Drezy and wild horses weren't going to keep him from her.

Which left James.

The thing down there, he would later admit, had looked rather like Drezy for a moment. After that it had begun to look like a human-sized column of melting pink candle-wax. What worried James most was that the rippling waxy thing smelled rather like fire-lighters. The paraffin odour reeked of potential disaster. James had always looked at those innocuous white blocks and told himself that there was a fire waiting to happen.

And, in his judgement, this was exactly what the thing at the far end of the corridor was. Literally. Fire waiting to happen.

He was bigger and faster than Martin, and was closing on him fast. Martin was almost within reach now and if James could just grab hold of his jacket, he could yank him off course, swing him into the wall and it would be over and done with. He leaned forward and stretched out his fingers. For a moment they brushed against the flying cloth of Martin's jacket. James grabbed and came away with a handful of nothing. In desperation, he launched himself at Martin's legs in a rugby tackle. A moment later he was trying to keep hold of one flapping trouser-leg and one shoeless foot.

A moment after that, Martin was down, skidding on the bare and dusty floorboards. The pickaxe handle thumped against the wooden wall panelling, but he didn't let go of it.

'You *cunt*!' Martin screamed, kicking out at him and crawling away as James tried to restrain him.

'It's not her!' James shouted as Martin broke away on all fours. 'It isn't her!'

Martin stopped of his own accord when he reached the shimmering patch of air that stood between the end of the hall and the flowing waxy column that looked like S'n'J.

'Oh my *Christ*!' he moaned. 'She's *melting*!'

'Get up!' James screamed. 'Quick!'

He was on his own feet now, but Martin was just kneeling there, one hand around the axe handle and the other clapped to the side of his face, expressing anguish like an actor in a silent movie.

Seconds, that's all! James told himself. *Seconds before we die!*

He reached Martin, took hold of the collar of his jacket and hoisted him to his feet.

'OUT!' James screamed into Martin's face and began to drag him back up the corridor. Martin didn't resist, but he didn't help by walking either. He'd gone board-stiff and James had to pull him along by the armpits. His heels made tracks in the dusty floor. Half-way down the corridor he lost his other shoe.

'Oh, *no*!' Martin moaned in a pained voice.

James glanced up. For a second he saw Drezy. The haziness had gone and she stood there before the black emptiness, her shirt moving as though tousled by a breeze. She looked like someone playing Peter Pan: she stood tall, her hands on her hips and her feet planted firmly on the ground. A faint smile played on the edges of her lips.

But Peter Pan, to the best of James' knowledge, had never been surrounded by an aura of fire.

The flames around her weren't the gentle orange flames you would have associated with the smell of fire-lighters. They were blinding and they burned with the ferocity of an oxy-acetylene welding torch.

In the moment before he started to charge backwards down the hall towards the door, dragging Martin with him,

James revised his opinion. She didn't look like Peter Pan at all, she looked like an angel of death.

'Essy,' Martin moaned, but there was no trace of her there now, just a human-sized column of roaring flame.

And it was moving towards them. Inside a second it was moving almost as fast as he was dragging Martin away from it. It didn't sway and dance like the tornadoes had done earlier, but came in a dead straight line as if it was following a wire.

When he saw the bottom of the stairs beside him he realized that he was only ten feet or so away from the door.

And he also knew that behind him, the door would be closing.

He tore his eyes away from the approaching column of fire and glanced over his shoulder at the door. Purple blotches swam in his vision. The door was open. Outside on the forecourt the air seemed dark, as if it were dusk already and James thought he could see frost twinkling on the ground.

And as he turned his head away to see how near the fire was, he saw the door begin to move. He dropped Martin – who fell heavily and stayed there – scooped up his crowbar, darted across to the door and wedged the crowbar into the chink of light that was left around the edge of the frame.

The door came into contact with the crowbar and James pushed against the piece of hardened steel, trying to lever the door back. He might as well have tried to prise up a corner of the World Trade Centre.

The door bit into the hardened steel of the crowbar, crimping grooves into it.

'Martin!' James shouted.

Martin was on his feet now, glancing from the column of fire to the door and back again while he hopped from foot to foot. He looked like a man who had suddenly found himself standing on a griddle.

'Through here!' Martin suddenly shouted and thrust open the lounge door, pushing at it hard as if there was a great resistance.

Behind it was the sea.

But it wasn't a view of the sea from a hundred feet above as in the book pages James had read, it was the sea bed.

The lounge was under water.

Martin yanked his arm out of the water and stared at it with a comical expression of disbelief as sea-water dripped from his suit sleeve.

The sea was sliced off at the frame of the door and hung there in a flat sheet that wavered slightly like the surface of a big soap bubble. The door was behind the shimmering surface, about two-thirds of the way open.

James glanced down the hall at the pillar of fire and noticed that it had slowed. It hadn't stopped moving entirely, but it looked as if it was struggling up a steep hill.

James peered past Martin into the dim green of the sea bed. There was a solitary crab scuttling sideways across a flat patch of sand. About twenty feet away something that might have been an eel flashed past a tangle of rock.

Martin looked over at James, his mouth dangling, his head shaking slightly. The pickaxe handle dangled in his left hand.

'Ideal,' Martin said distantly and took a deep breath.

Then he turned away and thrust his head and shoulders through the door and into the sea.

A second later, he withdrew, gasping.

He shook his head, spraying water. 'No good,' he said. 'Thought we might swim it, but it's too deep and too cold. You can't even see the surface from here. We'd die.'

James glanced over his shoulder at the approaching flame, then back at the crowbar wedged into the door. In another three or four seconds the door would bite through the bar. But in another three or four seconds this would hardly matter, because by this time he would be too busy being burned to death to care.

Martin turned towards the column of fire. 'It's going to go out before it reaches us,' he announced confidently. 'He hasn't got the power to keep all this happening.'

James took no notice of him, just leaned on the crowbar.

'He can't keep it all going,' Martin said. 'Something's got to give.'

And the column of fire broke into a thousand tiny balls of

flame which collapsed to the ground and spread out like a wave. James glanced at it as it sprayed up the side of the wall and the side of the staircase, then started to roll towards him, moving faster now that its height had been reduced.

Many of the tiny balls of flame were winking out, but there were going to be enough left to engulf him and Martin, James knew.

He leaned hard on the crowbar and the door began to swing open again.

'Quick!' James screamed, already forcing himself through the narrow opening, but Martin was right behind him.

Outside the house the ground was crusted with frost.

The marble-sized balls of fire followed them out of the house and flowed down the step. Most of them extinguished themselves in tiny puffs of smoke when they hit the frosty ground, but some survived, and speeded up. These broke into two groups, one of which tracked Martin, and the other of which targeted James.

'He can't have the power!' Martin complained, dancing away from the sizzling gobbets of flame.

His breath making white plumes in the freezing air, James watched the leader of his group approach him. The house had got hold of the story and had taken it over. The house was providing the power now, draining its reserves. And James thought that if E really did equal MC^2 those reserves were going to turn out to be pretty near infinite.

He stamped on the first tiny fireball as it reached him.

Smoke and steam hissed out from beneath his baseball boot and his foot got very hot indeed.

He expected the ball to eat its way through the sole of his boot, but when he took his foot away, the ball didn't stick to it. It lay on the ground smouldering, no longer a ball of fire but a badly charred cockroach.

'Beetles!' Martin shrieked from behind him. 'They're fucking beetles!'

James dodged the next one and saw Martin who was standing his ground and using his pickaxe handle as a club on the approaching balls of fire. Sparks flew when he hit them.

James hefted his crowbar and whacked the flaring roaches away from him. There weren't many left now. All across the forecourt they were winking out like sparks from a Brock's skyrocket.

'Did it!' Martin bellowed triumphantly and then said in an astonished voice, 'Oh my good God!'

James stamped on the last of his group and turned to see what Martin was yelling about.

'This isn't possible,' Martin complained, coming up beside him. 'It just isn't fucking possible. He can't be doing it!'

Martin was literally steaming. Like a racehorse. His face was dark and angry and James was relieved to see that he'd come back to himself after the episode inside the house. He no longer looked like someone who had tripped off the edge of sanity and wasn't coming back.

'Look!' he said and stabbed a finger out across the bay.

In a line across the bay from the castle to the rock on which the house stood, the sea had been sucked up into a peak, just as Drezy had claimed she'd seen. Vapour was rising from it as if it was purposefully being sucked up into the cloudy sky. James could see a distinct line in the cloud that corresponded to the ridge of water. Along that line, angry cloud was swirling.

'He's changing the fucking weather, that's what he's doing!' Martin complained bitterly. 'He's already made it cold out here. You know what he's going to do, don't you?'

James nodded. He knew exactly what was happening. In the book, the man who lived in this house was called Mr Winter.

'He's going to make it snow,' Martin said. 'It's only October, it can't possibly snow.'

'Oh yes it can, my little pals,' a voice said from behind them.

They whirled round.

Billy-Joe stood behind them, his face blank and his head stoved in.

He was carrying a fire-axe.

'It can snow, but you won't be around to see it,' he said,

and his mouth moved out of synchronization with the words. It was like watching a film that had been badly dubbed.

He hefted the axe and grinned.

'Fuck off, Billy-Joe,' Martin said in a voice of pure disdain. 'Mad axe men have been done to death. Where the fuck have you and Peter Perfect been hiding for the last twenty years? Don't you know *anything* about the genre in which you're working? It won't wash, I'm afraid. The fire beetles were pretty good and the underwater lounge was excellent, but this is pure cliché. Now stop it at once.'

Billy-Joe glared at him. 'I had you down for a prize cunt the first time I met you,' he said, his lips still moving out of synch. 'And Janie's told me all about what a wanker you are, too. Now, I think that a selfish bastard like you ought to be punished. That's *punished*, not published. And that's what I'm here to do.' He took the axe in both hands and raised it above his head.

And to James' dismay, Martin walked right into his range.

'Martin!' he warned, but Martin merely made a flapping motion with his free hand – presumably because he wanted to indicate that he knew what he was doing.

Martin stopped right beneath where the axe would fall. 'What a crap line,' he glowered. 'I don't know if you're inside that smashed-up skull, Billy-Joe, but if you are still in there somewhere, I have something to tell you. I know how much you hated books and writers and editors and the whole back-slapping literary shebang. So you should know this. Inside that house, there's a total arsehole with literary pretensions using your mouth to speak to me. In *his* voice. He isn't even bothering to use your voice, Billy-Joe. And he has the worst line in dialogue since Lulu Kaminsky. Think about that, Billy-Joe.'

'You're dead,' Billy-Joe said and the axe went right down behind his head for a good long swing. His head was high and the front of his body was curved back, tensed to strike.

'So are you,' Martin said and swung the pickaxe handle upwards with his left hand.

The end of it caught Billy-Joe underneath the chin. With a great deal of force.

Billy-Joe toppled backwards to the ground.

'That one's for Janie,' Martin snarled. 'I know what you used to do to her, you motherfucker!'

He turned to face James, a triumphant look on his face. 'Now he'll get up again, just like they do in all those crap zombie movies and horror books,' he announced.

But Billy-Joe didn't get up. He lay there on the ground looking very broken. His limbs quivered and his face twitched.

James went over to where Martin was standing, gazing down at the man.

'Go away, Billy, you're dead now,' Martin hissed.

Billy-Joe's eyes blinked open. His lips worked and a shard of tooth came out and lay on his chin. 'Hurts,' he said, and this time his voice was his own.

'I'm sure it does,' Martin said. 'Janie used to hurt after you'd beaten her up.'

'Kill me,' Billy-Joe whispered.

Martin shook his head. 'You're already dead. You're dead and he's let you go now. It doesn't have to hurt any more. Go home.'

And Billy-Joe's eyes closed.

Martin looked up at James. There were tears in his eyes. 'He deserved worse,' he said acidly, then turned towards the house. 'So much for your axe-battle climax!' he yelled.

At which point the door slammed shut and the big gold knob began to melt.

'He's on the run now,' Martin observed as a toffee-like strand of golden goo descended from the knob. 'It's all coming apart.'

The melted metal pooling on the step began to rise, as if it was filling an invisible mould.

'What the Sam Hill is *that*?' Martin shouted, stabbing an angry finger towards the door. He had stopped steaming now and begun to shiver.

The air temperature, James noticed, was falling rapidly. It wasn't just cold out here, it was bitter and the ground was crusted with frost.

The golden liquid was now pouring steadily from the door

knob into a shape which looked not unlike the paw of a huge animal. James thought he knew what that animal was going to turn out to be. He'd read about the were-lion embossed into the door knob, and now he was seeing the gargoyle figure forming in front of him. One of the back legs was already complete.

James' mind railed against the fact that so much liquid was pouring from one molten door knob, but it was happening in front of him. The other leg was now finished and the molten gold was flowing into the shape of a tail. And the tail was already swishing from side to side.

'I think we ought to retreat,' he said, glancing at Martin.

'It won't hurt us,' Martin said.

James turned to him. 'What do you think it *will* do then, serve us tea and cakes?'

'Look, I'm an editor and I will not allow a door-knob gargoyle to come to life in any story that I get sucked into. I won't do it! Now quit it, Peter Fucking Perfect!'

'Martin! We'd better run!' James insisted.

Martin turned to him. 'Where to?' he said. 'I can barely stand, let alone run. If it comes, we have to kill it. If we don't, we die. That's the top and bottom of it, James boy. That's showbiz.'

'Split up,' James said. 'It can't go for both of us at once.'

Martin looked at him hard. 'Good plan,' he said bitterly. 'One of us gets torn to bits.'

Over on the doorstep, the back end of the lion was already formed and struggling to pull away from the stream of gold. The back legs were pacing like a wild animal behind bars.

'It's a male,' Martin observed, hobbling away from James. 'If you can get behind it, whack it one in the bollocks.'

Martin went about twenty feet across the gravel, adopted the pose of a baseball batsman ready to strike, the pickaxe handle over his shoulder.

James stooped beside Billy-Joe's dead body, put down his damaged crowbar and picked up the fire-axe. It was new and had a keen edge. He would do better than whack the were-lion thing in the bollocks, he decided. If it came near him, he would take its genitals right off. *Instant sex change,* he told himself and managed a grin which must have looked similar to the one he'd seen on Martin. A smile of hopelessness.

The lion now existed from its tail to its throat. As soon as there was enough of its neck for it to roar, it started. The noise was terrifying. Beneath James' feet, the ground shook with the sound.

'It sounds pretty pissed off,' Martin said in the silence that followed.

'Empty vessels,' James called back amidst the following bellow.

Martin turned to him, grinning. 'Do you realize we're going to have to fight a door knob? Have we gone fucking crazy?'

'Not as crazy as some,' James returned, nodding towards the house. Suddenly he began to feel a little better. He didn't know if it was the interplay between two doomed men, or what. All he knew was that he'd do his best and that he wasn't going to be beaten by a door knob, for God's sake. How would that look as an epitaph: *Here lie the remains of James Green who was torn to pieces by a door-knob gargoyle. He fought and lost.*

The lion, when it was complete, was totally golden. Its eyes, its teeth, its claws. A travesty of a real lion, its head seemed to be all jaws and teeth. It did not look at all noble, more like a beast that had been designed and built in hell.

It roared and reared up on its hind legs like a frightened horse, swiping at the air in front of it, struggling forwards against the molten gold that was still pouring into it.

And then it was free.

Somewhere out to sea, thunder cracked.

And in the forecourt of Black Rock, it began to snow.

The snow fell in huge blinding flakes that blurred James' vision.

And the golden animal charged out from the doorway, steaming as it met the snow, leaving melted footprints in the frost.

It got to Martin in three huge bounds.

James saw Martin's axe-handle fly and heard the deadened

thud as it stove into the lion's head. Then the lion was rearing up and slashing with its claws.

James hammered across the forecourt, bringing the axe up as he ran.

Martin screamed and struck out again.

The lion bellowed, backed off and leapt at him.

Through the blinding snow, James caught glimpses of the beast hitting Martin in the chest, and Martin falling.

As James arrived, the lion sank its teeth into Martin's leg. James saw his chance. The lion's hindquarters were facing him, its tail was up and it was male. James heaved the axe at its testicles. Golden flesh split, steaming yellow liquid poured out and the lion roared in what James hoped was extreme pain.

The animal turned towards him, but he was ready and waiting for it. As its paw came up, claws extended, James struck again. The jarring shock almost tore the axe from his hands. He backed away as the lion slashed at him, its paw now half severed and its claws retracted. The hot yellow liquid was pouring from the wound.

The lion snarled at him and turned away. It limped past Martin who was trying to get himself up off the ground, then turned around and crouched. The moment that James realized it was not sitting down because it was hurt but because it intended to pounce, it was in the air.

It came down on Martin and its jaws locked around his injured leg.

'GET IT OFF ME!' Martin shrieked, thumping at its head with the pick-axe handle. Around his legs the snow was red with his blood.

James leapt over his body, skidded to a halt beside the lion, brought the axe up over his head and brought it down with all his strength into the lion's backbone.

The lion screamed, but it didn't let go of Martin's leg.

Martin screeched.

James stood astride Martin, aimed and whacked the axe down into the lion's face. Steaming yellow blood poured into the snow, mixing with the red from Martin's leg.

The lion raised its broken head.

James hit it again.

The lion howled, long and hard.

And then it ceased to exist.

What it had done, however, remained.

'My leg. Fuck fuck fuck. It *hurts*!' Martin squealed.

James knelt beside him. Martin's right leg was so badly mangled between the knee and the hip that it was difficult to tell which bits were the material of his torn trousers, and which were torn pieces of flesh. There was an artery gone in there somewhere, James knew, because down by Martin's knee, blood was jetting, just like it did in the films.

'It *hurts*!' Martin moaned again. His jacket and shirt were in ribbons too, his chest was badly cut and there were four puncture marks on his left hip but these wounds were not the important ones. The important one was the artery. That was where Martin's life was pumping away from him.

'We've got to get you to hospital,' James said, pushing his thumbs into the knee wound. It didn't clamp off the flow of blood like it did in the movies; all it did was make Martin scream and make the blood squirt out under high pressure.

'Get in there and get Essy!' Martin moaned. 'Don't worry about me. He'll be weak now. Just get in there and get her out!'

'You'll die!' James said.

Martin pushed himself up on his elbows. 'Everybody dies,' he hissed. 'It's just a question of when.'

'I can't just let you die,' James said.

Martin gritted his teeth. 'Then pull my belt off me and put a fucking tourniquet around my fucking knee, you wanker! Don't you know *anything* about first aid?'

Working quickly, James got the belt around Martin's knee and pulled it tight. It didn't stem the flow of blood entirely, but it had subsided quite a lot.

'That'll be fine,' Martin said. 'Now get in there and get your Drezy, we can fight about who gets to keep her afterwards. And if you're not out in five minutes, I'm getting up, going back to my car and driving myself to Barnstaple hospital. So hurry up.'

James doubted that Martin could stand, let alone walk. It was all just courageous talk. But it worked.

James reached the door, took hold of the door knob – from the centre of which the were-lion glared sullenly at him – and pushed.

The door, as he had anticipated, remained firmly closed against him.

He turned round to glance at Martin and couldn't see him through the flurries of snow that were falling.

He already knew that the fire-axe wouldn't take the door down, but there didn't seem to be any other way. He stood back and swung the axe.

He might just as well have tried to chop the barrel off a Chieftain tank. *In fact*, he decided, inspecting the spot where the axe had struck, *you would have probably had more success doing that.*

He swung the axe again, at the door knob this time. He thought he saw sparks and a few glittering flecks of gold falling, but when he looked, the knob was as undamaged as the door itself had been.

Defeated, he glanced at the snow behind him – which was rapidly turning into a blizzard – then he balled his fist and knocked gently.

And the door opened.

The hall was as bare as it had been earlier. James went inside. The first door he opened was the one that led into the lounge. This time there was no sea bed in there. It was just an ordinary empty room. He went to the far end of the lounge and looked out of the back window. Outside, above the overgrown garden, the sky was clear. There was a profusion of wild spring flowers growing in the garden. The sea down behind the rock was calm.

James hurried back to the window which looked out on the forecourt. It seemed impossible that it was winter on one side of the building and spring on the other.

It *was* impossible. It was spring on this side of the building too.

And there were other changes: the forecourt was no longer covered in gravel; there was a barred gate across the entrance;

the bushes that ran around the perimeter of the property were gone. And last, but hardly least, there was no sign of Martin.

I've gone back in time, James told himself. *Back to before Peter Perfect moved in. That's why there's no furniture or fittings in here. That's how the seasons have changed. The bushes around the perimeter haven't even been planted yet. What year is this then?*

What year it was didn't matter, he knew. The important thing was finding out if there was a link from where he was now to the time at which he'd entered the building. Drezy wasn't going to be back here in nineteen hundred and whatever it was. From where he was standing she was in the future.

What if you can't get back to where you started from? he asked himself as he hurried back down the lounge towards its rear door. *It might be eighty-odd years ago out there.*

He thrust the thought out of his mind and began to search. The entire building was empty but in the room upstairs, the one that Drezy said was Peter Perfect's writing room, he thought that when he listened carefully he could hear echoes of Drezy's voice.

But there was no hole in the fabric of reality to crawl through, no veil whose corner could be lifted to allow him under.

Eventually he gave up listening for the echoes of the future and went back downstairs, to where the closed front door was waiting for him.

He reached out and took hold of the cold door knob and the door opened.

The blast of cold air and snow that shot in at him almost knocked him over. Outside, a blizzard was in full swing.

James turned back, but the interior of the house was still in the past. There were no fixtures or fittings, no deep pile carpet. The house wasn't going to let him in and that was that.

He ran out into the snow – which was ankle deep – and headed for the pink-tinged patch where Martin lay. He was half-buried. His eyes were closed and snow had settled over his eyelids and down the line of his nose.

'Wwwww?' Martin murmured in a shuddering questioning tone.

'I couldn't get her,' James said, kneeling in the snow beside Martin and sitting him up. 'The house is flexible in time. It let me in but on the inside it's years ago. Before Peter Perfect came. I couldn't find a way to Drezy.'

'Gotttaaaahhh,' Martin shuddered. His head fell against James' chest.

James shook his head. His eyes blurred with tears. 'Can't do it,' he said. 'And anyway I'm going to have to get you out of here before you die. I'll come back afterwards. And I'll keep coming back until I get Drezy back. I swear.'

He stood, hoisted Martin up, put him over his shoulder and began to walk back towards the car.

This was the result of acting like a book hero, he realized as he trudged up towards the car. If he hadn't been so stupid last night, none of this need have happened. He could have stopped Drezy coming here.

But it was too late for this now. You only got one chance and if you fucked it up, that was tough. That was real life. One time only, no replays.

He reached Martin's car and propped him up against the side of it while he yanked open the car door. Martin was too far gone to even squeak at the rough treatment his leg was receiving as James put him in the car.

James got in, started the car, pushed the heater controls to maximum, turned on the fan, selected reverse and looked up . the hill over his shoulder. It was a long, steep backwards drive to the top and there was snow on the ground. There wasn't so much of it up here, but enough to make it difficult.

But James thought he could manage it.

'You're going to be OK,' he told Martin and began to drive.

I'll come back, he told himself as he reversed away from Drezy. *Hang on Drezy, I'll come back!*

Chapter Thirty-three

The Story's End

The words she had written earlier rang through S'n'J's head as she stood at the window watching James carry Martin away through the snow.

And now that power was draining away. There wasn't enough of it to hold everything in place, she thought to herself bitterly as James and Martin reached the gateposts and slipped out of view behind a swirling blanket of falling snow. For someone who was now supposed to be mortal again and rapidly losing his grip, Philip had just managed a mind-wrenching show of force.

Powerless to intervene since the door had closed on her, trapping her in the work-room, S'n'J had stood at the window watching it all fifteen feet below her on the forecourt. She'd witnessed the whirlwinds and when James and Martin had survived them, she'd cheered and punched the air with her fist, knowing in her heart that her piece of writing was going to come true.

She'd heard what happened when the door opened for them downstairs, and above the constant wail that Janie had been making – and still was – she'd detected the sounds of raised voices and another voice that sounded like Billy-Joe's.

Then her intuition told her that Philip *was* losing power and in a moment Martin and James would be charging up the stairs to rescue her.

But it didn't happen.

Instead, they began to shout at one another, their voices tight with panic. And as she listened, trying to work out what they were saying, the whole house seemed to shift on its foundations. And S'n'J began to *unhear* what James and

Martin had already said. Their calls and responses replayed themselves backwards, fading away. It was almost as if they were being thrust away from her, backwards in time.

No time passed at all before they came sprinting back out of the house with a thousand tiny balls of fire chasing them. Then, out there on the forecourt, Martin and James were obviously readying themselves for an attack which was going to come from the vicinity of the front door. S'n'J could only make guesses as to its nature.

Her mind really began to reel when a black printed line of music appeared in the glass of the window in front of her. She could not read music at all, but she knew what tune she was being shown.

The notes all looked solid and as if they were three-dimensional rather than flat print. In a daze she reached up and touched the cool glass, expecting to feel ridges. But the notes were *inside* the glass.

This didn't stop them from playing their tune for her when she ran her finger along the staff that contained them. The tune was the Peter Perfect rendition of 'Frosty the Snowman' and the moment she heard the melody, snow began to fall outside and something golden that looked like a lion with its grace and nobility removed sprang from the step, roaring.

S'n'J began to scream when the lion-thing found Martin, then clamped her mouth shut because she could feel the house siphoning the scream away from her and feeding on it. Downstairs in the cellar, Janie's screams were growing fainter so there was a good chance Black Rock was going to run out of power if, for once in her life, Sarah-Jane could keep her terror under control.

Diamond Ambrose Anstey lay curled up on the floor beside the broken computer case and she focused on him.

'Get up dog!' she hissed, thinking, *I have no fear. Though I walk through the valley of the shadow of death I will fear no evil. I will fear no evil. I will fear no Philip.*

Diamond raised his head, cocked an ear, listened, then put his nose back under his tail.

Downstairs Janie suddenly fell silent.

S'n'J felt her die. The sensation was that of someone plucking a brief, sad glissando upon the strings of her heart.

Gone, S'n'J told herself and felt tears begin to fill her eyes.

Ten seconds later, the lion ceased roaring and S'n'J drew a deep shuddering breath. Were Martin and James gone too?

Ten seconds after that, she heard someone charge into the house and realized that, against all the odds, James had survived. A tiny flame of hope lit in her heart ... and was extinguished again when she called out for him because her voice caught in her throat and suddenly James was *un*running into the house, vanishing backwards in time again.

S'n'J turned to go back to the window simply because there was nothing else she could do.

And there was James in front of her.

'James!' she cried.

He looked directly at her but didn't seem to see her. He came towards her as she spoke again, and her hopes were dashed. He was here but he was not here. The surface of his body rippled as though he was made of gently stirring water and when he moved she could see through him.

'Where are you?' she moaned. 'I'm here, in front of you! Come back to me!'

She held out her arms to him as he came closer and her hands passed through him. The place where he stood was made of freezing air.

She followed James to the end of the room, yelling at him, then she followed him back again, to the door.

'Don't go out!' she wailed as he took hold of the door handle and turned it. 'I'm here!'

James opened the door.

Except that it didn't open. He looked as if he was miming the action.

Somewhere, S'n'J knew, in another time, the invisible door he was opening really did exist. She just couldn't see it because James was in the past or the future. All she was seeing was a reflection of James across time.

Eventually she looked out of the window again.

And there was James, outside again, walking away from her with Martin draped over his broad shoulder in a fireman's lift. She had been abandoned. She was stuck in the house with a god who had engineered her very existence and now there was nothing to prevent that god from taking that existence away from her again.

Suddenly she was angry. 'Get up, you mongrel!' she shouted furiously at Diamond. 'Ellen said to rewrite the book and follow the dog. Well, I've done my bit, now you just get off your canine arse and do yours. Get me out of here!'

The dog didn't move.

S'n'J felt tears of frustration spring to her eyes. She didn't know how she had any tears left to cry after all that had happened, but there they were, clouding her vision and burning her eyes.

'I'm frightened, Diamond,' she said softly, settling on the floor beside the dog. She put her arm around it. It didn't feel like a ghost dog at all. Diamond was warm and his short shiny coat was soft. She could feel big muscles beneath his skin.

'I'm not frightened of dying,' she sobbed into his coat, 'I'm frightened of having to stay alive for ever. As someone else. Sarah-Jane will never have existed. Everything I was, everything I could be, will be gone. Do you understand that?'

The dog lifted his head and turned it towards her. Diamond Ambrose Anstey opened his mouth and licked her face. Once. His tongue was rough. When she looked at him, his expression didn't look mournful at all, it looked playful.

S'n'J found a little smile quivering at the edges of her mouth. 'You stupid dog,' she said kindly, through her tears, 'You don't understand anything I say, do you? If I could, Diamond, I'd take you for a walk, teach you how to catch a ball and bark at intruders. Things like that. We'd have fun together.'

Diamond whined; a heart-breaking trill, deep in the back of his throat.

'It's too late, isn't it?' S'n'J said. 'For either of us. We're stuck here, aren't we? For what's going to be a very long time.'

'Not for Sarah-Jane Dresden, it isn't,' Philip's voice said from behind her.

She pushed herself up from the dog. Philip stood in the open doorway, a few sheets of paper and a pencil in his hand. He was smiling, but he looked flushed and his hair was tousled. This was the first time she'd seen him look anything other than as perfect as his pen name suggested.

'Tough battle?' S'n'J said, a glimmer of hope lighting again in her heart. The corners of Philip's eyes showed distinct crow's feet. They'd been there before, faintly visible in a good light but now they seemed quite deep.

Philip shook his head. 'Not so tough, Snowdrop,' he replied. 'I knew how it would all end. Like I told you, I've finished the book. Writing the pyrotechnics was the difficult part, not the bringing them into reality. All I had to do was work on Janie to make that happen.'

'She's dead, isn't she?' S'n'J said. 'You worked on her a little too hard, didn't you?'

Philip shook his head. 'I know what you're thinking,' he said.

'No you don't,' she cut in before he could tell her. 'Just tell me one thing before you do whatever you think you have to. Tell me how the book ended.'

Philip paused. The lines around his eyes seemed deeper still. There were creases at the corners of his mouth now, and S'n'J definitely hadn't seen those before.

He's getting older, she told herself. *He's ageing right in front of my eyes.* A question occurred to her then – one that she put straight out of her mind because it didn't bear thinking about: *If my creator dies, what will happen to me?*

'Well, I can tell you this. The house doesn't burn down and Martin and James and all the king's horses and all the king's men don't save poor Snowy.'

S'n'J tried to get up off the floor and could not. Her bad ankle shot horrendous bolts of pain up through her body when she moved it.

'The very end, I meant,' she said through teeth that were clenched against the pain.

'Now's not the time or place for that,' Philip said tartly and walked past her.

She followed his progress across the room. He was walking

like someone suffering from arthritis. When he lowered himself into his writing chair, he did it very carefully.

'Bad back?' S'n'J enquired, suddenly feeling a peculiar glee.

Philip ignored her and began to pick away the melted plastic that had dripped from the computer monitor on to his desk.

Why don't you just magic it away, I wonder, S'n'J thought. She tried to get her good leg under her to push her to a standing position, but her ankle complained ardently.

Over at his desk, Philip laid down a sheet of paper on the space he had cleared, pencil poised.

Don't let him start writing again! S'n'J thought and to distract him said, 'How old are you, Philip? Only you don't look thirty-eight any more. You look a little older. Forty-eight, maybe?'

'Shut up and let me concentrate!'

'Writer's block?'

Philip turned away from her and began to scribble.

'I'd say you were about eighty-five, in real terms,' she postulated. 'Without all the keeping young stuff you've been doing.'

'Shut up!' Philip repeated. His voice sounded rusty and a little quavery. Like the voice of someone very old.

'And I'll tell you something else,' S'n'J added. 'I think you're ageing very rapidly because the house doesn't have a human being feeding its furnace any more. Janie's flown away to heaven, hasn't she? And you used up all your power supply seeing off Martin and James. Now it's almost run dry.'

Philip spun round in his chair. He had aged another ten years or so. He was a man approaching sixty, and approaching it badly. His skin was dry and yellow and loose. He looked exactly like someone living on borrowed time. He grinned and his teeth were yellow too. His eyes were the only things about him which still looked young and vital. And terribly angry.

S'n'J felt a fresh thrill of fear. But she wouldn't let this stop her. 'You'd like to take me downstairs and feed me to the house, wouldn't you?' she said. 'Well go ahead, if you think

423

you have the strength!' she challenged. 'You can't though, because you're past it, aren't you?'

'I don't think so,' he said and held out his hand, palm up. A ball of dull red fire the size of an orange appeared.

S'n'J glanced at it, then looked back into his dark eyes. She held his gaze.

'I know your little secret,' she told him. 'You didn't finish the story, did you? You're lying about that. You had to melt down the computer to stop me writing any more because what I wrote became reality. That's why you're up here now with paper and pencil. Your tale is falling apart around you and you've come up here to try to stop the rot. Does that sound about right, Philip?'

'No,' Philip said quietly. Under the fireball his fingers were glowing red hot. 'How could a mortal human do this?' he asked, pointing at the effect with his pencil. 'What you wrote didn't come to be. Only what I write becomes reality.'

S'n'J glared at him. 'You wish,' she said.

'I think we should say goodbye now, Sarah-Jane.' And so saying, he flicked his hand towards her and the ball of fire rolled from it, flew half-way across the room, hit the floor . . . and fizzled out.

S'n'J glanced at the scorched piece of carpet. 'Oh dear,' she mocked. 'You seem to have stopped being omnipotent and started being impotent.'

But Philip wasn't listening. He had his back to her now and was writing quickly with the pencil. '"Sarah-Jane ceased to exist,"' he muttered.

And S'n'J felt something akin to an invisible shower of ice fall through her body. She suddenly felt empty and unreal.

Philip swivelled round in his chair. 'You're not still here, surely?' he said. 'How about if I add this?' he said, turning back. '"It took a few minutes for it happen, but Sarah-Jane could do nothing to stop it. She already felt unreal and the sensation was growing."'

'NO!' S'n'J shouted and tried to stand. She seemed to be more pain than person now, which wasn't fair. If she was fading away like the Cheshire Cat, her pain ought to lessen too.

'"In ten minutes, history would have shifted itself. The fabric of the universe was rearranging itself so that Sarah-Jane Dresden, who was brought into creation by Philip Winter, had never existed at all."'

S'n'J felt as light as her own shadow. Her good leg was under her now and she was pushing herself up in spite of the all-consuming pain from her bad leg. Her mind now held only one thought and this was wriggling like an eel trying to get out of a jam jar and back into the water.

'"Everything she had been, everything she might have become, would soon be gone,"' Philip said and added, 'I thought you'd like that bit. I heard you say it to the dog when I came in.'

S'n'J was on her feet now – or one foot and one column of raging agony. The rolling-pin was in her right hand and the two slippery words of her last-ever thought were pinned down inside her head.

GET HIM!

She walked across the room, moving silently and lightly. She was hardly any more substantial than a ghost now. She could hear no sound, feel nothing except the pain in her bad leg and the wooden handle of the rolling-pin in her hand.

Before her, Philip was bent over the desk, writing quickly. He was bald now, but for a few white hairs on the back of his head. His scalp was pale and dry. His clothes hung on him like a suit on a scarecrow made of sticks.

Each pace S'n'J took seemed to decrease her reality. By the time she got close enough to him to strike she felt no more substantial than a puff of air. Her body was fading away under her. When she raised the rolling-pin – which suddenly felt heavier than a sledge-hammer – she found she could see through her arm and hand.

Get him! The words rolled around in her empty mind like two marbles in the Hollywood Bowl.

The see-through arm brought the heavy rolling-pin up past her eyes and held it above her head.

'Philip,' she heard a tiny, distant voice say.

Philip turned round. Now he was a tiny, slack-faced old man whose toothless mouth hung open. So why did he look so fucking pleased with himself?

S'n'J brought the rolling-pin down.

She started to regain her reality the moment the rolling-pin stove into the old man's thin skull with a crack of splitting bone.

I did it! she told herself, pulling the weapon into the air again. *I made him human again! I wrote the god out of him!*

The crack of splitting bone resounded in her ears and it was a moment before she realized that she was not hearing his skull break at all, but the crack of the high-voltage power which was coursing from the room's back wall and finding the wound in Philip's skull.

S'n'J backed away, dismayed. She didn't know what he'd been writing on the page, but it was more than he'd told her.

The power suddenly ceased. Blinding fire danced in the wound she'd made in the old man's head and then Philip exploded in a blinding flash.

And when her eyes recovered, she screamed.

Instead of seeing the little old man lying dead on the floor as she'd expected, she saw *two* Philips. He had divided. Both men were half the age of the original and looked quite a lot fitter.

But if there are two, the total energy must be divided in half too! she told herself.

Both Philips grinned at her in unison. 'I saved the best trick for last,' they said.

S'n'J hopped forward and wrapped the rolling-pin around the side of the nearest Philip's head. He flashed and split into two twenty-year-olds.

S'n'J struck out at one and made two ten-year-olds.

The surviving twenty-year-old grabbed her arm. He was strong. S'n'J spun round at him, dipped her head and butted him in the nose.

When she hit one of the ten-year-olds into which he divided, it broke into two five-year-olds which existed for a moment then flashed like lightning and disappeared.

'Get away from me!' she screamed, backing towards the door.

There were now three Philips in the room, all coming towards her, all boring into her mind with their eyes. The same hypnotic eyes gleamed darkly at her from three faces of varying ages. Wherever she looked the eyes caught her, pinning her into position.

The ten-year-old came closer to her. 'Please don't hurt me,' this Philip piped in a frightened voice. His appealing little face and those searching eyes had her pinned. And if the others hadn't both said these words in unison, S'n'J might have been lost.

But the hypnotic bond broke when the room filled with voices all saying the same thing.

S'n'J struck out at the boy, who broke into two younger boys and flashed into nothing.

'You're dead, Philip!' she shouted and swung at the twenty-year-old, timing her return swipe so that it cracked through the heads of both ten-year-olds before they'd had time to form.

Then there was just her and one remaining Philip: the one closest to Philip's original age.

'Don't kill me, Snowy,' Philip said. 'You know what'll happen if you do, don't you?'

She nodded. 'I'll die.'

'That's right. Those created by gods can only exist while the gods survive, and I am your creator.'

He came slowly towards her. 'You don't want to die, do you?' he said.

S'n'J shook her head. His dark eyes were filling her, finding her soul. She started to become excited, suddenly wanting his body inside hers. Her heart rattled against her ribs and her mouth felt dry.

'We don't have to die,' he said softly. 'Neither of us do. We can both live. For ever if we want,' he continued, still approaching. 'We can be friends from now on. Can't we?'

'We can,' S'n'J said. 'If you promise not to change me.'

'I don't want to. Not any more. I understand now. You've taught me that things only happen once and I can appreciate that. Zara, my original Snowy Winter, has had her turn and can't come back. It's *your* turn now, Sarah-Jane. And I'd like you to stay with me until whenever you decide to go. Will you do that?'

'I will,' Sarah-Jane said and held out her arms to accept him; held them out high enough to wrap around his neck.

Philip came towards her.

'Just one thing,' S'n'J said as he walked into her arms.

Philip stopped. An expression of suspicion passed over his face and was gone. 'What is it?' he asked.

'I was taught how to lie by an expert,' she said.

In the split-second pause that followed, three things happened.

Philip's brow knitted in a display of puzzlement, S'n'J's hands formed themselves into fists and she brought both of them hooking in towards the sides of Philip's head.

There was a moment of searing heat, a blinding red flash, and glittering golden dust fell to the carpet where Philip had been standing.

'It's a woman's prerogative to change her mind,' S'n'J said to the remains of what had once been a god.

She checked herself, but she was not ceasing to exist now that Philip was gone. He might have brought her into being, but she existed independently of him now. Far from beginning to fade away, she felt a good deal more real than she had for what seemed like a very long time.

Put that in your pipe and suck hard on it, Peter Imperfect, she thought and flipped the finger at the golden stain on the carpet.

Over by the ruined computer case, Diamond Ambrose Anstey got up, yawned and made a show of stretching.

'About bloody time too,' S'n'J said. 'Let's get going, Diamond.'

Chapter Thirty-four

James Returns

There were a lot of people at Barnstaple Hospital who wanted to know what had *really* happened to Martin. James had concocted a story about a farming accident. He told the doctors that a combine harvester they were testing had run out of control, mincing Martin's leg, and had then caught fire. The medics, who seemed to be of the opinion that James was the world's worst liar, wanted to know why Martin was working on farm machinery dressed in a Savile Row suit. To which there was no acceptable answer. James had simply shrugged and asked for his own burns and cuts to be treated.

He let them take him to an A&E cubicle and when he felt the job was done, he fled. This could have gone better too. One of the doctors who'd been treating him saw him leaving and ran after him, shouting.

James quickly climbed into the Cavalier that Martin had hired and drove away. He didn't know what he could do when he got back to Black Rock – all he knew was he had to try.

The snow ran out on the edge of Tintagel, but it was drizzling all the way over to Barnstaple. James drove back carefully, trying to formulate a plan and failing. If this was a story, like it ought to have been, he would be receiving flashes of intuition. Ideas would come to him. He would know *exactly* what had to be done. But in real life those things just didn't happen.

I'll know when I get there, he assured himself doubtfully.

The weather front providing the snow was amazing to behold. It followed the boundary of the village exactly. On one side of the line it was snowing heavily and piling up, and on the side he was on not even a single flake blew across.

James pulled up on the edge of the weather and peered down the road towards the centre of Tintagel. The snow wasn't impossibly deep yet but it was bad enough to become stuck in your car.

He made it all the way down to the tight bend on which stood the King Arthur's Bookshop before he got into trouble. It was snowing harder here and the fall was much deeper – the front spoiler of the car was acting as a kind of plough.

Beside the bookshop there was a short steep descent into the car park where visitors to the Castle ruins left their cars. And for some reason, Martin's hired Cavalier wanted to go down into the car park, rather than round the sharp right-hand bend.

Each time James backed off from the corner and tried again to steer round it, the car headed directly at the car park entrance.

After the fourth try, he decided that this thing was bigger than both of them and he'd just have to walk from here. He also decided that if the car wanted to fling itself into the deep virgin snow of the empty car park, he might as well let it. He couldn't just abandon it in the road.

He steered round the corner again, and accelerated gently. The Cavalier nosed its way into the deep snow on the steep hill and began to slide.

Which was when James realized he'd made a bad mistake.

The parking area was also steep, inclined at an angle of perhaps twenty degrees towards the edge of the sharp drop on which it perched. The drop didn't go all the way down to the sea – there was a further stretch of snow-covered land before the ocean – but as the Cavalier entered the car park, turned sideways and began to slide, driver's side first, James knew that it intended to go all the way. Across the car park, across the rough ground and off the edge.

The car slowly moved sideways, pushing against an ever-increasing pile of snow that would soon bring it to a halt.

But this didn't happen: it kept sliding until the snow was piled up against it to the height of the roof and James could no longer see how far it was to the edge. He had to get out of the car, and fast.

He grabbed hold of the door handle, pushed the door, and shouted in terror when it didn't open.

The lock! his mind screamed at him. *The door's locked. Undo it!*

His fingers snatched at the lock, he pushed against the door, and then he was out of the car, rolling through the snow.

He found his feet in time to see the car vanish off the edge of the rough ground.

But it was what had happened to the sea that was really staggering. From the bay at the foot of the castle, to Black Rock and as far out as he could see the water had frozen into a flat white sheet.

James opened his mouth to express his disbelief, then closed it again.

A cock-eyed idea was forming in his mind. It wasn't the kind of flash of inspiration you would find in a story, and when he voiced it to himself it might have sounded supremely stupid, but it was all he had to go on.

You can get down there from here, he told himself. *There's a cave at the bottom of the rock the house stands on. The sea flows into it. What if there's a way inside the house through that cave? You could climb down, walk across the frozen sea to the cave and try to find your way up into the house from there. A kind of surprise attack.*

The doubting thoughts started almost immediately. *And what if you fall?* he asked himself. *What if you go over one of those rocks and break a leg? No one will even know you're down there. You'll die of exposure if you get hurt. And you probably will get hurt. You're injured and weak already and that's quite a climb you're looking at, even in good weather. Anything could happen.*

James shook his head. If anything was going to happen to him, it would just have to happen. He'd promised to do his best and he was going to do it.

For better or for worse.

At the section of broken wall he paused for a second, looking at the bay below.

Then he took a deep breath and started down.

Chapter Thirty-five

Escape from Black Rock (Slight Reprise)

Diamond looked at S'n'J, cocked his head and barked once in his deep voice. For the first time, she saw his tail wag. She assumed that this was the nearest thing she was going to get to congratulations at having wiped out Peter Perfect *and* Mr Winter *and* the story of Black Rock.

'Thanks,' she said to Diamond and hobbled towards him, glancing back at the work-room door which was closed firmly against her.

The house had begun to make noises. They were similar to the ones her flat made after the central heating had gone off: the sound of things that had expanded, under heat, contracting again. All through the house things were making little bangs and creaks. The sounds were undoubtedly caused by the departure of Philip's power. The house was settling, but each tiny noise seemed sinister.

She got the distinct impression that the building wasn't so much going to sleep, as ponderously waking up. She pictured the way the house looked from outside – like a huge and terrible animal, crouched waiting to pounce. Surely this was just an impression, not a pointer to the true nature of Black Rock?

Haunted houses were just places where ghosts existed. Surely it didn't follow that they became alive too?

But Black Rock is more than a place where ghosts gather, Drezy, she told herself. *Quite a lot more. Perhaps you should check what Philip's last written words were.*

'Just a second, Diamond,' she said, and hobbled towards the desk.

A tinny instrumental rendition of 'Frosty the Snowman'

accompanied her. It came out of the ceiling in several different places and each source was slightly out of phase with the next. And to compliment the sound effects, the room's walls lit with a blinding white light.

'Baby it's cold outside,' Philip's voice said over the music. 'Do you think it's gonna snow, Snowy?'

S'n'J snatched the piece of paper from the desk. Philip's scrawled handwriting was difficult to read. The words danced in front of S'n'J's eyes, blurring in the brilliant glare from the walls.

'Peter Perfect was metamorphosing again,' she read, squinting. 'This time the change was permanent. No matter what happened to him now, he wouldn't die. He would have total mastery of the power in the house. When Sarah-Jane hit him, he knew he would keep on splitting until his human energy was exhausted. Whereupon he would merge with the house. He might have lost a battle, but his little Snowy was going to discover that he had, in fact, won the war.'

She shook her head. 'No you don't!' she hissed and tore the sheet of paper into shreds.

On either side of her, the walls turned to huge sheets of glass. Behind the glass was clear blue sea and coral reefs, through which swam thousands of gorgeously coloured tropical fish.

S'n'J glanced through one of the huge fish-tank panes. She felt horribly dizzy. She could see for more than half a mile across the sea bed before the blue darkened and blotted out her vision. Overhead the music was still playing. And when she tottered round looking for the door, it was gone. There was no sign of it ever having existed.

'You have to stay in the house for ever,' Philip's tinny voice said over the non-existent Tannoy. 'The getting in is easy. It's the getting out you have to worry about. It can't be done, Snowy.'

Diamond barked.

S'n'J looked down at him.

The dog pointed.

At the wall through which Philip had earlier thrust his hand.

'Not through there. I'll die,' she said, remembering the way Philip's hand had glowed red hot when he'd withdrawn it; how the band of gold around his finger had become so hot it had dripped.

As if to show the way, Diamond walked under the desk and stopped with his nose against the wall, then looked back at her. S'n'J crouched beside him. 'I understand,' she said, 'but I can't do it. It'll kill me.'

Diamond turned back, put his nose to the wall, tensed his muscles and pushed forward. His snout penetrated the wall. His paws scrabbled at the carpet and his whole head slid into the wall. Where he stopped, looking as if he had been decapitated.

'*I can't!*' S'n'J wailed. Behind her, something began to crackle.

Diamond's body stiffened and he pulled his head back out to look at her. It wasn't red hot. Or even smoking. He barked.

'Are you trying to tell me that it's safe?' S'n'J asked above the steadily increasing crackling noise.

If he'd been Rin-Tin-Tin or Lassie, Diamond would have barked knowingly and wagged his tail while he looked from her to the wall and back again. She wouldn't have been able to miss the message. But this was not what happened.

The dog pushed his head into the wall again and struggled all the way through this time. S'n'J watched the wall close around the tip of his tail and finally glanced behind her, realizing that she could now smell smoke.

Something that looked like a brush-fire was coming towards her in a single line of low flame, leaving nothing but black ash in its wake.

S'n'J turned back to the wall, got on her hands and knees and pushed her head against it.

It was like crawling through a six-inch freezing jelly. On the other side was the master bedroom where Snowy and Philip had made love. It was snowing in there: on the floor and the bed, it was a good three inches deep. The upper third of the room was enveloped in thick, swirling cloud from which the snow fell like cotton-wool.

Diamond stood half-way across the room, pointing.

Shivering and with her breath pluming into the air, S'n'J crawled towards him. Her jacket lay on the floor in the snow. She picked it up, shook the snow off and put it on. It was better than nothing. Her other clothes and her shoes weren't there.

Diamond nosed at a spot of wall below the window. *I hope you know what you're doing*, S'n'J thought as she crawled through the snow towards him. *Because if you're wrong, there's a big drop to the ground outside that window.*

But there wasn't time to give the matter any further consideration, because Diamond was going through. S'n'J followed him, hoping for the best.

And came out in the bathroom beside the toilet bowl.

The bathroom was coated with clear ice. Huge icicles hung from the ceiling, like daggers waiting to fall. The floor was skating-rink smooth and numbed S'n'J's flesh. She crawled on to it, finding it difficult to keep her half-frozen hands and knees under her.

Diamond stood in front of her pointing the way they had come.

She followed him, expecting to end up in the bedroom again. She was surprised to find herself in the library.

It wasn't snowing in here yet, but the upper half of the room was in cloud.

Diamond was pointing at a large bookcase that took up an entire wall. The top of it was masked by cloud.

She forced herself to her feet and limped across, knowing exactly what she was looking for and knowing it was going to be on the top shelf. There was a stepladder at the far end of the bookcase. She got it and took it back to where the dog sat.

'Where are you Snowy?' Philip's voice called from up there in the cloud. 'You needn't think you can escape me just because you've found a backwater of the maze. Sooner or later I'll know *exactly* where you are.'

You wish, S'n'J thought, leaning the library ladder against the bookcase. When she began to climb, the rungs bit into her feet and the pain from her bad ankle made her want to scream.

At the top shelf, the swirling cloud was bitterly cold and made it difficult to see. She was pretty certain that ice was forming around her lips and that the moisture from her breath was crystallizing around her nostrils.

There were six thick manuscripts on the top shelf, wrapped neatly in brown paper. There was writing in HB pencil on each of them and S'n'J peered at it. The manuscripts, in which Peter Perfect had brought S'n'J and five other unfortunate girls into existence, were marked, *Snowy #1* through to *Snowy #5*. The sixth was marked *Diamond*.

She pulled down the one labelled *Diamond* and threw it to the floor. *There you go, dog*, she thought. *Tear that up and you'll be free.*

She followed suit with the other five manuscripts, then climbed down, wondering what she was going to do with all the paperwork. Philip had said that her story alone was a thousand pages long, and the package she had just flung down there felt like it. It was going to take a long time to tear six thousand pages into shreds.

She got off the ladder, wiped the frost from her face and crouched down beside the pile of manuscripts. Three of the six packages had burst open when they'd hit the floor and Diamond was sniffing them.

Don't worry dog, she thought, *we're about to put this right.*

She found the package marked *Snowy #1* and tore the wrapper off, wondering if this was the only thing linking her with reality. Would she cease to exist if she destroyed the makings of her own life? She hoped not. *You wouldn't just wink out of existence if you killed your parents, would you?* she reasoned. *So why should this be any different?*

She glanced over at Diamond, wondering if she ought to destroy a few pages of his story first, just in case. Then she felt horribly guilty and decided she couldn't. She pulled the first page from her own manuscript, fought off the temptation to read any of it and tore it in half.

Nothing happened to her.

She tore it into tiny pieces with no ill effect.

Then she picked up as much as she thought she could tear in half at one go and did this too.

The question was, how long would it take to tear up several thousand pages? Some of the stories were shorter than hers, but that still left too much paper for one woman and a dog to rip up.

Then she remembered what was supposed to happen at the end of every good haunted house story. The house burned down.

And Sarah-Jane Dresden suddenly had a flash of what felt like genuine story-book inspiration.

In her jacket pocket, tucked inside her wallet there was a book of Cars Inc. matches. The one that James had written his number on, what seemed like months ago. Her wallet was soaked, and inside it, the little booklet of paper matches was damp. S'n'J's heart began to sink.

She balled several of the manuscript pages and put a match head to the striking surface at the bottom of the booklet.

It left a red streak behind it. The remaining phosphorus on the tip of the match fell off when she tried again.

Bastard! she mouthed, but didn't say the word.

'Where are you, Snowy?' Philip's voice said.

S'n'J tried another match. The same thing happened, except that this time some of the crumbling pieces of head sizzled reluctantly as they broke away. The following match stayed whole, glowed incandescent for a moment and went out. The one after that actually lit, but went out before the stalk caught.

'I can smell something in the library,' Philip's voice announced. 'Something like burning. You wouldn't be down there making mischief, would you?'

S'n'J shook her head in reply and plucked out a match from the centre of the booklet. This one lit, guttered, and began to burn.

She touched it to the edge of a sheet of crumpled paper willing the tiny orange flame to grow.

Then she began to rejoice. *We've got ourselves a fire,*

Diamond! she thought, picking up another piece of paper and touching it off against the growing flame.

'YOU'RE BURNING ME!' Philip's tinny voice screamed. 'PUT IT OUT!'

He was in my book too, S'n'J told herself. *That's why it's so bloody long. He didn't just write down my story in it, he wrote his as well!*

She split up the stack of pages and started crumpling sheets of paper at random and throwing them on to the growing bonfire.

Overhead, the cloud began to rain.

'You *bastard!*' S'n'J screamed, glancing up at the layer of cloud.

It was thinning and now she looked, all that was falling was a thin drizzle.

The pages on her little bonfire hissed and spat where the rain fell, but there wasn't enough liquid to put it out. The fire was spreading rapidly now, becoming more fierce by the moment.

'PUT IT OUT PUT IT OUT PUT IT OUT!' Philip's voice screeched.

'Put it out yourself, if you're so good!' S'n'J shouted back, balling more paper.

The rain increased for a moment and then the cloud was gone.

What now? she asked herself.

The answer was nothing except the screaming of a man whose reality was going up in flames.

For the next five minutes, she worked like a Trojan, building fresh bonfires. But S'n'J knew she wouldn't be able to burn everything even if she stayed here all night. And she also knew that whatever she did the house wasn't going to burn down because the room was airtight. When all the oxygen was gone the fire would go out.

She balled one last sheet, threw it into the fire, then she set about spreading out as many pages as she could across the floor. The air in here, what little there was left of it, was already hot and choking.

She turned to the dog, and said, 'OK, we'd better get out now. We've done all we can.'

'DON'T! SNOWY! YOU'RE KILLING ME!' Philip's strangled voice screamed.

S'n'J looked up at the roof. 'Good,' she said venomously. 'I'm glad to hear that Philip. Very glad indeed!'

She hobbled over to the corner of the room where Diamond was waiting for her, got down on her hands and knees and followed him through the wall.

They came out into the hall from the door that led down to the cellar.

Diamond turned and pointed at it.

S'n'J looked at the door. The padlock was undone and the door was slightly open. 'I can't go down there,' she said.

The dog, evidently didn't care whether she could or not. He nosed the door open and started down the steep stone steps.

S'n'J didn't have any choice but to follow the dog, just as the ghost of Ellen had advised. But she couldn't walk down those steep stairs. She had to sit down on the top one and bump herself down a step at a time.

During the descent Philip's screaming ceased and the voice of the house and the rock began to make itself known to her. It was soothing and seductive and it didn't speak in words. It sang like a Siren in short bursts of pleasing tones that conveyed more information than Philip's thousand-page books. During the long slow passage down the steps S'n'J learned of delights which she hoped she would soon forget, felt emotions and thoughts stirring inside her which surely couldn't exist in an ordinary human being.

By the time she reached the cellar – where the voices of a thousand ruined bodies sang their sweet song of pain – she understood how Philip had come to kill the thing he loved most. Understood how he had wanted to become a god.

The cellar was a cube of fifteen feet or so. The overhead bulkhead that provided the lighting was out, but it was still easy to see. It was like the work-room upstairs. When you wanted light, you got light. Philip had evidently favoured subdued, romantic lighting.

There were manacles on three of the walls and a small wooden desk against the other. A big tape recorder stood on it; two huge microphones lay beside it. This wasn't plugged in, but its ready light was flashing and the VU meter needles registered S'n'J's movements.

He recorded what he did! S'n'J realized, and suddenly understood the sense of it. Then she was disgusted with herself. She only hoped she wouldn't be too warped when she got out of here.

Not when you get out of here, but if you get out of here, she told herself. *Not many people have walked out of this room alive.*

But Sarah-Jane Dresden was going to be one of them. She promised herself this.

Diamond was nosing the corners of the room as if he wasn't quite certain which was the right one.

There was dried blood on the floor, but the thing S'n'J had feared most was not here. She had dreaded seeing the ruined bodies of Ellen and Janie.

Diamond barked once and went to another corner where something glittered.

She limped over to it and crouched, tears already springing to her sore eyes. It was Janie's gold wedding band. It was all that was left of her now. S'n'J picked it up and put it on her own wedding finger.

Up on the bench, the tape machine began to roll.

The cell was filled with the agonized screams Janie had made. The stereo effect and the recording were perfect. S'n'J could almost see the victim manacled to the wall, tearing the flesh off her wrists as she tried to escape.

'This'll happen to you too, Snowy,' Philip's voice grunted over the screams. 'You won't get out. Getting in is easy. Getting out is impossible. We've seen to that, the house and me.'

S'n'J grabbed hold of the tape recorder and heaved it to the floor, killing it.

Over by the steps, something began to sound as if it was being pushed with a great deal of force. There was a creaking sound and dust began to bloom around the floor. The creaking became a dull rumble and the entrance to the cellar heaved itself shut.

Trapped! S'n'J told herself. *He fixed it so I'd be trapped.*

She turned away from the seamless wall of black rock that now covered the stairway to look at Diamond who was pawing at the far corner of the room and whining.

'Nice try, Diamond, but he's blocked off that one too,' she said and fancied she saw a look of canine dismay on his face. 'They'll find our bones here one day. Maybe in a thousand years or two,' she told the dog.

Diamond whined and pawed at his corner. Then he tried the next corner, then returned.

S'n'J watched him, crying silently. This was how her life was to end, watching a dog running from one side of a room to the other because the animal was too stupid to believe its exit had gone. He would do that until he dropped from exhaustion. And when he recovered he would try again.

And somewhere along the line he was going to get hungry.

S'n'J only hoped she died of asphyxiation before they reached that point.

'Diamond! Sit!' she commanded. 'Sit down and relax. There's nothing we can do. We're stuffed.' She sat down against the blocked entrance and closed her eyes.

And then Diamond was beside her, pawing at her.

She looked into that sad, lonely face. 'You want a pat, I'll give you a pat,' she said and did so, closing her eyes again. She was starting to feel hot and sleepy now, as if the air was already used up.

The dog backed away from her and barked.

When she opened her eyes he was pointing at her.

And wagging his tail.

'What?' she asked, suspiciously.

Diamond wagged and pointed.

It took her a while to catch on but suddenly she understood and she was crying again. With relief this time instead of despair.

Philip had closed off one of the house's metaphysical back alleys, but when the wall had formed behind them another had been created.

442

'You *good dog*!' she said and planted a kiss on his bony skull. Then she let go of him and moved aside.

Diamond leapt at the wall and vanished through it.

S'n'J got up on her hands and knees, and placed her head against cool rock.

She fancied she heard someone call her name as she forced herself through the rock. It was a distant voice, and sounded very sad. It was a voice that didn't belong to anyone she knew. It might have been, she told herself later, the voice of the house itself. And then she was falling.

She crashed down on to a sheet of ice which crackled and groaned under the impact. It was dark where she'd landed but there was a semi-circular light nearby. When her eyes focused, she realized she was no longer in the house, but in a cave whose floor consisted of frozen sea water. The air was fresh and cold and tasted of freedom.

S'n'J punched the air. 'OUT!' she yelled into the echoing cave. 'CAN YOU HEAR ME, PHILIP WINTER, YOU BASTARD? I'M OUT! DREZY IS FREE!'

She picked herself up, looking around for Diamond. He wasn't there.

And no reason why he should be. He's done his bit and he's a free dog now, she shivered. The ice was already biting her bare feet and she was only wearing her jacket and one of Philip's shirts.

She hobbled towards the entrance of the cave, suddenly remembering having seen it before. On her one and only trip to King Arthur's Castle she had spotted it from the hillside and had wanted to go down and explore. But her parents had told her it was too dangerous. The cave was in the rock on which the house stood.

Which means I'm walking on the sea, she told herself, glancing down at the crackling ice. She hoped it was thick enough to support her weight.

She hobbled out of the entrance of the cave into the worst snowstorm she had ever seen. It was snowing so hard that she couldn't tell whether she was walking out to sea, or in towards the land. She reasoned that if she'd seen the cave from King Arthur's Castle, it meant that the two faced one another and that the land should be to her left, so she turned that way and began to walk.

After a while she began to feel as if she was walking on stilts. The cold numbed her legs from the knees down. She stumbled and fell and picked herself up again, wondering if her bad leg was making her turn away from the land.

I should be there by now! she told herself, tripping again.

The next time she got up, the wind whipped the snow from her vision and she saw the little snow-covered beach that formed the tiny bay at the foot of the Castle.

I did it! she told herself, not thinking of the long and difficult climb up to the village.

For a moment, as she drew closer to the beach, she thought she saw a reflection of herself, limping towards her.

'Drezy?' a voice called.

Through the flurries of snow she saw the reflection of herself again, dragging its bad leg as it half-hopped, half-walked towards her.

'Drezy? Is that you?'

It was a man. Her hammering heart began to sink. It was surely Philip.

'It's me! Drezy! Over here!'

And there was James. He had come back for her. S'n'J had never been so pleased to see anyone in her life.

'James!' she screamed and increased her pace.

They fell when they flung themselves into one another's arms and rolled on the protesting ice, smothering each other with cold kisses.

The moment didn't last long enough.

'We have to get out of here,' James said. 'Before we die of hypothermia.'

S'n'J nodded. 'What happened to your leg?'

James grinned sheepishly. 'I fell, climbing down the rocks. Acting like a book hero. I'll be all right. Are you OK to walk?'

S'n'J got up, dusted snow from her numb hands and smiled. 'There isn't a thing on this planet that could stop me now,' she said.

They held each other as they walked back to the beach.

Chapter Thirty-six

The End of Black Rock

During the long, lazy days that followed her release from hospital, Sarah-Jane Dresden wrote the only other piece of fiction she ever intended to write. She and James were both kept in for a couple of days while they were treated for hypothermia and broken ankles, and afterwards they moved into her flat and acted like star-crossed (if somewhat delicate) lovers during the daytime and sex-crazed teenagers at night. In spite of the plaster casts.

And when James fell asleep, S'n'J sneaked out into the kitchen and, using a pencil and paper, wrote an end to Black Rock. She wasn't happy with her literary style, but as she constantly told herself, it was the thought that counted. And in her version, she had Martin make a speedy recovery.

In reality, it was going to take a miracle to make Martin's leg better and S'n'J didn't dare hope for one of those. She knew what hoping for miracles and magic could do to you.

The hospital had saved Martin's leg, but were doubtful about how useful it was going to be to him. The nerves were severed, apparently, and couldn't be reconnected. A good deal of the flesh of Martin's leg had vanished down the throat of the lion (or into the combine harvester if you happened to be a doctor). Martin didn't seem particularly worried about the prospect of losing the use of his lower leg. Or even if the whole leg had to be amputated. He didn't seem particularly worried about anything any more, and that was a miracle in itself, S'n'J supposed. Martin had changed. Radically and for the better. If it hadn't been for her aching love for James, S'n'J might have considered having him back.

In her story, Martin *did* regain the full use of his leg. He went back to work and she and James stayed here and stayed hopelessly in love.

And Black Rock sat on a part of Barras Nose, waiting.

It was this fact that had started S'n'J writing her story in the first place. The house still stood, waiting for the next Peter Perfect to arrive. And S'n'J wanted the building razed to the ground. Or pulled apart brick by brick and ground to dust. Or blown up with an atomic bomb.

Or, most fittingly, burned down.

And on the kitchen table, while James was asleep, S'n'J was furtively arranging it. In her story, she and James would come home one day to see the light flashing on the answering machine. And when she rewound the tape and played it, it wouldn't contain a rendition of 'Frosty the Snowman' or the voice of Peter Perfect, but the cheery voice of Martin, who would announce, 'Guess what, Essy! I've done the deal of the decade. Can you guess what it is? You can't can you? I've bought Black Rock.'

At which point there would be a pause in which S'n'J and James would look at one another in wordless horror.

And then Martin's voice would say, 'But not for the reason you're thinking. Now look, guys, I know you've both vowed never to go near the place again, but on Tuesday at six-thirty I want you to drive to the top of the track, walk down it until you can see the house, then wait there. I'll be down at the house and I'll be joining you shortly. And when I get there you're gonna see the sight of your life. The house is going to be rigged with incendiaries. The fucker is gonna burn, Essy. That's why I bought it, to burn it. We'll stand up there and watch it go, Essy, me, you and James, and we'll dance and sing and punch the air. We beat the fucker and now we're gonna burn it! And afterwards we'll have a celebration party. OK? I'll ring back later!'

It would never happen, of course. It was a nice thought, and S'n'J could imagine it vividly and it was what *ought* to happen, but it was just a dream. Things like this didn't happen in real life.

S'n'J finished her story the week after her plaster came off and she stashed it away in an envelope, and put it under her bed.

The miracle she really wanted happened a week later. Martin rang, drunk with jubilation. It took quite a while to get the story out of him, but the upshot of all his babbling was that his leg was going to be OK. He could feel his foot when they pricked it, he said, and he had told the last doctor who tried it that if he did it again he was going to need some serious orthodontic work to bridge his missing teeth.

S'n'J thought of her story, which had surely had nothing to do with it, and smiled.

A week after that, S'n'J and James came home from a shopping trip and found the answering machine light blinking.

They both stood and looked at it, guiltily.

James broke the silence. 'Do you know who I think left us a message?' he asked.

S'n'J shook her head.

'I think it was Martin,' he smiled, conspiratorially.

She looked at him, in open mouthed surprise. 'You read it!' she said, 'You found my story under the bed and you read it and you didn't even tell me!'

James grinned and nodded. 'You didn't even tell me you were writing it,' he countered. 'It was excellent, too. I told you you had talent.'

S'n'J took his hand and squeezed it, glancing from the flashing light to James' smiling face and back again and not knowing whether she ought to feel flattered or embarrassed or excited about the message that might be waiting there for her. 'It can't be, can it?' she asked. 'It can't have come true!'

James shrugged, grinning fit to burst.

'We'll be disappointed,' S'n'J said.

James shook his head. 'I don't think so,' he said. 'Wind it back and see if we've got a bonfire to watch.'

Sarah-Jane Dresden crossed her fingers, rewound the tape and hit the play button.

Hoping.

Forthcoming Vista paperback
horror titles

The Blue Manor Jenny Jones 0 575 60010 1

Vanitas S. P. Somtow 0 575 60051 9

The Eternal Mark Chadbourn 0 575 60062 4

Dark Terrors edited by Stephen Jones and David Sutton
0 575 60024 1

Fevre Dream George R. R. Martin 0 575 60005 5

VISTA books are available from all good bookshops or from:
    Cassell C.S.
    Book Service By Post
    PO Box 29, Douglas I-O-M
    IM99 1BQ
    telephone: 01624 675137, fax: 01624 670923

VISTA